GOLD CROWN

THE JACK OF MAGIC BOOK 5

GOLD CROWN

ALEX LINWOOD

GREENLEES
PUBLISHING

Published by Greenlees Publishing, contact@greenleespublishing.com

ISBN-13: 978-1-951098-14-8

Cover design by Dominic Forbes

For those who must travel a long ways...

The worst part was the smell. Once in a while a pile of splintered lumber that used to be a storefront or a house was moved, and once again the smell of the black acrid powder was exposed to the air, burning Portia's nose. The foul stench traveled surprisingly far once released, covering the area of several buildings, or more. It smelled of dead things and strange foreign dangers.

Portia straightened, taking off her rough leather gloves and easing her tightened back. She stretched first one arm behind her, then the other. The midmorning sun shone hazily through the low cloud cover over the harbor. Three hours of labor and she'd moved what looked like half a house of ruined wood. Red paper stuck out from underneath a broken plank to her left. She kicked at it. It was shop wrapping paper. This must have been a general store, but any food that was within it had been taken off by beggars and animals, leaving only what was useless to the poor population living at the edge of the capital city.

Rolling her neck, Portia stepped to the roadway that ran along the harbor seawall on the far side of the ruined structures. Further down other students worked, their campus robes long abandoned for dusty work clothes that could be repeatedly washed or even thrown away. A few docks still stood in the water, with even fewer boats tied up at them. Further out beyond the mouth of the harbor white sails gave away the location of the ragged remains of fishing boats still able to work to feed the populace.

Portia tried to dust off her britches and tunic but only succeeded in raising a cloud of dirt around her. Coughing, she gave up the task for hopeless. Her face felt tight with grime. It was not even noonday and already she longed for a bath. Turning to look up the hill behind the harbor she stared up longingly at the wall that marked the boundary of the Magic Academy. Never again would she complain about how much work her studies were.

Stepping out of the path of a horse-drawn wagon coming up behind her to collect yet another load of debris, Portia stepped back in the road behind it and continued on, looking for her friend and roommate Ella. It was nearly lunchtime, and uncharacteristically, Ella had not already sought her out first. They had been detailed to different areas that morning.

Ella was further down the road, squatting next to a young child dressed in linen rags. The little girl's dirt covered finger jabbed at the pile that Ella had been clearing. Several other students stood back and watched Ella and the young girl, neither willing to continue their work, nor comfortable enough to come join the interaction.

"Stop! That's my pa's. It ain't yours," the young girl said, her whole body shaking as she spoke while tears ran down her face, leaving light-colored tracks.

Ella smoothed a hand over the child's chest, stroking her and speaking softly. "I know, child, it's not ours. We are just cleaning up." Ella flipped her gold hair back as she spoke, its clean shine a sharp contrast to the destruction all around.

"What's this?" Portia asked as she reached the pair.

The child looked up at Portia while still pointing to the destroyed building. "That's my pa's." She stuck out her chin in open defiance. Portia pushed back an urge to smile.

"And so it is I'm sure. We're only helping. Where is your pa?" Portia asked, even as Ella quickly shook her head behind the child, too late to stop the question. The child's lower lip trembled and her face worked, but no further words came.

Realizing her mistake, Portia squatted down next to Ella and the child so their eyes were on the same level and spoke as soothingly as she was able. "No one is disputing the ownership. We are only here to help. Have you had lunch today? Everything is terrible without lunch, don't you think?"

The word 'lunch' registered in the child's eyes with a quick twitch. The second mention of lunch stopped the tears. Portia waited as the child thought about her words, finally giving a slow nod.

"That's what I thought. Shall we three go and get food and discuss how this property may be properly fixed up for your pa?" Portia asked. Ella rewarded Portia's idea with a sunny smile and stood, holding out a hand to the child.

The child had to think only a moment longer, then nodded again and held out her hand to Portia, then used her other one to grab Ella's hand. The three of them walked back down the street the way Portia had come, going to provision wagons that had been sent down by the school so the students and guards would not have to journey back for their midday meal. There was too much work to be done, and the school wanted the students back at their studies as soon as possible.

The sun was setting through their narrow window as Ella and Portia regained their room at the Pyromancy house, the house where all the fire wielding students lived together.

The smell of onions and hot stew flooded the entire building, making Portia's stomach growl in complaint, but she was determined to clean herself before sitting on any furniture, much less relaxing enough to eat. She didn't even want to walk into their room and track in dirt, only reluctantly entering to open her trunk to retrieve fresh clothes before heading to the baths. The scent was faint, but she swore she could smell that black powder on her skin and it made the back of her neck crawl.

Ella had raced ahead of Portia the moment she'd smelled dinner. She was already in the baths.

A blissful candlemark later, Portia sat, clean, on one of the long benches in the large dark wood and shadowed dining hall. Her tray was satisfyingly full with a large bowl of stew, crusty brown bread, and even some precious cheese the cook had found at the weekly market. She frowned as she thought of the young girl from that day—her dinner surely was not as good as Portia's, if she had anything to eat at all. Portia's spoon wavered over her bowl.

Ella eyed her from across the table while chewing a massive bite of bread. Then, as if she could read Portia's thoughts, she reached out and pushed Portia's spoon into her bowl. "Eat. You can't do anything for anyone if you're starving yourself." Portia looked up to argue, but Ella was having none of it. "Eat!"

Portia nodded and dipped the spoon in. Dinner was good. She couldn't remember the last time she tasted anything so good. Perhaps when she was a thief and never had enough to eat—then, yes, food tasted that good—but blessedly it had been a while since those rough days.

"Dead, you think, or captured?" Portia finally asked.

Ella looked up, puzzled.

"That child's father," Portia said. They never had a chance to talk that afternoon, not wanting to do it around the child during lunch, and afterwards they had their own work to do.

"Captured," Ella said. "He was not on the official roll, nor burned on the pyres, least that's what her mother said when she finally found her after lunch. I felt so bad for her mother. She looked barely older than us. Anyhow, that's why I'm so hungry. I could see in her eyes she was happy her child had had lunch, and yet—"

"She was starving herself," Portia said, a bitterness creeping into her tone. If that destroyed store had been the family's livelihood, then the child and mother were most likely homeless and starving without it. The kingdom had provided little for those decimated in the war, the student's labor being no small part of what they did give.

"Yes, she did look starving," Ella continued on, ignoring Portia's dark tone. "I gave her my afternoon snack and you know how I need my afternoon snack. My head was pounding by the time we got here for dinner. But it's all worth it. I wish I could have given her more. Those poor people."

Bile rose in Portia's throat and she had to stop chewing. While they were sitting here warm in their house, provided with hot food and a safe place to sleep, a good portion of the kingdom's populace had been dragged from their homes and captured as slaves and even now stranded in some foreign lands. And their own queen refused to go retrieve them. The safety of the pyromancy house suddenly felt bitter.

Liam and Richard came to join them, their own trays loaded high. They too had been working down the harbor but in the shipyard, having some experience with that before coming to the school. They were brothers but could not look more different. Liam usually resembled a colorful bird, with brightly colored hair dyed strange colors of blue, or pink, or aqua, or even a shiny silver that looked like metal, while his twin brother, Richard, resembled nothing more than a cuddly bear with a thatch of dark brown hair matching his dark brown eyes.

"How go your duties?" Liam asked as he slid next to Ella.

He tried to grab a roll off of her tray but she was too fast and swatted his hand away then protectively covered her food. She could outeat them all, and usually got there before they did to get the tastiest morsels. "Oh, come on, Ella, they only had winter wheat left and you know I don't like that."

"You should've gotten here earlier," Ella said.

"Please," Liam begged, while Richard shook his head and sat next to Portia.

"Only if you teach me how to make my hair pink," Ella said. She made this request near every time, and as every time before, Liam merely shook his head. "Fine, then eat your wheat," Ella said without mercy.

Liam gave her a sulky look. "You're mean, girl."

"You're a mean boy," Ella replied. "And I have lots of brown bread."

Richard noticed Portia's dark mood. He leaned in to whisper, "Any news?"

Portia shook her head. She resumed eating, not wanting to talk about it.

Mia, the last of their group, joined their table. She was the quietest of them, even more quiet than Richard, but was such a steady presence that nothing felt right until she was there. Her hair was the brightest flame-red Portia had ever seen, but Ella never bothered her about that because Mia's hair was natural. Liam's hair colors were magic, and Ella was determined to learn how to do it.

Portia let the conversation swirl around her. She couldn't stop thinking about the child from that morning, nor of the child's stranded father and all the others facing such a black future in a foreign land. She'd been in that foreign land and seen what their fates would be. It was not something she'd wish on her worst enemy.

"I want to talk to the queen," Portia said suddenly, halting the conversation at the table.

The others looked around to see if anyone had heard, while Ella leaned in and grabbed Portia's hand. "Portia, no," Ella said. "You may be their Jack, but she is still the queen. She has given you her answer. Do not try her patience."

"It's the only way," Portia said. She tried to keep her voice down, but the urgency she felt pushed from the inside as if she might burst. "She has the royal navy, the guards, the resources to reach the large splinter over the waters and to provide protection while negotiating with the—"

Liam's normally happy face darkened. "You can't negotiate with them, with the Dragonoids. We've lost too many. They had no interest in working with us."

Mia nodded.

"Maybe they'd have more interest now that we shut them out. Maybe we could *make* them have more interest." Portia grabbed her water glass and took a swallow, as much to stop herself from talking even louder as to give herself a moment to think.

"Yes, at what cost?" Ella asked. "We've already lost so many."

"And we could get so many back if we would only try," Portia said, putting her cup down harder than she intended.

The ring of Portia's cup landing on the wooden table rang out through the dining hall, and other students turned to look with interest. Mia looked down at the table while speaking quietly so as to not carry, "We are not the enemy, Portia. Please, be careful. Going against the queen could be taken as treason."

Portia breathed in deeply. She sat up straight, forced her face to relax. The others breathed in more freely and sat up themselves. Students at other tables slowly lost interest as no confrontation materialized and went back to their own conversations.

"That is why I wish to speak to the queen," Portia said. "There must be a way to convince her. These are her people that are missing. The kingdom to the south is missing their king, and many of their own people. Would they not want to go and retrieve him? And those to the north? Near the entire kingdom was decimated. We may have shut the splinter against these creatures, but only after they extracted such a huge cost against us. Is it right for us to abandon our countrymen only because we now feel safe ourselves?"

Ella, Mia, Liam, and Richard refused to meet her eyes. They had no argument against her words, and they all knew it. This was something that had to be settled with the queen, as terrifying as that was.

THE NEXT DAY was just as hot and sweaty, and smelled even worse. One of the metal balls from the enemy ships had decimated the building Portia was assigned. Black powder coated the ball itself, still embedded in the floorboards that had been pushed down into the cellar. The black powder left streaks on the damaged wood that had once been stained a beautiful red-brown in a deep swirling pattern. The powder residue exploded out on impact, contaminating every surface.

Portia hated it.

Not only was it foul smelling and hurt her lungs, it was dangerous. An open flame could ignite it and the entire mass would burst into hot flame faster than any magic she'd ever seen. She lost skin to it before; she did not want to die from it now that the war was over. Mostly over.

To make the day even worse, the image of the girl from the day before would not leave Portia. Even here, in the depths of the reconstruction area, the cries of the children in the refugee tents floated over them, a constant reminder of the misery some were still enduring. Between the foul working conditions and the foul living conditions of the displaced, Portia could feel no peace in the hard labor.

By the time the soldier dressed in the queen's colors walked through, ringing the quitting bell, Portia had a plan. She would clean up, then request an audience with the queen that very day. Unlike Ella, she could survive missing dinner, a thought that made her smile despite everything.

Portia reached the ornate cast-iron gates of the palace just as the sun was setting on the lands to the west, sending warm rays of light down in the harbor that gave the area a soft glow. The palace itself sparkled in the late evening sun. With its purple stone walls and towers it resembled a gigantic flower. A gigantic, deadly flower. The grounds were immaculate, further lending to its ominous presence in it having somehow escaped the recent battle untouched.

The guard let her in without complaint, much to Portia's surprise. The last time she had requested an audience she had been rebuffed and mocked and sent back down the hill away from the palace to the laughter of the guards behind. Perhaps word of her doings in the battle had earned her some respect with them. Still, the guard watched her with slitted eyes and looked quickly away as she turned to face him. None of the other guards would even look at her. A shiver went down her spine.

A servant dressed in velvet livery led her through the palace, through the grand entryway, past portraits of past kings and queens, but instead of going to the audience chamber, he took an unexpected turn and let her down a dark hallway to a brilliantly lit room ahead. Sounds of cutlery and china and loud voices drifted down the hallway to her. It sounded like a large party.

"Please wait here," the servant told Portia, then turned and entered the room, leaving her to stand outside. She didn't want to stand in the doorway and attract the attention of anyone inside, instead peering around it to see who was there.

There was no one she recognized besides Queen Lorica and her consort, Aldis. All of those within wore fine rich gowns and doublets, embroidered silks and heavy laces, all loaded with fine jewels of deep blues, reds, and greens. More jewels were in that room than Portia even thought possible to exist. Who were these people? Were these the nobles of the town that she had only heard of? Could some of these be the parents of students that she went to school with? Involuntarily she looked down at her own garb of green velvet. It was her finest, and yet she felt she should be a scullery maid by comparison with what she saw within.

Even so, it felt unsettling she didn't know any of these people. Despite her inappropriate garb, an urge to walk within the room gripped her, to find out who they were, but she knew, coming as she was begging for a favor, it would be a reach too far.

She was lost in thought when all within the room suddenly rose with a commotion and the queen appeared in front of Portia, giving her a start. She quickly averted her eyes and backed up to give the queen space to exit the room.

The queen was dressed in a fine blue silk brocade, with the deeper blue trim and sapphires sewn around the neckline and down the sleeves. Her dark curly hair was piled high atop her head and interwoven with the crown of gold ivy and leaves, studded with even larger sapphires. Portia wondered if it hurt to have such a heavy weight on the queen's head.

"Your Majesty," Portia said, giving a deep curtsy.

"My Jack," the queen said. She gave Portia a tiny nod then swept by without a backwards glance.

Portia watched the queen walk away with confusion, then glanced at the servant who waived her after the receding monarch. Portia scrambled after her, finding it surprisingly hard to keep pace with the swift queen. She could hear the servant's footsteps behind them.

A guard outside another room at the far end of the hall opened it in time so the queen could sweep in without modifying her pace. Portia made eye contact with the guard so he knew she was there and wouldn't shut the door on her face. Again, he wouldn't look at her, but he held the door while she passed through.

The room was a small lounge, tiny in palace standards, furnished with several small silk brocade couches and a sideboard with crystal glasses and decanters of dark liquid. The queen sat at one of the couches and waved the servant who had entered after them towards the sideboard.

"My Jack," the queen said, the thinnest hint of irritation in her voice. "You have come and requested an audience and I have become available."

"I apologize, Your Majesty. I didn't mean to interrupt your dinner," Portia said, almost stuttering on her reply.

"What exactly did you think I would be doing at this hour?" The queen eyed her over her crystal glass as she sipped from it.

Portia's face heated as she blushed. She hadn't thought at all.

"I apologize," Portia said, suddenly wishing she had not come. Still, people were depending on her. She should not be so childish as to want to run away because of a social error. *Social errors can cost you your life*, a voice within her head reminded her.

"Well?" the queen said, lowering her drink to her lap and staring at Portia.

"I have asked, no, I'm coming begging, that you reconsider opening the splinter between worlds to rescue our people. I've been told the other races do not do well there. It is not a matter of adapting, Your Majesty... I've heard that if the elves stay too long, they will die. We can't just leave them there. They are the ones that helped us to win." Portia's flush intensified as she realized she was telling the queen what to do. She must really have a death wish.

The queen had simply raised one eyebrow at Portia.

Portia waited, trying to not fidget, but then couldn't help herself and continued on. "I could not go through the splinter. I could stay here. Then I would be protected to close it again."

"You would ask that your fellow countrymen risk their lives in something you could not do," the queen asked.

"I would do it, in a heartbeat, but..." Portia stopped herself. They both knew the queen did not want her to risk her life. Portia was the only one who could permanently close the access between worlds. The Dwarven kingdom to the south was able to do it only by encasing them in stone and physically blocking them. The elves to the north and the west had once had the ability, but now only an elder, frail mage had that skill, and he was not able to travel. It was unknown why their children had lost that skill.

"It does not matter, child, if you stay in this world if they come back in again to make themselves unwanted nuisances," the queen said coldy.

Nuisances? People were dying even now from hunger, and more would die far away. This was far beyond a mere nuisance.

"Has anything changed since we last met on this issue?" the queen asked, pulling Portia from her thoughts. "Have others come forward with the ability to heal the splinters?"

"No," Portia said, the words coming out grudgingly while she thought of the starving child she'd met and others suffering without their loved ones. No one in the dining hall she had just witnessed appeared to be suffering, or ever had.

"No. Then why have you interrupted my dinner?"

"It's just that people are starving. Others will die in that world. Their captors are not kind. Do we not owe it to them to rescue them?" Portia asked.

"Do we owe it to them to die on their behalf? Do you think my subjects would want that for their queen? For their countrymen?" The queen spoke as if Portia were a tiny stubborn dog, not learning her commands well. She leaned into Portia. "They are all my subjects. I must balance what is best for most of them."

Portia looked down, furious. She wondered if it was what was best for most of the subjects or what was best for the queen. Another battle would cost men and resources, lumber and grain, and most of all, tax money. How much of the kingdom's tax money had been spent on the dinner for the peacocks in the other room wearing a kingdom's worth of jewels a piece.

"Yes, Your Majesty." The words were bitter in her throat.

A sound behind Portia caused Portia to turn. King Consort Aldis had slipped in the door behind them and was watching the interaction. Portia tried to turn to curtsy to him without showing her back to the queen. Instead, she stumbled awkwardly and faced neither one directly.

He waved her to rise and quickly crossed the room to stand next to the queen, at least letting Portia turn to face them both. "Greetings, Jack. Our guests grow restless and I had to see what was keeping my beloved queen." He gave the queen a warm smile, but she did not return it, instead maintaining her gaze bearing down on Portia.

"Make no mistake, my Jack, the kingdom is grateful for your assistance in our recent battle. However, as the caretaker of the people, my judgment is what decides how events further unfold. Do you think a blacksmith working at his forge would know the best way to protect a thousand citizens? Do you think a seamstress working in her den could decide issues of state? Do you think we are so similar that your judgment could be substituted for mine? That you, Jack or not, can balance all the complexities of husbanding a land?"

The queen's voice grew more strident as she spoke. Portia looked down as the tirade continued, unable to face the queen who was even more terrifying with the calmness of her countenance, even as the volume of her voice rose.

Portia fell to one knee. "I beg you, Your Majesty. People are dying. People have already died, but more will die even so of starvation. Those abandoned on the other side will waste away. We are not whole."

"Enough!" the queen said, rage in her voice, standing to tower over Portia. Portia didn't dare look up. She stayed on one knee, the back of her neck and shoulders tingling, almost waiting for a blow that she could swear the queen wanted to lay on her.

The queen breathed heavily, then walked away from Portia and back behind the couch, putting the furniture between her and her subject. Portia felt oddly relieved and abandoned. She didn't dare utter another word, nor did the king consort or the servant speak. All waited upon the queen.

In a much calmer voice, the queen spoke again. "I forget how you are still just a babe in school. You have done very well by our kingdom, but that does not change your youth and lack of worldly experience. The nobles of this kingdom are nobles for a reason. We know, and understand, all the needs of our people and the land and of diplomacy and of war. Things you cannot know at your age, and will never know." The queen stopped herself.

Portia still did not look up. Her jaw tightened so much it sent a shot of pain across her face. She knew what the queen was about to say but would not—that Portia could not know because she was not of noble blood. But she was of noble blood. She was of the most noble blood of the land, the once ruling house of Callac. They both knew that, and yet here she was, having only barely survived on the street as a thief, while the queen, who came from the lower house of Coverack, sat on the throne and dined on pheasant and boar.

"Stand," the queen said.

Portia did so reluctantly, only looking up at the last minute to search the queen's face. It gave away nothing. The king consort had stood watching, holding a drink of his own, but otherwise taking no part.

"I forgive you this time your youth and ignorance. We shall not have this discussion again. My word is law," said the queen, her eyes glittering.

Portia nodded and looked down. "Yes, Your Majesty."

"Leave now, and return to your house. Instructions will

come to you later," said the queen, her tone making it clear there would be no recourse to whatever dictates she sent.

Portia followed the servant out, leaving the queen and king consort alone. The servant walked off without a glance behind. Checking the hallway, Portia lingered at the doorway, pretending to adjust her shoe.

Inside the room, a cushion creaked as the king consort sat down.

"She is only a child," he said quietly.

"She is a child of Callac. And a Jack," the queen said. "The first alone is enough to..." The sound of the queen's fingers tapping on the arm of her couch filled the room.

"The people love her," he said, gently

"That is not in her favor," the queen said, her tone steely.

Portia glanced down the hall. The servant who was supposed to be leading her away was halfway down the hall. He'd notice her absence from her designation position behind him as soon as he turned the corner. She had just a moment more.

"Would you like a drink, Your Majesty?" the king consort asked as the cushion creaked again.

"Yes. And rouse Grania. I need to speak with her tonight."

Portia sucked a breath. Grania was Queen Lorica's master of spies. She ruled all the spies, every spy under her meekly followed her orders. Even some generals.

The servant was nearly at the end of the hall. Running silently on the balls of her feet, Portia caught up with him. She gave him a weak smile as he turned to check on her as they exited the hall.

2

The pyromancy house was quiet when Portia returned, the hallways dim and only lit by a few candles in iron holders in the wall, with some additional spilled light from the rooms where students had left their doors cracked open.

It was well past the mad hour right after dinner when energy was high and students ran through the halls, sometimes shooting puffs of fire just to startle their friends, no matter it being against house rules. Now, everyone was preparing for the next day and some students were already sleeping. The normally always loud kitchens behind her were quiet and dark, and the silence seemed to spread through the building.

Portia gently pushed open the door to the room she shared with Ella, trying to avoid the door's annoying squeak. Ella was not there, but instead a lithe figure lay on her bed, sandy spikes of blond hair pressed on her pillow, and worse yet, dingy gray socks on her bedspread. At least the shoes were still on the floor.

"Mark, what are you doing here?" Portia glanced behind her. "Does Ella know you're here?"

Mark sat up on the bed and gave her a wicked smile. "Do you mean, did she threaten to murder me if I did anything wrong or touched any of her stuff? Why yes, I do think she knows I'm here. Thanks for asking."

"She's not normally like that," Portia said. It was true. Ella was the sunniest person she knew, and seemed to make friends everywhere, yet somehow her back had gone up instantly in Mark's presence.

Mark murmured something under his breath and rubbed his hair, making it even messier. He had black circles under his eyes and his clothes looked uncustomarily wrinkled. Ever since they had escaped the clutches of the gang back in Valencia, he had been fastidious about his dress, as much as he could afford. Now, he just looked tired and rumpled.

"What are you doing here?" Portia said, repeating herself. "Sleeping in your own bed not agreeing with you?"

He looked up, squinting with one eye. "The bed is fine, it's the dreams I don't like much."

Portia nodded, then came and sat next to him on the bed. "Me too."

She didn't want to ask him what in particular bothered him, as it was most likely exactly the same as what bothered her—the plight of the refugees—and she was too tired to talk about it anyhow. The audience with the queen had left her shaken. The monarch had always seemed neutral, if not always the most protective of Portia's health, but tonight had felt different than any other time. It was almost as if Portia had personally irritated the ruler and provoked an especially harsh response.

"Actually, Ella asked me to come here," Mark said.

Portia pulled out of her ruminations and stared into his gray eyes. That didn't sound right.

"Apparently Hilda is looking for you and for some reason asked Ella to message me."

"Where are they now?" Portia said, looking around.

A knock came at the door and Portia looked up. A stout woman of middling years stood in the doorframe, her formal black robes from the day still on. Professor Hilda Griffiths was Portia's teacher and housemother. She was also the first person who had told Portia about the school. She gave Portia a tired smile. Ella peeked in from behind her, blocked from entering her own room.

"You're back, wonderful." Hilda entered the room and took a seat at Portia's desk, her robes billowing and seeming to envelope the wooden backed chair as she sat. Ella followed closely and sat on her own bed, her hands between her knees, staring at what was unfolding in front of her. Portia shot her a look, but Ella just unhelpfully gave her a smile back.

"What's going on?" Portia asked, concern plucking at her heart. Hilda normally worked in solitude in her own study at this hour. Portia could not remember a time when she'd seen the housemother roaming around so late. She shoved her own hands underneath her knees and straightened her arms to prevent any shaking she felt her body wanted to do, still reeling from her encounter with the queen.

"No worries, Portia," Hilda said, her tone soothing. "It's just that I got a message from the queen. For Cecelia's service in the war, the queen has granted her the boon of an escort to her home in Coray. You. The queen thinks this a great gift for you both, and she wants you to leave immediately. Isn't that great?"

Portia stared at Hilda, her mouth hanging open. Realizing it, she closed her jaw, then glanced at Ella whose face was neutral, and then at Mark, who just shrugged.

"I'm being sent away?" Portia asked, turning back to Hilda.

Hilda tilted her head at Portia and pursed her lips.

"I'm serious, am I being sent away? Portia asked. "I mean, couldn't this have waited until tomorrow?"

"The message came a few hours ago, but you were not yet back." Hilda adjusted her robes awkwardly. "I had to respond to the queen. They are expecting you at the stables in the morning. I believe this is for Cecelia's benefit."

Portia did not like the way Hilda's smile did not reach her eyes.

"Yes, well, I took a walk through the Academy," Portia said as she stood to pace the room. She had walked for several hours through the darkened buildings and trees of the Academy. It was probably the safest place in all of Coverack, with the charmed perimeter and the guards on duty and the constant flow, even at that late hour, of practiced mages. She had wanted to walk off some of her agitation after meeting with the queen.

"You are not being sent away," Hilda said.

Portia didn't believe her.

Ella bounced on her bed a bit, unable to refrain from speaking a moment longer. "Mark gets to go with you, lucky one. Once again, you're skipping school. I asked to come with, I really did, Portia, but Hilda was adamant." Ella's gaze turned to Hilda. "My grades are not that bad. I can afford to miss some school. Send me off on an adventure. Please?"

Hilda pursed her lips and then closed her eyes briefly for a moment before speaking to Ella. "My dear, this is Portia's mother, and they are going to a farm, I would hardly think that would be an adventure. And haven't you had enough adventure lately?"

"There is never enough adventure," Ella said, flipping back her blonde hair. Mark made a strange sound, then coughed exaggeratedly. Portia glared at him before taking her seat again on the bed.

"I mean it," Ella said, speaking over Mark's coughing. "Portia is my roommate. I can help guard her mother and stuff. I can study on the road." She narrowed her eyes at Hilda. "This is about my grades, isn't it."

"No, my dear, it is not, but we should speak about them tomorrow, nonetheless," Hilda said.

Mark choked back another sound. Both Ella and Portia glared at him until he smoothed his face into a neutral expression.

"So Mark and I?" Portia asked once silence came back to the room.

"Yes, dear. They are sending three of their best horses. I do not know if there will be other guards."

Between the two of them, Portia and Mark had considerable magic powers, but they had been at war for so long it felt odd to think about taking a journey in the countryside without guards. A tiny premonition of danger created goosebumps along her arms and the back of Portia's neck. She gave herself a quick shake, trying to rid herself of the feeling. Her always thinking bad things were going to happen was more than likely just the habit of her spending so much of her life living in conflict.

It didn't always happen.

Hilda stood from the chair, her robes flowing back down. She stepped to Portia and placed a warm hand on Portia's forearm, then leaned in and said quietly, "You are not being sent away. You will be back." She gave Portia a final pat on the arm, then turned to go.

Portia watched her leave the room, Hilda's robes billowing out as she turned past the door and walked away, her muffled footsteps of soft leather on polished wood echoing down the quiet hallway. Turning, Portia saw Mark and Ella, both with arms crossed across their chests, glaring at each other.

Yawning, Portia stuffed a few rolls in her pocket, and another warm one in her mouth. The faint smell of cinnamon filled her nose. The only thing missing was some butter.

It was not yet dawn outside. The kitchen of the pyromacy house was lit by three large fires, all of them with large cast-iron pots hanging over them, and more light coming from thick yellow candles burning in the wall mounts.

Dressed in the distinctive house red linens, the cooks and cooks' assistants bustled around the large wood tables, preparing not only breakfast but prepping for lunch and dinner as well. Carrying large trays and bowls and bundles of carrots by the greens and other foodstuffs, they wove their way around Portia and her large pack, now even fuller thanks to the bundle of provisions from the head cook. Hilda must have notified the woman last night, for it was ready before Portia even had to ask. It felt heavy enough to feed three people for a long journey. Portia winced at the thought of eating dried jerky for the entire way, but it was better than starving. Perhaps the cook had been creative in her provisioning.

Finding her way to the portal entrance in the living room, Portia checked herself one last time, patting for her knives strapped to her calves, and her larger one inside her waist, as well as for her precious sword at her back. She felt slightly silly bringing a sword of all things to a farm but could not bear the thought of leaving it behind. The copper blade and green sheath still looked immaculate, despite all it had gone through with her. Leaving it behind was akin to the thought of cutting off her arm and leaving that behind.

Finding all her weapons and her overfull bag where they should be, Portia took in a deep breath and walked to the portal's entrance, opening on one side in the large communal living room. It looked like an ordinary door, but the door led from the pyromancy house, the location of which was secret to all including its inhabitants, directly to the center of the Magic Academy, all through the use of magic. One step to the next brought a person through vast distances.

Portal magic.

Once again Portia sighed. It was one of the few magics that had eluded her. The living room was safe, even with the door there, because the door blocked those without permission from using it. This allowed the students a safe place to stay off campus, even with the anti-magic movement afoot. Not that that had been a worry lately, at least, but the school had not changed its system.

Taking one last look around, Portia walked through the door, exiting into the stone garden courtyard on the other side. Doors sprang from the stones in a random pattern, scattered along a swirl of darker stones inlaid on a background of light gray pebbles.

There was one door for each of the magic houses: pyromancy, cryomancy, metallurgy, those magics she didn't even know the names of yet, each denoted by a symbol on the outside depicting fire, or some other representation of the magic of its inhabitants.

Portia could have lived in any one of these houses, but that was unique to her as a Jack of Magic, and neither she nor the school had known that when she was first accepted. Most mages can only do one type of magic, and even though the most prolific amongst them could do more than one aspect of that. A fire-breather could not make duplicates of himself, nor could a cryomancy mage make a portal.

Not that Portia could make one of these local portals either, much to her chagrin. Apparently it was very specialized and required great deals of energy.

For this journey, it would be simpler to just ride a horse.

The stables were on the back end of the campus where the ground rose to the hills behind. There was a road that ran around the edge of the deep green grounds that allowed passage for horses and large wagons so they could make way without having to go between the stately old buildings in the central square.

Portia walked back to the stables, shifting her increasingly heavy pack to keep it from pulling too heavily on one spot on her shoulder. She polished off the rest of the rolls, regretting that she had not grabbed more. Her pride at not wanting to seem greedy seemed like a silly thing indeed now that her stomach still wanted more food. Surely the cooks would've understood that.

The sun was just rising on the sea's horizon behind her, sending yellow beams of light shooting ahead and onto the path and the trees surrounding it, and into the windows of the campus building which reflected the light back in blinding flashes of yellow and white. Even with the reflections, Portia was able to spot a glint in the path ahead. It shone like water, but there was no rain, nor even a hint of moisture on that dry summer morning.

Portia stopped, squinting ahead. It was ice on the path, edge to edge, extending ahead several horse lengths. She was already off-balance from the heavy pack. One foot on that ice would have sent her flying.

"Oh blessed be, can't we have any fun this morning, *commoner*?" a sneering voice said.

Portia turned. Behind her stood a tiny girl, all of seventeen or so, with black hair and one hand on her cocked hip.

Magisend Lucy Gwynn of House Riddlepit.

The girl tilted her head at Portia, then spoke again. "What, not happy to see me?"

"Depends, I guess," Portia said. She waved to the path. "Why the welcome?"

"Oh, I was just practicing. I wasn't sure you'd be coming this way," Magisend said. "Just lucky, I guess."

"Lucky?"

"Geez, commoner, loosen up. I wouldn't have let you step on it. This time." Magisend gave Portia a smirk. "I was just feeling nostalgic for old times."

"I can dump a bucket of water on you if you'd like. That seemed to be an old time too," Portia said, a smile growing.

"Nevermind, nevermind, nevermind," Magisend said, waving a hand. The ice behind Portia gave a crack and then a sigh. Portia knew that meant Magisend had released the spell and the ice was now melting in the summer morning's heat.

"In all seriousness, we need to talk," Magisend said.

"About?" Portia asked, curious.

"What do you mean 'about?'" Magisend said. "It's been

weeks, the Elven general's gone, that crabby archmage is gone—"

Portia laughed. "Archmage Vermeil?"

"Yeah, whatever. The point is they're not here and we haven't done anything. It's been weeks. Over a month. People could be…"

Portia crossed her arms. "Dying? Magisend, are you worried about people dying?" Portia leaned in and stared at Magisend. "You care." She said it as if scandalized.

Magisend glared at Portia. "Do you?"

That was too much. "Of course I care. I want to do something, but we have no resources. I tried to talk to the queen again—"

"Yes, I heard about that. Congratulations. I don't like getting up this early, thank you very much."

"No one asked you to get up this early. Why are you even here?" Portia glared at Magisend. The sun was warm on Portia's face and she was suddenly aware of how late it was getting. Cecelia and the palace guards who had brought her from the palace this morning were expecting her at the stables. She did not want the queen to hear she had arrived late. "Please explain in simple terms what you want."

"I heard about your phenomenal interview and getting sent away." Magisend glared at Portia.

"You said. How?"

"Nevermind how. I have my ways. I want to know what your plan is. What our plan is. Exactly. I want a plan," Magisend said, throwing one hand up in exasperation. "You're the one who can open the splinter, the only one."

Portia stepped closer to Magisend, her voice lower. "Are you crazy? Anyone could be about now. Quiet."

Magisend pursed her lips and lifted her chin, reminding Portia of the days when she had first met Magisend and Magisend had thought Portia not even worthy of kissing her gold encrusted boot. Especially after Portia had stolen all her linens.

Exasperated, Portia continued. "I have to go. The queen has ordered me to escort my mother to her farm. We'll talk when I get back. Maybe you can find a way to talk to the queen," Portia said, shifting the pack's weight and feeling even more anxious about the time ticking away.

"The queen," Magisend said back at her, lowering her volume, but almost hissing out the word.

"I have to go!" Portia said, then turned and walked towards the stables, carefully going around the edge of the path and making her way in the grass, wary about any possible lingering ice.

"We're not done with this!" Magisend called after her.

Snow came out of the blue morning sky and fell around Portia as she walked away, a cloud hovering over her head, and Magisend's laugh ringing out behind her.

"Crazy nobles," Portia said under her breath. She brushed the flakes away from her face and walked faster to get away from Magisend's created blizzard.

Mark walked up to the stables just as Portia approached, also carrying bags. One looked to be holding clothes while the other had a long loaf of bread sticking out of it. Portia was happy to see she was not the only one who had brought provisions. He nodded at her and walked to her side as she approached the large black double doors of the blue stone barn.

The courtyard of grass and tan gravel was empty. Portia had expected the horses to be waiting there. Portia pulled open the door, having to lean back against the weight of the enormous wooden panel to start it swinging, but there was no one inside. She could not hear the sounds of any animals.

A whinny caught her attention. She looked back at Mark. He pointed to the far side of the barn.

Two palace guards in dress uniform of purple with gold braid rode on either side of Cecelia, each holding the lead of an additional riderless horse. They had just come up the long road. Portia exhaled a sigh of relief. They were not late.

The guards had no bags on their horses. Indeed, there were only three sets of saddle bags: Cecelia's bulging ones behind her on her horse, and empty ones on the horses being led.

The guards were not coming with.

"Portia," Cecelia called from her perch, waving and looking for all her years like a little child given a treat. Portia smiled back at the woman who was her mother but felt more like a stranger.

The guards handed over the reins of the horses to Mark and Portia, then gave a nod before turning and leaving, not even waiting to see if Portia or Mark had any problems with their bags or getting on the horses. Portia huffed. Perhaps they had a hot breakfast waiting that they had to get back to or lose out. Or perhaps they were just rude.

Portia and Mark managed to get their bags settled and mounted their horses before Cecelia had the idea of getting off her own. Portia wasn't sure how good Cecelia was with horses and thought the less opportunity for getting on and off the better. From what Cecelia had told her, it could be a long three-day journey, or more. The woman wasn't sure since she had never journeyed there directly from Coverack.

THEY REACHED the city limits within an hour, exiting the gate on the western side under the early morning sun. Far from the battle-scarred harbor, the streets they had passed through looked as if nothing had happened: houses sat within their little plots, flowers and vegetable gardens out back, the cobblestone streets clean.

The section of the city they had passed through was the more affluent section of town, where the highest house nobles lived in mini castles, while the lower nobles had sprawling houses. It had become fashionable generations ago to go away from the noisy markets at the harbor. It had served them well when the attack had come from the sea.

Mark, Portia, and Cecelia had ridden in silence, the clop of the horses' hooves and the stones ringing out through the neighborhood. There were no market stalls here, nor cry of sellers, only the sound of birds and the occasional swish of a gardener's scythe.

Once free of the city, they rode single file. Outside the city's gates the road was flooded with people on the roads.

Most were dirty and carried small bags, some even without shoes. Refugees, even now. The people streaming towards Coverack were not allowed to enter on the western gate but instead guided by the soldiers to go around the city's walls and enter on the south. The soldiers had been yelling orders at those wanting to come in when they had passed through on their horses. Portia had received barely a nod when they passed the soldier at the iron gate.

Watching the refuges walk past, Portia's stomach clenched. It had been a hard month for most. Food had been burned in the field, and the thinnest of the people coming showed it.

The invaders had been merciless in destroying homes and crops—really anything they could find—though they had little interest in taking anything except for people, leaving those lucky enough to have escaped without food or shelter.

The kingdoms to the north and the south had been devastated. The kingdom of Haulstatt, Portia's kingdom, had gotten away with the least amount of damage of all the costal human kingdoms. It was where most of the refugees journeyed to.

Hours went by, and Portia felt herself swaying in the saddle, her eyes glazing over with the hypnotic noises of the horses' hooves and the buzz of flies in the dry fields. She knew she should sit up straight or pinch herself or otherwise make herself more alert, but it felt good to relax in the sunshine and half-doze in the saddle. An annoying voice kept poking at her consciousness and she finally turned her attention to it.

"Portia, do you know the way beyond Holne?" Mark asked.

"Not to the farm, no. But I know we need to go to Coray. We can ask at the guardhouse in Holne. They might know the conditions of the road beyond Holne." She glanced at Cecelia but did not say anything further. No point alarming the woman that they were vulnerable without guards.

"Right." Mark said. He looked better that morning. The dark circles under his eyes from last night lightened, his skin more golden than gray. He glanced at Portia, then away, clearly wanting to say something.

"Spit it out," Portia said.

"What is the deal with Ella?"

Portia squinted at him. "What do you mean?"

"Why is she always so mean to me?" He finally said in a rush, his face reddening, and he looked away. "She's so nice to everyone else." His words were barely audible.

Cecelia grinned.

"A little sibling rivalry here, huh?" Cecelia asked. "Or is it something different?" She pushed her horse in between Mark and Portia's, inserting herself in their conversation. Portia was impressed with her riding skills.

Mark glanced at Cecelia, then squirmed, his face turning even redder.

"I do think she wanted to come with," Portia said, puzzled over Cecelia's words. Ella and Mark were not siblings. What could Cecelia mean by that?

"Yeah, I think she thinks all we do is have fun on our trips, not risking our lives or anything. She should know better. She was on the ship. We all nearly died," Mark said.

They had nearly died, the ship taking on water, and only saved through Portia's magic in healing the hull.

"Maybe you should ask her direct," Cecelia said.

Mark grunted. "Nevermind."

"I've had a lot of experience with young people," Cecelia said. "Direct is usually best, though they might squirm. Got six on the farm." She glanced at Portia. "And now Portia will be seven."

"Six kids?" Portia asked. A strange feeling passed over her. Her mother had gone on and had six kids, as if she had never existed.

"Half of them be my husband's from before, with his first wife. Only three are mine," Cecelia said in a soothing tone, as if she could sense Portia's upset. "Life does go on."

Yes, it does go on, Portia thought bitterly, reminded of her conversation with the queen who had urged her to forget those behind, as apparently her mother had forgotten her, or at least been able to move on. Portia turned her face away and stared at the fields until her vision cleared again.

They journeyed for most of the day, stopping only for a brief respite in a small copse by the road. The refugees had thinned. None passed by them during the brief time they had stopped and eaten bread and cheese.

As evening came on, and the sun was setting in their eyes, they passed over the final rise before the long descent into Holne.

"Holy buckets," Portia said as they reached the top and looked down into the township.

3

"Did they empty out all of Jukhnovo?" Mark asked.

"Looks like," Portia said quietly.

They all gaped at the sight ahead of them. Holne was a tiny hamlet; at least it had been. What lay before them were fields and fields of tents where crops should've been, the white canvas of their entrance flaps blowing in the breeze. Fires punctuated the grounds, twists of smoke reaching up to the darkening blue sky, silhouetted against the oranges and reds of the setting sun.

Beyond the tents, some of the town's buildings were visible, as well as the light yellow of newly cut wood, already formed into the skeletons of buildings and houses. At least here there were horses, most hitched to wagons, pulling lumber in the well-worn tracks between the tents. An impromptu road formed.

And everywhere, so many people.

"Why would they all abandon their land?" Portia asked.

"They can't go staying where they were, not this year, not if all their crops were burnt," Cecelia said. "Those foul creatures were just downright mean. They didn't want the crops, but they couldn't just leave them could they?" Cecelia spit to the side, shocking Portia.

Mark appraised Cecelia. "How did you get captured? They attacked the coasts, and your farm is so far inland. None else of your family were taken, I think?" He gave Cecelia a questioning look.

She nodded.

"Then how?" he asked.

Cecelia gave a bitter laugh. "Vanity, that's how."

Portia stared at her. What an odd answer.

Cecelia patted Portia on the arm. "Truly, I guess it wasn't as dumb as it seems now, but I was caught because I was off buying fabric for my girls. Nothing in town matched my desires, so I talked my husband into letting me go for a week farther east, and east I went... right into the trap of the invaders."

"You couldn't have known," Mark said after a brief silence, awkwardly trying to comfort her.

"Perhaps not, but I'm not thinking pretty fabric is so important anymore. I'll be keeping my purchases closer to home." Cecelia said, giving her head a shake.

They rode down the hill, past the tents and to the town beyond. They lucked out to get two rooms at the inn off the main square, the owner behind the bar glad to see coin up front, paying customers being harder to find these days.

Portia left Cecelia and Mark at the inn to order dinner

and see the horses settled, and went across the square to the clothier she remembered from passing through Holne before. Something about Alice, the owner of the store, always felt comfortable to Portia. She'd always given Portia exactly what she needed. A small tugging on Portia's heart pulled her to the store yet once again.

The inside of the store was quiet, the last of the customers exiting as Portia entered, the small bell above the door chiming into the dimly lit room. Alice stood with her back to the door, tallying something on a ledger.

"Welcome back, Portia," Alice said before she turned.

Alice looked the same as she had always done, her hair impossible to discern either golden or gray, shining one way or the other depending how the light struck it. Her face ageless. She smiled warmly at Portia.

Portia felt suddenly shy.

"Hello again," Portia said, stepping further into the shop. Beautiful fabrics lay everywhere. She thought of Cecelia. Perhaps she should've asked her mother to come with her. Would that have only brought up bad memories?

Alice stepped forward and looked at Portia closely. "You still have your sword."

A vibration on Portia's shoulder made her jump, seeming to come through the strap holding her sword to her back, almost as if the sword knew it was being spoken of. She jerked the strap and it stopped.

"I do," Portia said.

Alice's lips twitched, and she looked away, her eyes twinkling. "I have something for you." She went behind the counter and reached down to pull out a bundle, then laid it out on top of the wood surface. Gently opening the thin paper wrapping, Alice revealed a deep purple garment. "It's not done yet. I was waiting for the thread to do the needlework, and it has just arrived."

"For me?" Portia asked, surprised. "How did you know I was coming?" She stepped forward to look at the garment. The color was so rich it seemed to suck in the light.

Alice paused for a minute, then answered lightly, "I was hoping you would come. You do like to travel."

Portia didn't bother to explain most of her travels were for the kingdom, or for her own safety. As much as she was drawn to Alice and her shop, she still wasn't entirely sure how much she should share.

"It will have embroidery of the stars and the moon, with this," Alice said, holding up a spool of thread of gold.

Portia gasped. "Oh, no, no. That is much too fine."

Alice smoothed the material and lifted it up to show Portia its form. It was a court dress, worthy of Queen Lorica's court. Below it in the paper lay fine petticoats with translucent material that looked like spun spiderwebs.

Portia wanted to touch the material, to finger the petticoats, but dared not. She was still dirty from the road and felt even more so in the face of such fine goods.

"No, that's not for me," Portia said. "I'm more in the market for another knife holster, or tunic and breaches. I need to be able to fight."

Alice lay the dress down again and folded it gently. "This is a weapon of sorts. You only have to know how to use it." She looked up and stared at Portia.

Not sure how to answer that, Portia cleared her throat and looked away. Somehow in the war-torn country, this shop was fully stocked with material.

"There is something you can help me with," Portia said, still staring at the piles of cloth.

THE HAMLET of Coray was little more than four or five low stone houses, covered in thatch, and a slightly larger structure that might have been a store. A scrawny horse was tied up to the hitching post outside of it. The horse rolled its eyes warily at the three of them as they rode through the dusty street, shifting from one side to another to keep them visible as they passed behind it.

No one came out to greet them, or even to see what the noise was. A curtain flicked in the general store.

So they had been spotted.

Whoever lived here was aware, but no one came out to greet them. This felt more ominous than facing bandits on the road, something they had miraculously avoided on the three-day journey. Portia had a strong desire to dig her heels into her horse's sides and urge it forward, but restrained herself. Cecelia seemed unconcerned, her eyes only forward on the road to the farm.

Cecelia turned and smiled at Portia, pointing the way unnecessarily, her horse already pulling ahead, sensing her rider's eagerness.

Forcing herself to breathe in slowly, Portia relaxed her shoulders back and rolled her neck. There was nothing wrong here.

Perhaps it was the hours of riding in the hot sun with no other travelers in sight, all while the cicadas screamed, that had pulled her nerves so tight.

It had been a hot dry summer. The crops next to the roads on their journey lay parched in the fields, the stalks of grain a light gold, while a constant haze of dust hung over the fields. Some fields edged towards the brown of dying plants, but blessedly most were not that bad and remained edible, and harvestable.

But just so.

The farmers could not have been happy.

Portia thought she could feel their angst in the air, a mood that tainted every living thing in the land.

And while she had been relieved to not encounter any trouble on the roads, she could not quite relax after seeing nobody at all, not after the first day of constant refugees on the road. Someone should have been out and about, but there had been no one but the flies and the merciless, forever-crying cicadas.

Lines formed between Mark's eyes as he looked around. His eyes met Portia's. He gave a brief nod. At least he, too, felt the tension.

They rode through the hamlet and up an easy sloping road. The trees grew more frequent, their shade offering the occasional coolness that had been missing before. More moisture hung in the air, seeming to come off the trees and floating over the gentle hills. Once Portia even thought she heard the burble of a hidden creek within the trees, but they passed by and soon the sound was gone.

Sheep dotted the land, their black legs working under fluffy gray clouds of wool. One black lamb cried loudly and ran in circles around three adult sheep, while three younger ones, all white themselves, chased it. The black sheep finally cried one last time before ducking in between two of the older sheep and then sticking its face out between the seeming safety of its elders. Portia couldn't help but laugh.

"You like our sheep?" Cecelia asked.

Portia turned to her in surprise. "These are yours?"

Cecelia raised her chin. "Aye, all that you see. Wonderful, isn't it?"

The only fence on the lands was the rough-hewn two level split-wood fence that ran along the road itself. It was one large farm. Portia had never known a landowner, much less anyone who had so much. Suddenly she felt she knew Cecelia even less than she did.

Mark whistled, appreciatively.

A biting anger rose in Portia's chest. She tried to push it down. While she and Mark had been fighting for their lives in Valencia, and often going to bed without a meal, lucky to even have a bed, her mother had been living in this seeming paradise. This could have been her life.

She didn't want to blame her mother, and yet, who else was there?

Portia blinked, trying to rid herself of her thoughts. She knew as well as anyone the thieves, beggars, and criminals in the streets. If Cecelia had been attacked and Portia taken from her, surely it was not Cecelia's fault.

Surely.

The creak of an unoiled gate rang out. Ahead, the wooden fencing gave way to a decorative iron gate that stood open. A tall bearded man, with a ragged wide brimmed straw hat and dark hooded eyes stared at them from the gate, waiting. He must have heard the horses approaching.

He held an ax ready in one hand.

Cecelia waved a handkerchief at him and squealed, not unlike a young girl. Portia stared at her. The man dropped his axe and ran down the road towards Cecelia, who managed to kick her horse into a gallop. They met in the road and the man swung Cecelia from the saddle in a large arc, kissing her as she slid down his arms to stand on the road in front of him. Portia and Mark stopped their horses, looking away awkwardly as the couple reacquainted themselves.

After several minutes, Mark cleared his throat. "Shall we?" he asked Portia.

Portia gritted her teeth and nodded, looking ahead and then quickly glancing away when she realized they were still kissing. Hopefully the sound of their horses approaching would get the couple's attention.

Alas, only another throat clearing from Mark was effective, their arrival having no effect upon the man and Cecelia. Finally Cecelia pulled away, then gently slapped the man on the shoulder.

"William, this is my daughter, the one I told you about," Cecelia said to the man, pointing at Portia. He narrowed his eyes at Portia and then gave her a quick nod. His eyes moved to Mark in an unspoken question.

"And this is her friend, Mark," Cecelia said, understanding her husband's look.

"Friend?" William asked, skeptically.

"We've grown up almost as brother and sister," Portia said, feeling the need to speak up for Mark. William looked even less welcoming to Mark than he had to her.

"Portia, this is William, my husband," Cecelia said, rubbing the chest of the man while beaming at Portia. She seemed completely unaware of the tension between the other three. Unaware, or simply refusing to acknowledge it.

"Well, I thank ye both for escorting my wife home," William said, almost as if thanking them before sending them on their way.

"You'll have plenty of time to thank her and Mark. They're staying a while," Cecelia said. She grabbed the reins of her horse that had been patiently grazing along the roadside. "Did you get my message?"

William nodded at her. "Aye, that was some time ago, and you made no mention—"

"No, there was no mention of Portia. That was a recent blessing from Queen Lorica. She has given Portia permission to stay here a month and take a break from her studies and get to know her mother."

A month.

William's eyes met Portia's. He knew as well as she did that the queen's blessing was also a command, clearly an unwelcome one to him. Portia wished to tell him she felt the same, but could see no way to do it without hurting Cecelia's feelings. Even so, she had not guessed it had been explicitly given as a month-long. Cecelia had not mentioned that.

William looked away, muttering something and walking back to retrieve his ax.

Mark groaned next to Portia, the implication of Cecelia's comments clear to him as well.

He leaned into Portia and spoke while keeping his eyes on William. "You either did something very bad to the queen, or something very good, and now here we are. Thank you for including me."

Portia hissed back at him, both affronted and wanting to laugh.

Mark only cleared his throat, straightening in his saddle.

"Well, I've learned my lesson about leaving you behind," Portia said tartly, before nudging her horse forward.

Mark laughed and followed.

But even his laughter only slightly loosened the knot around Portia's chest. They had already been set by a month-long delay in returning to rescue those left behind after the big battle. Staying here another month seemed impossible.

They reached the iron gate, held open by William. Portia

passed through, feeling William look at her more closely as she passed.

"You two are well armed for students," William said.

Portia turned back to the man now walking in the wagon tracks behind the horses. "We were protection on this trip as well."

"Fine weapons all the same."

There was a query, as well as an accusation, in his voice.

"The sword was a gift from the elves," Portia said, instantly regretting her words. She did not need to explain every little thing.

Not that the sword was a little thing.

It had been days since she'd practiced, and she could almost feel its rebuke. A few moments by the firelight of the camp, or a quick session in a courtyard were not enough. The sword had skills all its own, and Portia was not even close to catching up to it. She'd had to practice with a wooden sword just to reach a basic level to use it. Professor Terfel had trained her the best he could, but before he could find a better teacher, the war had happened.

At least she'd never lost it.

As if it would let her go.

William and Cecelia walked past Portia and Mark, their footsteps outpacing the leisurely pace of the tired horses. Cecelia, looking suddenly tired, led her own horse while William swung his ax as he walked.

The path led over a grassy field and topped a rise. On the far side lay a sprawling house, wider by far than tall, and unpainted, the wood dry and gray in the sun. The house looked like it had been smeared upon the land and was standing only out of spite.

A chicken ran out from one side of the structure and into the small fenced yard, followed by three young barefoot children, barely half height, their golden hair every which way, and laughter ringing out. An older girl followed, holding a basket.

"Mama!" one of the young children called, her voice much like the squeal Cecelia had let loose just moments before. The tiny girl ran to Cecelia, arms wide. The two other children, boys, followed. The older girl walked more slowly, matching Mark and Portia's careful scrutiny of the scene.

Cecelia grabbed the little girl and swung her up, causing the girl to shriek even more before she was enveloped in a tight hug.

A band tightened around Portia's heart. Had she ever run to hug Cecelia like that. Cecelia, her own mother. She didn't know what would be worse, not having done so, or having had a relationship like that and not remembering it. If she couldn't remember, did it even count?

"Portia," Mark said, his eyes concerned. He sat on his horse, waiting for her. She had stopped her own mount and not realized it.

"What?" she asked, and immediately felt bad about the edge to her voice. She couldn't stand the way he was looking at her. She felt too exposed.

Swinging down from her horse, she stretched and looked away from Mark, avoiding his gaze while grabbing her horses reins to lead it around him and down towards the house.

"Okay, then," Mark said under his breath, but followed Portia's suit and dismounted. His first few steps were unsteady, and he shook out first one leg than the other. They had been riding for hours, and this was the third day of it.

William had taken the reins of her horse from Cecelia. He stood by while she was swarmed by the three little kids, the girl in her arms, and two young boys who could have been her twins except for only a bit older. He turned at Mark's approach.

"We have no ostlers here, so you be needing to take care your own horses. Luckily we've got extra hay laid by, and oats too. I'll come show you in a while if you can't find what you're looking for," William said, pointing to the side of the house. "I've got chores yet, before the sun gets down, so take care of all of them."

William handed the reins to Mark, then walked off to the field on the other side of the house, adjusting his hat as he went.

"Cecelia's been gone for near half a year and she gets a five minute greeting?" Mark asked.

Portia squinted in the direction of the sun, still bright despite hanging low in the sky. "She'll be here when the sun is down," she said, unsure why she was defending the man.

Portia and Mark walked in the direction William had pointed. Upon closer inspection it wasn't a single house, but rather a house and a barn connected, sharing a wall and heat and resources.

She wrinkled her nose at the thought of smells coming over too.

No matter. It was a roof, not something she'd always had.

The inside of the structure was dim, having no second floor with an access door to let in light. Portia stood in the entryway and let her eyes adjust while Mark gathered the reins of all the horses and tied them to a post by the door.

Despite the small size, the space was neat and well organized. A shelter for chickens ran along one wall, most likely where the animals stayed the night, safely away from the foxes, with shelves and stacks of seed bag on the other side.

A lone horse wickered from the back, its nostrils flaring, smelling newcomers. It stood in a relatively spacious stall, with another one next to it vacant. The empty stall was well cleaned out. Mark rapped on the wood.

"Wonder if they had a horse die recently? Would be easier to plant with two pulling."

Portia put her hands on her hips. "How would you know?"

"I know things," he said, his voice serious, but his smirk giving him away. "I saw them on the road the same as you."

"Never mind that. Let's get them settled so we can eat. I'm starting to understand Ella more and more. Maybe it's the country air," Portia said. Her stomach growled in agreement.

"Nay, I just don't think there's enough food in the world." Mark looked through the shelving near the horse in the back after giving it a good neck rub. He found brushes and buckets, and a rain barrel of water. He tossed a brush to Portia.

"Wish we could magic this task," he said.

Portia looked around the structure. It was a pile of tinder

waiting for a spark. "No magic in here," she said. She didn't want Mark's lights to start a fire.

Between the two of them it was quick work to take off the saddles and reins, and feed and water the horses.

Mark brushed his mount, sending more dust into the air to join with the dry hay dust and dirt that had accumulated in the barn. The wide unsealed wood planks of its walls had narrowed as they aged, letting in thin streams of light that helped them see what they were doing.

"Are we really staying here a month?" he asked.

"We can't. I don't want to," Portia said.

Did she want to? Cecelia was her mother. Still, there were all those others trapped so far away from their own families. Why did she care about them so much? Her horse huffed and backed away from her. Portia forced herself to relax and not to brush so vigorously. The animal calmed down.

She'd been thinking the entire journey of how they could rescue the others now that they'd been sent from the city. She'd come up with nothing. Three days. Three days of regretting not following her friend's advice to not talk to the queen. Three days of not knowing what to say to Mark if he asked what her plan was.

"I thought you'd want to go, I mean, we've got plans..." Mark said.

Portia waited for him to continue. She finished brushing her own horse, then moved to Cecelia's. She kept her back to him, but could see clearly in her mind's eye his awkward stance as he tried to work up the courage to say something to her. After a few minutes of silence that pricked her nerves, she whirled to face him.

"What? Okay, spit it out," Portia said, her brush hand at her hip. She was hungry, and tired, and knew she was not acting as kindly as she could have.

"Well, okay then, it's just... She's your mother and you've asked her hardly anything this entire trip. This farm," Mark waved around them, "is so far away. When will the next time you see her be? Aren't you curious?"

That was not the question she was expecting.

"Curious? About what?"

"About your childhood? This is your chance to talk to your mother," Mark said. He didn't have to say the second part of that sentence, that he would never have that chance because he knew his own mother to be dead.

Portia's face heated. She turned away again before he noticed it. No matter how many times he told her he had forgiven her, she had not forgiven herself for leaving Mark behind, just as his own mother had done.

"About your father," Mark said, refusing to give up.

Her father.

It was as if an anvil grew in her stomach, its weight making her nauseous. Somehow, the thought of having a father felt so foreign. There had been a time when she'd wondered about her father, but that had been many years ago when she was a tiny child. She'd eventually banished those thoughts when they'd become too painful. Now, fathers were something that other people have.

Or had.

Was she curious to learn about her childhood and about her father? Was that the word?

No, what she felt was trepidation and fear. Compared to the sad tales she already felt so comfortable with, the great unknown was terrifying.

4

The inside of the farmhouse was as bright as the barn had been dark. Long windows ran along the wall, their shutters pinned back, letting in the last of the rays from the setting sun. Most of the family area was one big room, with the kitchen on one side and a large heavy table that ran from the kitchen into the living space by the fire.

Despite the small size of the room, there were two fireplaces, a larger one along the outer kitchen wall, and a smaller one more centrally placed. A bench with tools, as well as a spinning wheel and large wooden loom sat along the most interior wall of the living room. It was more of a workspace than a place of leisure. There were only a few hard chairs to sit in, beyond the seating provided by the benches at the dining table.

William lit several candles, giving the place a warm glow.

The wood of the table and the counters gleamed like

polished stones in the flickering light. The entire place was sparse, but spotless.

The family sat on both sides of the large wooden table, on two long benches.

Portia had tried to take a seat at the end of one bench, in the corner, but the quiet girl with the dark hair who had the basket earlier insisted she sit in the center. The younger kids sat close to Portia, so close they snugged their legs next to hers and she could feel the heat of their bodies. They stared up at her face, not bashful.

Mark sat across from Portia. Another young girl, golden-haired like the youngest children, had insisted he take that spot, telling him that she herself should sit next to him. She looked all of thirteen but had a ferocious glare that she'd trained on the little ones when one had tried to slide into her chosen seat.

The girl had given her name as Isolde, all while staring at Mark, then rushed back to the hearth to pull out a slightly blackened roast. She had nearly cut herself trying to prepare dinner while also keeping an eye out for the encroaching kids at the table.

The names Cecelia had listed off of her children made Portia slightly dizzy. There were so many of them. Stephen, a taciturn sixteen-year-old, looked like a mirror image of his father, William, if only wearing the more slender body of youth. Muriel, the quiet basket holder, was the eldest daughter of fifteen, and Isolde, the one whose eyes were only for Mark, was thirteen. Those three were William's children from a previous marriage.

There were three more, the children of Cecelia and William. Portia realized with a shock they were her half-siblings. Not only did she have a mother, she had brothers and sisters, at least half-siblings.

The youngest three, her kin, looked nothing like her, having the sunny hair and complexion more like her roommate Ella. Reger, the eldest son, was seven, followed by Hugh, a golden boy who never seem to stop talking, and lastly Tiffany, the baby of the family at four.

Reger had grabbed at Portia's sword when she had followed William into the farmhouse, nearly pulling her off-balance. The hilt was too high though for his small stature, and he was only able to pull it up a hand length before reaching the end of his tiptoes and having to release it, setting himself down with a hard thump on the wood floor.

"Is that a real sword?" he asked, the amazement on his face softening Portia's initial reaction to having her weapon yanked at.

She squatted to his eye level.

"It is, but it's very sharp. Never grab a sword or knife from anyone," Portia said, soothing her voice so the scolding wasn't so harsh.

"Dad lets me look at his knife," Reger said, pointing to William, who looked abashed.

"Your father is very nice then, isn't he?" Portia said.

"Yes, he is!" Reger said. "Dads are nice."

"That they are," Portia said, giving William a nod as she patted Reger on the arm and stood. She couldn't interpret the look he gave her in return.

Once seated at the table, all the children spoke at once. The noise and warmth and smells overwhelmed Portia after three days of solitude on the road. Or at least the last two quiet days.

Isolde had taken her seat next to Mark after putting the last of the food on the table, helped by her sister Muriel. Cecelia had claimed to be too exhausted from the road and promised she would cook tomorrow, and go back to all her normal duties. The dark circles under Cecelia's eyes stood in sharp relief in the candlelight, speaking truth to her claim. It had been a long three days of journeying.

William broke a piece of bread and nodded for the others to start, setting off a mad dash of dishes and spoons from the children scrambling to fill their plates before the serving dishes were empty. Isolde had made sure to fill Mark's plate for him, leaning in close.

Portia looked down to hide her laughter at Mark's pained expression. He looked like a deer before the arrow, not quite sure what to make of the thirteen-year-old determined to take care of him.

"This is a working farm, and if you're to be here, you'll be working," William said gruffly as he lifted a piece of roast with his bread and popped the entire thing into his mouth. "There be no lords and ladies here, no matter how finely dressed, nor what weapons you bear. You," William pointed to Mark, "what can you do?"

Mark looked over Isolde's head to William. "I can... I'm good with my hands."

Isolde's eyes went wide.

Portia clapped a hand over her mouth, then pretended to be coughing.

Mark kicked Portia under the table, causing her to cough for real on the turnip in her mouth.

"I mean, I've been trained as a page."

William did not look impressed.

"I can make sparkly light magic," Mark tried again, his voice rising in pitch.

"That be what they do in the city? Make sparkly lights?" William imitated Mark. "Tell me, young man, how be you feeding your belly on sparkly lights?" William continued, not looking up to see Cecelia waving for him to stop. "I'll tell you what feeds our bellies here. Sheep, and crops. You can help me feed the sheep tomorrow."

Mark nodded, then exhaled as William's attention turned to Portia.

"And you, child of my wife, what can you do?" William asked. "Are you good with your hands too?" He stared at her, both of his hands at the side of his plate and not taking another bite. Despite his serious expression, Portia couldn't help but think he was making a joke.

"I am. My magic is a bit more, though," Portia said. As soon as she said it, she knew she was showing off for the other children.

"William," Cecelia said, interrupting. "They are our guests."

"Nonsense, wife, they be family. And this family works." William's somber expression broke to one of his few smiles, and Cecelia melted near immediately. He turned his attention back to Portia. "You'll be doing milk duty. The girls will show you how." And with that, the discussion of the next day's chores was over.

Hugh, sitting to Portia's left, tugged on her sleeve. "Are you really my sister? Does that mean he's my brother too?" He pointed at Mark.

"Honorary brother," Mark said for Portia. "We're like brother and sister, but not by blood."

"Did you swear a secret pact?" Hugh's earnestness was almost Portia's undoing. She had to turn to face away to keep him from seeing her laughter.

Mark did much better than she. He nodded at the young boy soberly. "We did. We decided we were brother and sister, and so we are."

Isolde's relieved expression irritated Portia.

***

MUCH TO PORTIA'S RELIEF, bedtime soon followed dinner-time, those living on a farm having to get up early and make use of daylight. Cecelia showed her the space that she and Mark would have in the attic, a tiny space above the loft available for storage, or a visitor or two if they were small.

A small ladder led up to the attic from the loft, a semi-private space open on one end, the end that also doubled as the entrance. The rest was merely a long, shallow space that ran directly beneath the rafters. There was a small pile of folded fabric, a few burlap seed bags, and little else. The house had little storage space and apparently needed even less.

In the relative privacy given by the cover of the din of children fighting below over who had to do the dishes and otherwise prepare the house for night, Portia and Cecelia sat high above them, perched on the edge of the attic space, while Cecelia used a broom of long grasses to reach in and dust the area. It was too low by far to stand in. Cecelia had insisted, saying she felt much better after dinner, but the dark circles under her eyes were only deeper.

"Stop, please," Portia said, reaching for the broom. "I can do that."

Cecelia sighed, then pushed the broom to Portia. "Okay then. I'll admit I am tired."

"Cecelia," Portia said, then stopped at the tiny grimace that flitted across Cecelia's face. "Mom," Portia said, feeling ridiculous. She was glad the dim candlelight hid the flush of her face.

"That's better," Cecelia said, patting Portia's knee.

"I... I never asked you about Dad," Portia said. For some reason, she felt unable to meet Cecelia's eyes, and looked away, hoping for some information without having to ask even further. She had no idea why this terrified her, but her racing heart gave way to her fear. It pounded so loud in her ears, Cecelia could probably hear it.

"Your father," Cecelia said, then sighed, a long heavy sigh that reminded Portia of how Ella sighed sometimes when mooning over a boy.

Portia stole a glance at Cecelia, who was gazing off into

the distance. She wanted to scream tell me more, but concentrated on her breathing instead, willing some patience to come to her.

Her torment was rewarded. Cecelia sighed again, then leaned in to Portia, speaking softly.

"Your father. Your father was a wonder. He had a way about him, I swear, I've never seen anyone before or after. Mayhaps that's why you've done so well. You do seem blessed."

Well, that was something, but also nothing specific. Portia turned the broom handle in her hands, feeling the rough wood.

"But, but what was he like?" Portia asked, not even sure what she meant. "How did he earn coin? What did he look like? What happened to him?"

"Oh, child, so many questions, but I guess I should've expected that. I suppose you remember nothing." Cecelia leaned in and touched her forehead to Portia's while giving her a quick embrace and then leaning back again. "No, I'm sure not. Well, he was a gentle man and had a way with animals, which was a good thing, being he was a rat catcher and all—"

"A what?" Portia said, gasping.

"Oh, don't be like that child, it was a task someone had to do. Besides, that ridiculously soft man could never harm them. No, indeed, he catches them all then goes off carrying them out of town somewhere else. I swear, I think he taught them how to play dead, to be counted for coin by the city guards, before carting them off and shooing them off into the woods. I kept telling the man, they'll just come back to the city, but he ignored me, saying, they know well enough now. Still have no idea what he meant by that. I swear, sometimes I think he spoke to them and they spoke back."

Portia felt the air in her open mouth and shut it. Her dad was a rat catcher. At least he did not sound brutal.

"He had your looks too, a bit, not so fair as my three young'uns down there," Cecelia said.

They sat in silence for a moment, a silence punctuated by little Tiffany's scream letting the house know she was not pleased with having her face washed by her elder sisters.

"Is he...?"

"Dead?" Cecelia said, letting Portia not have to ask the rest. "Yes. I thought I told you that. He died from the plague that came through that year. Those years were bad with that. He didn't suffer, it happened so fast. There were times I wished I'd gone with him, but I had you to worry about, until..." Cecelia stared off into the space over the loft, her heartbeat showing in her throat.

"Until?" Portia said, unable to wait a moment longer. "They said I was found by a dead body. John, my... the person who took care of me for a while."

"I wonder if that was the person who kidnapped you." Cecelia picked imaginary lint off her gown and then brushed it away. "None of the guards would believe me. Not a single one. Or perhaps they thought it no matter to have one more missing child when everyone else is suffering so? I stayed for as long as I could, looking for you, but eventually I found work cleaning for a lady and we moved frequently. William found me on one of her farms and promised me a home of my own. And here I am."

Cecelia stopped picking at her dress and looked at Portia. "You must think me terrible, don't you? I didn't leave you on purpose. I promise you." Cecelia eyes were earnest and warm.

A lump formed in Portia's throat. "I believe you," she said.

And she did.

A BANG WOKE PORTIA. At first she didn't know where she was, wood planks dimly visible ahead of her as she blinked away sleep. It was not yet light out, the window visible on the other side of the loft still dark, only tinted with the blue of the predawn. Mark was still sleeping, wrapped tightly in the blanket Cecelia had given him.

He had wanted to sleep downstairs to give Portia more room, but Cecelia had insisted. Portia snorted. He was probably safer here, where Isolde couldn't reach him.

The banging repeated itself. It was coming from the kitchen downstairs. Portia leaned over the edge of the attic space and peered down into the loft. Even in the dim light, she could see that no one was sleeping in the beds below. The entire family was up.

She checked the light in the window again. Truly, it was still dark out. With a heavy sigh, she stuck her hand out and pushed Mark to wake him.

"Go away," he said.

"Rise and shine," she said. "Time to show your handy handedness, or something."

"Not funny," he said, his voice muffled by the blanket he was speaking into.

"Whatever." She ran her fingers through her hair and tried to straighten her clothes. There had been little privacy in the tiny house to change for sleeping, so they had both slept in their road clothes. Now, she wished she had made more effort to find a place to change. She felt dirtier than if she had rolled on the ground outside.

The house was more crowded than the thieves house they had lived in in Valencia. Portia shook her head at the realization.

Cecelia was at the counter chopping vegetables when Portia made her way down the ladder.

"Can I help?" Portia asked as she drew close to peer over Cecelia's shoulder.

"Yes, please. Mayhaps you can do that pile over there?" Cecelia gestured with her elbow to a pile of potatoes and onions. "I forgot how much this family ate. I confess, your queen, I say our queen spoiled me greatly at the palace. I forgot how much work cooking is."

"I'm happy to help," Portia said. She pulled both of her knives from her ankle holsters, grabbed a kitchen cloth and wiped them with water from the bucket by the sink, then got to work. Soon the cutting board she was working on was filled with finely chopped potatoes and onions.

"Is there anything else to be cut?" Portia asked. Suddenly,

she sensed many people behind her. Turning, she saw Cecelia, Isolde and Muriel staring at her. "What?"

"You can do my chores today," Muriel said.

Cecelia elbowed Muriel. "Never mind that, girl." She turned to Portia. "My dear that was some impressive knife work. What kitchen did you learn that in?"

Portia turned away, wiped her knives again. "No kitchen," she said, so quietly as to almost be mumbling.

"Oh, dear." Cecelia coughed, flustered. "No matter." Cecelia nudged the other two girls away before reaching for a huge cast-iron pan to fit in the holder over the fire. "There's no more chopping to be done, but perhaps you could help Isolde with the milking. Much can be done before the first meal."

Isolde did not look thrilled at having a helper but said nothing, only gestured for Portia to follow her out the door and around to the entrance of the barn portion of the structure.

"We'll grab some pails, then head out," Isolde said.

Portia looked around, realizing there were no animals in the barn to be milked.

"Where?"

"Not here," Isolde said impatiently. "There's no room for anything in here. There, out in the field. We can bring them closer though, so we don't have to carry things so far."

Isolde squinted at Portia. "Where's Mark?"

Portia grabbed two of the pails Isolde indicated.

"He's coming, I think," Portia said, then followed Isolde back out of the barn and towards the fields.

"What's his favorite foods?" Isolde asked.

Portia sighed. It was going to be a long morning.

Three trips, six buckets of ewe milk, and a soaking wet Portia later, they completed the morning milking. Apparently ewes didn't like cold hands. Portia pulled her tunic away from her skin, the cold fabric chilling her in the cool morning air. Isolde had been unsympathetic, scolding her incessantly about the spilled milk.

Portia thought Isolde was overdoing it until she saw William's thunderous look as they returned with the final pails of milk. He, Mark, and Stephen had just returned from checking on the herd in the far pasture. William's face had turned red, his lips thinned into white lines and his brows narrowed. Almost worse than yelling at her, he had said nothing, only giving her a curt nod, then walking past. Portia's heart raced. They were all going in to eat breakfast. She would have rather done anything else, no matter how much her stomach growled.

But practicality won out. Any food she had of her own was in her pack, inside the house and up two ladders. She had to go in and face the family anyhow, she might as well eat breakfast. Plus, the smell of fried egg and onion and potato was irresistible.

Luckily, or due to Cecelia's kindness, there was still food left when Portia raced down the ladders from changing, her wet clothes balled in one hand, a plain linen-wrapped package in the other. She put the wet clothes for washing in a pile by the door for after breakfast.

Breakfast was a repeat of the din of last night's dinner, although Portia was getting more used to the noise. The food tasted even better after having been up for several hours and working so hard already.

"You spilled milk!" Tiffany said, pointing at Portia and laughing. Portia's face turned red. She smiled at the child anyhow. Tiffany wasn't being malicious, unlike the scowl that crossed Isolde's face.

"It's okay," Cecelia said. "She'll learn."

"She better," William said, with a growl in his voice.

"William, sweetie," Cecelia answered, trying to sooth him across the table with her voice.

"Mom!" Isolde said. "You'd been the first to yell at me for such an error."

Cecelia shot a glance at Portia, then leaned into Isolde, reaching out to pat her hand. "Hush, now. You know better."

"And so should she," Isolde said, then gave Mark a knowing look. "I bet you know how to milk, with your handy hands."

"Isolde!" William said, throwing down his napkin.

Silence held over the table as the older children looked down, the adults glared, and the young ones looked from face-to-face, trying to understand what was going on.

"I don't—" Mark said, stopping when Portia kicked him hard. "Ow."

William took a deep breath, looked down at his plate and then up again at Portia. "You might not understand that, with your castles and your fancy clothes, but this farm, it be running in at the edge. We pay our dues quarterly to the local lord, and he not be understanding any spilled milk or accidents. There be six children to feed here. We have no extras for the ground."

"I'm sorry," Portia said. She did understand what it meant to not have enough. How weird and traitorous it felt to be thought of as the rich ones. "I have a few coins..."

William held up a hand. "It's not to that point yet, child." He glared at her and leaned in. "But I'll be remembering that if it happens again." Portia swallowed, only feeling she could breathe when he finally winked at her. A sigh from Cecelia's direction echoed her own sentiments.

"I do have something though that might help. I'd forgotten about it." Portia pulled out the package she'd stashed under her left leg while eating. It was wrapped in a rough brown cloth and tied with twine. She handed it to Cecelia.

"What's this, my child?" Cecelia asked, taking the package and looking it over with wonder.

"It's for the family. A gift, sort of," Portia said, feeling awkward.

Mark looked over, as curious as everyone else. She had not told him.

Cecelia pulled on one end of the twine, undoing the bow, then slowly peeling back the paper to reveal three stacks of fabric.

Portia had had no idea what they might want so had asked Alice to pick something young girls might like. Now, looking at the bright yellow and red fabrics, she felt that she had not bought something perhaps more suitable to the boys as well. At least Alice had given her a good enough price that she was able to buy enough for something for all the children if things were cut well. And it was precious new fabric, not a resewn dress or hand-me-down.

Muriel and Isolde leaned to look closer, while Tiffany clapped her hands and squealed. William grunted from his end of the table, but the line between his brows lessened. He concentrated on finishing the food on his plate, letting the girls fuss over the present.

Noticing Reger's pout, Portia poked him. "I'm sure there's enough there for a dashing shirt for a young man like you."

He moved his shoulder away from her offending finger but nodded slowly, then looked over the fabrics, considering his options.

Mark and Portia exchange glances. "Well done," Mark said quietly.

Portia had finished her breakfast, so she rose from the table, grabbed a bucket and her clothes to go outside to wash the milk out of them and lay them in the sun. Maybe it was the food, or the gifts, or finally changing her clothes, but the day was feeling more bearable.

Opening the door, she stopped abruptly. Instead of finding an empty yard and sunshine on the other side, an elf glared at her, framed inside the doorway, its arms crossed, and foot tapping impatiently.

5

Portia slammed the door shut. Her heart raced. She swallowed. Dimly she became aware of silence behind her. Turning, she saw the family at the table, some with spoons half up to their mouths, staring at her.

"Sorry," Portia said, apologetically. "I tripped. So clumsy." Her attempt at a laugh came out more like a whimper. Mark narrowed his eyes at her, but the rest of the family shrugged and returned their attention to the fabric and what was left of the food.

Turning back to the door, Portia took in a deep breath, and opened it again and rushed out, leaning forward like the figure at the prow of a ship and pushing the elf into the yard, pulling the door shut behind her.

Staggering back, the visitor's irritation quickly turned into a true scowl. General Lyren windmilled her arms and finally found her balance several horse lengths into the yard.

She was tall for an elf, coming nearly to Portia's height,

though much more slenderly built. She had even more metal bars, gold braid, and medals on her shoulder than Portia remembered from before, her uniform sagging with the weight of them. Her ears poked out from her short shaggy brown hair, giving the effect of a child in a parent's uniform playing dress-up.

"I am not amused, young human. Is this how you treat your generals?" General Lyren said, ignoring Portia's frantic motions to be quiet.

No one was coming out of the house, yet.

"Quiet, please," Portia said in a whisper, entreating the elf.

General Lyren's response was to suck in a lungful of air to speak even more forcefully.

Dropping the bucket and clothes, Portia rushed forward again, clapped her hand over Lyren's mouth, and physically corralled General Lyren around the bushes edging the front yard, putting the foliage between the house and themselves.

"What *are* you doing here?" Portia said. "How did you even know where we were?"

Lyren's eyes widened, then looked down at Portia's hand over her mouth. Portia slowly removed it.

Still looking down, Lyren breathed slowly several times. She brushed her uniform, removing a few leaves that had been shoved into her medals by Portia's rough treatment. Slowly, she raised her head and made eye contact with Portia. "Young human, you will not ever do that again, do you understand me?"

With Portia's panic subsiding, the gravity of her action

sank in and blood rushed to her face. Going around shoving generals was not something a person did. Not if they were a smart person, anyway.

"I'm sorry," Portia said. "I panicked."

"Why?"

Why indeed. Portia had been acting as if she was about to be caught thieving. She'd done nothing wrong. It was not a crime to have an elf visit you.

Was it?

"I don't know why. I don't know how they would take you being here. I'm not managing it so well myself. Why are you here?"

General Lyren opened her mouth to answer, but the creak of the house door cut through the birdsong in the morning air. They both peered through the bushes.

Mark stood outside, holding the discarded bucket and Portia's clothes, looking around questioningly, then his gaze stopped to focus on the bush Portia and Lyren were standing behind. He gave a curt nod, then tucked Portia's clothes into the bucket and carried it with him as he walked over to the barn, disappearing within.

Portia exhaled heavily.

"I am here because we have business, young human. I've brought word back from the royal house." General Lyren looked at Portia as if she were crazy.

"But how are you here, at this place?" Portia gestured to the farm around them.

The general folded her arms and gave Portia a smirk, then

resumed tapping her foot again. "I have my ways. Are you done interrupting me?"

Portia nodded, biting her lip as if to remind herself not to stop the general again.

"My king and queen also feel that our people should not be left behind, no matter how few. However, they are not wanting to risk open conflict with Queen Lorica and your kingdom. So I've been sent with word of their support to you specifically, and a few gifts to help." She fluffed her hair in an exaggerated way. "Me, being one of them."

Lyren surveyed the farm then narrowed her eyes Portia. "Why exactly are *you* here?" She put her hands on her hips.

Portia's stomach soured and clenched at the memory of her meeting with the queen. She looked away from Lyren. "I think I was a little too enthusiastic with my queen."

General Lyren made a clicking noise with her mouth, nodded. "You are a stubborn human. I only got the directions to you here, and a rather confused story of you irritating important people."

"Directions?"

"You can imagine my displeasure at finally reaching the fine city of Coverack, only to be turned around again for another journey. My horse was no more pleased."

Portia looked in the direction General Lyren was pointing.

A beautiful black stallion pawed at the ground, looking impossibly clean for having journeyed three days. It snorted and arched its neck, flicking its black mane in their direction before turning its back to them. Portia smiled at the affinity between horse and owner.

"Your friends are worried about you," General Lyren said. "Even that prickly one, Magisend."

Magisend a friend?

Portia shook her head at the thought. How odd.

General Lyren continued, unaware of Portia's reaction. "She was quite persistent in wanting information from me but I wasn't sure of her, so shared little. She did manage to get me to promise to alert her as soon as you were to return."

Portia's tongue was thick in her mouth. She loathed to say it, but had to share the truth. "The queen has given me a gift of the month here."

Lyren raised both eyebrows. "That's quite the gift." She sat down heavily in the grass.

Portia nodded miserably, then sat down next to Lyren. "I think we can leave here before then, and probably should, but it would be... not be smart for me to show up in Coverack before the month is up."

"No, young human, I daresay not. Your queen wanted you good and gone. I take it she has not reconsidered her position on those stranded in the other world."

Once again Portia shook her head. She played with a piece of grass in her fingers, feeling the dry stalk between her thumb and forefinger, the crunch of it when it bent. The dry dead fibers reminded her of the dry desert land of the others... the Dragonoids. It was so hot there, so desolate, so miserable. The humans she had witnessed there, shackled and imprisoned, had looked as if they were wilting in the heat like a stalk of grass scythed from its roots.

And it was worse for the others: the elves, the dwarves. Something about the lands wore on the elves and they did not survive there long. Similar for the dwarves. She had not felt well there herself, but she had not had to be there so long, nor was she forced to work, instead spending her days hiding from detection, and focusing on survival.

Worse yet, King Morgani, the king of the dwarves, was still there, along with his high mage. The cost to this world was so steep to have their people gone, Portia still could not understand her queen's reluctance to help rescue those stolen away.

She refused to think it was because it was somehow advantageous to her queen to have her neighbors to the south losing their leader, and to have her own people missing. What could be the advantage of that?

"Here," General Lyren said, holding out some small vials. They were delicate glass containers of green and red, with cork stoppers, tied shut with twine.

Portia reached out, wanting to touch them. She flipped her hand over and accepted the lot dumped into it.

"Don't lose those, they are hard to come by."

Portia looked up questioningly.

"They are anti-magic poison."

Portia dropped the lot of bottles, scrambling back to her feet.

"What are you doing?" Lyren said, leaning down to check that none of the bottles had broken.

"What do you mean, what I am doing? That stuff nearly killed me," Portia said. Her heart raced. How could Lyren have forgotten?

"Ah, no, my young human, that is not the same as what you were struck down with."

"How do you know? Did you test it on somebody?" Portia countered. She paced, unsettled.

"Not intentionally, no. But it has been tested." Lyren had a crooked smile. Portia did, and did not, want to know what that meant. "It's not from the cult, I promise you."

Portia looked at the elf skeptically. "I thought anti-magic was forbidden."

"Well, the anti-magic that kills folk, yes, that is forbidden to all. There are other magics though." Lyren patted the ground next to herself. Portia did not step closer. "Do you think the king and queen give away all their secrets so easily?" Lyren said, leaning in towards Portia and giving what Portia assumed was supposed to be a winning smile. It was rather frightening, so wide as to reveal pointed incisors to match her pointed ears. Her dangling earrings, hanging high on her pointed ears, also glinted in the light, making the elf suddenly look even more foreign than she already was.

"It's for you. Put it on your weapons, and scratch someone with it, and they can't use their magic. You spoke of the mages of the Dragonoids having some magic at least. This cannot but help."

Portia looked at the delicate glass vials, their faceted walls catching the sunlight and looking not so much like anything but beautiful jewels. Terrifying jewels, then. She remembered being deadly ill in the land of Rocabarra, the land of the elves, with her own magic gone from a weapon treated with anti-magic, with no idea if she would live to recover or not, or even when.

Lyren had said this was not the same poison. How much did she trust the elf? Portia searched Lyren's face, then slowly reached out and picked up the vials again. Her hand shook.

Portia folded her finger over the vials in her palm. This was a potent weapon indeed.

The door to the house swung open, and its inhabitants exited in a stream; William and Stephen heading to the barn, Muriel coming out holding Tiffany's hand, with Hugh and Reger trailing after her, and Cecelia and Isolde following with the gifted fabric and another bucket.

General Lyren rose from the grass, standing and brushing loose blades from her uniform. She nodded in the direction of the house and the family.

"Well?" she asked Portia. "Are you going to introduce me, or shove me into another bush farther out from the house? I'll not be telling them all your secrets, young human, not unless you force me."

Portia grimaced at General Lyren's empty threat. Despite dreading whatever sarcastic comments William would make on fancy generals from decadent lands, there was nothing wrong with having a visitor.

She hoped.

Cecelia took in General Lyren's presence without batting an eyelash, though Isolde peered curiously at the slight elf, evaluating her from head to toe over the washbasin where she was currently rinsing fabric. Cecelia said to tend to their visitor and come back when they were done.

When they found William in the darkened interior of the barn, working a long plow blade over a sharping stone, he merely grunted when General Lyren asked to borrow Portia and Mark for a bit that morning, and gave a nod. He was more reluctant to give up Mark's help than Isolde was to give up Portia's. William told them to meet the rest of the family at the planting field when they were done, the tone in his voice intimating to not take too long.

Luckily, Muriel and the three youngest were in one of the far fields, picking vegetables for the next meal. If any of the three littlest ones had seen their unusual visitor, there would have been a hundred questions to answer.

Portia, Mark, and General Lyren quickly settled the general's horse with water and some oats, removing the saddle. The horse shook itself all over and did its best to keep its back to all three of them. Portia raised an eyebrow at General Lyren. What had she done to this animal?

General Lyren waved off Portia's look.

"Some creatures, and by creatures I mean horses, are just like that. Never mind the attitude. I assure you, she is quite spoiled." General Lyren looked around the farm. "So, this is where your mother lives." She turned to stare at Portia. "Are you thinking of retiring to the country, young Jack?"

Portia scowled at the general. Lyren knew full well that

Portia wanted nothing more than to go and rescue the people left behind, and not while away her time on some idyllic farm. Not that the farm had been much in the way of relaxation, but rather nonstop work from before sunup until sunset.

She had more time off as a thief. Or even as a student.

Glancing around the farm herself, Portia saw none of the family close by, but that could change in a moment. Any candid talk should be done further away. She pointed to the road leading to the farm.

They headed down the flattened dirt tracks in the grass, walking three abreast, before turning off into the fields and towards a large copse in the distance. The trees provided wind protection to the fields, and shade from sun now high in the sky. They walked in silence until they reached the edge of the trees.

"Excellent, young humans. I feared it might be more difficult to gain your time and some privacy. Now let's plan," General Lyren said, a twinkle in her eye.

Mark sat down in front of a large tree, its trunk wider than him by far, and leaned back, stretching out his legs. He wiped the sweat from his forehead and pulled his shirt away from his skin. "Plan. Excellent, though we be few here."

Portia's eyebrows drew together. She sat down by a tree next to Mark's, rubbing her hands on her pants then forcing herself to stop.

There were only three of them here, having been cut off from the few allies Portia had back in Coverack.

"Is there any other news from the king and queen? Your king and queen?" Portia asked, looking up at Lyren.

Lyren nodded, then sat down cross-legged in front of Portia.

"Indeed, there is. They do support opening another portal, only they would rather it not be in the land of Rocabarra. At least having any new portal to the Dragonoids world over the seas would give us some protection, rather than having them pour out on lands," Lyren said. What she didn't say was that it would offer the elven kingdom even more protection because of their distance from the sea. Only the human kingdoms, and a tiny portion of the dwarven kingdom of Morgani to the extreme south, had exposure to the seas.

The people of their world had unified and beat back the Dragonoids from the shores of their lands, despite the strange black powder and fearsome weapons of their ships. Then Portia had sealed the portals into their world, blocking their enemy's access to further incursions. This had spared most of the human kingdom of Haulstatt.

The people further to the south, those in the kingdom of Lusatiana, had not been so lucky. Their capital, Rodaine, had fallen despite the enormous seawall protecting the city nestled deep in its harbor.

Once the seawall had fallen, the battle had been swift and one-sided. The city had been destroyed, and the invaders came ashore to destroy as far as they could reach. They had no interest in the crops or the goods of the land, except for grabbing as many of its inhabitants as possible.

All they wanted were slaves.

And those slaves were all Portia wanted to get back. She kicked at the dirt, once again cursing herself for her impromptu visit to the queen. Someone more skilled in diplomacy might have been able to talk their way into getting what they needed. Someday she would have skills like those.

The falling of the seawall had been sabotage, done by the same people who created the glass vials' anti-magic poison. Portia had seen them for herself and fought those enemies in both Lusatiana and the land of Rocabarra.

Portia grabbed a piece of grass and pulled it, twisting, from its roots. She and Mark had been on a reconnaissance mission in Lusatiana before it fell, gaining a huge advantage that way. They'd found out information about the cult that had sabotaged the wall, witnessed the Dragonoids invasion and freed would-be slaves, including her mother.

Looking up, Portia made eye contact with Mark. "Mayhaps we don't need a huge army. We could go and check things out. Maybe with enough information and stealth we can get our people without one."

He tilted his head at her.

She clenched her jaw.

"Okay, okay. I'm the one that wants an army. But we don't have one." She gave Lyren a side-eye. Lyren studiously ignored her.

Mark nodded, giving Portia a slow smile. They had been through thick and thin together. What was another adventure?

"Just the three of us?" Lyren asked, looking back and forth. "What about the others? There are allies in Coverack."

"A few. My friend you mentioned, she is the only one from a powerful local house, and even then I do not know how much she can control, or if it's all in the iron grip of her parents," Portia said. The Riddlepit House was more on the scale of a palace, that much Portia did remember from her one time scaling its walls.

Her other friends were from further away, outside the capital city proper. They could possibly bring help, but it would take time. If they had any resources to bring.

"Archmage Vermeil might have had more luck rounding up help than we did." Mark stretched back and leaned against the tree, rolling his neck.

"Is that a dig at the elves?" Lyren asked.

Mark looked up, surprised. "No, should it be? They did only send you."

"A full general, with poison," Lyren said, drawing herself up and looking down at Mark.

"Stop. Let's be serious. We have to do this. There is no choice," Portia said.

Lyren and Mark released their stares at each other and nodded at Portia. Portia inhaled, feeling an odd sensation in her chest.

Hope.

It had been a while since she'd felt that.

"Can you not do better than this, young human?" Lyren said, bending over and looking slightly green. The dry hot wind ruffled Lyren's hair, coating the strands with the fine yellow dirt that blew incessantly around them. The yellow dirt was in Portia's mouth and nose, and down the back of her neck. It clung to her eyelashes, giving the entire land even more of a yellow cast.

Mark did not look much better than Lyren, but he'd had the sense to pull a handkerchief from his pocket and drape it over his nose and mouth and tie it behind his hair. He squinted at Portia.

"What do you mean do better?" Portia said, rummaging through her pockets for anything to place over her mouth. Finding nothing, she settled for holding a sleeve up. Keeping her eyes squinted, she kept the worst of the grit out of them but could feel it getting thicker in her eyelashes.

They had decided to open a portal, right there in the copse. Just to make sure Portia could still open one to the world of the invaders. It was a terrible risk, one that Queen Lorica could never know about since she had explicitly forbidden it.

It was a musical magic that she had to sing. It had taken some time to remember the notes from memory, not having anything written down with her. But the notes had been burned in her brain enough by necessity and fear on previous occasions that eventually it did come back. She'd modified the magic tune only slightly to make sure it did not open in the same location as had the other portals into the Dragonoids' world.

It would do no good to open directly into a city of armed enemies.

While singing, Portia twisted her fingers into signs of luck that it would not open into some place worse, for she was guessing as much as anything. Fine tuning the end location of where the portal ended was beyond her. When they'd stepped through the swirling circle Portia had created, looking like nothing more than a tall lady's looking glass, their location was both better and worse than she had hoped for.

There were no ferocious creatures to cut them down, no weapons pointed at their heads.

But the land…

"This doesn't look like a land any creature could live in," Lyren said, gesturing into the wind.

The land around them didn't look like land, just piles of yellow sand as far as they could see in any direction. The sun above matched her hazy memory of the sun in the Dragonoid world, but there was so much flying yellow dust it was hard to be sure. There was nothing but swirling yellow dust, yellow sand in tall sloping dunes as far as they could see. A bleary hot sun beat down through it all.

No creature could live in such a place.

Still, the land itself felt dangerous. It would not do to be stuck here.

Portia did not want Lyren thinking she had done this by mistake. Anxiety pricked at Portia's neck. She knew she should not argue, even as the words forced themselves from her mouth.

"You want me to open a portal right into a city?" Portia asked.

Mark came closer, shouting into the wind. "No, no city."

Lyren, still hunched over and looking ill, paused, then nodded understanding without looking at Portia. Lyren looked ahead to move forward, patting the knife at her side to make sure it was still there.

Portia reached reflexively for her sword, but her hand swiped behind her head at nothing. The sword was still up in the loft in the farmhouse. Her knives were with her, but leaving the sword behind was foolhardy. She wiped her sweating hands futilely on her pants. Now they were sweaty and sandy.

Looking around, Portia picked the top of the nearest dune that sloped above them and pointed to it. The others nodded. They trudged to the top, hoping to see some landmark beyond the sea of sand. Turning to look, Portia was reassured to see their footprints still in the sand behind them. They were filling, but slowly. They would have some time before their path was completely lost to the swirling winds filling in their tracks.

Lyren walked unsteadily, staggering back and forth more than the force of the wind justified. Portia pushed hard into the sand to catch up with Lyren to peer into her face. The sand was difficult to walk through, each step resisting and pulling at Portia's feet. Her thighs burned with the effort it took.

"Are you okay?" Portia asked over the wind, dropping her sleeve so her words would carry better.

"I do not like this world," Lyren said, keeping her face forward and down, concentrating on walking.

Portia had heard about this. Her stomach clenched. There was something about this world that the elves could not well tolerate. Another reason for the urgency of their mission to rescue those taken, since the same was true for many others. Just time spent here could be a death sentence, without even the hard lick of a master's whip.

She rechecked their footprints behind them again several times just to make sure they were still there. They had to be sure to find a way back to where they had come from.

Portia lightly touched Mark's arm, then Lyren's, nodding to go back the way they had come.

They came sliding down the hill of sand, once or twice losing their footing. Portia swore the path they trod going up the steep slope was disappearing even faster than before.

Once at the bottom, their pace returned to the slow drag of walking through molasses. Portia breathed easier when the swirling portal became clearer as they drew near.

Lyren was ahead when they reached the portal, her lighter weight not sinking so far into the sand so her steps were faster. Suddenly, Lyren drew her knife and leapt into a defensive pose, all while still unsteady on her feet, ending with her nearly toppling over. Both Mark and Portia reached for their own knives and scanned the horizon to see what had alerted Lyren.

There were footsteps walking away from the portal.

Footsteps that were not theirs. They went in a different direction, veering off to the right and away from the high dune behind them.

Had the person been going into this world, or the one they had just left?

Portia and Mark's eyes met.

He bent down and looked at the steps more closely, touching one lightly.

"I think someone followed us here," he said. "I don't think it's someone from here going into our world."

"How can you tell?" Portia asked.

"The steps are deeper in the toe direction. It's so hard to walk here." He stood again, shielding his eyes with one hand, peering the direction the steps had gone.

Lyren pulled up halfway from her stance, her knife still held in defense but more loosely. Her face was gray, even under the yellow dust, but her eyes were alert.

Portia bit her lip while looking at Lyren then scanned around them.

"Wait here and guard the portal," Portia finally said to Lyren. The general looked like she wanted to argue but then just gave a curt nod.

Mark and Portia ran as fast as they could manage after whoever had come. It didn't take long to find someone huddled in the sand, their face hidden in their arms and hair blowing wildly. The wind was too loud to shout. It was only when they drew closer that crying competed with the whistling wind.

It was Tiffany, sitting in the sand, her knees drawn up with her arms around them and her head down. Her body shook with each sob.

Portia grabbed the child by an upper arm and heaved her up. Tiffany looked up in surprise, her sob stopping mid-cry, then her face screwing up and an even louder bawl coming out. She grabbed Portia by the waist and clung on so tightly that they both nearly fell over. Portia smoothed her hair and whispered soothingly in Tiffany's ear the best she could in the windstorm around them.

Finally, Tiffany's grip relaxed enough for Portia to pry one of the child's arms free so they could all walk back the way they had come. Mark grabbed Tiffany's other hand, and between Portia and Mark, they half-walked, half-carried the child back to the portal.

Lyren was still standing when they arrived back at the portal.

"Was there anyone else?" Lyren said as she resheathed her knife and pulled a cloth from her bag.

Portia shook her head, then realized they had not checked that closely. The footsteps had led directly to Tiffany. She'd not seen any prints. She thought.

She glanced at Mark. Mark shook his head.

Lyren knelt on one leg and wiped Tiffany's cheek, leaving a spot where the tears helped clean the dust from the skin. Tiffany hiccupped, the remnants of her mostly subsided crying.

"It's all right, tiny human," Lyren said. "Did you come with anyone else?"

Tiffany shook her head vigorously, her dirty yellow strands flying and hitting Lyren on the face. Lyren leaned back and spit out some dust.

"Are you sure?" Lyren asked again.

Tiffany nodded.

"How are you here alone?" Portia asked. The last time

she'd seen the child had been with Muriel and her two younger brothers.

Tiffany jutted out her chin. "I want to be with you."

Rather than argue with the child, Portia, Mark, and Lyren corralled her to the portal. Mark lifted Tiffany, carrying her on his hip as he stepped through. Portia and Lyren followed.

The other side was still the blessed clear day they had left, with no wind, in the cool shade of the copse.

Portia quickly sang the tune needed to close the portal, concentrating as the oval drew smaller and smaller. If she didn't seal it without defect, it could open again. The foolishness of opening such a dangerous thing so close to her mother slammed down on her. A vision of William trying to fight off an invader with the scythe from his field was an unwelcome thought of the future.

6

Portia put the last of her clothes in her saddlebags and patted the rump of her horse. It snorted in the early morning air, its exhalations curling wisps of moisture. Dew still hung in the blades of grass like small jewels, glinting in the early morning sun.

Mark was still saddling his own ride, running the leather beneath the horse and cinching it tight, while Lyren stood by her horse in the far corner of the yard. It had stubbornly decided to graze, even after a large breakfast.

"Are you sure you cannot stay longer?" Cecelia asked as she came to Portia and pressed a package wrapped in burlap and twine into her arms. Portia raised her eyebrows as she took it.

"Lunch, and then some," Cecelia said.

"Thank you," Portia said. She gave Cecelia an awkward hug while juggling the package.

"I just wish you could stay. Can you tell me why you have to go?" Cecelia asked. She stroked the nose of Portia's horse.

Portia shook her head. "It's an emergency. I'm sorry." She grabbed the reins of her horse and led it to the trough by the pump.

She'd not had the courage to tell Cecelia what happened. Even now, heat suffused her face. She ran the curry brush on the horse's flank while it drank, her back to Cecelia.

They had arrived the previous afternoon back at the farm with the very dirty Tiffany. Actually, they were all very dirty. After making sure that Reger and Hugh were accounted for, along with the rest of the family, they had rinsed down in the yard. The cold well water had washed the yellow from their hair and clothing. Portia's milk-soaked clothing from the day before still had not been washed, so she spent the rest of the afternoon working in the sun with the others in the planting field while her clothes dried on her body. Luckily it had worked, and she was dry by sundown. There'd been time to wash her other clothes when they'd gotten back for dinner.

Lyren approached, making a formal bow. "I would not require the help of your daughter if it was not truly urgent. My apologies for cutting short your time."

"The queen did grant Portia a month here," Cecelia said.

"The beautiful Queen Lorica is wise indeed, but things can change, and quickly. I will bring her back to you as soon as possible. The queen would not want her delayed," Lyren said, drawing herself up.

Portia coughed to cover her snort at the bold-faced lie. Her queen would want nothing of the sort.

Lyren's metal sparkled intensely in the morning sun. Portia wondered if she polished them every night. She looked intimidating with them, despite her small stature.

Muriel stood by, with Tiffany, Reger, and Hugh in tow. Isolde emerged from the house, and William and Stephen came from the barn to say their goodbyes.

William grabbed Portia by the shoulders and then pulled her into a gigantic bearhug, squeezing her surprisingly tight, a squeak coming out as air was forced from her lungs. "Thank you for the loan of the queen's horse. We'll take good care of her until you return," he said in Portia's ear so loudly the hairs in her ears buzzed. He pushed her away, holding her by the arms, before giving her a wink and going to slap Mark on the back.

Reger swung a stick at the tall grass in the yard with force. He kept glancing at Portia, Mark, and Lyren but did not come over. Portia walked over to the boy. She squatted down to his level.

"Practice hard, and someday you might have a sword of your own," Portia said. He looked up. A tiny smile appeared on his lips before he looked back down again shyly.

"That boy will be a farmer like the rest of us," Stephen said, his tone surly.

"Stephen," William said, warning in his voice.

Stephen threw up his hands but did not apologize. He joined the rest and gave hugs all around. Finally Portia, Mark, and Lyren mounted and rode down the tracks away from the farm.

They rode in silence until they reached the gate to the

road, where they stopped their horses and stood, evaluating the road left and right.

"Okay, we decided not to open any more portals by the farm, but where?" Mark asked.

"Somewhere where there is a force that can guard the gate," Portia said. "It's bad enough I'm going in, but we should be somewhere the portal can be closed either physically or with magic. Even if I die." She said the last so quietly she wasn't sure if Mark or Lyren heard her.

"Good thinking, young human. I would say my kingdom of fearsome warriors, brilliant generals and wise mages would be the top choice, if not for the very express order of my king forbidding it," Lyren said.

At Mark and Portia's look of consternation, Lyren laughed. "I might help you in your rebellious actions, but I will not go against my liege."

"Traitor," Portia said. Lyren shook her head at Portia, smirking. "Ay, that's the problem,"

"I don't think going back to Coverack's a good idea," Mark said.

"I wish there was some way we could get help from Magisend or even Mia's house," Portia said. "Others must want their people home."

"No one will openly defy the queen," Mark said softly.

Portia stopped her horse.

The three stood in the morning sun, the birds chirping in the trees. It was a beautiful morning in the green farmland. A normal day. Utterly unlike what they contemplated.

"What about Morgani?" Lyren asked.

"Queen Morgani does not want the portal either," Portia said.

"True, but her countrymen have experience closing them. Archmage Vermeil is there. His help alone would be worth it. It's possible he's found us more allies," Lyren said.

"Even if we can't get into the kingdom, we could find a desolate part of the mountain far away from any settlements," Mark said, his voice lilting up in suggestion.

"Then we're back to our problem of no one guarding the gate," Portia said.

"Dang it, Portia, why can't you really make two of yourselves for real," Mark said. Portia snorted.

"Morgani it is," Lyren said. "We'll find a way to get Archmage Vermeil to help us. I know how to work with these dwarves." Lyren made a clicking noise in her mouth, pulled her knife from her belt and flipped it casually in the air, catching it by the hilt and shoving it back in its place on her belt.

Portia thought she was kidding, but she wasn't sure. It wasn't worth asking.

They turned to the right, taking the road leading south, and set off, the clomp of the horses' hooves echoing over the land.

By late afternoon, the rolling green hills of the farmland had given way to thicker patches of woods, the occasional stone outcroppings becoming more frequent. A larger animal, a white goat, though too far away to tell for sure, stood at the top of one outcropping and then ducked away as they approached.

The thicker patches of wood now surrounding them were darker than the light green young trees of the copse on the farm. Here the light barely penetrated the thick interwoven branches of the tops of the trees, leaving dark shadows between the trunks and on the thick layer of dead leaves at their base. Portia shifted restlessly in her saddle as she peered into the trees, futilely trying to see anything within them.

The air itself was cooler, even on the road. The cool air poured out of the woods and onto the road, wrapping itself around them.

Earlier, when the sun was still high, they had taken a few minutes for a rushed lunch on the side of the road. Some cheese and bread chewed while standing up to let blood flow through their legs. The horses grazed and rested. But the break had not lasted long. There were precious few hours of daylight and they could not risk riding at night and breaking an animal's leg on some unforeseen obstacle in the path. It was near new moon and there would be little light to help them after the sun set.

General Lyren yawned, stretching her arms up and out, leaving her horse's reins draped loosely on the pommel, seemingly unconcerned about the darkness around them.

Mark's eyes met Portia's. He raised his eyebrows, then patted the knife at his side. At least he felt some of the ominousness that Portia did.

"If I remember correctly, we should be nearing the border

to Lusatiana. Are you sure, young human, that we cannot just take the road through the border town? I'm very much in favor of a hot meal and a warm bed, if not tonight then at least tomorrow," Lyren said.

Portia shook her head. "You are memorable, even if I'm not immediately recognized. We are often together. If enough gossip happens, and carries down the road as it often does with soldiers, word might get back to the queen that I am not where she thinks I am."

"Can't you just make yourself look like someone else? Or make her look like someone else?" Mark asked, nodding at Lyren.

"Hey, no need to mess with my appearance," Lyren said.

Portia held up her hand to stop their bickering. "I couldn't maintain it long enough, not without draining myself, dangerously so. The portal magic takes so much strength..."

"Fine, fine," Mark said. "We'll just remember you when we're safe with our empty bellies and our cold backs."

"When did you get to be so delicate?" Portia asked.

Mark smoothed down his tunic and tossed his head. "Since I became used to the fine life of eating every day and sleeping on something other than the floor."

"I don't know this area so well, but it seems to me if we cannot take the road we'll have to go through these woods," Lyren said, pointing to the ever thickening trees ahead of them due south, where the road veered off to the east.

The color drained from Portia's face.

"What? Why that look?" Mark asked.

"If I remember right, that's the Forest of Horrors. There

was something in a class about it one day, something about when the kingdoms split and it became part of the natural border between Haulstatt and Lusatiana," Portia said.

"Is that all you know about it?" Lyren asked, staring at Portia intently. "That's all they said about it in your class?"

"Well, no, I don't think so." Portia spoke down in the direction of her saddle. "I was rather sleepy that day."

Mark laughed, the sound ringing out, sending birds from their perches in the trees, startling them with the dark cloud of flapping wings. Even the horses jumped a little.

"Well, they know we are here now," Lyren said.

"Who?" Portia asked. She looked around, confused.

"Whatever is in these woods. Unless you think the horrors are the trees themselves that are going to reach down and attack you." Lyren looked serious.

Mark gave the woods a thoughtful glance.

The pit in Portia's stomach replaced the hunger she had felt moments before.

Rather than put off the inevitable until it was dark, they decided to strike towards the woods at the bend in the road. It would be even harder to make their way through the trees by horse than on the road.

They made their way through a small field of dried grasses that met the road and went to the trees. The closer they came to the dark shadowy woods, the more ill at ease Portia felt. She checked her sword again, then realized it would do her little good in a fight with the tightly set trees interfering with her swing. She would be much better off with a long knife.

They stopped and dismounted the horses, taking advantage of a break while Lyren ventured into the trees, trying to find a deer path or other way forward. Mark pulled an apple from his bag, took a bite, and then offered it to Portia. It was sweet and tart. She reluctantly handed it back after taking three or four bites.

"It will be tough going. And there were signs of things I did not like," Lyren said, coming back out of the woods again and brushing leaves and twigs off her pants and shoulders.

"Enough to not go in there?" Mark asked.

"No, we will go, but we'll be careful," Lyren said.

"Of what? What did you see?" Portia placed herself directly in front of Lyren, forcing her to answer.

"I didn't see it directly, whatever it is, but I did see long white scars on the trees, going higher than my shoulders. Something in there has a temper, and that something is not small," Lyren said, sidestepping Portia to go to her horse, and grabbed her water bottle. She took a swig, then replaced the bottle in her saddlebag.

Portia shivered. Normally she'd want to climb a tree, and secure herself there to sleep safely through the coming night. But they were trapped on the ground, along with the horses they needed to protect.

The trees were already blocking the sun, robbing them of even more of the day. They found a small clearing just inside the woods. It was not visible from the road but not so deep into the forest that they couldn't escape by running out of it. Mark and Portia gathered wood for fire while Lyren went deep into the trees and returned a while later with several rabbits slung from her belt.

It was quick work to prepare the rabbits and pull some other provisions from the package Cecelia had prepared for them. Even so, it was fully dark by the time they sat down to eat. The flames of the fire licked up, sending shadows dancing on the surrounding trees. A few stars were visible between the leaves above them when the wind rustled and blew the branches.

They decided to set a watch through the night. They would take turns sleeping. Portia had the first one. She sat with her back against a tree while Lyren and Mark laid down, pulling coats over themselves and sleeping with their heads on their saddlebags. The horses were nearby. Close enough to watch, but not so near as to be spooked by the fire.

The first few hours were fine. Portia stripped the leaves from twigs on the ground near her to give her hands something to do while her eyes scanned the woods. Her ears tingled with the effort of trying to hear the smallest sound.

But soon her eyes were drooping, and her head bobbed towards her chest as she fought off the sleepiness and the dreams that wanted to visit her.

Then a snuffling sound rang out in the woods. In Portia's bleary confused state she wasn't sure at first it was a dream or real.

Then she heard it again.

Closer.

Her eyes were open wide as she scrambled to her feet and pulled her large knife from its sheath. She looked around, trying to see what made the noise while she stepped as quietly as she could over to Mark and Lyren, nudging each one with her foot.

They woke easily and with one look at Portia, scrambled to their own feet and pulled their knives. The three of them stood around the fire in a circle, looking out. A horse whinnied, spooked by either the noise or the tension of their riders.

The horse's sound was met with a loud scraping noise from within the woods.

It sounded close.

Goosebumps rose on Portia's arm. Her scalp tingled, as well as her ears.

Besides the scraping noise, the woods were absolutely silent.

Anything, even an owl's call, would have been better than the silence.

The woods were listening.

Portia ran through the magic she knew that might be useful. Not fire, not in the woods with all the dry tinder on the ground, but perhaps ice, or creating duplicates.

Ice might be the best for this task, but it was the hardest magic for Portia and wore her out.

Not good if they were in a life-or-death fight.

"If it attacks, use your lights aimed at its eyes," Portia said to Mark under her breath. He nodded.

Lyren held a finger up to be quiet. The snuffling drew closer until at the edge of the light cast by the fire, a snout appeared, attached to two beady eyes and the largest boar Portia had ever seen. It had ferocious long curving tusks that glowed white in the firelight like bones.

It stared at the three of them, as if making a decision.

The decision was to charge.

With a nonhuman scream, it ran directly at Portia, its hooves scrambling in the dry leaves.

"Now!" Portia yelled.

Mark held his knife with his right hand. Using his left, he gestured to the beast. Flickering lights whirled around its head, darting at its eyes.

The beast screamed again, an angry howl of rage. It flung its head left and right, trying to free itself from the flickering lights.

But it did not stop running forward. It was on the path to run through Portia.

Portia made a gamble. She cast ice ahead of the beast's path. It coated the leaf-covered forest floor lightly at first, then grew thicker and smoother, turning the forest floor's sure-footing into a glossy frozen puddle.

The draw on her energy was excruciating, but she forced herself to continue, even while scrambling to one side. The ice had to be thick enough that the creature's hooves would not crush it and render it useless.

The boar was running full speed when it hit the ice. Its front legs splayed out left and right in a seemingly impossible angle from its body. Its chest hit the ice as its body tipped forward. It skidded to where Portia had been.

Portia stood nearby, panting. Blackness edged her vision.

At least it was off its feet. It gave them a few moments to regroup.

Then another snuffle sounded out behind her. There was more than one of them.

Mark looked to the sound, his eyes scanning the darkness. One of the horses tethered nearby reared up on its hind legs, its eyes rolling as it tried to see where the noise had come from.

Lyren motioned for them to stay and then ran directly towards the sound behind them. She was uncannily silent on her feet.

This left Mark and Portia to deal with the now enraged animal that had regained its feet. It swung its head between Portia and Mark, huffing and growling, noises Portia had no idea pigs could make. Its head stopped, its beady eyes fixated on Portia.

An ugly wrenching, tearing noise, followed by another inhuman scream came from the darkness.

Portia forced herself to concentrate on the boar in front of them. One strike with its tusks could kill.

She waved her knife back and forth, hoping to intimidate the animal. Her arm was shaking.

The horse leapt again. This time it snapped its tether. When its front hooves landed on the ground, it galloped past Mark into the darkness.

"No," Portia yelled. At the same time, the boar by the fire took off after the horse like a dog after a fox.

Almost without thinking, Portia flipped her knife to grab it by the blade and threw it at the boar as it passed by. It was so close she could smell the animal's scent and bad breath.

The knife whistled in the air, turning hilt over blade until it landed with a sickening sound deep in the boar's eye.

It veered with the impact, striking a tree, slowing it. It screamed a continuous shriek that chilled Portia.

Mark ran after the wounded animal, leaping onto its back as it staggered. Leaning forward, he slit its throat with one quick motion. The scream stopped, but it ran on for several lengths with Mark clinging on until finally it slowed then toppled. It was barely visible in the light cast from the fire.

Pulling his leg from underneath the animal, Mark nodded at Portia, who had run after him. They both turned to where Lyren had disappeared and ran.

They found nothing. They walked through the darkness. The lack of moonlight made the going difficult, Portia nearly falling more than once after tripping on hidden roots. Finally, a white glimmer shone on the ground ahead.

It was a boar's tusk, attached to a dead boar, sprawled on its side. The white wounds of deep cuts in the surrounding trees showed where it had struck many times.

"Where's Lyren?" Mark asked, his voice barely a whisper.

"I don't know," Portia said.

They searched around the fallen pig. Portia's stomach curdled at the thought of finding the general dead. If she had been severely injured, she couldn't be too far away.

But there was no one, and no sign of her.

Finally, when they got so far that the camp fire was dim in the distance, they turned back. There was no point in getting lost in the deep of the night. Plus, there were two other horses to look after. There was no reason to think there were only two boars in the huge forest.

Portia cleaned her knife by the fire, while Mark made quick work of butchering one of the pigs. They had a long journey and there was no point in wasting meat. If it had not been trying to kill them first, it would not have ended up being their dinner.

The meat was sizzling over the fire when a whistle rang out through the woods. The tune was oddly familiar.

Portia scrambled to her feet, knife out and ready. Mark did as well. They waited for whoever was coming towards them, for indeed the whistling was getting closer.

7

The fire flickered, sending warm reds and yellows dancing on the trees around them, and up towards the dark canopy above them, its light not quite reaching the blue-black leafy heights. The meat sizzled over the fire, frustratingly loud as Portia tried to hear more of what, or who, was approaching.

She made eye contact with Mark.

The whistling continued. A thin reedy tune that lilted and carried, almost happily, in the darkness.

It was accompanied by the clop of horse hooves dragging through the thick leaf cover of the forest floor.

Portia concentrated on her breathing. They both waited. The tune stopped. Only the crackle of the fire and the sizzle of the meat remained.

An owl called, "Who."

As if on cue, Lyren walked into the edge of the light of the fire, grinning like a child, and leading their runaway horse by a broken rein tied to a thin elven rope.

Mark and Portia relaxed their stance. Relief flooded Portia. Her visions of spending the next morning searching for a dead body seemed ridiculous now.

"Ah, dinner number two. Most welcome," Lyren said. She led the horse to its other two companions and tied it to a nearby tree. Her gait was uneven as she strode to the fire.

"You're hurt," Portia said.

"Only slightly," Lyren said, waving it off.

"Where did you go? Portia asked.

"I saw our poor horse take off, and you two do swift work with the remaining boar, so rather than waste time in a discussion, I retrieved our steed. I have no intention of walking across this land." Lyren sat down heavily on the stump by the fire. "It is beneath the dignity of the general to share a ride with another."

"Nice work," Mark said. He squatted back down by the fire and turned the stick of pork pieces over.

"Well you should say so, young human, for you would have been the one walking if I had not found it," Lyren said, stretching her legs out in front of her and crossing them at the ankles. There was a streak of blood soaking through the material of her left pant leg, glistening wetly in the firelight.

"Me?" Mark asked, looking up, surprised. "Was it my horse?"

"Is it your horse?" Lyren asked, her eyebrows raised.

"They're the queen's horses," Portia said, interrupting their sparring.

"No matter. I outrank you. Even this young human," Lyren said, jerking her thumb at Portia, "outranks you. Course it would've been you walking."

Mark snorted. He looked down and fiddled with the spit again.

"I should heal that," Portia said, indicating Lyren's leg. "It might be small now, but it could become much worse—"

"Yes, yes, yes. But don't wear yourself out too much," Lyren said, warningly. "We have many hours yet until dawn."

Luckily, the wound was shallow. Portia cleaned it with water, wishing for strong spirits, but having none. But they did have enough water to wash the deep scrape clean. She used a healing spell to mend the surface of the skin, but lightly to save her own strength. The wound only needed to stop the bleeding, and not be easily reinjured. Wrapping Lyren's leg in a handkerchief donated by Mark, Portia sat back when finished. The healing work had tired her, but not unbearably.

Besides, it was someone else's turn to keep watch. To her surprise, Portia fell into a deep slumber the moment her eyes closed. Mark sat at the edge of the fire, slowly rocking back and forth, scanning the woods while Lyren and Portia slept.

THE SKY WAS OVERCAST, with dull, puffy clouds reaching down low, as if wanting to touch the grassy hills, when they emerged from the dark woods two days later. The thick density of trees ended so abruptly it was as if they passed through a doorway into the farmlands beyond. Despite the grayness of the day, Portia still squinted, the light that much brighter than it had been in the woods.

They had managed to keep their bearings through Lyren's sure sense of direction, since the stars in the sky were so obscured by the trees it was difficult to know which way they were headed. They heard boars in the distance, but none had been so bold as to attack them. Even so, they had not slept well, keeping guard for both themselves and their horses. The horses had also suffered. They walked slowly, misstepping more than once on the treacherous roots in the forest.

"That is a trip I hope to never make again," Mark said. He rubbed his eyes and stretched his arms out, yawning. Even Lyren, normally so imperturbable, looked more relaxed.

They had long past left the rest of the pork behind, not able to take the time to smoke it. Their provisions were down to some stale bread and nuts. The last of the cheese had gone that morning.

The horses were just as hungry. They ignored their riders' commands as they walked to the nearby field, dipping their heads and pulling at the young tender grass.

"We are near the border, I can sense it," Lyren said.

Portia narrowed her eyes at her. There was something odd about the elf's sense of direction. She spoke of it as if she knew where she was by smell or some other inherent ability. Nothing had been said of this in her classes at the academy, but then it seemed there were many holes in its knowledge.

"Good, let's find an inn and a hot meal, and a bath," Mark said.

"We can't risk being seen," Portia said. "That's why we went through that whole ordeal."

"We can't risk being seen by *guards*, or the soldiers at the border fort," said Mark. "There must be some other hospitality that is completely and blissfully absent of soldiers."

"Mayhaps," Lyren said.

Portia sighed. She was so hungry and tired she didn't think she would be able to turn down a warm bed if it appeared in front of her. She'd save her energy for that fight if such an unlikely thing happened.

"Which way?" Portia asked Lyren.

Lyren pointed across the rolling green field in front of them. It was not long before the faint outline of tracks appeared cutting across the field, marking a road. Smoke coiled into the sky far ahead, its source hidden behind the curves of the hills ahead. After two full days in the dark forest, coming upon humans again created a different sort of anxiety.

The clouds gave a diffuse light everywhere, making it hard to tell how late in the day it was. They rode on, giving the horses their reins to stop and occasionally graze. Now that they were safe from the predators of the woods, it seemed wise to restore the animals in case they met different predators on the road.

There was little traffic on the road. Once, they passed a slow-moving wagon heavily laden with hay, pulled by an ancient horse barely up to the task. The driver, a middle-aged man with a low straw hat, chewed on a stalk of grass while he evaluated them. He gave a nod at Mark and Portia, then stared, surprised at General Lyren, as she came up upon him, last of their group of three.

"We should cover your ears," Mark said, smiling mischievously at Lyren when they had passed out of sight of the farmer.

"Do not try your luck," Lyren said. She lifted her nose and shook her head.

"We are trying to avoid attention," Portia said. The longer they rode, the more her thoughts drifted to a hot meal, even as she tried to push them away. If they could somehow disguise Lyren, then visiting an inn would be much less risky. If there was such a place around there.

"Hot food..." Mark said suggestively. "A warm soft bed."

"And who pays for such a thing?" Lyren asked. "My Rocabarra coppers would draw too much attention."

The money was different. If Lyren pulled Elven stamped coins from her bag, no disguise would prevent the interest in who she was and where she had gotten that money.

"I have some coin," Portia said. "The queen did gift me a small amount after the last battle." For someone who had no need of coin most days, living room and board free at the academy, Portia had managed to accumulate quite a bit. She thought it odd to have money after spending most of her life scrambling for bits of it here and there just so she would have enough to eat.

"Some?" Lyren asked with a laugh. "I'd say you have a good claim to much of the treasury, having saved the kingdom and all."

The coins in Portia's pouch were stamped with Queen

Lorica's likeness as the head of state. With a start, Portia wondered if any coins had ever been made with the likenesses of her ancestors, the House of Callac. They had once been the heads of the kingdom. Of all human kingdoms.

The sky dimmed to a dusky gray as the sun set. They rode on, the smoke ahead ever taunting. What had started as one plume curling up into the sky now was several spaced out. A small town ahead. They needed to decide what they were to do, either cut across the land again, or risk the settlement and any possible soldiers within.

Portia's stomach grumbled an answer.

Lyren and Mark both looked at the sound.

"Impressive," Mark said dryly.

"Oh, very well, no need to be so dramatic," Lyren said. She stopped her horse and leapt to the ground, handing the reins to Portia. She dug within her bags and pulled a few items out, then turned and carried them to a small grouping of nearby trees. "No peeking," she called out as she walked away.

Portia, confused, looked at Mark. He shrugged his shoulders. They waited.

A few minutes later, Lyren emerged from the trees again, her metal adorned uniform gone, replaced by leathers of soft brown, covered by a rough tunic of linen dyed deep blue. A matching leather cap sat low on her head, hiding her ears.

"Let us go see what we shall see," Lyren said, shoving her uniform into her bags and tying them shut, then remounting her horse.

They resumed their ride through the dusky evening, shadows in the nearby trees lengthening as the road ahead became more and more difficult to see. The smoke was closer, silhouetted against the last of the light in the sky. They should reach it before it was truly dark and too treacherous for the horses to continue.

THE MAN FLEW out the door, sprawling into the dirt in front of Lyren, Mark, and Portia. They had dismounted outside of the town and hidden their horses in some trees on the outskirts and then walked in. Lyren had not explained her insistence, except to say, "we should be far from any royal forces, but should is not a promise" and "caution never hurt anyone."

The man had been thrown by several strongmen, judging by the height he'd reached. The sounds of laughter and shouting poured out of the building while the door was open. Smoky yellow light silhouetted two men standing in the doorway, admiring their handiwork. Then the door slammed, and the night was dark again.

The man on the ground groaned, then twisted, struggling to find his way to sitting. He almost made it, bringing his upper body up, then giving up the fight and flopping back down with a loud hiccup. A moment later, a snore filled the night air.

The smell of ale billowed out from him, tickling Portia's nose. It was a sharp contrast to the wet smell of green grass and trees. Then another sour smell wafted across her nose. The man had not bathed in quite a while.

Besides the glow of yellow around the edges of the door, and some light slipping out around the window covers of the inn, the night was black. The clouds above hid all stars.

It was a tiny village, no more than a cluster of four or five houses close in, and a few shadowy buildings further away that were difficult to make out. This house of hospitality was barely bigger than the houses around it.

None of the houses had any light, even in darkening night. If they had inhabitants, they were hiding within, not even daring to light a candle. All fires banked. While getting closer they had watched the plumes of smoke wink out one by one as the darkness settled, until there was just the one left from the inn.

The only sounds in town came from the inn. Through the shut door, yells floated out to them, along with the sounds of dishes and glasses clanking.

"That is a rowdy bunch," Mark said. His voice floated in the air. It was so dark it was difficult to see him even a horse length a way.

"I can't imagine sleeping well with that," Lyren said. Even with her cap on, Lyren's earrings still tinkled when she moved her head. Portia wanted to say something about it, but didn't dare. If they went inside, it would be far too loud for anyone to hear anyhow.

They stood for a moment in the darkness. A third new smell reached Portia. Stew and fresh bread. They were not just selling ale inside.

Portia checked her knives, and the cloak she had tossed over her sword on her back. She drew the hood up. "Shall we?" she said.

"We shall, young humans," Lyren said. She moved forward and Portia heard more than saw her step over the drunk man. Mark followed, and then Portia.

When Lyren opened the door, a wave of noise came over them. Shouts, glasses clinking, wood chairs shoved across the floor. Burly men and women sat with tankards of ale, while a harried barman drew more, shoving them across the bar. There were more people inside than Portia would've ever guessed possible in this tiny town in the middle of nowhere.

"What the?" Mark said under his breath.

Just as quietly, Lyren answered, barely audible, "Bandits."

Portia's eyebrows drew together as she looked around. "How can you tell?"

Not looking at her, Lyren pushed through the crowd towards a dark corner with a few unclaimed chairs.

They walked past the bar to get there. There were not just coins on the bar, but chalices, knives, a few tools she did not recognize.

They settled on the chairs around the tiny table. Only then did Lyren lean in to Mark and Portia and reply. "Look at what they're paying with."

Stolen goods.

"Where are we?" Portia asked Lyren. Lyren's sense of direction was so sure, perhaps she knew even where they were exactly.

"We're on the edge of Lusatiana," Lyren said quietly.

She needn't have bothered to be so discreet. A shout came up behind them, and two men were fighting. The meaty sound of fist meeting face was followed by the roar of cheers as spectators egged them on. Finally, one man landed on the floor and did not rise again. He, too, was taken out the door, this time dragged. The door slammed again, and the room went back to its normal roar.

Portia thought furiously. Why would it be so wild here, now? Lusatiana was a normal kingdom, with the ruler and soldiers and citizens.

Her heart skipped a beat. It *had* been a normal kingdom, before it had been ransacked by the Dragonoids. Its capital had been razed by their strange black powder weapons from their ships, the lands burned.

Who knew what was left of its army, if it had fled, or been killed. There had been no harvest this past year, which meant no grains to support the people.

Those left behind must've suffered greatly, and now these raiders were coming in to steal even more.

A middle-aged woman came to their table. An apron around her waist indicated she was a waitress. Her hair stuck out in straggly wisps in the moist heat of the room, her plump face flushed red.

"What cha want?" she asked, gruffly but not unkindly. The man behind her poked her in the arm. She pushed his hand away without even looking.

Rather than shout over the din, Portia pointed to a nearby dinner plate piled with food and then held up three fingers. The waitress nodded. She turned to go, but Mark waved and then pointed at a mug, also holding up three fingers. The waitress waved acknowledgment and left, swatting at the man trying to poke her again. He yelled after her in frustration.

"At least it smells good," Portia said. Her mouth was so dry it was becoming difficult to even speak. They had run out of water on the road and she reminded herself to never again let their water skins go empty before dark.

The food was hot and good, the bread soft, the stew salty and spicy. There were even chunks of potatoes and fresh vegetables and a dab of butter. The tension in Portia's shoulders and neck relaxed as her belly signaled its happiness. She was concentrating on dipping a torn piece of bread into the stew and picking up a chunk of meat when a fist hit their table. Their glasses jumped, sending a puddle of ale on the table that ran towards her legs. Portia backed up quickly, her chair hitting the wall behind her, trapping her, but she managed to twist in her chair and avoid most of the spilling liquid.

Reluctantly, Portia took her eyes off her beautiful plate of food and looked up into the bloodshot eyes of the large man. He was wide and stout, his black hair short and sticking out in wild spikes. He leaned forward intently to stare at the three of them.

"And'a who gave you the right to be here?" he asked, his voice slurred.

He gripped the table with both hands, his meaty fingers wrapping around it. He looked like he wanted to pull it from them, along with the food and drink on top of it. His rolled up shirtsleeves revealed thick hairy forearms. A dark shadow on his left inner forearm caught Portia's attention. He shifted, and the light hit the shadow.

It was a diamond tattooed into his skin. It was the mark of the cult.

A gentle pressure settled on Portia's foot. She glanced at Mark and Lyren, and the subtlest motions told her it was Lyren. The pressure was steadying.

"We're just here for the food, relax, my man," Mark said, his tone artificially light.

"That's not the question I asked, son," the man said, leaning into Mark, looking as if he might even spit on him. Portia held her breath.

"We're just customers," Mark said, keeping his tone the same, even with the man so close that his breathing ruffled Mark's hair with each exhalation.

"Says who?" The man's voice rose. Others in the tavern turned to look, the din slowly quieting.

"These coppers," Portia said quietly, laying a scattering of them on the table.

The man twisted his head to stare down at the coins and then back up to Portia. "So much money for such a little thing. Did anyone'a explain to you the admission price here? Payable to me." His mouth twisted into what was probably supposed to be a smile. It couldn't have been less inviting if he had had fangs hanging out of his mouth.

"We're not paying extortion," Lyren said, her voice steely.

Her words carried through the room. Now every single person was turned to them and staring. Even the bartender, glass in hand, stood with his mouth open, before he slowly backed up, getting as much distance from the confrontation as possible.

"Admission. It's admission. Think of it as a tax, like you fancy city folk like to have," the man said. He tried to lean over Lyren too, but she was sitting the exact opposite side of the table from him, making his position awkward.

Lyren slowly and coolly crossed her arms, leaned back. "No."

Portia lifted her foot, pushing against Lyren's, trying to get her to stop. Turning to Lyren, she said through gritted teeth, "We're trying to avoid attention."

Lyren pushed Portia's foot down with surprising strength as an answer.

The man lunged at Lyren, his hands reaching for her neck. Lyren slid down in her chair, escaping below his grasp. Having overextended himself forward, he lost balance and fell heavily on the table, but he finally managed to grab Lyren's arms. Slithering back while still holding on to her, he regained his footing, then tugged to pull her across the table.

But Lyren didn't move, no matter how hard he pulled. Her legs were wrapped around the base of the table. The more he pulled, the more the table pushed into his own belly.

Mark and Portia had leapt back. Portia had reached for her knife, but one glance at watching faces stopped her from pulling it from its sheath. No one else had drawn weapons. If she did so first, she could set them all off.

Mark glanced back and forth between Portia, the man, and the audience. He followed Portia's lead of not drawing a blade.

The man yanked at Lyren again, his face red, eyes wild. This time Lyren let go of the table and she came flying over it with his pull. The man did not expect the resistance to be so suddenly gone and flew backwards, crashing into the patrons and chairs behind him, and then landing heavily on his backside.

Lyren scrambled on top of him, her motion so fast it was a blur, ending with her knee on his chest and one of his arms twisted so tightly it looked as if she would break it.

Sweat broke out over the man's face. Lyren gave his arm a further twist. He whimpered.

Somewhere in the back of the room a fork landed on the floor, its tines vibrating, the only sound in the room.

"Perhaps you would accept this exercise as our price of admission to this wonderful tavern," Lyren said calmly. When the man didn't answer, she twisted his arm again. He nodded. She let go of his arm. He flopped back down, laying his head on the floorboards and panting heavily.

Lyren rose to her feet, surveying those watching. "My apologies for disturbing your evening." She looked to the waitress standing by the bar and motioned with three fingers for her to come by to settle the bill. Before Portia could even warn Lyren, the man rolled to his side and then grabbed Lyren's ankles as he sat up, yanking hard to topple her over.

As if anticipating it, Lyren leapt back, but not quick enough. The man had firmly grabbed one ankle and twisted. Any other person would have landed sprawled on the floor, but Lyren leapt up with the man's twist and spun horizontally, twisting her ankle out of the man's grasp and finishing the spin to end with her feet below her once again.

Taking only a second to pull her leg back, Lyren then kicked the man in the chest, using the weight of her entire body. He flew up and landed into the chairs and tables of those behind him. People rose up, cursing, as their drink and food went flying, coating many of them with their own meals.

Portia wanted to stab the man, like she never wanted to stab anyone before. Mark stood nearby, so close Portia could feel his warmth, only belatedly realizing he had one hand on her arm, pulling her back.

There was something dark on the floor by the man. It looked familiar.

Portia gasped, then looked up. General Lyren's distinctively pointed elf ears, graced with earrings and chains, twinkled in the yellow candlelight of the tavern, exposed for everyone to see.

8

Only the crackle of candle flames, and the drips of the remains of the spilled ale falling off tables, made a noise in the dim smoky room. Portia pulled her eyes from Lyren and scanned the room. As one, the people stared at Lyren, most with their mouths hanging open. A few men had the angry scowl of fear that some have when they see something new. Elves were not much seen around here. What were the stories they told of them, Portia wondered, to elicit such a reaction?

The man sprawled on the floor, the one with the diamond tattoo of the cult and whom Lyren had dispatched so easily, roused himself, moaning as he sat up. His noises broke the spell in the room. The others pushed forward, hands holding weapons that glinted menacingly in the candlelight. It was an odd mixture of men and women wearing mostly rags, yet also wearing the odd fur lined vest, or leather tooled embellished jacket, or cap stitched with gold thread. Some had rare blue-dyed linens. The finer goods were stolen, Portia guessed, for they were much too nice for any average folk she knew, being more the realm of noble houses. Judging by the molted outfits on the crowds, no one had managed to nab a complete set.

They had refrained from entering the fray when they thought the man was just picking on a little human. Now they knew it was something other than that, they had permission to strike at the newcomers.

Portia wrenched her arm out of Mark's hand, and pulled out her knife, standing in defensive mode. The screech of metal on metal told her that Mark had pulled his own blade, followed by Lyren.

The three of them stood in defensive posture, arrayed in a semicircle against all those in the tavern.

The waitress and bartender ducked behind the bar.

"Magic?" Mark asked under his breath.

"Too many, unless we want to burn the house down," Portia said.

"No need to be that extreme, young human. The poor barman owns this place. Let's not ruin his livelihood," Lyren said.

Portia could not believe what she was hearing. First, they were only here for a meal, and to not attract attention, and now that Lyren had firmly gained the attention of every single person in the bar, and perhaps some of the wild animals outside and two fields away, they were to use restraint in defending themselves. A strange sound filled her ears, and Portia was shocked to realize she was growling. She snapped her mouth close.

One man charged directly at Portia, his knife near large enough to be a sword. He yelled, spittle flying from his mouth.

Portia blocked the blow, barely, wishing desperately she had the sure blade at her back in her hand. It was too tight in that little inn for a sword fight, and she was too close to Lyren and Mark to swing properly, but it would have felt better regardless.

Others followed the man. The three of them held the attackers off, blocking, twisting, occasionally drawing blood. It was an even match. Too even. Had they not been trapped in the corner of the room, they might have better luck against the horde against them.

And it was only getting worse. The attackers pressed in. Portia's elbow struck Mark's, impairing both their blows against the enemies. On Portia's other side, Lyren was so close that Portia's hair blew with each stroke of Lyren's blade.

They panted and swung, keeping off the rabid crowd, but just barely.

"Okay, maybe some magic," Lyren said.

Portia and Mark glanced at each other, and Portia gave him a nod. He raised his left hand just as the exterior door to the inn crashed open.

Yells from outside startled those by the door, and then heavy, burly men, wearing brass plate and armed with swords came pouring through the door.

Soldiers.

"Perfect," Lyren said.

Portia understood immediately. "Now!" she yelled to Mark.

He cast his left hand and sent his light moats flooding into the room, concentrating on eye level.

Portia imitated his magic, creating more lights, but hers so fine they were like clouds of colors, swirling reds, dusky yellow brown clouds of dim lights. She first surrounded the heads of those nearest to them, then concentrated on those by the door.

Scanning the room, she saw one window along the long wall they were trapped by. It was covered in dark material, a dingy tapestry, but she'd seen it move when the door had swung open, for the window was not well sealed.

The soldiers pushed further into the room. Their swords made quick work of the smaller knives of the customers. The yells of the soldiers had started as the intimidating tactic of warfare, then had turned into true rage as they found those within the tavern unexpectedly armed and already fighting.

Portia elbowed Lyren and Mark, then nodded at the window. The three of them pushed their way along the wall.

Using the confusion of the lights, Portia turned at least one customer against another as they slipped by. She wanted to use the suggestion magic that the three of them were not there, but that was no sure bet. They could just as easily be killed by an accidental swing where someone thought it was empty air as by an intentional blow of someone trying to run them through.

It was just too crowded.

They had to get out.

They had to get away before the soldiers saw them.

Finally, after what seemed an eternity of struggle against

the crowd of foul smelling bodies, they were by the window. The others still hemmed them in, lashing out with their blades. If they turned their backs long enough to get out the window, someone would surely manage a strike against them.

Mark grabbed a table by two legs. It was small enough that he could lift the entire thing to head level. He swung it like a scythe at the heads of those around them. A sickening crack told of at least one connection. Most of the others backed up. He then threw it at the rest, those who had refused to move. It was enough to knock the front people back and down onto of those behind them.

Using the moment of distraction, Lyren ran a few feet then leapt up to a horizontal position, using both legs to kick directly into the center of the tapestry covering the window. The tapestry and Lyren disappeared out the window, along with a muffled tinkling of breaking glass.

Portia sucked in her breath, surprised.

"Go!" Mark yelled.

Checking first that no one was close enough to hit her, Portia leapt out the window headfirst. She avoided most of the glass and rolled to one side, getting out of the way just in time as Mark followed. His feet landed with a thunk in the soft dewy grass outside.

Lyren was crouched, waiting. She pointed to the woods. The three of them ran across the low field behind the inn.

They went into the dark woods, going several trees in, then stopped. They'd lucked out—no one had run directly into a low branch and knocked themselves out. It was still an early moon, and there was even less light deep in the trees of the forest.

Portia leaned forward, her hands on her knees, panting. Lyren and Mark also breathed heavily into the misty night air.

"Well, that was a nice quiet meal," Portia said, an edge to her voice.

Lyren hissed a warning.

They all held their breath.

Someone was walking on the edge of the woods, beating along the trees with a stick. They paused by the three of them, but did not enter the woods. Portia said a silent thanks that there was no strong moon that night.

After several minutes, the person left. They waited another candlemark and heard no other sounds.

Lyren tugged at Portia's sleeve. "Put your arm on my shoulder," she said in a whisper. "Have Mark do the same to you."

In such a formation, Lyren led the three of them slowly through the woods, winding their way through like a snake, feeling their way to their horses. If they had left the horses outside the inn, the soldiers would've seized them. Portia hoped the horses had been good and quiet and not drawn attention to themselves, unlike their riders.

The horses had been good. They were still in the little clearing just inside the forest on the other side of the village. As if sensing the need for quiet, Portia's horse greeted her only with a quiet huff of air through its nostrils. They untied their mounts and led them slowly through the trees for a little distance longer, once again following Lyren.

When Lyren nodded her satisfaction that they were far enough away, they led the horses from the forest back to the barely visible road. The lighter areas worn from wagon wheels teased at Portia's vision. She wondered if she was only imagining she could actually see it.

Even back on the road, they still walked, leading the horses. They had a better chance of finding any dangerous holes this way, safely guiding their horses around them.

In the distance, the sound of metal striking metal rose and fell. They were still fighting at the inn.

After what seemed like forever of slow plodding through the black night, Lyren led them off the road again to another section of forest nearby. They entered.

Lyren indicated she would keep the first watch.

The exhaustion of the battle, the use of magic, and the terrifyingly maddening effort to walk through the night without breaking either their legs or their horses' finally sank into Portia. She no sooner laid down, then her eyes shut. A half-panicked thought of Lyren not being able to defend the three of them was not even enough to keep her awake.

The last thing she remembered was Mark's snore before consciousness left her.

They made their way into Lusatiana, across burned and half regrown fields, past abandoned farm houses, past burned villages. They wound their way south, avoided the fort at the border. Between Lyren's hunting skills bringing in rabbits and other small creatures, and their luck in foraging in the fields, it was enough to feed them for the several-day journey south. They had avoided most buildings, not sure if the scavengers and raiders were done with them yet, instead opting to camp in woods when they could find them. Lyren's sense of direction drew them south and east.

Topping the crest of one hill, Portia recognized where they were, overlooking the long descent into the valley of the city of Rodaine, or what had been the city of Rodaine, the capital of Lusatiana.

They rode closer. It was not directly on the way to the kingdom of Morgani, but Mark and Portia remembered the great city as it had been. And the attack upon it. They convinced Lyren a sidetrack for scouting purposes was worth it. Really, Portia was just curious, but she'd never admit such a thing to General Lyren.

Some of the buildings still stood, so it wasn't until they were quite close Portia realized the entire city lay abandoned. What was standing were the burnt shells and half walls of buildings, only blacked sections on the ground marking others that had burned away completely. No ships anchored in the harbor, save for the wreckage of one, its mast poking through the green-black waves that crashed over it. It would not resist the water for long, and soon even that remnant would disappear.

They walked through the debris of what had been the city. Here and there, oddly, some areas were cleared completely of destroyed lumber. Someone had been scavenging here, and not just for gold cups and luxury goods within the houses. The areas of gravel swept clear, almost as neat as the palace garden, sent a chill up Portia's back. It was almost worse than the silent streets and the lack of citizens. Someone had been here.

Someone might still be here.

Mark motioned down what had been one of the main roads. Their horses' hooves clapped on the cobblestone streets, echoing madly off the empty city and bouncing off the few buildings still standing. They were not being discreet.

Portia wondered if it wise for them to be there at all. The sun was still high in the sky. As long as they got out of there before darkness came in they should be all right. The road out of the city was across the long field, and while it might be difficult for them to escape notice, it would be equally difficult for someone to follow them on the sly.

"Remember my old page days?" Mark asked, his smile a rebuke to Portia's feelings of ill foreboding. Perhaps she was overreacting.

"Yes, and that creepy person who worked there," Portia said, giving a small shake.

"I didn't think they were that bad," Mark said.

Portia squinted at him, then looked away.

"I want to go see if they have any of the goodies there that I remember. Mayhaps the raiders missed something." He pressed his heels into the side of his horse, urging it forward. Portia and Lyren increased their pace to keep up. It would do no good to become separated in this place.

They reached the building that was mostly intact, only its front blackened and seared as if it had been pressed up against the fire and charred. It was the building Portia barely remembered, though it looked little like the gaily painted structure she remembered Mark dragging her into. There was nothing left of the obnoxious sign with gold paint hawking the services of the pages and messengers within.

"I'll be back," Mark said. He dismounted his horse and tied the reins over what was left of a post and ring. In a blink, he pulled open the charred door and then disappeared inside.

Portia exhaled heavily. She wished he hadn't done that, but she'd been too slow.

Portia and Lyren dismounted as well, stretching and twisting. They'd been riding for hours. There was nothing here for the horses to graze, unfortunately, but they wouldn't be here long.

"Perhaps we should go with him?" Portia asked Lyren, unsure.

Lyren looked up and down what was left of the street running between destroyed buildings. "We could, but then who would watch the horses? Chances are we'd run into someone out here before he would just happen to find someone in that building. I didn't hear anything, anyway."

Portia paced, then walked to the door and opened it and peered inside. It was dark, the only light streaming in from an upper window, dust motes floating in the air. What had been the floor of the upper level was gone, and the window had been part of the second-story. Mark was not in the space. There was a door far at the back, ajar. He must be back there.

Something dropped in the back, the sound echoing around the structure. Mark's muttering followed. Another crash. It didn't sound like a fight, rather like someone walking into piles of goods in the dark. What was he after?

Portia pulled her head back out into the sunshine. Lyren was sitting on the remains of the porch of the building, her legs dangling over the side, swinging and kicking. Portia took one look back at the building, then came and sat next to Lyren, wiping a spot clean before dropping her legs over the edge and swinging them as well. The blood flowed to her feet. It felt good.

"Why did you pick a fight with that guy?" Portia asked.

Lyren turned to Portia and raised her eyebrows. "What guy?"

"That cult guy. The one at the tavern before we got to Lusatiana."

"I didn't pick a fight with him. I just stopped one," Lyren said, explaining as if to a child.

"Yeah, the thing is, see, there were no weapons out until whatever that was happened," Portia said. Why did it feel like they were not talking about the same thing?

"The fight started long before the weapons, young human. If we had let that man bully us and take money and mark us as victims, it never would've ended. He and his cronies would've followed us through the countryside if they could. It was best to decisively discourage that. Ideally forever," Lyren said.

"Forever? You mean kill him?" Portia's brow furrowed.

"Ideally, no, but the defeat had to hurt enough to not want to do it again." Lyren swung her feet faster and looked out over the ruined city. She looked even more like a child than before.

Lyren had kept her uniform in her bags since that evening at the tavern which was for the best since the flashy medals on the shoulder of the uniform would've been visible for miles, like signaling mirrors. The cap that she'd rescued from the tavern floor was pushed low on her forehead, hiding her ears.

"I don't know, I don't think we would've ever seen him again," Portia said. "Wouldn't it have just been easier to give him a coin to make him go away?"

"In the moment, yes, but what of the many moments afterwards? When he is bonded to you as a source of coins and the pleasure of bullying, when would it end? Once is never enough. Especially when things were not going well for him otherwise, for then he would come after us even harder because he would know for sure it was an easy win. Don't you see, the price has to be paid sooner or later? It's better to pay it sooner, because in the end it's cheaper." Lyren sighed after her long speech, then lay down back on the porch, putting her hands behind her head and closing her eyes, her heels resting on the edge of the porch.

Portia wanted to lay down too and relax in the sun, but one of them should keep an eye out for possible attackers. She chewed her lip and thought about what Lyren had said about paying the price sooner rather than later. It was a rather cold calculation of how to deal with people.

Had she been doing things wrong the entire time?

She'd always kept her head down, unless absolutely pushed. Maybe that had been a mistake. Maybe acting decisively right away was better, even if it seemed overkill in the moment.

The door behind her slammed. Turning, Portia saw Mark blinking in the sunlight, his arms cradled around masses of clothes jumbled together, soft leathers dyed red, brown, and black, airy linen so thin it almost looked like fog, bundled in creams and whites, other clothes in jewel tones of blue, yellow, and red. Any one of the pieces looked like it could've been worn by an attendant in Queen Lorica's court.

"What is all that?" Portia asked, scrambling to her feet.

"We all had to dress the part to be pages to the gentry of the town. I knew some of the others were getting help with their clothes, more than I was. I thought I saw the goods coming from the back of the building." Mark beamed, extremely proud of himself.

Lyren opened one eye and looked at Mark and his arms full of loot, then shut it again and went back to resting in the sunshine.

"What are you going to do with it all?" Portia asked.

"Keep what fits, and what I can carry as gifts for others," Mark said.

"Finding food would've been better," Lyren said from her position on the ground, her eyes still closed.

Portia shook her head. She went to Mark and touched some of the light linen. It was like airy gauze, but still had some stiffness to it. It felt tough. She'd never seen any fabric like that before. Taking the material from Mark's bundle, it turned out to be a long airy petticoat set, several layers deep. He must be holding an overdress that went with it.

"Want it?" Mark asked, one eyebrow up.

Of course she wanted it. Spying a deep blue and gold

threaded garment from the pile in Mark's arms, Portia grabbed it and pulled, letting the length unfold. It was an overdress that would work splendidly with the petticoats. Her hands curled around it. "Mine."

Lyren perked up when knives clinked, tumbling from the depths of Mark's bundle and onto the porch near her ear. They were tiny decorative knives, with carved gold handles and golden sheaths.

Mark held up one of the knives. "Supposedly for opening letters, but they were made mostly just to impress the clients. I wonder if they're real gold?" He bit down on one, then stopped and rubbed his jaw.

Portia laughed. "All showing and no substance, huh?"

"Whatever, it's a beautiful show. Good enough for me." Mark pocketed a few of the knives, startled by Lyren's hand bolting out and grabbing a few for herself. They left one for Portia, and she took it, looking at the tiny thing. It was nothing like the larger knife she kept strapped to her chest, or the ones on her ankles, but she was not one to turn down a gift weapon.

Despite Lyren's grumbling about leaving room in the packs for food, they packed up what they could of Mark's haul. He put on a new outfit of burgundy and gold. He looked even fancier than he had the first time Portia had seen him dressed in court clothes. He did not stop smiling the entire time, even as they rode out of Rodaine and up the long craggy road towards the Kingdom of Morgani.

The trees grew thicker and wider, their dark brown trunks now an arm span wide, reaching high to the sky, holding a canopy of leaves blocking the light. What had started as small green shrubs dotting the stony fields outside of Rodaine had grown into narrow adolescent trees here and there, finally clustering together, then forming a dense intimidating forest the higher they climbed the mountains towards Morgani.

The road had been quiet, only the clop of the horses' hooves ringing out. At first, the sound of the sea behind them had been a backdrop of reassuring noise, but it didn't take long before that was left far behind. Now it was just the hooves, the birds calling, and an occasional huff from a tired horse.

It was midday, but they were so far in the thick of trees that the road itself was shadowed. Portia wished Mark and Lyren would make small talk and break the silence, yet at the same time was grateful they did not. It was better to be able to hear if someone was approaching.

Any one of the trees could've hidden an attacker. The trees were not so large as to be able to hide a horse, yet.

"So, where is this kingdom of Morgani?" Mark asked, trying to make a joke. "Is it the kingdom of leaves and dirt?"

Portia glared at him. He shrugged.

But he had a point. Where was it?

She'd been in the kingdom of Morgani once, but had entered through a splinter deep in its heart underground. She'd left it through a hidden exit in the mountains.

How arrogant of her to think it would be so easily found just because she needed it.

She nudged her horse, urging it to speed up and catch up to General Lyren. Lyren did not glance at her, instead holding up one hand to keep the silence and giving her head an almost imperceptible shake.

"Soon," was all that the elf said. She didn't even look at Portia.

They continued on.

Portia's scalp itched. She wanted to scratch it, but was loath to move her arm. She kept her right hand close to her knife. The strap holding her sword in its scabbard was loose for an easy draw.

She felt eyes upon her, more than the birds and the small ground animals. She imagined the very trees watching them, eyes in their trunks moving to watch them pass.

Under her breath, barely audible, Lyren said, "Roll up your sleeves. Both of you." Even as she spoke, the elf did the same herself, working fast so her hands were free as quickly as possible, her sleeves secured above her elbows.

Portia shook her head but she did as she was bid, as did Mark. Their skin glowed in the dim light, calling attention to itself.

Only the snick of a blade leaving its scabbard warned her when a group of dwarves dropped from the surrounding trees, landing softly. The dwarves circled them, a half-dozen ahead, half-dozen behind, and even more scattered in the trees on either side, twigs breaking under their landing.

9

Not one sound came from the forest around them. Not a bird call, not the rustle of a ground animal, not a leaf falling. The shadows of lush canopy overhead felt even more ominous than it had a moment before. Now, rather than a welcome reprieve from the blistering sun, it was the hiding spot for dangerous creatures who could drop at any second.

Who had dropped.

Only the breath of the dwarves around them, and their horses and their own labored breathing sounded in the air.

The horses had stopped without a command from their riders, unsettled by the sudden appearance of the dwarves dropping from the sky. It was a testament to their good nature that they did not buck, but waited uneasily for their riders to figure out what to do.

No doubt there were more dwarves further ahead, and more behind that had not even revealed themselves. More everywhere.

This must be Morgani's guard.

Portia sucked in her breath. Her hand gripped her knife, but she did not draw it.

Lyren and Mark also held their position.

All waited.

As if on a signal, the dwarves pulled themselves up from their battle stance. Several still stood at the back, out of reach of the riders, their long swords held at the ready, but the others sheathed their blades. They walked several steps closer to the riders, then stopped out of reach of the horses' hooves. There was battle experience there telling them just how far that was.

One stepped forward. He looked familiar.

His paunch was gone, and his face thinner and more tired looking, but it was Commander Kerat, the first dwarf Portia had ever met. His blue uniform hung poorly on his frame, as if he'd lost much weight only recently and not yet had time for alterations.

He smiled at Portia. It was a weary smile, but one none the less.

"Aye, welcome back, Portia, closer of portals. You've good company with you today." He nodded to Lyren. "It helps to know the humans were not of the cultish variety, no?"

Lyren nodded back, holding up one arm to show a clean forearm.

Mark laughed, held up both arms, then rolled down his sleeves, fixed his outfit to look proper again.

How long had the dwarves been watching them? Portia pursed her lips, making a note to ask Lyren later how she knew they were surrounded. She did not like getting surprised like that.

"Hello, Commander Kerat. You've a good memory," Portia said. It was awkward looking so far down at Kerat. Making a decision, she dismounted her horse. She still towered over the commander, but not so ridiculously so.

The dwarves around them did not move, friendly faces or not. The three of them were not continuing on, at least not at the moment. That was fine, since they didn't know exactly where they were going anyhow. At least Portia didn't think they did. She glanced at Lyren.

Lyren's expression was unreadable.

Mark and Lyren also dismounted their horses.

The dwarves' line bulged, allowing them to lead their horses off the road and tie them to a nearby sapling. Portia stretched, killing time, waiting to see if Lyren would bring up their reason for coming first. Lyren definitely was more diplomatic than she was.

At first she thought she was to be disappointed. Lyren made inquiries about the royal family, knowing more members than Portia thought possible, and then about the dwarves in general. Kerat answered her questions graciously but kept glancing at Portia.

They were sitting on an outcrop of rocks, Lyren, Portia, Mark, and Kerat. The rest of the dwarves were nearby, but kept a respectful distance. They were not a part of the conversation.

After the fourth question about yet another general, Portia

cleared her throat. Lyren stopped talking mid-sentence. They all looked at her.

"We need to go to Morgani," Portia said.

Kerat raised his eyebrows and then gestured to the land around them, as if to say, 'you're here.'

"You know what I mean," Portia said. Why did this feel like she was being so rude? No matter. They had to do it. "We need to be in the real Morgani." She pointed to the ground.

Kerat appraised her, waiting.

He knew very well that she meant the underground passages that comprised the Dwarven kingdom. Where the citizens lived, where they magicked and gathered and had things like portals and defense. The surface was reserved for the humans and the elves and the animals, which was why this large defense party greeting was such a surprise. But Kerat was not helping her at all.

Instead, he watched her.

"We need to see Archmage Vermeil. We need to be in the real kingdom." Portia's face flushed. She was not explaining things very well, but the last time she'd seen Queen Morgani, the Dwarven queen, she'd been strictly against opening another portal to the Dragonoid world. Even with King Morgani and their Archmage trapped there.

Would Portia telling the truth now instantly banish their chances of getting the help they needed? For help they did need. From the Archmage of the dwarves, and from their warriors.

"Aye, that's what I thought, but we needed to hear it first," Kerat said, explaining nothing.

They sat in silence until Portia could take it no more. "Why?" she asked.

"There have been raids, lots of them, on our herds on the surface, and some trying to find a way into the lands. Someone spread rumors that we mine gold and diamonds." Kerat snorted, then threw a rock down the side of the hill by the road. The horses jumped when the rock clattered against some trees. "We just want to live unharassed, and that's hard to come by these days. Diamonds and gold be cursed."

"Harassed? From the Dragonoids?" Mark asked, leaning in to hear Kerat's response.

"Ha! They're long gone, from what's we've heard, though they are the responsible party, no?" Kerat didn't look to them for an answer, only staring into the woods. "Burning all the farmlands and houses of our neighbors and leaving them bereft and starving. And now the neighbors, humans who never had much use for us lowly dwarves before, are now looking to us for help. We've not had much in the way of extras to start with, and now with our sheep getting killed and so few of our warriors here to help because..." Kerat glanced at Portia, then looked away, not finishing his sentence.

Portia knew why he stopped talking.

He could have finished his sentence by saying 'so many of our warriors are trapped in the other lands because someone closed the portal on them unexpectedly, cutting off their chance of escape.'

That someone being Portia.

Portia's stomach twisted in a knot. She wanted to make it

right. She was here to make it right. If only their queen would listen.

Mark looked at Portia, and then at Lyren, confused at Kerat's unfinished sentence. He'd never been to Morgani before. He didn't know what Kerat looked like before. How thin and starved the dwarf looked now, by contrast to the plump being he'd been. How all the dwarves looked so thin, at least those she could glance at without attracting notice.

Blessedly, Mark had the sense to not press for an answer right then. Perhaps he saw something on Portia's face. Portia knew she was not one to be able to hide her true thoughts on her countenance, something she'd wished more than once was otherwise, but for once it was useful.

Portia sucked in a breath, determined to make her case getting help from the dwarves when a screech and a banging noise came from behind them. It sounded like an extremely angry animal.

A booming reverberated around them, bouncing off the mountains and back to the trees again. Somewhere in the woods a tree fell down, its leaves ripping and tearing down through the tightly set branches around it. It landed with another boom that echoed in the forest and beyond, seemingly through Portia's very chest.

She leapt to her feet, along with the others.

Holding a hand out for them to stay, Kerat ran to the road and joined his men. A few ran down the road, but most melted into the dark shadows of trees and disappeared. The crown of leaves atop the woods they entered rustled and moved high above, though there was no wind.

Portia drew her sword and crouched, ready, as Mark and Lyren did too. They formed the defensive circle that was starting to feel all too familiar.

"Should we follow?" Mark asked, his eyes scanning the woods in the direction the dwarves had run off to.

"No," Lyren answered. "They know these woods better than we do. If they need help, we'll hear soon enough, but I doubt that will be the case. Besides," Lyren turned to wink at Portia, "if we run off, we'll stress out the two dwarves assigned to watch us. They are already upset at us outnumbering them."

"How—" Portia started to ask, but stopped when Lyren cut her off with a shake of her head. Portia growled, but turned to watch the woods again. Whatever would happen, she was ready.

Their breath and her own pounding heart were the only sounds Portia heard.

Nothing happened for minutes. Her heart calmed down. The woods remained a silent witness to whatever was happening out of their sight.

Portia rolled her neck, willing herself to relax and not overtire her muscles before she needed them.

One of these days, she would get Lyren's secrets of how she knew things that seemed impossible to know.

Portia's sword vibrated, sending a shiver up her arm. Was she imagining it? It felt like it was pulling in one direction. She shifted her grip and thought the sensation gone. Still, the hairs on the back of her arms rose.

She squinted to focus better in the dim light within the trees. Nothing. Even in the high noon sun, the woods lay dark and cool.

It revealed nothing.

Portia huffed.

Mark paced behind her. He faced the mountains, on the far side of the dirt road. The mountains that held the dwarf stronghold, at least if Portia's sense of direction was right.

Lyren looked between the two directions.

A whistle sounded through the trees. It rang on like a long clear bell, then stepped up in frequency like a lute player's fancy slide.

"I'm betting that's the all-clear signal, young human. Care to wager?" Lyren smirked at Portia.

"Ha! Perhaps Mark would take you up on that," Portia said. She'd hold on to her coin, thank you very much.

Without realizing she had done it, Portia found she was standing at ease. Lyren apprised her, then nodded and also relaxed.

Mark glanced back, saw them both out of battle stance, no longer with one foot in front of the other with their weapons held at the ready. He looked about, trying to figure out what had happened. There was nothing to see but the shadowy woods and the road leading off into the distance and down the hill out of sight. Nonplussed, he stood as well, but his eyes darted from Portia and Lyren to the dark woods and back again. He could not quite relax.

"The whistle," Portia said to him. His brows furrowed

before clearing. He nodded, then stood, lowering his weapon but not sheathing it.

A fine mist of dirt drifted on the road in their direction. It came from over the hill where the dwarves had run to. Something or someone was on the road.

A female's shrill voice cut through the woods. "Enough! Get your hands off me this instant!"

Any response to her demand was too quiet to hear.

Her yells echoed again, impressively loud for still being out of sight. "I am not the bad guy. I gave you the bad guys, wrapped and ready to go!"

"And we thank you for that, young miss, but we don't know you here, and there have been bad things happening as of late from..." Kerat's replied, his voice calm.

The dwarves came over the hill, surrounding a small girl with dark hair and a fierce scowl. They also led three riderless horses. A thin scarlet and yellow twisted rope, fine as a lady's belt, wound around the girl's arms, pinning them to her side. It looked too delicate to physically hold her so. Commander Kerat walked next to the prisoner, deferentially speaking to her.

Portia gasped.

The girl looked up and met Portia's eye.

Mark whistled, then laughed, turning away. "No way" he muttered so that only Lyren and Portia could hear.

Lyren sighed. "Impressive. This, I did not expect." Lyren sheathed her weapon and crossed her arms, awaiting their approach.

Portia could not wait so calmly.

She stepped into the road, walking briskly, almost stomping, to meet the group, her sword still out and swinging dangerously. Blood roared in her ears. She reached the cluster of dwarves around the girl, then refused to budge from her spot on the road, forcing them to stop.

"Magisend Lucy Gwynn, what are you doing here?" Portia demanded, surprised at the anger in her own voice.

"The question, Jack, is what are *you* doing here," Magisend said, matching Portia's anger and then some.

"It's a party," Mark said, calling from where he and Lyren stood watching. Portia ignored him.

"I'm..." Portia started, then glanced at Kerat. They hadn't gotten to that part yet, and she didn't want to blow it. "I'm trying to work out our plan."

"Here? Without me? Without the others? Are you nuts? Don't commoners ever think?" Magisend said, looking down her nose at Portia. It seemed impossible to be that haughty while at the same time a captive. Of course Magisend could pull it off.

Portia gripped her sword tighter. One stroke would be all it took.

Magisend smirked. Was she daring her?

Looking away, Portia forced herself to exhale, then concentrated on relaxing her shoulders. She breathed in and out three times.

Kerat stared at Portia, concerned.

"Commander Kerat, we are here to seek the assistance of

your kingdom in retrieving those of our lands lost to the Dragonoids. And your people as well," Portia said, nodding at the question posed by his raised eyebrows. "We know full well that Queen Morgani was opposed several moons ago, but things might have changed for your people since then. And we're desperate." She said the last line quietly, her face reddening at the admission.

"Aye, things have changed indeed," Kerat said softly. "You'll be speaking to the queen on that matter. I can make no promises for our people."

"And Archmage Vermeil?" Portia asked.

"And Archmage Vermeil," he said.

Magisend blew her bangs up and out of her eyes. "Well, that's all well and good. Now please untie me. I am a *noble* from the kingdom of Haulstatt. You restrain me at your own peril."

Portia bit back a laugh at the consternation crossing Kerat's face at the demand of his prisoner. She was not the only one Magisend drove mad.

"Aye, maybe, but just to be safe, we'll be letting our queen decide," he answered, walking away before Magisend could reply. Another dwarve held tight to the loose end of the rope and kept Magisend from following, leaving her to glare daggers at Kerat's back as he went to speak to the others.

"How are you here?" Portia asked, still confused, but not quite so angry.

"I'm here looking for you, of course," Magisend said, sniffing.

"But the last time we spoke, you knew we were going to Cecelia's farm," Portia said.

Magisend laughed, a beautiful light laugh so unlike her normal speech. "Commoner, do you still think I get intelligence from only your word? I am a Riddlepit! I have sources."

Portia's mouth dropped open.

Relenting, Magisend lowered her chin and spoke in a quieter tone. "How many elf fights do you think happen in these lower kingdoms? It's a wonder the royal guard isn't here."

Dread sank into Portia's stomach like a stone. If Magisend had known the fight in the tavern many days ago meant Portia was in the south with Lyren, then could her queen, Queen Lorica, know the same? Had Lyren paid her respects to the human queen when she was looking for Portia in Coverack. Portia glanced back at Lyren.

Magisend said even more softly, "I don't think she spoke to the queen."

Portia's eyes rounded at Magisend guessing her thoughts so exactly.

"My question to you," Magisend said, her voice returning to its normal condescending tone, nodding at the three horses Mark, Portia, and Lyren had ridden in on now tied to a nearby tree, still heaving loaded with their packs, "is how I have arrived at the same time as you? What else have you been doing?"

Glancing at the dwarves surrounding them, who kept their eyes studiously focused on the distance and not on the two conversing girls, Portia shook her head. It was none of Magisend's business.

Magisend narrowed her eyes at Portia's reticence.

"Why would you even think this is where we were going?" Portia said, avoiding the question.

"Because I know some of the folk involved, remember?" Magisend said. She tilted her head, making it clear she was waiting for an answer from Portia on her earlier question on where had they been.

Portia pursed her lips. They locked eyes for a few seconds.

Portia looked away first.

"Fine. I'll tell you what I've been doing," Magisend said in her highest haughty tone. "Fighting off foul smelling ruffians, that's what. With no help from these folks." Magisend leaned to one side and jerked her body, pulling the end of the rope wrapped around her from the hands of the dwarf holding it.

He grunted, then picked up the end of the rope from the ground, not even deigning to look at Magisend.

Magisend turned red, then a scary shade of white. Her fists clenched.

Portia stared at the rope. It looked so delicate that Magisend should just be able to pull it off. Magisend could have just frozen them all with her powerful cryomancy magic. Why hadn't she?

"Anti-magic something. I don't know, but while it's on, I can't freeze these soldiers into the next world," Magisend said, seeing Portia's stare.

"Probably for the best," Portia muttered, turning away so

she didn't have to see what terrifying expression that conjured on Magisend's face.

THEY STAYED ON THE ROAD, the humans and Lyren riding their horses, the dwarves walking. The sun was working its way to the west, blocked now by the high mountains. A strip overhead was all they could see of the clear blue sky, now darkening to a deep bluish black, for it was blocked on one side by the dense forest, and on the other by the mountains. The air cooled nearly immediately as soon as the setting yellow orb disappeared behind the mountain and a brisk wind picked up.

Kerat had arranged for a squad to go back and retrieve the two men Magisend had frozen to a tree before the dwarves had come upon the battle. Magisend had been so irate at the men for daring to attack her that she'd not only frozen the men directly to the tree, securing them high up on the trunk, but then blasted the top of the tree with so much ice that it bent away from her, length by length, until it was leaning over sideways. When the wood could take no more, it broke asunder and the top part crashed down to the forest floor.

That had been the crash they'd heard in the forest.

The two men had been so terrified that they would land underneath the tree they were frozen to that they had soiled themselves. It was either skill on Magisend's part, or sheer luck they had not been crushed under the tree whose trunk was a full arm span wide. There would have been little left of them.

Portia suspected it had been skill on Magisend's part. Magisend had shown some restraint, but just barely. Rubbing her neck, Portia thought of her own torments at Magisend's hand. As bad as it had been, it had never been so outrageously lethal.

The smell of the men's soiled pants added to their acrid body odor. Even the horses they had been bundled on, all while firmly tied up, had danced uneasily as the men were loaded, their nostrils flaring. Portia did not envy the stableman who'd be tasked with cleaning those saddles.

The dwarves had cut away the foresleeves of the men's shirts even before they were completely free of the ice attaching them to the tree. Each of them bore the mark of the cult tattooed into their flesh. That, and Magisend allowing Kerat to check her own arms to see there was no mark, was enough for him to relent on releasing her from the lasso.

Or perhaps it had been a word from General Lyren, for the general did know Magisend. Portia was too tired to ask, nor did she care.

Her thoughts were on how to convince the queen of their need for assistance.

None of the dwarves looked well fed. Instead, as a normally stout race, these looked more like the waif-like elves in the north. Suddenly, Portia wished their saddlebags were full of food instead of fine cloth.

They stopped on the road, in front of a dirt path that

veered off to the right and wound along the steep face of the cliff now towering over them.

Kerat waved his hands in a complex pattern, eluding Portia's observations despite her best effort not to miss it. A flash of light erupted from the ground ahead of them, blue tinged with red sparks. The illusion of a narrow dirt animal path winding on the steep gray rock disappeared, leaving a rough-hewn gash in the mountainside, covered by an enormous timbered door.

The hidden entrance to the Dwarven lands. Unlike the first such secret passage she'd seen, though, this one was rough and ugly, pick marks streaking the stone. Gaps showed between the thick timbered door and the stone around it. This was the servant's entrance version, compared to the fine opulence of the first gated entryway she'd seen, with its rock carvings and finely tooled door.

This entrance looked like it had been made in a hurry.

Inside, it was even rougher than on the outside. The dwarves lit torches waiting in iron holders just within the entrance, and the light flickered on angular walls cut into the mountain, jutting veins of harder rock still sticking out into the corridor. The creators of the passage had not taken the time to smooth the walls, instead just making it large enough for horses to pass single file and that was all. Those traversing the passageway had to duck and weave around obstacles.

The dwarves took the lit torches from the wall, the flames dancing from the breeze flowing through the tunnel, even with the door shut behind them. Dim blue-tinged spots on the ceiling tickled at Portia's vision. She stared at one spot, nudging her horse ahead to block the light from the torch-bearing dwarf behind her so she could stare at it better. Once directly below it, a white dot of light shone down on her from the center.

A star.

They were air vents. The blue was light from the night sky high above them, shining through holes burrowed through the thick rock above.

That was how they were not dying in the closed tunnel lit by air hungry open flames.

They plodded on in the dim tunnel, the rhythmic gait of the horse and the monotony lulling Portia to sleep. It was so dim there was little difference between keeping her eyes open or closed anyhow.

A noise disturbed her dreams. She woke, blearily, to a cacophony of dwarves crowding around her horse and the horses of Magisend, Lyren, and Mark.

The dark tunnel was gone. They stood in a huge cavern with door-sized openings set into the walls of the caverns, arranged like floors of a house. Walkways ran between the openings, and ladders provided access to the levels above and below.

Dwarves stood close around them, mostly women, children, and old folks, peering with a frank curiosity Portia did not remember from her last visit. All the dwarves were painfully thin. Their clothing was clean, but mended many times over, the rough stitches and patches visible even from a distance.

"Portia!" a voice called to her. Confused, Portia turned

around in her saddle, looking here and there to the faces around her. None seemed familiar.

"Portia!" the voice called again. A chittering followed.

The crowd parted slowly. Footsteps echoed throughout the cavern, but before the owner appeared, a small creature dashed down the opening in the crowd and ran up Portia's horse's right front leg, too fast for the horse to react, except to step backwards until Portia restrained it. The creature scurried onto Portia's saddle, then leapt up onto her shoulder and buried itself in her hair at the base of her neck. It chittered in her ear.

Archmage Vermeil walked into view, his robes swishing with each purposeful step. He towered over most of the other dwarves. Portia knew from experience he towered over her too, especially when angered. He didn't look angered now. Indeed, his smile was the biggest she'd ever seen on his face.

But even his smile couldn't hide the hollows of his cheeks, showing in stark contrast in the flickering torchlight. Portia's heart hurt in a way she had not felt since leaving Coverack. What had happened here in the moons since they closed the portals?

"Portia, welcome!" Vermeil said, reached up to help her down from her horse. His outstretched hand prompted a loud protest from the creature under her hair, followed by it sticking out its head and baring its teeth to Vermeil.

"Chit! Whatever are you doing? Get down right now!" Vermeil said, pulling his hand back.

The creature emphatically said no, clear even to those not of its own species.

Portia laughed.

Mark and Lyren watched, amused. Thank goodness neither one of them had the tendency to scream at the presence of small creatures, unlike some of Portia's past companions.

Magisend was not amused. She crossed her arms, then cleared her throat, staring down from her saddle like a queen on a throne.

Vermeil caught this from the corner of his eye and turned to Magisend. He gave her a beautiful flourish of a court bow, right down to the offer of a kiss on her hand. She visibly melted under the flattery and stretched out a hand for his attentions. Portia bit her lip to not laugh again and undo all the poor archmage's hard work.

They dismounted their horses. While Archmage Vermeil flattered and soothed Magisend, Portia stood close to Lyren and Mark and spoke under her breath while still smiling at all around them.

"Where is Kerat and the rest?" Portia asked, while giving a nod to a youngster that wanted to pet her horse.

"They took the prisoners somewhere and asked that we wait here. We would have woken you, but it was to only be for a moment or two," Lyren said.

Mark chuckled. "Yes, we would have woken you, but the soldiers were so amazed by you sleeping in your saddle that we couldn't bear to take their amusement away."

"Mark!" Portia said out loud, startling those around her.

"What? We all need some fun now and then, no?" Mark

held up his hands in askance while stepping back out of Portia's reach.

Turning her back on Mark, Portia reached up gently and extracted the animal from her shoulders. It was the same two-fist-sized ball of fur she'd met the first time she was here. She'd no idea it liked her that much. Well, that was not entirely true. It had bitten Archmage Vermeil quite hard to protect her on her first visit, but in its defense, the archmage was trying to kill her.

Blessedly, she and Vermeil were on the same side now.

At least they were the last time they'd spoken. That seemed ages ago now.

"I'll take that now," Vermeil said. He stood behind her, one hand stretched out. Chit, the furball, walked daintily from Portia's hand onto Vermeil's and then crawled up the arm of his robe and settled on his shoulder.

"I guess you two are on better terms these days," Portia said.

"We do fine."

Vermeil was just as tall as she remembered. Portia stepped back so she wouldn't have to look up at such a steep angle to converse with him.

"Can we talk?" Portia asked him.

He shook his head almost imperceptibly. "Of any pleasantry you might like, of course," he said. "I just got word of your arrival, as did the queen. She is expecting you as soon as your escort returns."

Portia looked down to hide her scowl. They would have

no chance to come up with a plan together before having to speak to the queen.

"Has there been any change?" Portia asked. She sensed more than saw Mark, Lyren, and Magisend watching their conversation. Thankfully, they did not crowd her and Vermeil, but instead hung back and entertained the dwarf children around them.

"Not overtly," Vermeil said. "But things have not been comfortable here, as you might have noticed. No one expected the chaos and lawlessness in Lusatiana. It's affected us greatly, I am afraid to say. We are lucky to have had the reserves that we did, for they plundered our aboveground farmlands."

Portia stared at him. "All of them?"

"As much as they could reach. It seemed out of viciousness as much as anything else for what they couldn't take, they burned," Archmage Vermeil said.

"Why? If they were starving themselves?" Portia asked.

"Some indeed were starving. Others... others had this madness. Like those two Magisend struck down. The ones with the tattoos. They seem to think they're fulfilling some prophecy by continuing the work of destruction that was done in Lusatiana."

Kerat and a dozen of his squad returned, ending their conversation. He waved them on, after taking the horses' reins and handing them to an older dwarf who bowed respectfully and walked off leading the horses and several children to care for them.

They walked as a group through several large caverns, the dwarves that had surrounded them melting away until it was just the humans, Lyren, Vermeil, Kerat, and his men. The caverns felt emptier than last time Portia had been here.

The last cavern opened up to the exterior of the underground Dwarven palace. It looked the same as last time except the large ferocious creatures guarding it were no longer there. Their absence chilled Portia. Now only thin dwarves stood holding their pikes on either side of the entranceway.

They walked in silence through the corridors of the palace. Even Magisend kept quiet, her normal brashness subdued by the summons.

In the throne room. the queen sat on the dark wooden throne. Few ladies attended her, another marked difference from last time. No crowd stood in audience.

Dark circles shadowed the queen's eyes. Even she seemed thinner than before, her auburn hair duller. As before she wore the finest robe of all the dwarves, but it, too, showed mending, even if the stitches were finer than for the common folk.

After they were announced, and had bowed and curtsied their greetings, the queen waved them forward.

"Why are you here?" the queen asked without preamble, her voice tired.

Lyren stepped forward, bowing once again.

Before Lyren could speak, Portia stepped in front of her. "We have come to ask your assistance, to guard a portal, while we retrieve our people. And yours," Portia said quickly, matching the queen's candor.

Lyren pursed her lips in surprise, but merely nodded when the queen looked at her for confirmation.

The queen's gaze returned to Portia. Her jaw worked, the flexing muscles showing in her cheeks.

No one else moved. Even Chit, who was still on Vermeil's shoulder, stayed still. Portia forced herself to breathe so she would not fall over in a faint. Her breath sounded loud in her ears.

The queen thrummed her fingers on the arm of her chair.

The queen's gaze drifted over the visitors, her attendants and subjects, before her eyes settled back on Portia's. A chill ran down Portia's back.

"We have conditions," the queen finally said.

10

The throne room felt silent and heavy. Portia's legs trembled. Thankfully, it did not show through her pants and long tunic.

The queen stood from her throne, the first time Portia had seen her do such a thing. Walking down the long shallow stone steps at the front of the dais, the queen stood in front of Portia. She, too, was surprisingly tall for a dwarf. Her eyes were just above Portia's. The scent of grass and flowers flowed from her robes, reminding Portia just how close the queen stood.

"The conditions for our people are not onerous, but they will be met," the queen said. "We need safety here, as well as our people returned. Our soldiers are reduced. Those we have spend too many hours protecting our lands. We cannot maintain a full-blown war."

Portia nodded, barely able to look at the queen. She

concentrated on a crack in the tile floor in front of her while the queen spoke.

"Do you understand?" the queen asked.

"Yes, Your Majesty," Portia said. "It will not come to that. We can open a splinter out of sight and do things with stealth." Portia hoped she sounded more confident than she felt.

"See that you do. Archmage Vermeil will notify you when our preparations are complete. He will consult with you as needed," the queen said.

Lyren stepped forward. "Perhaps Your Majesty would like an update on Portia's abilities—"

"I'm well aware of her abilities," Queen Morgani said, an edge to her voice.

Portia looked up, surprised.

"Yes, Your Majesty," Lyren said, stepping back.

The queen walked past the group, exiting through a door off to the side of the large room. Her attendants followed after in a crowd, leaving the throne room empty except for the subjects and petitioners.

Lyren exhaled with a loud sigh.

"Didn't think you had it in you, commoner," Magisend said, not unkindly.

———

THE BREAKFAST ROOM of the communal living space given to them by the dwarves was a long open cavern, roughly several wagon lengths long, and a wagon length wide. It was also their dining and sitting room, for the guards outside the door had discouraged any wandering within the Dwarven kingdom. It was barely big enough for Portia to practice her swordsmanship after she pushed the long table and benches to the side of the room, tucking them in under the tapestries depicting scenes of the lands above hung on the wall. There was little other furniture, save for a chair or two tucked in the corners.

Working through her exercises and footwork, Portia wished for a sparring partner. Lyren would only work with her for three candlesmarks a day and then claim exhaustion—an exhaustion Portia wished she could feel, instead of the nervous energy and torment of waiting for preparations she had no part of.

Portia, Mark, Lyren, and Magisend had spent much of their time in this long room in the long days they waited for preparations to complete. Lately, Mark had taken to helping the patrols above ground. Portia had wanted to join them but was talked out of it by Lyren, and even Magisend. She was too important to risk fighting ruffians in the fields. Magisend claimed she had done her duty already, so did not join Mark.

Lyren managed to evade the guards and disappeared for long stretches each day.

Occasionally Archmage Vermeil would stop by to update them. He had been fascinated by the anti-magic vials Lyren had given Portia. It worked completely differently than the rope they had used to restrain Magisend. After much discussion, they decided coating their blades would be the best use of it, if needed at all. Portia could not remember much magic in the Dragonoids' world.

Indeed, it had been difficult for her to do magic there at all, especially cryomancy with the dry air and lack of moisture anywhere. Would Magisend fare any better?

"I think you're just skipping school." Mark's voice drifted into the breakfast room from the hallway. "What I don't understand is why you brought no one else?"

"I have noble duties that call me from school often. My duty to the house of Riddlepit is more than reason enough to leave the campus. I can leave without much remark," Magisend said.

Portia pulled up from second position and let her blade drop as Mark and Magisend walked in the room. Mark chewed an apple, one of the bonuses for helping with the patrols. He tossed another to Portia. She caught it with her left hand. It felt firm. Her mouth watered even as she set down her blade on the long table. The dwarves had done their best to feed them, but there was not much food to be had for anybody.

Magisend had already eaten her apple, the seeds in her hand the only thing left. Portia snorted. If they'd been back in Coverack, a maid probably would have taken the seeds from Magisend already, and wiped her hand as well.

"Yes, but isn't Mia also a noble person? Wouldn't her absence also go unnoticed?" Mark asked between bites of apple.

"She's of the country nobles. There is a difference," Magisend said. She sniffed at the paltry business dealings of countryfolk.

"Help is help," Mark said. "There's a whole school of students there."

Magisend crossed her arms, the seeds falling to the floor, while her eyes flashed. "And I thought we were going to be subtle and sly. Pray tell, how can we do that with the whole academy of students tramping through the countryside?"

Portia sighed and turned her back on both of them. She tried once to interfere in their discussions before she realized they enjoyed arguing.

A knock on the doorframe interrupted this time.

Archmage Vermeil and Kerat filled the doorway, more soldiers behind them. Even Lyren was back, talking with some in the hallway.

"We are ready. We've permission to bring you now, if you can," Vermeil said.

Portia grabbed her sword and was at the doorway before he finished his sentence.

A DAIS SAT at the far pinched end of a large tall cavern, growing much wider further from the raised platform. Over the dais and reaching back into the wall above it, carved out to make room, heaped rubble and rocks, held back only by a thin wooden shelf. Ropes hung from either end and ran back along the cavern walls to the far wide end of the cavern. The ropes connected to the wooden shelf. A pull would dislodge the shelf, sending the heavy rock debris on whoever stood on the dais.

On the cavern ground, stone walls faced the high dais, long arrow slits built into them, just wide enough for the heavy shaft of a crossbow bolt. Behind the walls, and set slightly above, sat mechanical bow machines, secured behind large stone embankments. Heavy ropes coiled in piles in front of them, ready to be wound around massive wooden barrels to store ratcheted tension. Once wound, a single lever would release the ferocious energy, flinging ten arrows forward at once from each machine.

All weapons focused on the platform.

Archmage Vermeil and Kerat led the way into the cavern, followed by Portia, Magisend, Mark, and Lyren. Lastly, the rest of that Dwarven guard accompanying them followed.

Mark whistled. "I think I know where you're supposed to open the portal."

Portia nodded. So much lethal weaponry focused at that point. May no one slip and accidentally fire.

Fear descended on Portia like a wet clammy blanket. Her scalp tingled and her stomach ached. Either she'd forgotten, or willfully ignored, the danger they were putting themselves into.

Queen Morgani was making no such mistake.

"Impressive," Lyren said. She walked to one of the archery machines, examining its workings, while carefully keeping clear of the sharp arrows mounted at its front. It was not primed for battle, but the elf took no chances.

"We needed defenses, powerful defenses, that could be manned by just a few," Kerat said.

"I'll be here as well, for the queen will not let me go,"

Vermeil said. "I can create stone barriers to the splinter, but that takes time, sometimes much time as you know."

"Aye, we'll give you that time."

"Wait, aren't you supposed to provide our cover?" Magisend asked Vermeil archly, her hands on her hips.

"Of course, of course," Vermeil answered, with infinite patience. "I'll return here after that. It is the only exception the queen will allow. It will not take long."

Much as she hated Magisend's attitude sometimes, having that question answered helped. Portia knew it would be better to not have to defend a splinter, for if the dwarves were successful, there was still the question of them getting back again from the foreign world, not to mention getting out possibly hundreds of others.

"It might be harder than you think," Portia said. "Do you have a second mage to help, in case it is difficult? I could barely do magic there."

Magisend snorted.

Portia ignored her. Just wait until Magisend experienced it for herself.

"Um, no. I'll send for one. My apologies, I should have thought of that," Vermeil answered Portia. He, too, did not even give Magisend a glance.

One motion from Kerat sent a soldier running. Vermeil nodded thanks.

Another troop of dwarves arrived and flowed around them, entering the cavern. They took their positions at the weapons without a word from Kerat. Several grabbed the ropes leading to the wooden shelves holding back the rock.

The whole Dwarven crew moved smooth as clockwork. Most were young females. Some were older, with gray hair sticking out from underneath their leather helmets.

The strongest of the soldiers arrayed themselves in a semicircle on the floor of the cavern, swords drawn, facing the dais. The first line of defense.

Portia and the others had taken the time to get their weapons and cloaks before traveling to the cavern prepared by the dwarves. Kerat gave Mark, Portia, and Magisend each a small bundle of food, a veritable fortune in the starving kingdom, for which Portia was grateful. Food was just as difficult to get in the Dragonoid world. Stealing for it would be another needless risk of getting caught. The food bundles fit neatly into the leather shoulder bags they each wore.

Hopefully the food would not be needed, for this trip should not be that long. They planned a scouting mission to track where the splinter Portia created was set, and how far it lay from the cities, for surely that was where the captives were.

Kerat had mentioned the possibility of the captives sent out to work the farms.

They had no answer for that. There was no time, under any plan they could come up with, that would allow combing the countryside for prisoners.

So this trip was to find out where the splinter was relative to the cities, if they could figure out such a thing. It would be bad luck indeed to open to some remote area like the first one Portia had back on Cecelia's farm.

No, Portia shook her head. She'd risk an opening closer to

the edge of the city. It was worth it, for there was no point going at all if they could not find their kin. She clenched her fist.

They'd long since decided Lyren would not accompany them venturing through the splinter, for she became too ill in the Dragonoids' world. Her presence would be more a liability than an asset. They could not focus on helping or protecting her while also scouting out the world and plotting a way to rescue their people.

After hearing Portia's tale of how she had disguised herself, the queen had provided long lengths of brown linen. It was finer than the linen Portia had used, but close enough to match. Portia was grateful for the tight weave, for it would protect much better against the hot stinging sun of the Dragonoids' world. Sun strong enough to burn within minutes of skin exposure.

Finally, the second mage arrived, breathless, and dressed in a shoddy imitation of the brown robes Portia had directed the seamstresses to make for those going into the world.

Portia led the others towards the dais. Goose bumps rose on her arms as she mounted the steps to the platform. Magisend, Mark, Vermeil, and the other mage hung back on the cavern floor, despite their plan of coming with her. It was smart of them to not risk their necks standing under the rock avalanche waiting to happen, but it made Portia feel even more alone and exposed to be up there by herself.

Pulling a parchment sheet from her bag, Portia reviewed the music notation she kept from long ago of the sounds of the song that would open the splinter to the Dragonoids' world.

Working from memory at the farm had not served well. She would do better this time. Taking one long last glance and muttering to herself the melody, she then closed her eyes and looked up to memorize the sound.

After a moment she carefully folded the paper, then slipped it into her bag. Singing the magic required to open the splinter, she at first felt nothing, sending a shot of panic through her chest, but she kept going. A few notes later the vibration began, slowly, quietly at first, rumbling in her chest. It was working.

A shimmering opaque oval outline appeared mystically in front of her, barely visible at first, but growing stronger as Portia continued the song. Mist swirled on the surface of the outline, moving faster and growing more agitated as the outline itself solidified.

Finally, when the reverberations in her chest grew until her whole body shook with the melody, Portia knew it was complete.

She stopped singing. The silence in the cavern felt louder than her melody had been. Turning, she saw everyone staring at her and the splinter behind her.

The opening to another world.

Waving them onto the platform, Portia stepped back so there would be room. Archmage Vermeil and the other mage shook their heads, as if shaking off the spell, and ran up the stairs first, followed by Mark and Magisend. Soldiers followed.

General Lyren gave a salute from the cavern floor.

Portia stuck the tip of her sword into the swirling oval.

Perhaps she should have brought a staff or spear for this and not risked her precious weapon. But nothing happened to it, no enemy strike, no grabbing from the other side. Withdrawing her sword, Portia turned and looked at the others.

All were ready.

Portia stepped forward to step through.

"Wait," Kerat called from the cavern floor. "Let them check first." He motioned to several soldiers who ran up the stairs.

"No, it's not—" Portia started.

"It's necessary. The queen will have my head if I let you walk into a dangerous situation. You created this opening and are the only one who can close it permanently," Kerat said, his tone brooking no argument.

Portia acknowledged his point with the tilt of her head and stepped back to let the soldiers through. They disappeared one after the other through the swirling oval. Not a sound came back to them.

Several minutes passed. Several long minutes for Portia to regret more and more letting others take the risk for her, for a task she alone had set for herself.

Finally, one of the soldiers poked her head through the oval and gave a curt nod, then stuck one arm back into the cavern and motioned for the rest to follow.

The far side of the portal opened into a thin forest of sorts. The woods were tall narrow yellow trees, the trunks barely an arm width, but the only foliage being a spray of fern-like leaves at the top. The land around rose and fell in gentle hillocks, mercifully blocking their location from most directions. It was a fortuitous place to have opened into.

Now if their luck would just continue with the splinter opening close to a city.

Portia picked the nearest hilltop and walked towards it, wanting to get a view. Mark and Magisend followed slightly behind, flanking each side, their weapons drawn, their eyes scanning. Two soldiers came as well.

Portia looked back and held her finger to her lips for quiet. It was hard for such a large group to be silent, but they had to try.

Meanwhile, Archmage Vermeil and his mage assistant worked at creating a spell over the portal behind them. If all went as planned, it would be invisible to anyone except those looking for it and knowing its exact location. It, too, was musical magic, but they sang so quietly Portia could hear nothing from them just ten paces away.

Realizing that, Portia sliced a cut on the nearby trees with her sword as she walked, reaching as high as she could reach. Marks for their journey back to the portal, but not something so obvious as a sign at eye level, for the Dragonoids were roughly as tall as she was.

No, they were taller.

Portia shook her head in frustration at her own error. Reaching higher with the sword, she continued with the marks but made them smaller. There was not much choice, because marks low down would be instantly visible for someone watching their footing through the tree roots.

As they neared the top of the hillock, Portia motioned for

the two soldiers to stay behind. They were not dressed appropriately, and would be instantly recognized as invaders, or worse yet, taken as escaped prisoners, for they clearly were not Dragonoids.

The soldiers pressed their lips together in an angry line but did not argue. They stopped and watched as Portia, Magisend, and Mark dropped to their hands and knees and crawled to the top of the hill to peer over.

The hillock overlooked a gentle slope that ended abruptly at the top of a cliff, revealing a huge drop beyond, then a vast plain of yellow and gold sand and rock. In the middle of it lay a city, with an enormous blackened field next to its walls.

A burned and scarred battlefield.

It was the inland city that had the last portal Portia had been at, the one she and Ava ran through, desperate for their lives, while shot at by the enemy soldiers.

Portia exhaled and looked down, not believing their luck. It could not get more perfect.

Except they had to get to the city. It was surrounded on all sides by open spaces. The forest she had seen before was on the far side.

Magisend and Mark took it all in. They'd never been in this world before.

A cloud rose up at the entrance of the main gate of the city, far down below them. A large cloud.

Someone was leaving the city and kicking up a lot of dust.

It was probably just a coincidence, for how could anyone see them from so far away, their heads just rising above the hillock? The city guard could not have spotted them. Still, Portia felt a sudden urge to get out of there.

She scooted back down the hill, pulling at the sleeves of Mark and Magisend to get them to come with. Making their way back to the portal, they found Archmage Vermeil and his assistants already gone, back within the portal as promised, their work complete. If Portia hadn't known the portal was there, she'd have walked right by what looked like a thicker patch of trees growing on the side of a steep hillock, with debris clogging the ground, discouraging anyone from walking that way.

It was all an illusion.

Two soldiers stood guarding outside the magic, their eyes scanning the woods. They nearly jumped out of their skins when the group came back. The humans and dwarves all went back through to the Dwarven kingdom. Portia insisted no one stay behind.

Kerat and Lyren stood waiting, appearing not to have moved from the cavern floor since they left.

MAGISEND THREW down her spoon into her bowl. They were back in the common room of their quarters, having dinner and planning the next move. Kerat promised to join them afterwards, along with Vermeil. A modest dinner of mushroom meatloaf, some precious green vegetables, and potatoes was long gone, the plates scraped clean. Only a grain pudding remained on the table, not yet decimated by the hungry travelers.

Oil lanterns hung on hooks in the wall, sending flickering shadows across the room. Lanterns hung in only half of the available brackets, and to conserve oil only half of those burned It left the room with a dim, dangerous feel.

Magisend, Mark, Lyren, and Portia sat at the table, two to a side on the benches, huddled together as much for warmth is for companionship.

"Absolutely not," Magisend said. She glared at Portia sitting across the table from her.

"Why?" Portia asked, setting down her own spoon. "You'd get their language. You'd have that advantage."

"And you have, what? What would you pluck from me with this magic spell to instantly transfer languages from one mind to another?" Magisend asked, contempt in her voice, and something else Portia could not quite place.

"Nothing," Portia said, instantly regretting it.

"See? You're not even being honest." Magisend folded her arms and lifted her nose to look down at Portia.

Portia curled her fists. "How am I not being honest?"

Magisend raised her eyebrows, tilting her head. "Really?"

Mark leaned back and away from Magisend sitting next to him, as if she were burning hot and he was too close to the flame. He exchanged a look with Lyren across the table.

"How? How am I not being honest?" Portia repeated.

"Portia," Magisend said, her voice drawing out Portia's name. "The Dragonoid you put that spell on also learned your language at the same time. It is *not* a single direction spell. You know that."

"We speak the same language!" Portia yelled. She wanted to slam a fist down on the table. How could Magisend be so unreasonable?

"Okay, then, dearest one, tell me what other knowledge it would pluck from my brain to share with you," Magisend said, her voice level and infuriatingly controlled. "Some magic, perhaps? Family secrets? The color of my undergarments?"

Mark sputtered at the words undergarments, nearly choking on a bite of pudding.

"Nothing. It wouldn't share anything. It's not like I care what color you wear under your tunic, anyhow," Portia said.

"You don't *know* that it wouldn't share anything else. You didn't know it would share our language with the Dragonoid. Admit that." Magisend leaned in close, glaring at Portia. "Admit it."

Portia hadn't known. She'd used the magic spell she'd learned in the Elven kingdom to steal the Dragonoid language from one of the captive invaders. To her horror, it had learned her language in return. They had to isolate the prisoner after that, being careful not to speak of any plans in its presence. Since they didn't butcher their enemies, it still lived. If it managed to escape and return to its own world, it would have much too much knowledge to share as it was.

It had been a dangerous mistake.

Portia's face heated, the flush reaching even to her ears and neck. She couldn't maintain eye contact with Magisend, finally looking down at her plate. "I admit it," she said softly, the words bitter.

The lanterns flicked in the silent room. A guard from outside the door peered in at the sudden quiet, making sure all inside were alright, then quickly stepping back out of view when all four turn to stare at him.

Finally, Portia grabbed her spoon and ate the rest of her pudding, shoveling it into her mouth, not tasting a bite. It only made her nausea worse.

"Well, I'll do it," Mark said, trying to take a lighter tone to break the tension. "It's not like I have any fancy secrets anyhow. I very much want any advantage I can get." He gave Magisend his winning smile, and then a wink, leaning in close. "I'll tell you the color of my undergarments, without a spell."

Magisend's eyebrows shot up and her eyes widened as she stared at Mark. Letting out a huff, she threw her napkin down next to her plate, rose from the bench and exited the room. If there had been a door, Portia was sure she would've slammed it so hard it broke the hinges.

"That was not helpful," Portia said.

"No? At least it was fun," Mark said. He grabbed the serving dish of pudding and scraped the last of it onto his plate.

"What is the significance of undergarment color?" Lyren asked, her eyes flicking between Mark and Portia.

"Nothing, nevermind," Portia said. She kicked Mark under the table. Hard. He stubbornly did not react.

"Where is Magisend?" Kerat asked from the doorway. Archmage Vermeil stood with him, both of their faces serious.

"She needed some air. She'll be back soon," Mark said airily. Portia hoped that was true.

Kerat and Vermeil entered, sitting at the table close to Mark and Portia.

"The queen agrees with the proposed plan, with one condition," Kerat said. Both he and Vermeil looked uncomfortable.

Finally, Vermeil spoke. "She agreed that not sending any more of our people is a good idea, considering how ill-suited for the world our constitution is. While we are not weakened as quickly as elves—"

Lyren snorted.

"It is difficult for us to maintain fighting shape while there. Just that time I spent casting the spell exhausted me near to collapse, I'm afraid to admit," Vermeil continued. "However..." He dropped his gaze, refusing to look at Portia.

"However?" Portia said, prompting.

"She's decreed I should close the portal the best I can if you don't return within a moon. We will not leave it open forever. You say the city is nearby, correct?"

Portia nodded. A moon should be plenty of time. It would take a day, perhaps two, if they were extremely cautious in their approach. She couldn't imagine anything taking so long, unless they were captured, and then a year's worth of moons might not be enough.

"Close it, how?" Mark asked.

"Encased in rock," Kerat said. "It's not as good as

removing it completely, but it should withstand most all of their weapons. Located as you say, I doubt they would drag their most ferocious of machinery up the cliff."

Portia's brows knitted. They might be underestimating the determination of their foe, but she was not going to say such a thing to Kerat, for it would only make him less likely to let her go. It was a near miracle they would let her go at all, considering she was the only one capable of permanently closing the dangerous portal.

"Fine, that's not a problem," Portia said, smoothing her expression into a smile. Hopefully it didn't look as fake as it felt. "We won't need near that much time."

Kerat nodded. "We need to work out a signal of what you should send through the portal before entering yourself. It would be good to know friends are entering and not an enemy."

"Excellent," Mark said, pushing away his plate. "Those arrows look sharp. I've no desire to become a pincushion."

Vermeil laughed. "Indeed, not."

"Is the plan still to leave before dawn?" Portia asked.

"Yes. As near as my crew could tell, their dawn should be close to ours. With any luck, you'll have a moon to help light your way down the hill to the city."

Portia nodded. They had just enough time for a quick sleep before leaving to take their chances in the dangerous world of the invaders.

11

A quarter moon shed some light on the forest of thin yellow trees in the Dragonoid lands. The odd shaped leaves at the top waved in the dark early morning breeze, sending strange shadows all around them. Portia determinedly nicked the tops of the trees as they walked, as she had done the first time they had entered the world, her sword biting into the soft wood. The marks were barely visible in the dim light. She grimaced.

An odd fragrance floated in the air, an acrid floral scent, something she had not noticed when they had visited earlier. Perhaps it was the cooler evening air that supported it, so different from the blasting heat of the sun that dried everything, leaving only a hot burning in her throat. The tree leaves had provided little shade earlier, but the brown linen robes had done their jobs and protected their skin. No one had arrived back in the Dwarven caverns with their skin burnt.

At least she thought not. Portia'd not thought to check the Dwarven guard.

Following her, Mark trudged along, his normally sunny disposition marred by grumblings at a headache caused by the magic Portia used to give him the foreign language. Portia did not remember feeling ill after the same spell had been cast on her, but perhaps she was not as skilled with it as the elf had been.

Of course, the only other person she'd used it on, the captive Dragonoid, had not complained about Portia causing him pain. Even if she had given him a headache, it would have been the least of things he would've been enraged about.

They trudged along, picking up their feet slightly more than normal to avoid getting them tangled in the roots of the trees that ridged the ground around them.

Blessedly, Magisend did not mock Mark for his pain, nor call out his decision to get the language as a bad one. Perhaps she didn't think it mattered since he wasn't of noble blood.

Portia shook her head. Now was not the time to think such thoughts. Here, they were a team. For good or ill, their lives in each other's hands. Still, it was better for two of them to have the language than just her. Three would have been best, but Magisend made it more than clear that would never happen.

Arriving at the hill overlooking the city, they dropped down and peered over the top. Far below, torches burned in the night air like fireflies, reflecting on the city walls. The city's gates were not yet open.

Pink tinted the sky to the east, or at least the direction

Portia thought of as east, since the sun was clearly coming. With any luck, they would find their way down to the city while it was still difficult to spot movement in the hills. They didn't want anyone to know the direction they had come from for fear of revealing the portal.

The hillside sloped down to the drop-off ahead, a bare grassy area with few trees. The land to the right was barren, but on the left the trees were thicker, and there was even some other greenery lower down. They made their way left and started down the hill.

Keeping the shrubby plants between themselves and the city as much as possible, they walked on in the dim light. Portia winced with each step as her foot crunched down on dead undergrowth and dried leaves. At least a dirt path would have been quieter.

"There aren't any big wild animals here, are there?" Magisend asked, her voice low. "An animal trail would make this easier."

"Only if the animal didn't try to eat us," Portia said. She had only seen one large creature in these lands. One had been enough.

"Weakling," Magisend said.

She could put a sneer in a whisper. Impressive.

Portia blew out her breath, concentrating on the steepening path in front of her, pretending that Magisend didn't exist behind her.

The hill ended in a gully below, bone-dry. They stood just within the last of the trees before the drop into the packed earth bottom of the gully. On the far side ran a dirt road. All around, the sky brightened with the coming sunrise.

Down the road, away from the city, a puff of dirt hung over the surface of the road, barely visible.

"Hurry," Portia said. "Check your robes first."

Portia checked to make sure that all of her skin was covered by the brown linen robes provided by the queen. She pulled the deep hood up over her head and then pulled it forward, hiding her face. It obscured most of her view except the ground directly in front of her.

Mark and Magisend did the same with their own robes. Peering under her hood, Portia checked their work before giving the thumbs-up, her thumb just a peak in the fabric of the brown robe that covered her hand.

Picking their way through the gully, running when the ground was flat enough, they made their way to the other side. Mark tripped once and cartwheeled forward, arms wind-milling, but managed to right himself before wiping out in the dirt. They scrambled up the far side of the gully, dusted them-selves off, then walked casually down the road in the direction of the city, as if out for an everyday stroll.

Portia wanted to turn and look behind to check the progress of the travelers causing the cloud behind them so badly that it almost felt like a physical itch she could not scratch. Gritting her teeth, she kept her head facing forward and listened for any noise coming up behind them.

With any luck, it'd be a wagon coming to market and not a squad of soldiers intent on causing trouble.

Luck was with them. The rumbling behind them turned

from a vague noise to the distinct creak of wheels on gravel and rock. Several animals pulled the wagon, that much she could tell from the strike of their feet on the dirt, much louder than any human or Dragonoid would be walking.

Mark, Portia, and Magisend crowded to the side of the road, making room for the cart coming up from behind. As animals drew next to them, Portia snuck a glance. They looked like horses, but different, like a child had drawn a watercolor of a horse, distorting it as children's drawings do.

The animal snorted and look back at her. Portia quickly looked away, not wanting to provoke it.

The animals and the cart it pulled moved further ahead on the road. Portia exhaled in relief that the driver had not greeted them.

Heavy ceramic jars nestled in dried grass on the back of the long, low cart behind the single occupant, a Dragonoid driver sitting on a bench in the front, idly holding the reins and chewing on a stock of grass. He, too, had a brown linen robe on, but with the hood pushed back, enjoying the cool morning air before the sun rose. The scales on his skin glistened as if oiled. Magisend gasped quietly as it pulled past. Portia elbowed her for silence.

Magisend, Mark and Portia picked up the pace, falling in line behind the wagon.

They wanted to be close enough that the guard at the city gate would think they were with the driver, but not so close as to agitate the driver himself. Portia cursed not having the time to watch more traffic on the road and see what the customs on the road were there.

More wagons rolled behind them.

Just as the sun broke through over the horizon, another road joined the first, then both turning to the shimmering city walls. The second road had much more traffic. All the drivers and other walkers wore similar robes to what Portia, Magisend, and Mark had on, with only a few having the hoods pushed back.

Once the sun rose, nearly all the hoods came forward.

The knot in Portia's stomach loosened a bit. She no longer felt like she was going to vomit immediately. Now they all looked the same. Well, almost.

The others walking on the road—while dressed similarly—stood much taller, towering over the three of them. Most stood at least an arm length taller.

Portia's head was at chest level to a group that passed them, walking briskly down the center of the road. She kept her gaze downward so it would be even more difficult for any curious traveler to see her face. Hopefully Mark and Magisend were doing the same.

They would have to pass as children if they wanted to be mistaken for Dragonoids at all and not as runaway humans.

MUCH AS THEY TRIED, they could not keep up with the wagon and its load of jars. It pulled ahead, growing more distant. The other passing wagons thinned as the sun rose, no doubt all rushing to market and not wanting to miss the crowds.

"Move it," a growling voice called from behind in the Dragonoids' language. Portia rushed away from the center of the road to the side, but almost not quick enough, feeling the air rush as a draft animal nearly ran her over.

The driver continued on, flicking his whip at the animals.

"Jerk," Magisend said.

Portia grabbed Magisend's arm and squeezed, hard. Magisend had to be quiet. Talking in the common human tongue would give them away in a second.

Magisend tried to pull her arm away. She drew in a breath to yell back.

"Halt," another voice called from behind.

Magisend stopped struggling.

The hairs on Portia's neck rose. A chill came over her skin. The clatter of the wagon passing had drowned out most other noises. She had no idea who was behind them. How foolish to be caught out so. This part of the road, so close to the city, ran through a wide flat plain, leaving no place to hide even if they ran. Besides, running would just invite suspicion.

Portia took a deep breath and stopped, still holding on to Magisend. Mark nearly stumbled into them, pulling back at the last second. The three stood clustered in a group on the edge of the road.

Portia turned slowly.

Three large soldiers paced the road, taking near half of it. They had the half robes and breast plates of the warriors she'd seen during the war. Their powerful legs were bigger than her waist. Deep hoods hid their faces, adding to the ominous look.

"*Where are your parents?*" the one in the center asked.

The language itself was so naturally aggressive it was hard to tell the tone of this particular speaker. He had not insulted them, at least. Perhaps he was in a good mood.

A growl followed. The soldier rested his hand on the knife at his belt.

Or perhaps not.

Portia let go of Magisend's arm, pointed down the road towards the city.

"*Speak,*" the Dragonoid commanded.

Deepening her voice the best she could, Portia spoke back in the painful Dragonoid language, the guttural hiss and growls digging at her throat and larynx. She tried to lower her tone. "*They told us to meet at the gate. We wanted to walk.*"

Portia's heartbeat thudded in her ears. The Dragonoids exchanged glances.

"Are you all the same kin?" another of the Dragonoids asked.

The word he used for kin also meant cave, the two meanings flashing in Portia's mind as he spoke. She thought he meant family.

The Dragonoid on the right stepped forward, as if anticipating an incorrect answer.

Before she could answer, Mark stepped forward. "Yes," he said, his version of the Dragonoid speech much lower and more resonant than Portia's. He added a spitting sound at the end that sounded like an insult.

The center Dragonoid dropped his hand from his knife at that, his stance relaxed. The Dragonoid who had come closer fell back in line with the other two. He nodded at Mark.

"Don't stray from the road. Killots are afoot. Hurry," said the Dragonoid. While it wasn't yet friendly—the language didn't allow for that, it seemed—this was a better response.

The Dragonoids moved on, leaving Mark, Portia, and Magisend breathing heavily.

"We better hurry, no?" Mark said in the same language.

Portia nodded, even more angry at Magisend. If Magisend had spoken in the human common tongue just a hair later, they would have all been caught. It was just by luck they avoided that.

They hurried on to the gate, careful now to avoid the center of the road and any more late wagons that might be rushing down it.

"What are Killots?" Mark asked.

"No idea," Portia said, *"but if they are worried about them, they can't be good."*

Magisend made sounds of frustration at not under-standing what they were saying. Portia elbowed her in the ribs, and she quieted, blessedly. It was her own fault she was ignorant. Riddlepit, indeed.

A bottleneck of wagons and travelers crowded the gate into the city. Guards flanked either side of the road, waiting in two lines.

Part of the battlefield from the previous splinter was visible from the road, the ground scarred and blackened, as if large fire pits had been set here and there, with an enormous one in the center of the devastated area. The blackened earth was in sharp contrast to the yellow sun-bleached sand and dirt everywhere else. A few gouges, several hand lengths deep, in the blackened sections showed more yellow dirt beneath.

There was no other sign of battle. No soldiers, no tents, no weapons of war.

It was almost unnerving not seeing the soldiers here. They had to be somewhere, and now she had no idea where.

They reached the front of the line at the gate. Blessedly, the guards looked tired and waved them through after a cursory glance. Portia exhaled, but her heart didn't stop pounding until they walked several streets into the city, keeping close to the wagon ahead of them. Crowds pushed in the streets, a surprising number of pedestrians considering the roads had not been full. The wagon parted the crowd for them and they slipped through.

Further from the gate, the crush thinned. When the wagon turned off into a narrow passage between two buildings, Portia, Magisend, and Mark continued forward.

Portia guessed which way to the city center.

No one bothered them as they walked, everyone keeping their heads down and walking quickly. There was little chatter on the streets, and only the occasional cry of a child.

One such child, dragged along by its mother, stared at them. As it passed, it reached out a scale-covered hand to Magisend's robe. It grabbed a handful of the material and pulled.

Magisend grabbed the robe back with two hands, just in time to keep it from being pulled from her, only slipping upwards in the back and showing the back of her boots. Magisend growled impressively low and deep, then yanked the material back. The child screamed as the fabric pulled out of his grasp.

Portia sucked in her breath.

Mark shifted, fumbling underneath his robe for a knife.

No no no. They could not get in a fight here. Portia reached out to stop him.

But the mother didn't even spare a glance, yanking her child forward and walking briskly. The child continued screaming, its robe falling back, its eyes tearstained as it pointed at them all while being dragged away.

Portia slowed at that finger pointing directly at her.

Magisend roughly pushed her forward to keep walking. Mark was already two steps ahead.

Portia scowled. Since when was Magisend better in the heat of the moment than she was? Portia walked faster, pushing sideways against Magisend to move her out of the center of the street. It was childish, but Portia couldn't stop herself.

They kept on, pushing further into the heart of the city.

The streets in the city center were weirdly deserted. Storefronts faced most streets, but the stores were empty of customers. Boards covered the fronts of many. Only a few pedestrians walked the streets, sometimes disappearing around the corner when spotted, as if not wanting to be seen.

Large metal pens filled a central square ringed by store-fronts. Slave pens, with tall narrow bars and barred roofs and straw covering the dirt floors.

Every single pen, empty. Not a human, not a dwarf, not even a Dragonoid walked the grounds.

Bits of broken baskets littered the ground. A small animal rustled in a pile of discarded pottery in a corner, running into unhealthy looking bushes when they drew near.

Where was everyone?

Mark held his nose with one hand, the sleeve of his robe disappearing under his hood. There had been slaves here recently. No one had bothered to discard the dirty straw at the bottom of the pens when they'd left. Portia gagged at the smell.

"What is this place?" Magisend asked. Portia whirled to her, hissing to be quiet.

Magisend waved to the empty space around them. All the nearby stores fronts were dark and empty.

"Slaves," Portia said in common, hoping the one word was enough for Magisend to understand.

Magisend put her hands on her hips, irate. Like she was happy with this?, Portia thought.

"Where are they? Do you think they killed them all?" asked Mark, his voice small. He looked around nervously, then stepped close to Magisend and Portia. "Do you think they're that vicious?" he asked Portia.

"Don't be ridiculous, no business person would destroy their own resource like that," Magisend said.

"How would you know? You're a noble," Mark said, irritation in his voice at her butting in.

"What do you think nobles are, Commoner?" Magisend said, drawling out the last word, miraculously keeping her voice low. Back in the caverns, she would have been much louder.

"Stop," Portia said. She needed quiet to think. "Magisend's right. They wouldn't just kill them, not without some terrible reason. We have to find where they are."

"What possible reason could they use for killing prisoners?" Mark asked.

"You know, spite, irrational anger, plague. We killed all our cattle one year when they thought the plague was coming from them," Magisend said, relishing Mark's spooked reaction.

"Magisend, stop," Portia said, admonishing as loudly as she dared. Those two couldn't stop even here. They were going to get them all captured.

They searched through the city, finding their way to a busier section. They found the market where the farmers had set up, selling strange looking vegetables and strips of meat hanging from hooks, leather and fabric goods, long, dangerous metal utensils and pots, perhaps for a kitchen or a barn, and other things she did not recognize at all. But nowhere did they see signs of any humans, or any other captives.

Portia took advantage of the crowded market conditions to pluck a few coins from a lady's purse, taking other coins from the pocket of a distracted merchant.

Mark did the same, slipping his hand out stealthily and pulling back quickly. If she hadn't known the techniques herself, Portia never would have guessed he was stealing.

Magisend walked with them, oblivious to their industry,

concentrating more on keeping out of the way of the Dragonoids. She backed away so obviously from each possible contact that Portia finally grabbed her, and held her still, making her walk forward and endure the slight touches. Magisend growled in irritation but did not yank herself free.

"Shall we eat?" Mark asked in the growling and spitting language of the Dragonoids.

Portia nodded. They should have enough coin now, and there was no surer way to get information than from someone deep in their cups.

They walked to the tavern that had rows of tables and benches outside, extending out into the courtyard. They picked a table near the edge of the market, just a few steps away from the crowd.

The table and benches were half-full with scattered patrons, a few in pairs but most sitting alone. The sun beat down on the tables so the hoods stayed up, another reason to not go inside. At the nearest table to them, a tipsy Dragonoid leaned heavily on a fisted hand, its elbow on the table, while his other clawed and scaled hand curled around a glass with just a few dregs at the bottom.

Mark held up a hand, getting the attention of the server who wound their way over, the normal brown robe that most citizens wore replaced by one with stripes of rusty red and brown. The same colors that hung on flags outside the doorway.

"Three good cups, and one for that one," Mark ordered, pointing at the drunk patron.

The server nodded, barely slowing down before turning

right around and going to the door of the establishment and entering.

"*What are we having?*" Portia asked, the question short, but still enough to hurt her throat trying to wrap around the strange language.

Mark shrugged.

The server delivered the glass to the Dragonoid at the next table over first, then pointed at Mark. The patron looked quizzical, then picked up the glass and gave them a nod before taking a sip.

Their own glasses were dropped off seconds later, the server rushing off without a question. Portia's stomach rumbled, but they weren't really here to eat.

They sat in silence, patiently sipping the tall glasses of cool, weak ale, almost a fruit juice. The sweetness went down well in the heat of the day. When the Dragonoid had finished half of the gifted glass of ale, Mark stood and went to join him.

Portia and Magisend waited and watched.

Mark and the Dragonoid spoke in the low spitting language, the occasional exclamation coming through, but most of the words unheard from their seat only a few arm lengths away. The Dragonoid shook his head vehemently, then slammed a fist on the table. Magisend and Portia jumped, but Mark seemed unfazed. A second later Mark also slammed his hand on the table, delighting the Dragonoid who laughed and clapped him on the back, then reached to pat him on the head.

Magisend tilted her empty glass, tapping the edge on the table. Portia ignored her, sipping the remains of her own drink. Magisend leaned in, pushed the glass directly in front of Portia, and tapped harder. Portia turned away from her, looking over the patrons in the courtyard. Magisend huffed behind her, then leaned into her, nearly knocking her off the bench.

A server came out the door, delivering a load of drinks and food to one of the tables. Magisend stood, rocking the bench they were sitting on, held up her empty glass and waved it, her sleeve nearly falling down to reveal her arm.

Portia grabbed the table to steady herself, then looked up to notice Magisend's sleeve. She grabbed Magisend around the waist with both hands and pulled her physically down, nearly toppling her to one side when Magisend stubbornly refused to bend her knees.

Still holding the glass, Magisend turned to Portia and shoved the empty glass close to Portia's nose.

"*Fine*," Portia said to Magisend in the Dragonoid tongue, adding an insult at the end she would never translate. Turning to the server, she called out "*Two more.*" She didn't know if there was a more polite way to ask. Her voice sounded high-pitched and weird, no matter how she tried to lower it.

Turning back to Magisend, Portia glared. It was impossible to make eye contact with the deep hoods hiding their faces, but she imagined Magisend wilting under her burning eyes. She was going to kill her when they were alone. What did she think she was doing?

The server paused, looking in Portia's direction, then nodded slowly. They disappeared within the tavern. A strange feeling came over Portia after the server's lingering attention.

She might have made a mistake and given them away.

Pulling a coin from her pocket and laying it on the table, Portia took Magisend's glass from her hand and thumped it down on the table, then yanked Magisend to her feet. She walked to the exit quickly, tapping Mark on the shoulder as she went.

Pulling Magisend along, Portia walked quickly through the crowds in the square towards a quieter portion of the city. It would be better to hide in the masses, but she needed to have a talk with Magisend and could not do that with others around. Speaking in the human common tongue would give them away immediately.

Mark caught up with them soon after, breathing heavily from running. They found a quiet spot in a large expansive park. Other smaller Dragonoids in their brown robes ran and played on what look like playground swings and slides. They blended in here since all around were smaller beings in brown robes playing, with only a few supervising adults on the far end of the park.

They sat on the edge of the gently sloping hill, far enough from the playground to not be overheard.

"Are you trying to get us killed," Portia said, her temper still hot, "or are you just stupid?" Not the most diplomatic she'd been.

Not diplomatic at all.

"Watch your tongue, commoner," Magisend said. She

brushed off imaginary dirt and leaves from her robes, then sat with her legs crossed, staring vaguely off past Portia.

"Oh no you don't," said Portia. She moved directly into Magisend's line of sight. "First off, I'm not a commoner, we can stop with that right now. Second, even if I was, that is no reason for being treated poorly. Third, our lives are on the line here, as well as all the captives. You will behave better. You will follow directions. You will—"

"Portia," said Mark, softly. He leaned in to break her eye contact with Magisend.

"What?" Portia asked. She had the presence of mind to lower her voice, but just barely.

Mark nodded to a group of young Dragonoids crossing the field diagonally, coming towards them. They would soon be within earshot.

Portia nodded, then leaned back. Beneath the sleeves of her robes, her hands clenched and unclenched as she tried to release the tension she felt in her back and her stomach. Trying to release the fuzzy rage she felt towards Magisend. Perhaps it wasn't all Magisend's fault. It was scary being here. They all needed to work together.

The group passed without even giving them a glance. Portia breathed easier. Not trusting herself to say anything to Magisend, she turned to Mark.

"What did you learn?" asked Portia.

"There are no slaves or captives here in the city at all. At least there shouldn't be any." He held up a hand to forestall questions. "Apparently they've all been called to the capital city. Something about riot or rebellion control. I couldn't tell really, the word he used for it was weird. The word also meant the turning of the seasons. Anyway, he was drowning his sorrows in a much stronger drink than we had. All of his slaves were taken without payment."

Taken?

None here?

This was not good. Should they go back to the portal and let them know and get reinforcements, or should they get more information first?

Magisend's haughty voice interrupted her thoughts. "Well let's go get them then."

Despite her anger at Magisend, Portia had to admit that was the most straightforward path. They could just go get them. Even so, she wasn't ready to acknowledge Magisend yet, so continued her questions to Mark.

"How far to the capital?" asked Portia.

Mark shrugged. "I hadn't got that far. What happened? Why did we leave in such a hurry?"

"Magisend wanted a drink." That wasn't the full story. "She wanted a drink, and I tried to order one, and I think the server got suspicious at something I said or how I said it. It didn't seem wise to stick around and find out if I was right," said Portia.

"Oh, I think you might've been right. Just as I was leaving, several dressed in those striped uniforms came out, making a beeline for the table. Luckily, I was far enough gone to blend into the crowd. Thank goodness everyone here dresses alike." Mark stretched his arms, then laid down on the gentle sloping hill.

"See, this is what happens. We have to be careful here," Portia said to Magisend. She was going to keep blaming Magisend even if it was something she had done to attract the server's suspicion. "Have you ever had to be careful in your life?"

"What do you mean, careful?" Magisend said, drawling the words out.

"Watch what you say, watch how you behave," Portia said.

"Why would I do that?" Magisend asked, confused.

"Even around your parents or the teachers?" Portia could not let it go.

"My parents give a goodly sum to that school, so generally no, that is not a concern," Magisend said, also leaning back and laying on the ground, putting her hands behind her head.

"Even with your parents?" Portia asked, incredulous.

The silence dragged on so long Portia thought Magisend was not going to answer at all. Finally, Magisend said in a quiet voice, "Sometimes around my parents. They say they are waiting for me to prove myself, not that I know exactly what that means. Nothing in school has seemed to be it, so why bother?" She did not sound happy.

<hr>

THE SUN WAS high overhead and beat down mercilessly. They shifted to a position just below a stone wall ringing the park that lent a sliver of shade, the only shade available. There were not even the slender yellow trees like those at the hillock by the splinter.

Perhaps they could have hidden under the playground equipment, for as the heat of the day increased, the number of others around them disappeared. Portia envied their ability to disappear into cool houses.

They ate and drank from the supplies Kerat had given them.

Once the day cooled, they would find a way to learn where the capital was, and then start for it. Right now it was too hot to do anything. Even under the sun-shielding robes, Portia's skin burned to the touch. Sweat soaked her back. Her ankles felt damp in her boots. The worst was the heat pushing down on her so much breathing felt difficult.

Portia lay on her side, stretched out along the wall, trying to get as much shade as possible. Magisend and Mark did the same further down. The exhaustion of just breathing in the heat, and excitement from earlier overwhelmed Portia. Her eyes slowly shut.

What seemed like a moment later, pebbles rained down on her head. Then a larger stone hit the wall behind her and bounced off, striking her shoulder, causing a shooting pain where it hit her shoulder blade. Portia sat up, blinking, trying to focus on the mirage of the shimmering air.

It was still midday.

The heat felt even worse, if that was possible.

A group of young Dragonoids walked towards them. One led the pack, several steps ahead and walking with a determined gait, visible even through its robes. Further down the wall, Mark stood, shaking out his arms and legs. Magisend sat up slowly.

Portia scrambled up, checking for her knives and sword.

Seeing their victims rise, the group spread out, right and left, forming a wide V behind the leader, blocking any chance of running. One of the Dragonoids threw up a large rock and caught it repeatedly, all while staring at them.

Except for the gang arrayed in front of them, the rest of the park was empty. Heat shimmered the air, rising from the scrubby green growth and bare yellow dirt patches.

Beyond the park, wide avenues ran in front of large estates. Walls lined most of the streets, giving the houses within privacy. It also gave the park users privacy, something Portia was especially grateful for now.

If it came to blows, it'd be hard to hide their humanness.

The wall behind Portia threw a larger shadow that it had before. The sun hung closer to the horizon, and at their backs, giving them the advantage over the newcomers.

The Dragonoid tossing the rock feinted throwing it at Portia, then laughed when she jumped.

Portia's hand opened and closed on empty air, very conscious of the deadly blade strapped to her back.

"What do they want?" Magisend said in a semi-whisper. She had moved down the wall to Portia, carefully facing the attackers the whole time. "Give them some money and make them go away."

Portia shook her head.

If this gang had wanted to steal from them, they wouldn't have woken them up. No, they were in it for some form of entertainment. Which was only fun if the victims were awake and not enjoying it.

"You're ugly and you're in our way," Mark called out, in the Dragonoid language, his tone impressively deep and aggressive. He spoke so aggressively spittle flew out of his mouth along with the words.

He, too, had moved closer to Portia.

Sparing a glance, Portia estimated the wall behind them was the height of two men stacked. Too high to jump easily. They were good and well trapped by the dozen or so Dragonoids in front of them.

The leader slowly walked over to Mark, each lingering step a mockery of Mark's aggressive tone. *"What did you say, vermin?"*

"You're ugly and stupid," Mark said, doing his best to match the indolent attitude of the aggressor.

"And you're dead," the leader said. He lifted a hand, preparing to signal an attack.

Mark burst out laughing. He even pointed, then bent over laughing. He slapped the wall.

Portia and Magisend looked at him like he was crazy, as did the gang members waiting to beat them up. The leader looked especially affronted, placing both hands on his hips.

"Stop that abominable noise now, vermin," said the Dragonoid leader.

"Then stop being so stupidly funny, coward," Mark said, standing, his laughter finally under control. *"Coward."* This time, his voice dripped with contempt.

"You are so dead," said the Dragonoid.

"You keep saying that. Are you going to call your dad to come beat us up? Is this your gang of protection? Are you so pathetic? Such a..." Then Mark said a word that Portia could not translate in her mind to common. It was something akin to a plant being pulled from soil, utterly dependent on its environment. It was the ultimate insult to Dragonoids.

The effect was instantaneous. The languid attitude of the Dragonoid leader was gone in a heartbeat. He rushed forward, grabbed Mark by the collar and slammed him into the wall behind. Blessedly, Mark's hood fell further forward, and he was not immediately exposed as a human. Portia wondered what the Dragonoid thought of Mark's light weight. Even the adolescent Dragonoids weighed probably twice a human.

The other Dragonoids stood, uncertain what to do without a signal from their leader. Portia pulled her sword from underneath her robes, the slide of the metal on the sheath a welcome sound.

At her side, Magisend pull a knife of her own, impressively long and dangerously curved.

Mark pulled up his leg. Bracing against the wall, he kicked the Dragonoid's stomach. The Dragonoid's grip on Mark's collar loosened.

Mark dropped like a stone out of the leader's grip, then rolled away sideways and back up on his feet. Now several lengths separated the two. Mark was no longer trapped by the wall.

"Since you want a game, let's choose a fairer one. Something you can show your worthiness. Isn't that better than hiding behind your friends?" Mark said "friends" the way Magisend said commoner to Portia.

The Dragonoid liked it even less than she did.

The Dragonoid growled and spit, slowly circling Mark. It pulled a knife of its own, wickedly jagged. It looked unclean.

Portia's stomach turned. Whatever muck was on that blade would kill even if the knife stroke didn't.

"What say you?" the Dragonoid asked, finally.

"A wager. A battle. You and I and a bet," Mark said.

"You have nothing I want" the Dragonoid said.

"No? Right now I can say you can't beat me. You want the victory," Mark taunted, his tone sounding so relaxed.

Portia had no idea what game Mark was playing at, but it had bought them some time. The rest of the Dragonoids were not attacking, yet.

Magic was difficult to do in this world. They'd not taken the time for Portia to let Mark and Magisend experiment and see for themselves. Now Portia regretted that. Hopefully Mark wasn't counting on magic to save him. Or them.

"What bet?" the leader asked. His gang formed a ring around him and Mark. Only the rock thrower held back, keeping an eye on Portia and Magisend.

"I win, you... buy us dinner," Mark said.

Dinner?

"*Ha!*" The Dragonoid snorted and howled. Portia and Magisend exchanged confused glances.

Then it hit Portia. It was laughing.

The leader stopped laughing. "*Dinner. The dead don't eat,*" he said. "*This is a cheap bet. If I win, you're dead.*"

"*Brutal,*" said Mark casually. "*You guys play rough here.*"

"*No interference,*" Mark said, pointing to the others ringing them.

"*Who's going to tell?*" the leader retorted.

"*Your mind every night when you go to sleep and know that you're a coward. They,*" Mark motioned again to the other gang members, "*will always know you couldn't do it on your own. How long will you be leader then?*"

That elicited a growl, then a nod.

Portia's breath hitched in her throat. She didn't want to watch this fight. To her, Mark was always that tiny kid she'd found on the street, standing by his dead mother's body. The kid who relied on her protection for all those years in the gang of thieves. Watching him hurt or injured here would be unbearable.

Mark and the Dragonoid circled each other, their steps slowed and controlled.

Sweat dripped down Portia's back. The heat shimmered around everything.

The leader rushed Mark again. This time Mark stepped aside, then swung out a foot in a low arc, dragging the leader's robes under his own feet and tripping him.

Angry shouts rose from those around at Mark's quick motions.

The leader didn't even stop, turning like a bull and charging again. Anger made him even clumsier.

Mark danced to the side, this time in the other direction. Again, he tangled the robes of the leader with his foot.

Again, the leader stumbled, then recovered. He turned to charge again.

This time the Dragonoid took his time, moving more slowly. His dirty knife waved back and forth. His hood fallen back, he watched Mark closely. The scales of his face shone rainbow colors in the sunlight.

Mark charged. He picked up his own robes with his left hand, then ran up the body of the Dragonoid like it was a statue, kicking down the attacker's knife arm with one step along the way. He slapped the top of the Dragonoid's head before leaping down the other side.

Portia's mouth hung open. How? How much did that Dragonoid weigh that he wouldn't topple over with someone climbing on him like that?

That Dragonoid must be massive. If he pinned Mark, that could well be the end.

Magisend sucked in her breath next to Portia. "I had no idea he could do that."

"Me either," Portia said.

They had both spoken in common.

Realizing their error, Portia glanced to their guard. Luckily, he stared at the two battling it out. With any luck, he'd not heard them speaking a tongue they shouldn't know.

The Dragonoid reached up and rubbed his head, then roared in fury. He stomped towards Mark. The dirty knife swung in wide, aggressive arcs.

He tried to steer Mark to the wall. To pin him there. Mark was too quick, ducking away, and dancing just out of reach.

Sweat darkened the shoulders and back of Mark's robes.

Mark danced backwards. This time his foot caught on a large rock behind him. He stumbled backwards, arms windmilling.

The gang leader charged. He yelled a triumphant battle cry.

Mark dropped, tucked down and rolled out of the way.

The Dragonoid tried to change course but had too much momentum.

He ran by Mark, his knife reaching and just catching Mark's robes. It caught. The fabric of the robes stuck in the jagged edges and tore.

Mark danced back. Portia could not take her eyes off the jagged hole in his garments.

While the Dragonoid slowed to turn and charge again, Mark ran forward, dropped his knife and grabbed the rock. He whirled like a shotput thrower with the rock in both hands and unwound, sending the rock to the back of the Dragonoid's head.

He had his knife back in his hands before the rock made contact.

It landed with a soft thunk squarely on the back of the scaled head. The Dragonoid turned slowly, stunned. It let out a strange keening noise, then fell over.

Mark turned to Portia and Magisend. "Now!"

Portia grabbed a handful of dry earth and threw it at the eyes of the gang member guarding them.

Magisend tried to do magic but nothing came from her fingertips. She looked stunned, then angry.

"Nevermind that, run!" Portia yelled at Magisend.

The three of them ran diagonally across the large park to the nearest avenue. To the nearest walls they could jump over.

Luckily, they had the advantage when it came to speed.

Plus, the gang members behind them had been momentarily stunned by the defeat of their leader. Portia spared a glance back. Most stood over the body, while one or two others watched them run away. It was only when they neared the far end of the park that some of the gang members started chasing after them.

Mark picked one of the lower walls ahead, darker red stone bricks topped with yellow granite capstones. The roof of a house set far back in the lot peeked over the top.

Hopefully no one was looking out their windows.

He leapt to the top of the wall, then turned to extend a hand to Portia, yanking her up. Magisend followed.

They dropped down to the other side.

A beautiful courtyard laid with large tile mosaic filled the yard. Huge chairs sat in a circle.

Blessedly, it was empty and quiet.

They ran along the wall, hunched low so as to not be visible from the street, going to the back of the house. There, they went over the wall again, exiting into another wide empty boulevard.

They crossed the street and climbed over another wall and repeated the journey to the back of that property.

They didn't stop until they had gotten far from the park, and could no longer hear the cries of their pursuers.

———

OUTSIDE THE CITY, in a meadow hidden from the road by a clump of trees, the air was much cooler. Almost bearable. It helped that the sun was near setting, its rays blocked by the tall trees behind them. Constant chirping flooded the meadow, no doubt from insects hidden in the dried grasses.

Miraculously, a stream wound through the trees, winding in the direction of the city. Precious blue waters, only slightly muddied in the whirling pools at the edges. The rest clear and beautiful. Green plants dotted its edge, lucky in their proximity. Everywhere else the plants were near brown and almost dead.

"A miracle," Magisend said, dropping her bag and then kneeling down by the water. She lay on the bank, stretching her body out over the waters and alternatively drinking and scooping up the water to wash her face.

Mark and Portia joined her.

Nothing had ever tasted so good.

While the water was not ice-cold, it was still cooler than the air. It felt amazing on her face, washing away the sweat and dirt, cooling in the breeze.

And drinking. It went down too easily.

Portia drank until her belly was so swollen with water she

thought she was going to throw up. She sat with her back to a tree, her hand resting on her belly until the feeling passed.

They'd managed to exit the city in the crowd of farmers leaving for the evening. The yawning guards had not even spared them a glance. Before exiting, they had stopped just long enough at the closing market to buy some food and find out the direction of the royal city.

Portia gained the directions by talking in a cutesy child's voice to an old Dragonoid standing hunched over a display of hard little bread loaves. The Dragonoid took Portia's coin, then looked her over. She shoved two small loaves into a bag, held it clenched in her hands while she described the directions to Portia.

Finally, when she was done, she held the bag out to Portia, but high enough that Portia couldn't reach it.

"Promise me you'll get your parents' permission before running off," the Dragonoid said.

Portia nodded enthusiastically. The woman did not lower the bag.

"I promise," Portia said, her throat burning with the effort of speaking in a strange tongue.

The merchant dropped her hand. Portia snatched the bag from her and disappeared into the crowd before the old Dragonoid could make another demand.

Portia had fumed about the merchant's condescending attitude the whole way out of the city.

Portia grabbed a dry tall stalk of grass, peeled the base and stuck it in her mouth. It didn't taste bad. She liked watching the little seed heads at the end wave around in the breeze.

Leaning back against the tree, she felt the sweat at the back of her neck and along her body dry as the cooler air flowed over her.

No more walking in the sun.

"Seven days, huh?" Mark asked Portia. He, too, leaned against a tree. His hood back, his face bright red, either from heat or from sun, Portia could not tell which.

"Wait, just to get there?" Magisend asked. As she recovered from the hottest part of the day, her haughty attitude came back more and more. "They're going to close the portal after a moon. Maybe we should go back and tell them."

Mark languidly waved away her concerns. "We'll make it."

Magisend glared at him. "How do you know? Things haven't exactly gone smoothly so far."

Portia rolled her head in Magisend's direction. "And whose fault is that?"

"Oh, spare me. Did I conjure that gang into being?" Magisend crossed her arms.

"Don't worry, Portia can just open a new portal from the capital city," Mark said.

Magisend turned to Portia, squinting her eyes. "Can you do that?"

"Yes," Portia said.

"Back to where we came from?" Magisend asked.

Portia closed her eyes and sighed.

"Back to where we came from, exactly?" Magisend asked again.

Portia slowly banged her head against the tree once, then

opened her eyes. "No, not exactly, but close enough. We will come out somewhere in our world."

"Somewhere. Oh great, let's make sure it's in the middle of the sea and we can all drown. Or how about some forsaken island no one will ever find us all," Magisend said.

"You are the positive one." Mark shifted from the tree and lay down full-length on the ground, propping his head on one hand. "Why did you even come if you have so little faith in Portia? Why is it so important to you?"

Magisend looked down, picking apart a plant she had plucked from the ground next to her. "None of your business."

"Considering we all rely on each other to survive, perhaps it is my business." Mark stared at Magisend, who refused to make eye contact. "Why is this so important to you?"

"That is a good question," Portia said.

They sat in silence as Magisend continued tearing apart the plant.

"Someone I care about was captured," Magisend finally said in a rush.

"I didn't hear about any nobles being taken from Cover-ack." Portia sat up, her curiosity piqued.

Magisend glared at her. She slammed the plant pieces down on the ground next to her and pulled out another plant, its roots dangling and dropping dirt.

"Kinda hard on the greenery. Their life is tough enough here as it is." Mark looked dead serious, but Portia knew he was joking. Would Magisend?

No.

Magisend threw the plant in his direction. But still, she did not pull out another one.

"So if not a noble from Coverack, then who?" Mark asked.

Magisend crossed her arms and stared sullenly ahead.

"Who do you care for?" Mark said teasingly. His tone was light, but he watched Magisend closely.

Portia watched, transfixed.

But Magisend simply moved away from her tree, lay down on the ground and rolled over, her back to them.

Portia chewed on the grass and leaned back. She closed her eyes. Who could it be that Magisend would risk so much for? At the Academy, she only seemed concerned with her fellow nobles. Certainly she never let Portia forget her station.

The rest of the day passed in a haze of naps, each taking turn keeping watch until the night was full dark. The moon came out, shining down on the meadow. It easily gave enough light for them to pick their way back to the road and their journey to the capital.

THEY CAME upon the capital city just as light was dawning in the high mountains. The city nestled in a high valley surrounded by mountain peaks. A singular main pass between two peaks rising on either side formed the entrance. The mountains around rose so densely that if there was another pass on the far side of the city, it must be much smaller, or be hidden as several small routes.

The city itself sparkled under the sun, as if each building

was made out of glass or gemstone. Some reflected watery blues and greens and reds, pure colors diluted by the intense sunlight saturating the city. Other buildings reflected a rainbow shimmer like that of an abalone shell. Golden iron-work trellises adorned each wall, adorned even the gates on either side of the road topping the pass high above the city. It flaunted its wealth everywhere.

It was nothing like the dirty stone towns of the lower plains.

"Wow," Portia said. Mark and Magisend stood on either side as they stared down at the city below.

They had given up the purely nighttime travel as the road started ascending the mountains. It was too dangerous, the risk of a rockslide too great, to feel around in the dark on the side of its steep peak. They climbed the mountain for two days. What travelers had shared the road were not interested in them. No one so much as spoke a greeting.

Compared to the others on the road, they had little to be of interest. They still wore their dusty brown robes disguises. But here, even the wagons making the climb into the city were ornate and beautiful. The other travelers wore multicolored beautiful robes, some having embroidery trimming the sleeves and hems. Portia, Mark, and Magisend were not as well-dressed as even some of the servants accompanying these travelers.

They descended down the road, past the unmanned peak and through the ornate gold gates. They joined a long caravan of wagons and walkers. The guards, dressed as finely as the city itself, in orange uniforms with gold colored breastplates, waved them through. Another section of the gate area was reserved for those exiting. By contrast, the exit was backed up, and guards were meticulously going through each wagon and bag.

Portia squinted against the glare in the courtyard. Not only was the sun intensely bright, the light also bounced off the gleaming walls of the city buildings.

Blessedly, there were huge awnings painted dark on the underside that stretched out over the pedestrian walkways of the streets. The shade made it bearable both for vision and for heat. Some pedestrians chose to walk in the middle of the street, ducking the wagons, and soaking in the sun, but they were a small minority.

Portia glanced at Magisend. The small girl looked studiously forward. She had promised to behave better in the city. Portia was skeptical. Short of opening a splinter and pushing Magisend through it, there was little choice but to trust her. Still, it put Portia on edge not knowing if she would give them away in some stupid way.

Despite the glamour of the city, it was laid out similar to the other towns they had been in. They would not be so easily able to exit and reenter, so it was important to find a hiding spot in this town if they had to stay for several days.

They decided to look for the sewers, much as Portia had survived her first time in this world. Mark and Magisend thought it a great idea, although Magisend was not too keen on those other inhabitants that might be running around.

Portia walked in front of the other two, looking for an entrance to the sewer system. It didn't take long to find one—a long trench cut into the paving at the edge of a little trafficked street.

The sewer entrance had a golden iron gate on it, but it was only held in place by two small pins.

Portia checked around with a quick glance. There was no one about. She squatted, took her long knife, and flicked out the pins, grabbing them and putting them in her pocket.

The gate grating was surprisingly light. Portia lifted it from its brackets and handed it to Mark, who wrapped part of his robe around it, hiding it from a casual glance. Portia dropped a pebble into the black hole. The echo came back quickly with a solid ping of rock on stone. The sewer wasn't flooded, nor was it terribly deep. Portia jumped down into the darkness.

Mark handed down the grate to her. She was just barely able to reach it on tiptoes. She set it against a curving wall, barely visible in the darkness, then stepped back out of the way. Magisend jumped down, followed by Mark.

"Now what?" Magisend ask.

"We scout the city," Portia said.

"From here?" Magisend asked, incredulous.

"Well, this is part of the city," Mark said, drawling slowly, an excellent imitation of Magisend's own contemptuous tone.

"We just need to map out some escape routes, and if it's possible to exit the city from this system. Going out the gates doesn't look so easy," Portia said.

"I noticed that," Mark said, now serious.

"Probably to keep slaves from escaping," Portia said.

"Agreed," Magisend said, surprising Portia.

She checked her knives and sword to make sure all were present and where they should be. Mark and Magisend followed suit.

Their eyes adjusted to the dimness of the sewer system. The light from the hole above bounced around on cream colored tile. Even down here, in a place most citizens would never see, it was beautiful and well maintained. The tile that lined the walls and floor was nicer than the interior of most homes in Coverack.

Portia huffed. These creatures had all that wealth and yet they stole from others.

Or was that how they got so much wealth?

Portia shook her head. That was something to think about another day. They had a lot to do, and little food left for the stay. Their hunts had yielded less and less as the road ascended the mountain. Not only did they need to find the lay of the town, they needed to get some food and water.

Mark set faintly glowing dots intermittently on the wall as they walked, a form of his magic, to mark their path so they would not get irrevocably lost. He strained with the effort of setting each light pink dot, high up on the wall, to mark the way they came. Sweat dotted his brow, even in the cool air of the sewer. The dots should last a week or two, perhaps less in this strange world where magic was so much harder to do.

They quickly found the market, the din from the busy square above audible even in the sewer system, echoing around the tile walls and drowning out completely the ever present sound of dripping water. Here, a small river of runoff took the middle of the sewer, but was easy to avoid by walking to one side. The system looked to be built to handle huge floods that came with the snowmelt of a high mountain town.

Blessedly, it was summer now.

The grated opening into the middle of a market square was far too busy to exit from, but they found another, quieter, access point a few streets over in what looked to be an alleyway between two tall building. The ceiling of the sewer was low enough they were able to crawl out easily into the alleyway after unfastening the grate from below.

Portia replaced the grate when all three were out, but did not replace the pins. These, too, made their way into her pocket.

Huge crowds filled the market square. Children ran everywhere, nearly the same size as Portia and the others. This allowed them to blend into the crowd, despite their small sizes, except for them looking like near beggars by comparison to the citizens of the city.

Rather than risk getting caught stealing, they bought supplies from vendors by pointing and dropping coins into outstretched hands. No one questioned why their hands never appeared from beneath their robes, the vendors' eyes far too focused on the payments.

It was easy to eavesdrop, listening as they walked through the crowd. Someone yelled about the lack of an auction, the lack of slaves. "Royal privilege" spat another, as if a swear. One higher voice whined about how many there were sitting wasted and none to be had for the folk who need them. Lastly, "Just go look at the pens," came the grumbling and growling complaint.

Portia's ears perked up at that, but she couldn't find the speaker fast enough. They were lost in the swirl of the crowd. Somewhere around here were pens of slaves.

Mark nudged her, telling her that he had heard too.

They circled the market area of the city, making wider and wider circles. If slaves were part of the normal commerce, they shouldn't be too far from this area. The city itself was concentrated enough in its narrow little valley to not have many different marketplaces.

It didn't take long to find what they were looking for.

They turned the corner, Portia chewing on a roll she had purchased earlier, it balling dry in her mouth, making it hard to swallow. But that was not why she stopped chewing, her mouth hanging down.

In front of them, in a square near as large as the main market square, were pen after pen of slaves.

The pungent aroma of bodies sweating in the sun and sickness and death washed over them. Magisend gagged under her robe next to Portia.

They stood and stared.

Uneasy guards paced in front of the pens and all the entryways to the square. It was crawling with guards. Banners flew above the pens, reminding Portia of the banners of her own monarch.

Banners proclaiming these slaves royal property.

Several of the guards eyed the three of them standing conspicuously in the middle of the street.

There were no other citizens in the square. The only

beings in the square were guards, and the poor captives stuffed in the pens behind them.

Just with a quick glance, Portia spied one dwarf amongst the captives. They were packed so tight it was hard to see beyond those at the neared pen.

"Hey, move along!" a guard yelled, angrier than the usual Dragonoid speech, which was usually pretty dang angry.

Portia turned to walk along the outside of the square, pulling at Mark and Magisend along the way.

"No, back! No one is allowed here, not even some spawn," another guard yelled, more exasperated than angry.

Spawn?

He meant kids. Them. Growling a little, Portia turned away along with Mark and Magisend. They found their way back to the quiet sewer entrance. Dropping down in the quiet coolness, Portia breathed in deeply to calm herself.

"Did you see how many there are?" Portia asked. "Lorica must know how many citizens are missing, and yet they did nothing?" Portia paced back and forth, too agitated to stay still. She did not wait for a response from either of her companions. "So many. We'll never get them back to the splinter a week away. We'd need an army alone to free them."

Portia continued pacing until she was too worn to take another step.

She plunked down on the sewer and leaned back into the cool curving wall behind her. Closing her eyes did nothing to banish the sight from her mind.

"Morgani gave her support because we said we could do it

without an army," Mark said, gently reminding her. It felt like a slap. Portia indeed had said that.

"Clearly that's not going to happen," said Magisend, indolently dismissive of the whole thing.

Rage filled Portia. It was rage at those beasts above, rage at the whole unfair world, rage at her childhood, but most of all, right now it was rage against Magisend and her blasted noble attitude.

Portia scrambled to her feet and grabbed Magisend by the collar with both hands, pushing the girl back against the wall. "Enough," Portia said, her voice low and barely controlled.

"Portia," Mark cautioned, but she ignored him. The rush of blood in her ears thrummed.

"Magisend Lucy Gwynn of the House Riddlepit, if you so much as say one more negative, unhelpful thing I will open a portal right here and now into the coldest part of the world and shove you through to never be heard from again, do you understand?" Portia felt out of control.

It also felt good.

Magisend stared at her with stupefied eyes for a moment. She looked down at Portia's hands, then back up into Portia's eyes. Then one corner of her mouth lifted. "That's genius, Portia. Now open the splinter in the square and send all those slaves through. I'll gladly join them."

13

Like all Dragonoid cities Portia had seen, walls surrounded this city. Here, in their chosen location, the ground lay level and the streets ran perfectly straight, but peering over to the far side of the wall circling the city revealed a long deadly drop into gray rock and mists far below, terrifyingly high. It was utterly unlike the two other cities she'd been in.

To add to the strangeness of the city, other sections of the wall far from that spot backed up directly to the mountains that rose high above, making the wall itself almost redundant.

Even with the strange features of the land and surrounding mountains, the wall itself—constructed from massive, evenly carved yellow granite blocks, topped with golden iron work—created a beautiful symmetry running around the city.

Portia could admit that much from her vantage point on top of the wall, gazing out over the city, the dramatic mountains around it. Below on the city street, Mark held one of her legs firmly, while she leaned over the abyss and looked down.

At least no one could surprise them by coming over the wall into the city, not here.

Not unless they had wings.

So it was just a matter of keeping an eye out for anyone inside the city spotting them. That would be easier here than in most other areas of the city.

They had found long, low warehouses to the west of the city gate. The structures had few doors, no windows. Long, hulking walls of stone and brick built right up to the roadways in between. Not even a hand's breadth of space wasted.

The warehouse area stood close to the city's entrance, a convenience for merchants. Items came into the city and were stored not far from the gates. From there, transport was only as needed, and only in the right direction. What suited their mission was that the area was also far enough away from the stores and houses of the city's residents as to be deserted at the end of the long work day.

It was a perfect location for Portia to test making a splinter back to their world.

They'd decided it best to test it that evening, rather than in the thick of the guards, while also trying to help thousands of prisoners escape.

Portia glanced at Magisend below, standing next to the wall. The tiny girl scanned the area around for anyone coming.

Magisend had not apologized when Portia finally released her collar earlier underground. Nor had Portia. Neither one had spoken a word about it through their quiet dinner in the sewers. Mark, for once, did not joke either.

Portia bit her lip, then jumped down from the wall, landing with a soft thump next to Magisend.

Magisend turned and gave her a nod.

For the time being, anyhow, they were working together as a team.

Mark pulled his longest knife, and Magisend followed suit. They both stood, their backs to Portia, watching for intruders.

Portia turned to the wall.

Taking in a deep breath, she closed her eyes and asked for a good aim. She was not used to opening a portal to her world from anywhere else. She knew the tune to get to the Dragonoid world well, even having some help from Magisend in writing it down, but this. This was from memory.

And a lot rode on her doing it right.

Not just for them, but for the hordes of prisoners needing help. At least the three of them had known the chances they were taking. The prisoners had been taken against their will.

Closing her eyes, Portia listened to her heart for a few minutes, then began singing, barely loud enough to hear. Concentrating on the part of the melody she'd heard in the Dwarven kingdom so long ago, she hoped that would bring the portal close to Morgani. They at least would have some idea how the portal came into being, knowing that Portia was on the other side.

As always, the magic pulled at her energies, feeling like a water soaked woolen blanket pulling her down, sucking at all her strength. It was much worse here in this world than at home. Much, much worse. She'd forgotten how much worse.

Her fingers and feet tingled, a numbness traveling up them. Her arms and legs trembled. She still stood, not trusting herself to take a step. Besides, it felt as if she would be running through quicksand if she had to move at the moment.

It was not a good way to feel, not when opening a new portal when you were not one hundred percent sure what you'd find on the other side.

The magic shimmered in front of her. Difficult or not, she was able to do it. Focusing on the swirling oval in front of her, she thought of home, and of getting there, and the notes she was singing, but mostly hoping she would not mess it up.

Finally, the resonance in her chest vibrated.

It was finished.

Leaving off the singing, Portia shook her arms and legs, willing the feeling back into them. It didn't help, but she felt better trying.

Mark turned back to check on her. He looked up at the swirling oval and nodded.

Portia pulled her sword and tested the opening, slowly extending the blade inside and pulling it back out. She lay her palm flat to the blade, feeling for heat, or coldness. She threw a stone through. It did not bounce back.

Mark shrugged. He stepped to the portal, and with a wink to Portia, stuck his head through.

His whole body quivered and his arms shook wildly.

Panicking, Portia pulled him back out, terrified of what she might see.

He silently laughed, collapsing to the ground.

Portia glared at him, then crossed her arms.

"It's fine, I don't recognize it exactly, but it looks like home," Mark said quietly, still laughing, wiping a tear from his eye. "Oh, come on, we can't have any fun?"

Magisend huffed, but when Portia turned, she thought she saw Magisend hiding a smile.

Sticking her own head through the opaque mists, Portia looked around. The land looked more like the grasslands near Cecelia's farm than the hills and forests by Coverack. It wasn't the mountains or caverns of Morgani. A flutter of disappointment fluttered in her chest. She pushed it away. It could have been worse. At least it was the right sort of area.

She thought.

No, if Magisend wasn't allowed to say negative things, neither was she, even in the privacy of her own thoughts. The splinter she'd made was good enough. It looked like their world, so surely it was. They just didn't know where yet.

A high-pitched whistle bounced off the warehouse walls around them, the volume growing and growing. Portia's ears twitched, then started to hurt. Mark and Magisend crouched into ready position, scanning around them.

No city dwellers were visible, yet.

As quickly as she could, Portia sang the magic to close the portal. Sweat broke out on her neck and back as the oval shrank in on itself, closing infuriatingly slowly. They couldn't leave it here unattended for Dragonoids to find. That would be a disaster of the worst sort, no matter what land or country it went to. And if they stayed here to defend it, as unlikely as it was the three of them could do so, they'd risk being caught.

The portal was the size of a dinner plate when the echos of footsteps echoed down the street. As of yet unseen masses of Dragonoids were running, their heavy footfalls echoing off the buildings and the city walls in a maddening cacophony.

The noise tore at Portia's nerves.

Only a fist size remnant of the portal remained when runners rounded the corner.

Mark cried out and pointed. He and Magisend adjusted their stance. They were tiny compared to the massive creatures running towards them.

Portia didn't dare look.

If she broke her concentration now, or did something wrong, not only would the portal not close, it would explode. It would send all three of them tumbling down the steep cliff on the far side of the wall.

It would also send all hope of rescuing the prisoners down the wall along with them, to die a brutal death in the gray rocks below.

A hissing noise caught Portia's ear from behind her. She wanted to look so badly but didn't. Her eyebrows bunched together as she concentrated on the tiny little remnant of the portal, until finally, it snapped shut with a little pop. A blast of hot air flew out from the closure spot, sending her hair flying.

Not even taking a moment to breathe, she whirled, drawing her sword as she went. Twenty or so armed attackers ran towards them, swords and knives held high.

Behind them, two more Dragonoids ran, but these held

blue glowing staffs. They wore intricate stitched robes of purple and gold. They looked important, the staffs dangerous.

Magisend was down on one knee, her knife on the ground beside her. Hands out, she sent ice out towards the attackers.

Or it would have been a thick rope of twisting ice if they had been back in Coverack.

Instead, here, only a mist came from her fingertips, barely blowing forward. Magisend's face twisted with effort. She hunched over, her hands in claws.

The mist carried forward slowly, moving like a cloud. It coated the stones ahead. The ice flakes on the pavement sparkled in the last of the late day sun just reaching over the wall. The ice coating reached near the entire width of the street.

The lead attacker reached the slick stones. His feet slipped out from underneath him. Falling backwards, his arms swung wildly for support. He found it by grabbing a fellow runner on each side. Then all three went down, knocking even more over in a tangle of legs, weapons, and oaths.

"Run!" Mark yelled.

Portia pulled Magisend's sleeve, yanking her from the deep magic trance. The girl's eyes slowly focused. Portia impatiently lifted Magisend to her feet and pushed her to Mark, then picked up her knife.

They bolted down a side street, away from the scrambling and falling Dragonoids.

Moments later, the high-pitched whistling stopped. Portia's ears still hurt with it, even after it halted.

They turned another corner. Part of Portia knew they

should be quieter, not slapping the pavement with their feet, but it was hard to run silently on the unyielding surface.

They ran down another long block between the warehouses. Portia scanned the walls. All frustratingly smooth. Then, up ahead, a black line zigzagged up the wall of one of the buildings.

She slapped Mark's arm as they ran and then pointed at the thing on the warehouse wall ahead. "Look," she said. He glanced, then gave her a devilish grin and picked up the pace.

Magisend started to lag, her feet slowing. Portia was impressed she could run at all. She grabbed the tiny girl by the wrist and pulled as she ran.

To her credit, Magisend kept her feet under her, but just barely. She was too exhausted to even yell at Portia.

It was as Portia had hoped. The black line zigzagging on the side of the warehouse was the shadows from an iron ladder leading to the roof. The rungs were much higher than any human would use, but still climbable.

Mark sheathed his knife, then leapt up and grabbed the bottom rung. He pulled down the ladder until it clanked at its end stop. It was still almost a full man's height above the ground. He had to pull himself up with his arms, then bring a foot up.

The rungs were spaced for Dragonoids.

Standing on one rung, the next closest was at Mark's waist. Pulling himself up with his arms, he was able to bring first one foot up, then the other.

He went up two steps, then paused and came back down.

He reached out a hand.

Portia lifted Magisend up to Mark's outstretched hand. He lifted Magisend easily up to the first step. Then he brought her up with each step he took himself, lifting himself first, then pulling her up after.

Portia was able to grab the first step on her own and then climb after them.

Their breath came in ragged gasps.

The sun set below the wall, deepening the dusk around them. A yell down the street punctuated the shadowed streets.

A wind blew, chilling the sweat on Portia's neck.

Something whistled in the air, coming towards them. Portia's shadow flashed on the wall in front of her. Instinctively, she tucked in and ducked, gripping the bars tightly. Above her, Mark and Magisend did the same.

A ball of fire hit the wall far to her right. Fire exploded outward. Heat blasted her face and neck, even in her defensive position. For a moment it was hard to breathe, then the heat passed, and the cool air reached her now stinging face. A flake of ash floated by.

Gray smoke followed the explosion, tainting the air. It smelled of garbage and stung Portia's throat.

"Holy mud snakes," Mark said, climbing again. He pulled himself up furiously, yanking Magisend up after him. Portia chased after.

The smoke smelled of that dangerous black powder they'd seen before in Rodaine. A Dragonoid weapon.

But it also smelled of magic. A tingling in Portia's nose

and fingers told her it was magic with a surety she could not doubt.

Someone down there could do magic here, easily. Or at least more powerfully than they could. They topped the roof just as another whistle sounded. A waist-high wall surrounded a flat roof. They crouched behind the wall, covering their heads with their arms.

This time the fireball flew above and then skittered on the roof top, exploding and sending the gray smoke past them.

Crouching, Portia ran the length of the wall to the next building over. Mark and Magisend followed.

Shouts bounced off the walls of the warehouse below. It was difficult to tell where it was coming from.

Reaching the end of the building, Portia crouched in the corner, then cautiously peered out over the wall facing the other building. She didn't dare look over the side the fireball had come over.

Stacks of small barrels filled the narrow alley below. The next roof over was at least a full length away. She could jump it with a running start. Probably.

But then there was Magisend.

Portia turned back to see how she was doing. Magisend slumped against the low wall, breathing heavily. She looked up and met Portia's eye. Magisend's eyes were clear and alert, but she looked exhausted.

Before Portia could stop him, Mark popped up and glanced over the wall in the direction the fireball had come. He looked around quickly, then dropped back down again.

"Well?" Portia asked, leaning in to Mark to keep her volume down.

"Ten, perhaps? Some in fancy robes. I lucked out. They were looking down the wall to where we were before. Back at the ladder," Mark said quietly, breathing heavily between each sentence.

"They could have sent more around the building," Portia said.

"If they're smart, they'd attack from all four sides," Magisend said.

Portia glared at her. Whose side was she on?

"What? It could happen. We should be ready," Magisend said, not even bothering to glare back. She leaned her head back against the wall, still winded.

"She's right," Mark said.

Portia closed her eyes for a moment, thinking.

There were too many to fight, at least directly. Maybe they didn't need to fight.

She opened her eyes again, surprised by the dense stars overhead. She'd been too distracted to notice it was fully dark out already.

The moon had not yet risen.

The perfect time for a ruse.

"Could you get their attention?" Portia asked Mark.

"Why?" Magisend asked, incredulous.

"We're going to go over that wall," Portia pointed to the wall behind them, "and leap over to the next building. I want to make sure that they can see us."

Magisend's mouth hung open. Portia gave her a smirk. She couldn't help it.

Mark elbowed Magisend. "Not really us."

"Oh, Mark, you hurt my feelings," Portia said. "And I do such good work."

A more serious tone in his voice, Mark said softly, "Do you really think you can do three duplicates? Here?"

Portia bit her lip and nodded. There was no choice

Magisend looked more confused than ever. One eyebrow arched. Her arms crossed.

"Just be ready to run back the way we came," Portia said to Magisend.

Concentrating on the open roof in front of them, Portia conjured three images just like them, duplicates. Fake Portia, fake Mark, and fake Magisend. The images were wavering and not quite solid. Portia pushed more magic into it, hating the sickening feeling of illness it gave her in this land. The images solidified. The fake Magisend even stood with one hip cocked and her arms crossed, a snarl on her face. Portia wanted to laugh. The real Magisend did not look amused, looking even more like her duplicate than before.

Satisfied, Portia gave Mark the signal. He stood and banged the hilt of his knife on the wall in front of him, waved his arms, and yelled. Matching yells came from below. They had spotted him. He danced back away from the edge of the wall, and then ducked down to crawl back close to its protection, out of sight of those below. Grabbing some loose gravel from the rooftop, he threw it over the edge of the wall. The pebbles bounced on the ground below.

Portia grabbed a handful herself and threw it over the other wall. A shout from below told her at least one Dragonoid had entered the alley and was getting a rock rainfall. Perfect. A witness.

Concentrating on the duplicates, Portia had them run back to the middle of the roof to get a believable running start, then run to the edge of the roof and leap over and onto the next building over. They sailed over, one after the other, in a beautiful arc. They looked so believable, Portia could almost feel the wind through her hair as if she had really jumped over the space between buildings.

Angry shouts from below greeted the sight.

Portia sent the duplicates running along the edge of the rooftop of the next building, plainly visible to those below. The Dragonoids below gave chase. It was difficult for Portia to see to the far edge of the next building, it being lost in the shadowy distance. They needed to get out of here before her duplicates did something stupid in the darkness, out of her supervision.

Portia pointed to the ladder they had come up, back along the building they were on. The three of them ran crouched low, still hiding behind the wall. They reached the ladder. A quick glance over the wall showed no one on the street below.

They scrambled down, half falling, half climbing between the gigantic rungs. The metal slammed into Portia's legs and shoulders. She tried to minimize the impact, more to be quiet than worrying about bruises.

They ran through the streets, searching for the sewer opening that they had used in this area. Between the darkness of night, and the dizzying chase, Portia could not orient herself. Luckily, Mark had no problem, and after two or three turns, he brought them directly to the entrance.

One by one, they dropped down into the tunnel below the street. Mark replaced the cover, aligning it in place with a snap.

They ran down the sewer itself, their feet slapping in the shallow puddles they couldn't avoid. Even here, it felt important to get more distance.

After what felt like many candlemarks, they finally slowed, letting their burning lungs catch up.

"Did you see those strange blue staffs?" Portia asked, still struggling to breathe.

"Yeah, that looked like magic," Mark said.

"How much magic do they have?" Magisend asked, stopping.

Portia flinched as the memory of the Dragonoid she burned so badly came back to her. Even if it had been trying to kill her with a fireball of its own. Letting her own footsteps slow to a stop, she turned back to Magisend. "Fire magic, that is for sure. Although the one I saw had to use a wand to do it."

"So those staffs are like super wands?" Mark asked. He circled around the two girls, found a dry spot to sit down, then flopped back against the tile wall.

Oh great. More powers in the hands of their enemies.

"Maybe," Portia said. "Remember, we only saw them do magic back in Rodaine. I think. We have no idea how strong their magic is here in their homeland."

Portia's back hurt, the muscles cramped from running and

from tension. Her head hurt too. Why couldn't this rescue mission just go smoothly?

"I hope it's just as exhausting for them as it is for us," Magisend said, irritation in her voice. She sniffed and crossed her arms.

Portia wanted to laugh but didn't dare. She turned away so Magisend couldn't see, not that there was much risk in the dim passageway. The dots of Mark's magic dots gave more light than the intermittent grates opening up to the city above now it was dark outside.

Portia and Magisend joined Mark, resting and leaning against the wall. There was no place they needed to be at the moment, and here was just as good as anywhere else to recover.

Portia shivered, dreaming of a land of white snow everywhere. Of crystals of it in her hair and down her back, on her bare arms. Something nudged at her, abruptly ending her dream and urging her to wake up.

Opening her eyes gave her little to see. It was dark everywhere. She blinked, confused. Then she saw one of Mark's faintly glowing dots attached to the sewer wall in the distance and remembered where she was. She must have fallen asleep.

Water dripped, the noise echoing off the tile walls. Turning, she reached out and felt Mark's foot. Magisend slumped on his other side, a faint bundle of clothing and dark hair. They were both sleeping.

Shaking her head, trying to lose the confusion of sleep, dread filled Portia with the mistake they had made of not setting a guard.

What had woken her?

As if in answer, running footsteps echoed through the sewer, the noise bouncing in all directions.

Portia rushed to her feet. She pushed Mark as she rose, then leaned over him and slapped Magisend's arm to wake her.

Panic filled her. They were in a long continuous dark tunnel. Foolishly, they had selected a spot to rest with no branching tunnels nearby, no routes to choose from when running away, even if just to confuse any possible pursuers. If they didn't get moving, whoever was coming would see them, and worse.

"What?" Magisend asked, still sitting, and looking up sullenly at Portia.

"Get *up*," Portia said to her as loud as she dared.

Mark was already on his feet, his knife drawn. He turned his head left and right, trying to figure out which direction the running was coming from.

Magisend glanced up at him, then scrambled clumsily to her own feet, moving slightly aside so as to not stand up into his knife.

The faint pink dot at the far end of the tunnel flickered and dimmed. Splashing, then a deep growl and curse came from the same direction, along with the slap of feet on the tile floor.

Portia, Mark, and Magisend turned as one and ran as fast

as they could in the other direction. Portia couldn't remember much of the details of this tunnel. There were fewer branches in the sewer system on the edge of the city, that much she did recall.

They ran in the dark, trying to not trip over each other and their accursed robes, now wet and dragging from the water. Portia's hood flopped down in her eyes and she flipped it back. Better to see and not wipe out than to worry about what their pursuers might spy.

They ran and ran.

Those behind gained on them. Portia's scalp and ears tingled. She tensed for a knife in the back, or for a hand to reach out and grab her. It was unnerving to have an enemy at her vulnerable back.

Just as she decided to turn and fight, her foot tripped on a large stone in the middle of the tunnel, an aberration in the normally spotless system.

She went down in a tumble of robes and knives and sword into the ice-cold water. Water ran down her back, soaked her scalp as she flipped head over feet.

Mark and Magisend's footsteps receded into the distance.

Time seemed to slow down.

Portia felt like she was moving in slow motion. She sat, felt for her weapons in the hands-deep water, then turned to the direction of the pursuers.

Only to be smacked in the head by something sharp and painful.

Blackness filled her vision.

14

Portia awoke, her head throbbing so intensely she felt nauseous. Something globbed and stuck in her right eyelashes and cheek, keeping her eye from opening all the way. She tried to reach up but found her wrists tied with a thick, rough rope that dug into her skin. More rope wrapped around her ankles.

Whoever had brought her here had leaned her against a dirty tiled wall before tying her up. It looked like the same tile as in the sewer system, but not as well maintained. Broken and cracked tiles dotted the wall. Pieces of debris scattered on the floor. Dirt coated everything.

The room stretched out wide and high, the ceiling lost to darkness above. A few candles burned in holders on a rough wood table in the middle of the vast room. Other candles sat in candleholders placed directly on the floor, having no other furniture to put them on. A few chairs scattered in the room.

The room shifted in and out of focus. Portia closed her eyes again.

———

"I said, get your hands off of me," Magisend said. "My hair is not a toy." She sounded beyond annoyed.

Portia opened her eyes. Her head only mildly throbbed, no longer shooting pain into her brain.

Mark and Magisend sat next to her in the candlelight, also tied and propped against the wall. A semicircle of candles surrounded the three of them, making it difficult to see beyond it.

On the far side of Magisend, a small Dragonoid, child-sized, perhaps as big as Magisend if she had been standing, stood over Magisend, staring at her hair. It turned its head this way and that, staring at the fine black strands hanging in Magisend's face.

It reached out tentatively to touch Magisend's hair. Magisend leaned to one side, then the other to avoid its touch. "Stop it!"

"It doesn't understand you," Mark said, his voice horse.

"Then you tell it!" Magisend yelled, exasperated. She leaned so far she toppled onto her side. The Dragonoid made a croaking sound, then squatted and petted Magisend's head. "Mark!" Magisend yelled.

Mark sighed. "*Stop hurting her*," Mark said to the Drag-onoid, in its own language.

It looked up, surprised. Its tongue flicked out. The scales

in its face looked almost iridescent in the candlelight as it examined Mark. *"I'm not hurting her,"* it finally said.

"You are," Mark said. *"Stop it."*

"You can't tell me what to do," it said, now getting angry. It touched Magisend's hair with one finger while staring at Mark.

"It can't. That is true, Issakson, but now is time to go," a deeper, much more aggressive voice said from the darkness, the words spitting and popping.

The small Dragonoid jumped, then deflated. *"Yes, Father."* It gave Mark a final hiss before stepping over the ring of candles and stomping away.

Mark looked at Magisend, then glanced at Portia. His eyes widened when he saw Portia's eyes were open.

"Tell me how you escaped. I'll not keep asking nicely," the voice asked from the darkness.

Mark turned to the voice. *"You keep asking the same question, and I keep telling you the truth. We didn't escape from the pens. We are not slaves. We came to save them,"* Mark said back in the harsh language, the last accents barely audible from his tired vocal cords.

"There is no other way you'd be here," it said. *"I grow tired of this."* A chain dragged across the floor out of sight.

"I opened a portal," Portia said, barely able to get the words out. She struggled to sit up straighter. Her body hurt all over.

A shuffling in the darkness met that, then footsteps coming closer. A huge Dragonoid, bigger than she'd ever seen, stepped into view just within the ring of light cast by the candles.

Divots in its face marked where several scales were missing. A long scar cut across its chest, the scales severed, a thin white line of scar tissue breaking up their pattern.

"*We have lost enough, do not think to threaten us with more,*" it said to Portia, its black eyes glinting in the candlelight.

A shiver went down Portia's back. "*I'm not threatening. You've seen all our people in cages. How can you say you've lost enough?*" Portia said. Almost instantly, she regretted it. Already, she was fighting with their captor and she didn't even know what it was talking about with 'their loss.'

That chain in the darkness rattled her. She didn't want to see it used on Mark.

Or herself.

She bit her lip to physically stop herself from talking.

"*We have lost warriors and sons and fathers. Enough,*" it said. "*We don't want any more portals. If what you've said is true, we should kill you now for our own protection.*"

"*What?*" Mark said, his voice pitching upwards and cracking with the strain.

"*You are the ones that opened a portal and attacked us. We just want our people back.*"

"*We did not attack you,*" a younger voice said quietly. An adolescent Dragonoid stepped forward. Mark's size. "*Our emperor did that.*"

The large Dragonoid placed a protective arm around the younger one.

Another child.

The enormous Dragonoid peered at Portia, then Mark. *"He made our people go on pain of death. We did not choose."*

"Then why are you blaming us for everything that happened to your people?" Portia asked. So much for not making things worse.

Mark shot Portia a look. She ignored it, despite it feeling as if her face were burning from his gaze. Guilt.

The large Dragonoid crossed its arms and stared at Portia. The younger one looked up at its parent, expectantly. Portia wondered what it hoped for as a response, if anything at all. Did it hope to see Portia struck down for her insolence?

Magisend struggled back to an upright position, her shifting on the floor breaking the silence. She managed to sit up and wiggle back next to Mark despite the bonds on her wrists and ankles. Dust coated one side of her face and body from the floor.

"What are they saying?" Magisend asked. She flipped her hair back.

Were nobles not afraid of anything?

Or was waiting just too new of an experience for someone of her rank?

Portia pulled her eyes away from Magisend, despite her fascination. Here, Magisend wasn't the dangerous one. Or the most dangerous one.

"They're discussing killing us because of the portal," Mark said quietly. The Dragonoid's gaze shifted to him.

"Oh, great, your fault again, *commoner*," Magisend said, shooting Portia a contemptuous glance.

"WHY ARE YOU EVEN HERE?" Portia shouted at Magisend, her voice exploding out of her chest surprisingly loud. Even the large Dragonoid jumped.

All eyes fell on Portia.

Portia shook, surprised at herself as much as any of them. Adrenaline coursed through her veins. Her face heated.

The blood rushing through her ears sounded so loudly it reverberated in her head like a waterfall. At the bottom of the world.

"*My apologies, sir,*" Portia said to the large Dragonoid looming over her, speaking in his language as respectfully as she could. What would someone like him want? "*We understand your pain at losing those close to you. We have the same pain. We are trying to fix it. It has nothing to do with taking your people from you. Only our own.*" Portia did not finish the thought, only taking your slaves.

"*What about our people?*" the creature asked.

Portia closed her eyes for a brief moment. "*I only know of one prisoner.*"

"*Liar!*" shouted the adolescent Dragonoid. "*Abwola is missing, and Herx and—*" The larger Dragonoid silenced the younger one by pulling him close with one arm and hugging him tightly. The younger one resisted, then accepted the hug for one brief second before running off, knocking over a few candles in its path. The flames flicked and died in the dust.

"*We were only trying to protect ourselves. You came into our world, not the other way around,*" Portia said.

"*The others came here. Uninvited. We heard tales of their*

demanding black powder. Weapons. Threatening those who didn't turn them over," the large Dragonoid said.

Dwarves.

Suddenly Portia wasn't just mad at Magisend.

"*It's not what we want. We want only our people. We do not want the others to have the weapons either, any more than we want you to use them against us,*" Portia said.

Mark turned to Portia, a questioning look on his face. She gave her head a subtle shake. An explanation would have to wait for later.

If they had a later.

Taking the Dragonoid silence as an invitation to keep talking, Portia inhaled deeply. "*We want to get our people, all of them, even the shorter others that came for the weapons, bring them back home and then seal the worlds between us forever. It has brought only pain to both sides,*" Portia said.

The large Dragonoid snorted. "*You have no argument from me on that, but the emperor would look unkindly at you stealing his property.*"

Portia tilted her head, not understanding.

"The emperor seized all the slaves," Mark quietly reminded Portia in common.

How loyal was this Dragonoid to his emperor? Filth covered the room they were in. No fine furniture graced the floors. If the emperor was awash with wealth and power, he was not sharing with the one in front of them.

Portia took a gamble. "*Would his losing this property help you?*"

The large Dragonoid rocked back on its heels, looking

down its snout at Portia. *"Clever one, you are. Perhaps. Perhaps not."*

Another tack then.

"We were attacked when making a passage home. Do you know how they knew where we were, or if they knew what we were doing?" Portia asked. Clearly not everyone in this land was on the same side. How much would he give away?

A lot.

"If you did portal magic, then yes, they would know. There are few here who can magick. Those who can, can also sense others who can do it as well. This is why the emperor requires lifetime service from all with skills in the fantastical arts. Death is the sentence for anyone caught hiding their children who can magick. Immediately, in front of all witnesses possible." The Dragonoid dropped his head, then walked away after that long speech. He returned with a huge wooden chair, placed it in front of them and sat.

"All magic?" Mark asked?

"They say all, but I am not so sure," the large Dragonoid said. A dark look passed over him. Even with the strangely warped features and lizardlike appearance, it was obvious something troubled him.

"You knew someone who could do magic." Portia said, guessing.

The Dragonoid nodded, his expression darkening.

How much dare she risk?

All of it.

"You are not loyal to this emperor, are you?" Portia said, more of an assertion than a question.

In the calmest, most chilling speech she'd ever heard in the language, he replied, "*You have landed in the middle of the rebellion that will kill him.*"

Mark blew out a long low whistle.

Magisend, impatient at not understanding any of the conversation, elbowed him. "What?" she demanded.

"Rebels," Mark said to her in common.

Magisend considered the word, then stared at the Dragonoid. As if making a decision, she gave him a huge, broad smile, pouring on the charm, even while half covered in filth. "Well hello, enemy of my enemy." She turned to Portia, who stared with her mouth open. "Portia, be a good subject and negotiate an alliance with this fine creature."

Did nothing ever faze Magisend?

The Dragonoid stared at Portia, its head tilted as if waiting for a translation. Portia swallowed. No way she was going to pass that on word for word. "*We would like to work together,*" she managed to get out.

It nodded.

THEY SAT at a large table on the edge of the enormous room, perched on chairs far too high for them. Portia, Magisend, and Mark pulled apart the chunks of bread, topped them with cheese and shoved them in their mouths, chewing furiously. The large Dragonoid watched, bemused. The younger ones had returned, and they sat, one to each side of their father, watching the humans with fascination. The eldest of the two still looked sullen, but had perked up when Mark had shown him a pair of dice in his bag. He had given them to the young Dragonoid, a gift that earned a surprised glance and a quick grab. The dice disappeared in the Dragonoid's closed fist.

They had come to an agreement that they would work together, the three of them and the Dragonoid rebels, pending Portia proving herself. They needed to see that she could do what she said she could do. That her magic would open the portal between worlds, and more importantly, seal it behind them. And that the magic would lure the royal guards when needed by the rebels.

In return, the rebels would not involve the humans in their war. They'd let them escape unharmed, as much as possible. It was up to the humans to run fast.

Portia had thought that fair. As long as the Dragonoids didn't interfere. They had not counted on any help when they came to the Dragonoid world to begin with.

The agreement had not reached the return of their weapons, but the enormous Dragonoid had promised they would do so if she passed the test. Portia looked longingly at her sword resting on the floor by the wall. She felt naked without it.

She was just grateful they had thought to dig around in the water for all her possessions after knocking her out in the sewer tunnel. The rebels were nothing if not thorough, no matter how surprised they had been in finding loose humans running around in their secret hideout.

There was always some test. The familiar dread and fear

filled Portia's belly. Even after all this time, it was still terrifying to have a dangerous trial.

Why did real-world tests usually turn out to be so dangerous, and possibly fatal?

"I still don't understand why I should be the hostage," Mark said after he swallowed an especially large mouthful. "If you're going to do something dangerous, don't you need a bodyguard?"

"What am I?" Magisend asked. "A decoration?"

"Yes, a noble." Mark burst out laughing, inhaled a bit of bread, and coughed. He leaned down, gasping and trying to clear his windpipe until Magisend slapped him on the back so hard the chunk of bread flew from his mouth to the ground, and almost knocking him down with it.

He looked up in surprise, his mouth a round "o".

Magisend smiled sweetly back at him. "Just trying to help."

Portia sighed. She exchanged a glance with the large Dragonoid. Was he smirking? Portia glanced at his two children. He probably knew exactly what was going on between Magisend and Mark, even if he didn't speak the language.

AFTER THEY FINISHED their much overdue lunch, Magisend and Portia prepared to go to the surface. Two Dragonoids would escort them through the sewers to an opening by an especially accessible grate where they would wait and observe.

Portia's task was to open a portal, even just a partial one, and then close it again to see if the royal guards and mages came. The two Dragonoids would help them flee through secret passages they knew well, an advantage Portia hoped would be enough for them to get away. . She could still feel the heat from the fireball of the first attack, the skin on her cheek still stinging and feeling raw, even days later.

She wondered if her face was as red as it felt.

The Dragonoids agreed to let Magisend come with Portia.

If Portia's magic did not draw the royal mages, then it would be Magisend's turn to try. Portia knew it was foolish pride to not want Magisend to have that chance. She wanted something that Magisend didn't have.

Suddenly she felt like she was five years old. Her face reddened, and she turned away from Magisend as the flushing hurt her already pained cheeks.

Portia pulled the green and red faceted vials of anti-magic poison from her pouch. Blessedly, they had not broken in her collision in the sewer. She handed one to Magisend, who opened it, gave it a sniff. Magisend then slowly poured a thin line of it along the edge of her knife blade. Taking a rag given to her by the Dragonoids, she carefully smeared the poison on the metal, turning the rag to soak up excess, all while carefully avoiding letting it touch her skin.

It took surprisingly little to talk the large Dragonoid leader into letting them have their blades back for this task. As long as Mark did not have any weapons, and he was guarded well by one of their own, the Dragonoid was satisfied.

Currently, Mark's guard was the adolescent with the dice.

He sat close to Mark, throwing the dice and then showing Mark the results. They discussed them intensely. It looked like two brothers playing a game, and not captive and mortal enemy. Portia shook her head, but could not hold back a small smile. As much as Magisend could insult anybody she met, Mark somehow was the opposite. He could charm anyone.

If Portia had half his people skills, perhaps she could have gotten the queen to take on this mission instead of having to go behind her back.

Taking one of the red vials of poison, Portia held it over her sword. For some reason, she felt anxious about treating her precious blade with anything. It was her most prized possession. She cleaned it meticulously, even when exhausted and wounded from battle. She probably treated it better than she treated herself. Her stomach wobbled, felt unsettled.

As if sensing her unease, the sword vibrated just the slightest. Without being able to say why, Portia suddenly felt it was okay. She poured a thin line of the sticky black substance on the blade, letting it spread. Holding her own rag above the coppery blade, she watched, fascinated, as the black oil thinned and coated the weapon as if it had a mind of its own. The rag was only needed to wipe off the most excess of drips.

Grimacing, she replaced the sword in its sheath. The holder for the sword would most likely need to be replaced since the poison would contaminate the beautiful green leather. It pained her, but she told herself to grow up. There was much more at stake than a piece of pretty attire.

A slam came from the hallway outside, then running feet

and another door slam. One of the guards standing at the door peered out into the hallway, then exited, leaving a sole Dragonoid with a rusty spear to watch over them. Portia whirled and stared towards the exit. They'd only been allowed outside the room for quick restroom breaks, and then only escorted. She had no idea where in the city they were. Mark and Magisend had been led back blindfolded after their capture.

She hated not knowing where they were.

And now something was going on.

Portia quickly treated her knives with the poison, inwardly grimacing at the hurried work. She put on her baldric, her small bag of other tools, then checked her camouflaging robe.

She and Magisend went to stand by Mark, the small Dragonoid looking up at the two of them suddenly crowding his prisoner.

The Dragonoid leader came back into the room and walked briskly to the far side to grab a rolled tube of paper from a pile on the floor in the corner. It turned to leave again, but Portia stepped to block its path.

"What's going on?" she demanded, speaking in the guttural language.

The Dragonoid tried to step around her. She danced backwards to keep facing him and not letting him get by.

"What is going on? Tell us," Portia demanded again, ending with an insult to get his attention. She'd insult his line back to their origins as a smear of mud in the ancient seas if she had to in order to get a reply.

The Dragonoid paused. It could have just swiped her

away with one gigantic hand, but did not. *"They are moving the slaves. The empress and number one mistress are fighting for control. The mistress wants to dump those of the empress off a cliff, along with her guards."*

Portia paled.

Magisend, not understanding what the Dragonoid said, elbowed Mark. He told her in quiet whispers. She held back a shriek with one hand.

The Dragonoid tried to get around Portia again. Awakening from her shock, Portia blocked him again.

"Let us go now. We have to go to them," Portia said.

"You have to prove yourself first," the Dragonoid said, dismissing her.

"No! We have to save them." Portia put her hands on his chest, trying to stop his forward motion. Instead, her feet slid backwards across the floor, leaving white streaks on the dirty tile.

The Dragonoid flipped his head in annoyance. He stopped, grabbed both of Portia's wrists, and pulled her hands from his chest. He could have lifted her high above with just one hand.

"I am not risking all my people, my sons, my daughters, over what a stranger says they are. You must prove yourself." His eyes burned into hers. He held her wrists so tightly, they ground together, sending shoots of pain up her arms.

She stared back.

He was so close she could feel the heat coming off of him. The scars on his face were even more terrifying seen so close. One knife line ran along his jaw, where a half hand width over it would have slit his throat. His breath blew her hair back.

The Dragonoid's son made a whining sound, moved closer to Mark

Portia breathed heavily, feeling the eyes of all those around her.

"Fine, we'll do it now, but we go right after," Portia said. *"Now is your time to attack. Now or never. We will not help you if our people die."* Portia's eyes glittered back.

The Dragonoid growled, grinding his teeth together.

15

Dragonoids poured into the once empty room. They wore armor and bore weapons, most looking like they had been discarded by a far richer army, or waiting to be fixed by some blacksmith. It was a ragged crew.

More candles had been lit, but their holders had been pushed out to the base of the outer walls to be out of the way for walking, leaving the room with weird dark spots in the middle. Strange shadows flickered on the ceiling from the cobwebs above.

Mark gathered his things. As part of their negotiation, he was to come with Portia, along with a stronger escort to help them. The escort also had the duty of disabling the humans if they were liars about who they said they were, but that part had been left unspoken.

Once the action started, there would be no time to come back to these headquarters.

The Dragonoid leader, called Issak by the others, stood in

front of a map at the table, smoothing down the rolled edges. Several Dragonoids with chevrons on the shoulders of their rough homemade uniforms stood back waiting while Portia's group gathered around the table first.

"If approved, you will open the portal here." Issak pointed to a section on the map. The spot showed a wide wall, with what looked like several large buildings across a street. The buildings provided the perfect cover for archers to lie in wait.

A chill went down Portia's spine. The Dragonoid rebels truly better keep their word on leaving the slaves alone, for if not, they could easily pick them off as they ran for the splinter.

"Back off once it's made. Hide it if you can, because the royal mages will come quick. We'll have some help for you." Issak stared at Portia intently.

The word 'some' was not lost on Portia. Much of this they would have to do on their own. And with that horrid magic detecting ability of the emperor's mages, it was impossible to do this rescue sneakily. Three humans with no magic against an empire was not even close to a fair fight.

But there was no help for it.

Portia dropped her eyes to study the map, trying to memorize the location while Mark translated for Magisend. The Dragonoids that were to accompany them stood behind, listening.

"Lead the slaves to the splinter on our signal." The leader poked the map for emphasis. *"Otherwise, you'll walk into a battle, do you understand?"* What he didn't say, but was equally true, was the battle would be between two sides who

cared little about the humans and their concerns. Better to stay out of the way.

Portia nodded.

Handing Portia the rope she'd requested, the Dragonoid leader dismissed them. She shoved the rope into her bag and walked away slowly. The waiting commanders watched her, blinking slowly.

They would not speak a word until she and the other humans had left. They were taking no chances with the humans knowing their plans in case they were captured, or worse, turned out to be spies.

Giving up on eavesdropping, Portia exhaled and then picked up her pace.

They stepped out of the large room. The Dragonoid escort started running down the long hall to their destination. Portia gladly ran too, finally on their way to doing something. Mark and Magisend fell in line beside her.

They made their way through the sewer tunnels, for the large room had been part of that system. Their route snaked and turned on itself so many times Portia lost all sense of direction. She couldn't tell if it was necessary, or a precaution. Hopefully, just necessary. They didn't have time to waste on foolishness.

Finally, they reached a portion of the tunnel where the ceiling came lower. The branching out of other tunnels had dropped a while back. They must be near the outer walls of the city.

The tunnel widened further, and the ceiling lowered until

they were ducking to walk. All except Magisend, who smirked at Portia, then gave her a wink.

They reached a wide, grated opening to the sky above. It was so low it was easy to grasp the bolts holding it down. Portia's hands easily fit between the wide bars.

Opening the grate, Portia stuck her head out to look around. She gasped.

Instead of the constant gold and brown stones and dirt of the dusty city elsewhere, this was clean swept and manicured. And green.

Even in this space-cramped city, this neighborhood had wide spaces between large sumptuous houses that peered over tall walls. Carved stones decorated the walls between swirls of finely worked metal that decorated every surface available.

There were even little plants growing in pots along the street, as if the neighborhood had a gardener.

Why here? It was so quiet. So idyllic.

Then she let out a sigh of appreciation.

This was not the neighborhood to just happen to run into guards. No. If her magic could call the mages to chase after her, this was the perfect place to test it. The emperor's mages and guards would have to work hard to come out all this way.

They'd have to be looking for something, or someone.

It also gave Portia and her crew time to hear the attack coming and escape. She hoped.

Magisend poked Portia in the leg. "What do you see?"

"The perfect place for a test," Portia replied. She climbed out of the sewer. Belatedly, she checked her robes to make sure they covered her completely. It would be strange to see anyone coming from out of the street, but at least she was not immediately identifiable as human. A Dragonoid poked its head out of the sewer opening, keeping an eye on Portia.

Portia looked around. She picked one wall.

She had been thinking of where to open a portal to for this test the entire time they'd been running. If they were attacked so quickly that she couldn't close it, it was critical that it not go to any place she knew. Certainly not back to Coverack. She tried to remember the sounds of one of the portals from the Dwarven kingdom, the one with the blowing sands. The world of nothing.

Humming the tune to herself, she tested out the melody. It sounded right.

Standing close to the chosen wall, she sang the music, invoking the magic. As always, it drained her, but not so badly as usual. Perhaps it was knowing they were so close to succeeding in getting everyone out. Perhaps it was the adrenaline rush in knowing battle was coming. Either way, she was grateful for the strong vibrations in her chest.

The swirls appeared quickly. The oval looked like a doorway forming in the beautiful wall.

Portia spared a glance behind her. The Dragonoid still had his head out of the sewer, looking around. She considered telling him to either emerge fully or duck down, but didn't want to interrupt her spell once it started. Portal magic was dangerous. The faint scar on her hand ached in agreement.

Turning back to her work, she vowed to ignore him. It was bad enough she also had to listen for the emperor's mages and guards while she worked.

They didn't keep her waiting long.

A clanging sound came from the far distance. Also, the high-pitched whistle alarm she recognized from the attack in the warehouse area.

Quickly as she dared, Portia changed her tune for the magic. No longer did she invite the opening into another world, but sang for its healing as fast as she could.

The clanging drew closer.

Portia hopped from one foot to the other while she worked, her anxiety keeping her from standing still. She tried to look around while also concentrating on the portal, her eyes straining to catch sight of any approaching guards.

The wretched portal in front of her resisted closing. She'd never turned a spelling around mid-casting before. Was there some special trick to this?

Perhaps she should have tested that out first.

Too late now.

A whistling overhead announced the arrival of a fireball.

It hit the tower of an enormous house just one house over, making Portia jump. The fireball exploded out around the tower, completely enveloping it for a brief moment of reds, oranges, and yellows before diffusing out into the air.

A squeak escaped Portia as the heat reached her, setting off the pain in her face again. Luckily, she had just completed the spell. The resistant little portal finally closed, much as it had struggled.

She turned and ran for the sewer. The Dragonoid standing in the middle of the opening stared at her dumbly.

"Out of the way, you enormous beast!" Portia yelled. Below, yells from Magisend and Mark echoed her.

Finally it moved, just as Portia reached the opening. She jumped down into the open hole, not even checking if anyone else had foolishly stepped in the way. Landing with a thump, she grabbed the grate and threw it up and over the opening.

She set it in place just as a fireball smashed into the nearby street. The heat hurt her fingers.

Pulling them back, she stuck them in her mouth and cursed, but just for a second.

"Run!" she yelled. As a group they fled.

BY LUCK OR BY CUNNING, Portia didn't know which, for she didn't lead, they made their escape back to the center of the city. Here, the sewers were dense mazes of tunnels branching off here and there, deep water they had to pick through in some places, other sections dry.

No one pursued them through the sewers, a blessing. The most important task lay ahead. Portia wanted to conserve her strength, and that of Mark and Magisend.

The Dragonoids that flanked them walked silently, only slightly less threatening now they had seen the truth of Portia's magic. The two Dragonoids that walked further ahead, leading the group, talked between themselves. Portia wanted to push her way up to them and demand to be included in their planning, but even that was too much work at the moment. She had her instructions from the leader.

Nothing ever went according to plan when it came to battles anyhow.

"Now what?" Magisend asked Portia. The Dragonoid next to Magisend gave her a glance for speaking in common but did not say anything. Portia took that as permission.

"Now we get our people back," Portia said.

Mark slapped her on the back. She could imagine his smile, even if she couldn't see it in the darkness. Only a little light fell into the section of the underground sewer they were currently in, making navigation especially tricky.

"How are we gonna do that, if every time you open a portal we get blasted?" Magisend asked.

"Well, there aren't that many of them that can do magic, and our good fellows here," Portia waved at the Dragonoids, belatedly realizing Mark and Magisend probably couldn't see her hands in the darkness, "absolutely can't stand those guys. Hopefully they'll get them out of our way."

"And if not?" Magisend asked.

Portia sighed. "Then we'll have to fight, or outsmart them, or run."

"You should be excited, Magisend," Mark said. "This is your chance to prove you're not just a decoration." Portia didn't need to see him to hear the laughter in his voice.

Neither did Magisend.

"I'll kill you," Magisend said, splashing her way over to where Mark's voice had come from. He splashed away.

Magisend sounded angry. Truly angry. Perhaps it was the stress of the day, or anxiety about what was coming, but she sounded like she really wanted to hurt him.

The timing could not have been worse.

"Mark, Magisend," Portia said, calling as loudly as she dared, her voice low and serious. "Someone might hear you. Do you want us to fail? We could die here."

They stopped their chase. An awkward silence fell as Mark and Magisend fell back in line, one on either side of Portia. Goosebumps rose on Portia's arms. She didn't like being in between what felt like a coming storm.

The two Dragonoids ahead stopped under an especially large grate. Light from the street above fell in long streaks across their heads, shining down through the metal bars above. The calls of market vendors and the moan of rolling carts floated down from the street.

Portia guessed this was the large market close to the slave pens. She walked up to one of the Dragonoids standing underneath the large grate. *"Won't we be seen if we emerge here?"* Portia asked, pointing upwards.

The Dragonoid growled, as if affronted that she had spoken to him. *"No one should notice."*

Portia waited for the rest of the explanation. He only glared at her. Impatient, she opened her mouth to ask how no one would notice when an explosion ripped through the air above.

Screams replaced the normal market cries above. Running feet and roaring draft animals completed the chaos.

Another explosion sounded.

As if that was a signal, the two Dragonoids reached up, one on each end, and unfastened the gate. They lifted the monstrously large piece of metal slowly and set it down along the wall of the sewer.

"You will not be able to retreat this way," one of the Dragonoids told Portia. They must intend to close it back up after them.

Portia nodded in the darkness, then remembered they probably couldn't see her. *"Fine. We hope to not be back anyhow."*

"Good," one of the Dragonoids said, but something in his voice made Portia think it was a well wish for their success. Gratitude filled her heart at even that encouragement.

Then another explosion went off above, bringing her back to their mission.

"Now. Hurry," a Dragonoid called from underneath the grate. He held his hands cupped for Portia to step into. Two of the escort had already climbed to the street. If they were up there guarding the hole, that would explain how no one had fallen in yet.

Not bothering to answer, Portia stepped forward and put her foot in the Dragonoid's hands and stepped up. It was like stepping on stone. He was so strong his arms didn't even waver as he took her weight. He raised his hands and lifted her above his head quickly. Portia felt like she was flying to the surface. She struggled to keep standing straight so she didn't lean over and bash her head into the ceiling on her way up.

The opening blessedly was behind one of the larger stalls of the market, shielded from the central square and most other directions by the thick stand of tents around them. The two

Dragonoids already on the surface grabbed her hands and lifted her, placing her gently on the ground to one side.

Mark and Magisend followed, then the grate cover and several more Dragonoids. The Dragonoids set the heavy cover back and refastened it. They saluted Portia, then ran off without a word.

Portia watched them go, shocked.

"Well, I never," Magisend said.

For once Portia agreed with her. The Dragonoid rebels had gone from threatening to disable her, or even kill them, to leaving them completely on their own, all within a day.

Weren't they supposed to escort the humans to the slave pens?

A loud crying pulled Portia's thoughts from the strange behavior of the Dragonoids. A child ran back into the space between tents, sobbing in that strange Dragonoid way. Mark started to run over to it when an adult Dragonoid followed the child. Mark stopped, thankfully not having gotten too close.

The adult grabbed the child by the wrist. *"No son, not this way,"* it said, then yanked the child back the way they had come. It did not even spare the three of them a glance before it exited back into the main square, its child in tow.

Portia blew out a breath, relieved and shocked.

"Let's go see if it's this chaotic at the slave pens," Portia said.

They emerged into the chaos of the central market. Smoke filled the square, obscuring much of it. Broken squashes smeared in long yellow streaks and rolling and dropped fruit littered the ground. Other food stuffs Portia couldn't recognize lay smashed and trampled in the dirt, along with broken table boards. Most of the customers had already fled, leaving the decimated vendors and their families wandering dazed in the debris.

"What's the smoke from?" Mark asked.

Portia shook her head. She didn't know. Hopefully no more explosions were planned for where they were now.

"We've got to move," Portia said.

Straining to orient herself, Portia looked up at the surrounding buildings. Guessing, she pointed to one main street coming off the square. The three of them ran, going from one tent edge to the next, staying out of sight as much as possible. Not that a tent would offer any protection against an explosion.

Once they exited the square, the going was much easier, no longer having to pick their way over debris on the ground. Those that were on the street running were much more concerned about getting themselves to safety than having any interest in what three young Dragonoids might be doing.

Portia rechecked her robes to make sure she was completely covered, then spared a glance for Mark and Magisend. They were filthy, but otherwise fine. They were near indistinguishable from any other child running from the chaos.

She had guessed right on the street. A unique building with a spire, just as it had been drawn on the maps, sat at the end of the road ahead. That building was part of the square of buildings around the slave pens. It was only a few more blocks to their destination.

Now, instead of tents and vendor tables, they ran past businesses in permanent buildings. The inhabitants were either bolting their doors, pouring out to peer down the street to try to figure out what just happened, creating clusters of gawkers that they had to run around.

Then more explosions rang, this time from in front of them. They were close enough that Portia could smell the foul black powder. Mark grunted next to her. He recognized it too.

She'd forgot to ask the rebels about the black powder weapons. Apparently they had it. Portia growled at the missed chance to learn more. Mark gave her a questioning glance, but she shook her head. Later.

Most of the Dragonoid business workers who had run out into the street rethought their choices and ran back in. In moments, few were left on the street.

Another explosion rocked the city, this one so close Portia's ears rang painfully. The vibrations shook her and ran through her chest, making it feel like her heart had stopped beating for a moment. She stumbled in the aftershock, nearly tripping over Magisend, who did go down.

Mark and Portia pulled Magisend up and they kept running. Portia pointed to a large entryway of a business at the end of the block. They ran for it to hide and take the situation's measure before running into the next intersection. The building with the spire taunted them ahead. So close, and yet so impossibly far.

"Now what?" Magisend asked after they made it safely into the alcove, huddling together as far from the street as possible.

Portia intentionally didn't look at Magisend, not wanting the irritation she felt deep inside to show on her face. She was the leader, this was part of the deal. Even when she didn't know what to do next.

Squatting down, Portia leaned out to look at the intersection and the next block. Only faint puffs of gray smoke drifted down the street. It was ominously quiet.

They couldn't sit there forever.

Taking a deep breath, Portia stepped into the street and waved Mark and Magisend to follow.

They made their way down the next street, and into the next intersection. The silence and lack of anyone on the street made Portia's skin crawl more than the explosions had. It was like waiting for something awful to happen, but not knowing what.

Cautiously, they made their way to the last building before the square holding the slave pens. They could not yet see into the square, but even here, being so close to so many packed together nearby, they should hear something. No sounds hung in the air, leaving it unnaturally quiet.

An enormous wave of fear ran over Portia at the thought the slaves might already be gone. She felt dizzy and sick to her stomach.

Were they too late?

Peering slowly around the corner, Portia exhaled at the sight of the packed pens. Slaves pushed up against the bars, gripping them tightly, their eyes wide with fear. All absolutely silent.

There were no guards.

None in the entire square. Where could they have gone? It was almost the moment for Portia to open the portal that would call the emperor's mages, setting the trap for rebel soldiers. Only after that were they to unlock the cages holding the prisoners, but this was too big an opportunity to pass. They could run now and unlock the gates and then deal with the portal. It wouldn't take that long, Portia told herself, even at the same time wondering how much of that was a lie.

It would work, if only the prisoners would understand and stay put.

If they could hold back the panic and trust her.

But they had no clue who she was, or why they should believe her.

She was just some kid.

Portia's mind felt like it was going to explode trying to solve the problem, and quickly. They only had moments. And if she chose wrong, and the prisoners panicked and ran, they'd never gather them all up again and get them home. They'd be lost forever, or even die today here in this square.

Portia bit her lip, thinking. She stared at Mark and Magisend. Mark could help unlock some of the cages. She didn't think Magisend could do anything, not as a thief anyhow. It wasn't worth the risk of doing magic to try to freeze the locks open. Their magic was a call for the emperor's mages and it had to be done correctly, when they were ready.

"We're going to open the cages," Portia said.

Mark raised his eyebrows. He heard as well as she that they were to set the portal first.

Portia gestured to the cages. "There are so many of them.

And the guards are missing. The explosions mayhaps worked too well for the leader's plans. If we are going to have any chance of getting them all, we have to unlock all those cages. You're going to help, Mark."

Mark looked uncomfortable, considering Portia's words. He glanced at the packed cages, shifted his weight, then gave a single nod.

Magisend watched, glaring, with her hands on her hips. "We can't screw this up."

"You're right. These people need you to command them and tell them what to do. Make them trust that their nobles have come to rescue them. They'll listen to you," Portia said to Magisend.

Magisend opened her mouth to argue, then realized what Portia had said. "You're correct," she said, sounding surprised she agreed with Portia. Her arms dropped. A smile replaced it, only to falter a second later. "What *are* they to do?"

"They're not to open the cages, no matter what happens, no matter how much they want to panic, not until the moment we give the signal. They run too early and the portal's not clear, that have no place to go and the guards will be after them," Portia said, thinking furiously.

"What signal?" Magisend asked.

Portia waved that off. "Tell them they'll know when they see it." Portia hoped she could keep that promise. "The guards could come back any moment. We have to go."

Digging in her bag, Portia pulled out a lockpick, and a second one she handed to Mark. Thank goodness for spares and being prepared. She raised her hand and signaled to go.

Mark, Portia, and Magisend ran for the cages, crossing the dusty yellow ground between the buildings and the metal pens. It felt like they were running into a bear trap without the free will to avoid it. It was impossibly convenient to have no guards here.

It *was* too impossibly convenient.

Two guards, pacing deep within the corridors between pens, came running at the sound of their footfalls. They must have been left behind to guard over captives while the bulk of the soldiers ran to deal with explosions. They slowed when they saw the three of them, but did not attack, confusing Portia.

Oh. The soldiers thought they were Dragonoid kids.

Portia slowed. Mark and Magisend followed suit, slightly behind her. Portia turned her head and whispered to Mark. "Ask about your mother. You're looking for her" Her own hood interfered with her vision but she saw Mark's hand flick acknowledgment at her request.

For a moment, Mark did nothing. Then he called out in a little Dragonoid kid's voice to the soldiers, all in their language. *"We're looking for my mom."*

One of the soldiers tilted his head at Mark's voice. Even with Mark dropping his voice lower, it must not have sounded quite right. *"You should not be here,"* it growled.

"Please, can't we just look? It's scary out there," Mark said.

Underneath her robes, Portia clenched and unclenched her left hand, her right still clutching the lockpick. The Dragonoids towered over them. Even her sword might not be enough of a weapon if it came to a fight.

The two soldiers resumed walking towards the three of them, an anger and purpose in their step that wasn't there before.

"You were told to leave," a second Dragonoid said. "So leave. Now."

Portia turned her head slightly, whispered back to Mark and Magisend, "Split up," then gave a hand signal.

The three bolted, far faster than the Dragonoids could pivot. Portia to the right, Mark to the left, and Magisend crazily darting between the two soldiers and disappearing into the maze of pens behind them, leaving the Dragonoids to roar in rage.

Running to the rear of the square, Portia wove between pens just in case one of the Dragonoids had picked her to follow. After the third such veer, she glanced back, breathing hard. No one came behind her.

The humans in the cages around Portia stared at her, wide-eyed. Dirt and worse filth coated their skin and clothes. The smell turned Portia's stomach. The prisoners barely had room to stand, much less anything else. Most had a wild look to their eyes.

They stepped back fearfully when she approached the door. Portia grabbed her hood and pulled it back for a second so they could see her face, before quickly pulling it back forward. Their eyes widened even more, and someone from the back gasped. Portia held up one finger to her mouth for silence.

Hopefully they spoke common.

"I am going to unlock the cage, but you cannot leave until we give you the signal. If you do, they'll just capture you again," Portia said. They stared at her blankly. "Do you understand?" Portia asked. Finally, a tall emaciated man by the door gave her a nod.

It would have to do.

Checking for pursuit once again before starting, Portia picked up the bottom of the heavy lock wound around two bars, keeping the door shut. It looked strange, but it had a hole for a key. How different could locks be?

She dug around the hole set on the face of the heavy lump of a lock with her pick. Thankfulness filled her heart when a soft click told her the lock worked like other locks she had tried before. After that, it was quick work. The lock bottom fell free from the top. The mechanism hung open. Portia set it back quietly against the bars and gave the prisoners another finger over the mouth, a reminder to be quiet.

She moved to another pen, and then another, completing her work quickly. Once, a guard came running around the corner and she had to run to disappear down another route between pens. If the square had not been so enormous, it would've been utterly impossible to hide from the guards like this.

And the prisoners helped, once throwing rocks and yelling to create a distraction when it looked like Portia was not going to be fast enough in fleeing.

Working her way to the front, Portia saw Mark on the other side of the square, working the locks just as she did. He gave her a quick wave and moved on to the next pen, hidden from view.

They were going to get all of them. Portia's hand shook as she worked, her anxiety ramping up the closer they got to succeeding. Once, a prisoner gently placed a hand on Portia's while Portia worked. Portia looked up in surprise, the warmth from the prisoner's hand oddly calming. It was an older woman with a thin blue shawl over her head. She smiled at Portia, revealing several missing teeth. Portia nodded and smiled back, feeling suddenly shy. She moved on quickly.

Just as Portia finished with the last lock on the row of cages she was working on, a cry came out from the center of the square. Then a smashing noise and a scream.

A scream that sounded like Magisend.

Portia bolted towards the sound, not even bothering to hide, instead tearing through the center of the passageway, dirt flying up behind her.

There was a small clearing in the very center of the pens, with paved stones set in an exact square. In the center, a metal rod stood waist-high. A heavy ring hung from it. A line of prisoners strung out, one chained to the next by the wrist, led from the ring out in a long line between pens. Some in the line were crying, their tears making tracks in their dusty faces. One woman was on her hands and knees, vomiting. The prisoners attached to her had to bend down, the handcuffs attaching them pulling and cutting in their skin.

A strange silence hung in the air. Despite the pens packed with prisoners, their gaunt facing staring out, their hands hanging onto the bars, not a one made a noise. Not a cry, not a yell, not a plea. It was as if they were all enchanted.

Or terrified.

The door of one pen stood open, a guard standing in the center with one arm held stiffly forward, blocking the prisoners inside. The prisoners stared at something behind the guard, shifting to see around him. Portia followed their eyes.

Another guard, a set of handcuffs dangling from one arm, was whirling around in circles at the edge of the clearing, his other hand trying to grab at the arms around his neck. Someone was on his back, trying to strangle him. Someone tiny by comparison.

That someone was Magisend.

The struggling guard, unable to get a good grip on Magisend's small hands, finally whirled and slammed its back to the bars, smashing Magisend in the process. Magisend screamed.

The tiny girl hung on even tighter. Her hood back, her humanness clear for all to see. Magisend tilted her head and stuck her face in the neck of the Dragonoid. Was she trying to bite the Dragonoid's nonexistent ears? It was like watching a mouse try to subdue a cat.

The second guard pushed the remaining prisoners back into the pen and flicked the lock over the door. He turned, trying to decide between grabbing Portia or helping his friend.

Portia made it easy for him. She pulled her sword from beneath her robes, only getting tangled for a second before she ripped through the brown linen with the blade. She circled the guard, putting herself between him and the fighting pair.

"Are you nuts?" Portia called to Magisend, keeping her eyes on the now approaching guard. He didn't even bother pulling a blade. Portia narrowed her eyes at the insult.

"No. You're slow. What took you so long?" Magisend

asked, gasping, trying to speak casually. The creature slammed her against the bars again, and Magisend screamed.

Goose bumps ran down Portia's arm.

The guard facing Portia ran, lifting his right arm to backhand her. Closer, Portia could see the dun colored plating that ran along his body, on his arms, and even in tiny segmented sections covering each hand. He didn't need to draw a weapon. His whole body was covered in one.

Gritting her teeth, Portia lightly danced to one side, letting the momentum of the Dragonoid carry him past her. He howled in rage at the miss.

They played this game several more times, Portia's breath ragged with the effort. Worse, Magisend had not made any sound for a while. Dodging yet another attack, Portia glanced over. The Dragonoid Magisend had been fighting stood, brushing its shoulders. Below it lay a crumpled pile of brown linen and a bit of dark hair.

Portia's heart stopped for a moment. It was difficult to breathe.

The Dragonoid trying to hit Portia yelled its rage one more time, but this time it was Portia who howled louder. She screamed.

Surprised, prisoners who weren't already watching the battle came to the edge of the bars to stare.

Even the Dragonoid tilted his head for a brief second before shaking his surprise off, slapping his fists together and then running to Portia. He was learning to not run so fast, to prepare for her to dance away.

This time she didn't.

This time she ran back directly at her opponent. He hesitated just a split second at her unexpected action, at the tiny opponent in front of him running towards him like she was going to smash him over a cliff. That little hesitation fueled Portia even more. Rage thrummed up through her sternum and out her arms and legs, guiding her every motion, guiding her sword arm.

Dodging to the left just a half step at the last moment, Portia dodged the Dragonoid's swing, then came back to the right and ran up the guard just as she had seen Mark do once. She willed herself to fly up him, and so she did. At the apex, she swung her sword down with both hands, hilt first, into the back of the Dragonoid's head.

Using her momentum, she jumped off behind the Dragonoid and turned, her feet skidding in the dust. The Dragonoid turned on his heel to face her, dazed and off-balance. He lifted an arm as if to strike, nonsensically since he was so far away, before he crumpled down in a pile.

Portia stood panting. If that hadn't worked, she would've run him straight through. She shook at the terrifying depths of her own rage.

It took a moment for the red to clear from her vision.

Magisend.

Dreading what she might find, Portia lifted her eyes. Instead of seeing a slain Magisend laying in a puddle of blood, her eyes alighted on Mark standing over the other downed guard.

Portia ran over to him.

"What?" she asked, barely able to get the word out.

He nodded to Magisend crumpled on the ground on the other side of the enormous guard. He must have heard the screaming too.

Portia whirled to the pile of collapsed pile of linen that was her school enemy. Shocked, Portia realized she also thought of her as her friend. No, that couldn't be right.

Magisend slowly moved. First an arm, then slowly lifting and rolling herself to a sitting position. The skin around her eyes was turning black. One nearly swollen shut. She patted her arms and legs, then grunted with satisfaction that nothing was broken.

Portia offered an arm. Magisend peered up at her, then took it. Portia leaned back and lifted Magisend to standing.

"What happened?" Portia asked Magisend. She glanced around. There were no more guards. Yet.

"Nothing," Magisend answered.

"Nothing?" Mark asked, incredulous, as he wiped the dirt from his knife. The guard he'd disabled lay at his feet, uncon-scious, but still breathing.

"Couldn't very well use magic, could I?" Magisend said as sarcastically as she could, her voice rough and breaking. "Even I can't fight off that many fire balls from the emperor's mages. You two are too slow. I'd have you in stocks at home."

Portia and Mark exchanged glances. Even for Magisend, that was odd.

Magisend limped over to the woman who had been on her hands and knees in the dust. The woman had stopped vomiting nod her fellow prisoners had lifted her to standing. She swayed uncertainly on her feet.

Magisend staggered over to the woman and walked directly into her arms. The woman and Magisend clung together, the woman weeping into Magisend's hair.

***

PORTIA AND MARK WATCHED, their mouths agape, at Magisend and the woman.

"I guess we now know who she's here for," Mark said softly.

"Who is she?" Portia asked.

"I don't know, but it doesn't matter if we don't get going. We'll all die here together." Mark glanced around the pen, then checked his weapons again. "We're late to open the portal." He paced a few steps, uncertain which way to go.

They couldn't afford to lose the rebels' help, not after what they'd seen that morning of the firepower of the emperor's mages.

"Right," Portia said. "Did you get your side all unlocked?" She motioned to the pens.

"Yes, though I'm not sure how much I trust them to not bolt early. I mean, the fear of the guards can only last so long when there are no guards to be seen," Mark said.

Was he really wishing for more guards?

Portia stared at him. He shrugged his shoulders.

"Let's hurry then," Portia said.

They ran to Magisend.

"We have to go," Portia said to Magisend's back while

Magisend still hugged the woman. The woman stared at Portia, tears staining her face.

Magisend released her hold except for one hand on the woman's hand. She stared at her intently. "Remember the instructions. You must wait for the portal to be open and clear. For our signal." Magisend glanced at the rest of the prisoners around them. "All of you."

Portia ran to the lock fastening the line of prisoners to the pole in the middle of the square. It was quick work to pick. They didn't have time for her to release each set of handcuffs so they had to make do with pushing the whole group of prisoners into a nearby pen, and setting the door shut, making it looked as if it was locked when it was not.

Before closing the door to the pen, Magisend stepped inside, grasped the woman tightly in a hug. "I'll see you soon on the other side."

Portia stood by the door, waiting for Magisend to complete her goodbye. On her way out, Magisend bumped into Portia, then stopped, her mouth near Portia's ear, standing too close for anyone else to hear. "If you breathe a word of this to anyone, I'll have my father get your head as a decoration for my front door. On a pike. Jack or no. Do you understand me?" Magisend said.

Portia nodded. Magisend walked on. Portia rubbed her neck.

She did not understand Magisend nearly as well as she thought she did.

THEY RAN through the empty streets of the city. It had been some time since the last explosion, and citizens were starting to venture out of the buildings. Portia gritted her teeth. Hopefully they had not taken too long with unlocking the pens and jeopardized the plan.

It was only several long blocks to the planned location, but felt like forever. Walking away from the prisoners felt wrong. The prisoners were still at the mercy of the Dragonoids, and Portia was going in the other direction.

What was the plan, to kill some of the prisoners? Portia shook her head. Focusing on that was not going to help them. She intentionally breathed in deeply several times to calm herself. They had a plan. They were going to work the plan.

"Did you see any dwarves?" Mark asked, pulling her from her thoughts.

"No," answered Portia, frowning at the word. "Did you?"

"A whole mess, and some elves. The dwarves were huddled together, and none too friendly, I must say. But at least they understood common. I made sure of it." Mark adjusted his belt again as he looked around nervously. His linen robe had a long rip on one side, making it difficult to hide his human skin.

"Oh good. Were any of them King Morgani?" Portia asked.

Mark shot her a puzzled look. "I have no idea. I've never met him."

Magisend snickered from behind them. She still limped but was managing to keep pace, if just barely.

That proved Magisend's brain wasn't damaged, Portia thought, not entirely displeased.

The huge wall Portia remembered from the map loomed ahead. It was larger than it seemed from the map. She could open a portal the size of a warship on it.

The buildings across from the wall were equally huge. As they walked to the front of the buildings, Portia glanced up. She thought she saw an arrow tip, but it disappeared into the shadowy darkness of the window.

A wide courtyard filled the space in front of the wall, the ground dusty and yellow. The wall itself was uncommonly plain for the city, utilitarian, as were the buildings around them.

The empty courtyard provided no place to hide. Portia gritted her teeth. They didn't even have shields to protect themselves. If the emperor's mages arrived too quickly, they would be caught out in the open.

But they didn't *all* have to be.

"Stay in the cover of these buildings," Portia said, motioning to the inset entryways of the buildings.

Mark shook his head.

"Don't argue, I need to concentrate. You can help me better keeping an eye out back there," Portia said, not bothering to look back as she walked towards the wall. She heard rather than saw Magisend go to Mark and whisper furiously in his ear.

If only the two of them could do duplicate magic, or some ruse to confuse any attackers, but only Portia could. And she had other magic she had to do.

Squatting down to provide as small a target as possible, Portia concentrated on the magic, on the tune she had to sing. The one she had used in the earlier test in the warehouse district seemed close enough. She hummed it out loud, to remind herself of it, before breaking into the magic song.

The vibration in her chest telling her the magic was working did not come as quickly as it normally did. She'd already worked the spell once that morning, then spent time running and fighting without a rest. Her body was not happy.

Portia clenched her hands and then forced them open again. She'd get a rest when this was over. She'd sleep for a week and chuck anyone who tried to stop her.

That was later. Now she had to coax the magic into being. Reluctantly, it came.

Swirls appeared on the wall in front of her, tenuous as always, growing slowly more solid. Portia focused on the swirls on the edge of the portal, watching it solidify. Watching it come into being.

Then the whistle alarm came from behind her. The sound bounced off the wall, piercing her ears.

Portia jumped. Already. They'd detected the magic, and all too soon they would discover her. Sweat broke out on her brow as she stared at the still translucent portal. Stopping now would be disastrous. The portal would explode. It could kill those for blocks around. Including herself.

No, it needed to be finished. It needed to be open for those depending on her.

She could not shut it again, even if she had the energy to do so.

Portia tucked her head down and put her hands over her head, bracing for impact. Her skin goose bumped in anticipation of the fireball hitting her and enveloping her in flames.

She sang on.

The portal vibrated and hummed in return. It was almost ready.

A blast hit a building a block away. Portia jumped, this time faltering in her song. The portal wobbled, almost like a mirror dancing on a table before toppling over to shatter into a million pieces.

Portia stared up, horrified, almost forgetting to sing. She hiccupped, then quickly started the magic again.

The portal kept wobbling.

She kept singing.

Then, like a petulant child, the portal slowly stopped wobbling and calmed down. Portia sang and sang until her throat felt coated in sandpaper, until her breath was ragged, her head light.

Then it was done.

Portia fell back onto her butt.

The portal shone silvery in the late afternoon sun, standing out against the yellow dirt around them. She'd placed it perhaps too high to easily step into, but she'd toss the prisoners in if she had to.

She turned to look behind her. Then gasped.

Mark and Magisend stood surrounded by an army of Dragonoids, their weapons held high. Portia's heart raced in panic until she noticed the mismatched weapons and the homemade uniforms.

It was the rebel army.

Mark waved furiously for Portia to come away from the wall.

Slowly Portia rose. Every muscle hurt. Even her hips hurt. The blood rushing to her feet was an agony so intense she almost fell again. Stumbling, she ran back away from the wall.

Leaving the portal open and unguarded.

Suddenly, it occurred to Portia that this was a really stupid thing to do. This was exactly what Queen Lorica had warned against—another opening to their world, one that was not guarded on the other side.

No, no, no. Panic pulled at Portia.

Something fell into the courtyard from the building ahead. Portia looked up. Archers stood in every window, their bows pulled back and ready, their arrows trained into the courtyard. Portia breathed a sigh of relief when the arrow tips did not follow her path. They were waiting for the emperor's soldiers.

They did not have to wait long.

The whistle alarm sounded again, closer.

Another fireball flew through the air, hitting the wall further down. It exploded, sending flames splashing out along the wall like spilled lantern oil. Cracks laced the wall where the ball had hit. Broken bits of rock fell down.

Then the soldiers arrived. And kept arriving. What seemed like hundreds of them raced into the streets, filling the courtyard. The rebel army ran out to meet them.

Further down the street, in the crowd of the approaching army, glowing blue staffs bounced along above the soldiers' heads. The emperor's mages were coming. Their fireballs already rained down on the battlefield.

One of the rebel Dragonoids pushed Portia back to the rear of the crowd. He motioned to the building behind her. *"You've done your part, now get out of the way,"* he said.

She shook her head, but he held up one hand. *"Your people need you, no?"* he asked.

Portia nodded dully, finally understanding. She ran back to the building. Mark and Magisend stood halfway in the entryway, casting magic into the battlefield from their spot in the back. Mark threw lights into the eyes of the attackers, Magisend slicking the ground underneath their feet.

At Portia's questioning look, Magisend shrugged. "It's something. Those stupid mages are already here. We might as well help."

Scrambling to think what would work best, Portia came up with duplicates of her and Mark and Magisend. She made the duplicates run into the middle of the battlefield to get the enemy's attention and then run off.

The duplicates wove through the crowded field, dodging the swords and knives of fighting Dragonoids as they went. A knife going through their phantom images would have given away their unrealness. Portia sent the duplicates within a horse length of the emperor's mages. The mages' staffs wavered at the effrontery, then the mages turned and watched incredulously as the duplicate humans ran by, blatantly throwing off magic lights and ice.

Then the mages gave chase.

Soon the emperor's soldiers noticed fireballs no longer

came to their aid. Whether out of fear or anger, or thinking there was a better target, Portia was not sure, they ran after the mages and the duplicates. The rebel army followed the retreating soldiers, wild cheers of victory on their lips.

Portia nearly fainted from the effort. She'd never done so many kinds of magic at once. And never from so far away. The connection to the duplicates felt thin and tenuous as they ran away, but she didn't dare release it just yet.

Scattered fighters remained in the square. The archers above picked off the emperor's soldiers where they could. Soon even the archers within the buildings came out and chased after the rest of the army.

What had been a careful plan was breaking down into citywide chaos.

Now was their chance.

Portia motioned for Mark and Magisend to follow and she ran back to the pens. They didn't dare send up a magic signal overhead for the prisoners so had to run from pen to pen, telling them now was the time. The prisoners didn't have to be told twice, pouring out of the cages.

"Stay with us," Portia yelled, struggling to be heard over the noise of so many moving people.

Portia led them back to the portal, while Mark and Magisend checked the cages and made sure they didn't lose anyone. The crowd of prisoners straggled out into a long line, heightening Portia's anxiety. There were so many of them. How were they going to get them all through?

When they got back to the square, Portia realized that in the mad rush of the battle she hadn't checked the portal. She held out a hand to stop the prisoners, before she turned to face the shimmering oval on the wall.

As always, she tested it with her sword, before sticking in her head to look around. Mild yellow sunlight shone down on waving fields of grains, surrounded by lines of dark green trees. It was the same grasslands she remembered from the first time. The portal did let out somewhere into their world. She pulled her head back out.

Another whistle siren sounded, sending a chill up Portia's spine.

And even if it didn't, staying here had to be worse.

Portia waved the prisoners forward. A shorter woman squinted at Portia and hesitated, reluctant to go through the strangely shimmering mists. A man yelled from behind her.

Not wanting to push the woman and cause her to dig in, Portia waved the man around. He gratefully pushed his way to the front of the crowd. Sensing Portia's problem in getting the crowd through, he turned and yelled to those behind them. "I saw her test it. She's from my kingdom, I recognized the accent. Follow me, or stay here and be slaves on this miserable world—but if you do, get yourselves out of the way of those who want to be free!" He gave a wave and then jumped through the portal, almost dancing on the way.

A cheer came up from behind him. People shoved and pushed their way to the front, making Portia yell to go more slowly so as to not kill anyone. The crowd swelled, shoving the woman who'd been reluctant to go up against Portia. She smiled at Portia apologetically, then looked longingly at the portal.

"Will you go now?" Portia asked her. The woman nodded.

Portia held out an arm, stopped the flow of people and nudging the woman into the line. Once the woman was on her way to the wall, and the gateway to their world, Portia pulled back her arm. The crowd flowed to the wall, rushing to fill the gap Portia had created. Men helped women through. Weaker prisoners leaned on stronger ones. A few even carried those too weak to walk on their own like sacks of flour slung over their shoulders.

Straggling near the end of the line, dwarves and elves came amongst the humans. The dwarves walked as if drugged. The elves could barely walk at all. It wasn't even clear if they could see, for they held on to the tails of the shirts of those in front of them, gingerly stepping so as to not fall down.

Portia directed some of the healthier looking humans to carry the elves. One dark-haired young man scowled at her before bolting for the portal and jumping through, causing those he'd cut in line to yell angry curses. The others, though, did help the elves.

One unusually tall dwarf passed by. Portia nearly mistook him for a human. Her heart leapt when she realized her mistake. She knew one dwarf who'd be very happy to see him.

The dwarf next to him wore an especially fine woolen tunic, the paisley pattern visible even under the dry yellow dirt encrusting it. Portia put a hand on his wrist, stopping him. He paused, then slowly looked around, as if trying to wake from sleepwalking.

"King Morgani," Portia said respectfully.

The dwarf stood perfectly still. If from shock, or lack of understanding, Portia could not tell.

Portia looked around. No soldiers fought nearby, but they could return at any moment. She bit her lip, then turned back to the Dwarven king.

"My apologies, Your Majesty, we shall talk on the other side," Portia said. "Have a safe journey home." She pulled back her hand, giving a respectful bow.

Magisend approached, along with some of the stragglers. Mark came along from a different street, corralling a few prisoners who had panicked and bolted.

They were so close. Just a few more to get through, and then they could go through themselves and shut the portal from the other side. The tight nerves around Portia's chest relaxed just a little. She hadn't realized she was holding her breath until she could breathe again.

Magisend helped the stragglers through, gently holding out her hand for each one as they walked through. For some it was almost a reverent touch, having a noble help a commoner home, for even here, in a strange land, with both commoner and noble alike covered in dirt from their trying times, it was clear who was who. No amount of dirt could hide the finery of Magisend's clothing. No amount of dirt could hide the holes in the rough spun of the commoners. Even here, they gazed at Magisend with something akin to awe.

Portia pulled her eyes away from the strange sight. Something had pricked along her back, a feeling warning her. The square was empty. Perhaps too empty, for not a single archer stood in the windows of the buildings across the way.

Turning to look around to examine the rest of the square, her eyes met Mark's. He, too, looked anxious, shifting from foot to foot, while waiting for those he guarded to get their turn into the portal. He spared Portia only a quick look before his eyes darted around, also searching.

Something fluttered down to the shoulders of the old woman standing at the entrance to the portal. It floated and flipped like a feather, turning in slow motion in the warm afternoon air.

It was a burned piece of parchment. Her stomach sinking, Portia slowly looked up to the top of the wall high above the portal. Glowing blue staffs bounced at the top of the wall, held by someone on the far side, getting higher and higher. A purple linen hood, trimmed in gold, rose above the wall next to one of the staffs.

A rough scaled hand pulled the hood back. Enraged Dragonoid eyes glared down at Portia. The emperor's mage lifted his staff to strike.

17

Portia could feel the anger and rage pouring down from the mage above her, its eyes rimmed in red, its hand holding the blue glowing staff high above to strike.

Time seemed to slow down around her. Even the dust motes hanging in the dry afternoon air moved slowly, glinting yellow gold in the sunlight. The prisoners stepping through the portal moved impossibly slow. Mark opened his mouth to say something but Portia couldn't comprehend over the roaring in her ears, the adrenaline pouring through her veins.

Instinctively, Portia put up both hands to block the mage's strike, raising her sword as she did so and alarming the prisoners around her. One noticed the mage above and screamed. The prisoners pushed and stampeded to the portal, their orderly line gone. Magisend helped shove them through. Mark dropped back to stand with Portia, his arms also up to strike.

A ball of fire formed at the tip of the mage's blue staff,

rolling and glowing, the flames licking in circles as it expanded. The mage held the staff up higher as the ball grew, keeping the fireball from enveloping its head.

A flick of its wrist sent the ball racing towards Portia and Mark.

Still chanting her magic, Portia shut her eyes, bracing for impact, even as she sent out a thin stream of ice, willing it to form into a shield.

Ice magic. It was the most effective of all against fire. It was the hardest for Portia to do in this land. Even Magisend, for whom ice was her specialty, had struggled to form even the thinnest cloud of ice crystals here.

And Portia was tired. She had done more magic this day than ever before. Not even during the battle at sea had she done so much. But there was no other choice. Tears ran out of the corners of Portia's eyes at her exhaustion and her effort.

The ice raced up to the mage, spreading out just as the fireball impacted it. The ice itself disappeared near immediately in hot steams of vapor when the fireball hit it.

But it lasted long enough to stop the fireball's descent, making it explode high in the air above them, blasting out hot air as it disappeared.

The hot vapor sucked away Portia's breath for a moment, sending her hair in wild swirls around her face, but blessedly, it was not hot enough to blister skin.

The prisoners kept moving. One, the corner of his robe ablaze, had thrown off the garment and stomped on it, before giving up and running into the portal dressed only in his under tunic.

Only a few prisoners remained.

Magisend stared at Portia, her eyes wide.

Portia waved her through. Better to have at least Magisend on the other side to fight off any Dragonoid mages who might claw their way into the portal.

Magisend hesitated, looking up at the mages above, and then Portia and Mark.

"Go!" Mark yelled. "Get them all out, then guard from the other side."

Magisend gave a quick nod. She ran and grabbed the last two prisoners by the wrists, pulling them roughly to the portal and then pushing them through. She took one last look at Mark and Portia and then jumped through herself.

Now to get her and Mark out.

Hands shaking, Portia resheathed her sword in the short breath they had before another fireball came.

"No," Mark said under his breath. He looked behind them. Portia followed his eyes and saw three staggering prisoners limping along, clinging to each other. The two on the outside carried a third who appeared to be unconscious.

No no no no no.

"Go get them," Portia said to Mark. Before he could argue, she danced back and yelled up to the mages on the wall high above them, waving her hands furiously.

The angry eyes above glared down at her.

"*Tell me I can't do magic, eh?*" Portia called up. "*Just because you do as you are told like good little pets doesn't mean I have to.*" She sent light motes up towards the mage, more to infuriate them than do any real harm.

At least five blue staffs raised in response. The mages above crowded around, focused on Portia.

It was an intimidating sight. Not only were they huge, but their magic was impressive and fast and hot. And they hated her.

Portia pulled a knife from her ankle holster. Focusing on the lead Dragonoid's eyes, she threw the blade. It whistled end over end to its target.

The Dragonoid flinched, lightning fast reflexes.

Instead of the blade striking home in a soft eye, it skittered over the rough scalp of the Dragonoid. A few scales flew into the air.

Portia held her breath.

Enraged at her daring, the Dragonoid raised his blue staff to strike her. Except now the staff was just a dull black stick, the blue glow gone. The Dragonoid didn't notice until it flicked its wrist and nothing came down upon Portia's head.

The mage looked up at the dead staff. It shot Portia a look of pure rage, raising the staff to throw at her. Someone behind him pulled him back before he let loose. The other mages pushed to the front of the wall.

Seeing his chance, Mark ran to the prisoners and dragged them to the portal. Portia didn't dare glance, only seeing from the corner of her eye.

Not wanting to lose all her knives up the wall, Portia focused the light motes in swirls around the other Dragonoids' heads, trying to distract their concentration as the fireballs grew. She pulled her other ankle knife but held it in reserve, for when a really dire moment came.

Except now felt dire. Five fireballs hung in the air above her, growing steadily stronger.

Five

She'd barely been able to stave off one.

Mark better not look up and do something stupid, was all she could think.

Mark and the prisoners got to the portal. The two walking prisoners and Mark lifted the unconscious one and pushed him over the edge of the portal.

One of the prisoners, a tall scraggly one with rags tied on his feet for shoes, dressed in a torn tunic, looked up. He saw the mages, then glanced back at Portia. Suddenly, the prisoner stepped back behind Mark and the other standing prisoner and shoved them both through the portal, sending them head over feet into the swirling mists.

A moment later, the square was filled with Portias. She gasped. Everywhere she looked there was a duplicate of her. She had not done this. Making eye contact with the prisoner, she realized they had come from him.

Quickly thinking, she stopped the light magic and made duplicates of the prisoner, as many as she could manage. The square was filled with them, just as earlier in the day had been filled with soldiers and guards. She sent the prisoner duplicates running, scrambling here and there. The prisoner followed suit, sending the Portias everywhere.

Howls of rage came from the wall above. The mages looked down at the chaos below them. Fireballs flew down the wall, thrown seemingly at random to hit the figures below.

She didn't dare run forward into the portal just a few

lengths away. The fire was raining too heavy and thick directly in front of it. The prisoner himself had long since fled from it, racing away from the flames and heat.

Portia stepped back reluctantly, still considering dashing through the wall of fire, but her courage ran out when the scalding air washed over her. Her skin felt as if it was crackling, the pain unbearable. Her robe smoked from the heat.

Retreating, Portia ran back to the buildings across the square.

Hiding in the entryway, out of direct sight of the mages above, she felt for the portal with her magic. It answered her touch, vibrating in her chest. Even from this distance she could affect it magically.

The safest thing she could do for her world was to close the portal now.

At least the guards stood by the other portal to the Dragonoid world. This one had nothing on the other side to stop the invaders from pouring back through except Mark and Magisend.

Her heart stopped a beat at the thought of closing the portal with Mark on the other side. No, he had Magisend. Besides, he had to guide the prisoners home. He'd be fine.

And she'd be fine, too. She'd find a way back. She'd done it before.

Pushing all other thoughts away, Portia concentrated on closing the portal.

The fireballs exploding in the dirt of the square faded away. The yells faded to silence. The world tunneled down to just her and the portal.

Closing her eyes, she willed it to close.

To heal.

To be done.

It hummed resistance, though not so strongly as the others had. Then something snapped inside of the portal, and inside her. It felt right, but also shockingly fast.

Portia opened her eyes. The wall ahead of her held only smooth brick, cracking under the current barrage of weaponry.

The portal was gone. She exhaled heavily, half victorious, a half cry of despair.

Footsteps entering the alcove startled her. She looked up into a familiar face.

"Peter," Portia said.

The prisoner in the torn tunic nodded. He held out a hand. "Portia."

THEY RAN through the sewer system, their feet kicking up water in the dim cool tiled tunnel, the battle far behind them.

The duplicates would fade away without them continuing to pour magic into them, but they should last long enough for Portia and the prisoner to get away.

Not the prisoner. Peter. The Black Cat gang member she never thought to see again.

Her breath ragged, Portia stopped running, bent over panting. Peter stopped as well. He sounded even worse than she did.

"Why?" Portia asked between gasps.

Peter glanced down the tunnel behind them. One of the rags he used for shoes had unwound, flopping soaking wet behind him. He stooped over, grabbed the loose material, squeezed the water out and wrapped it around his foot again, tying it tightly.

"Why?" Portia asked again.

Peter sighed. "Why what?" He stared back the way they'd come.

"Whatever that was." Portia waved back the way they'd come. "Because you almost killed me once. It would have been so easy for you to walk through that portal and not look back." Portia straightened up, the burning in her lungs eased. She wanted to grab him and force him to look at her. Instead, she stretched her neck and back.

"Easy in the moment, yes. And then I'd have the rest of my life to think about it. I've done that once." Peter tried to sound casual.

"Once? Is that all?" Portia was not going to let him off that easy.

He glanced into her eyes, then quickly away again. "Right. Maybe more than once."

After an awkward silence, they started walking again.

Portia wasn't sure, but she thought they were going towards the city gates. If they could just get out of the wretched place, they'd have a chance of making it back to the one portal still open a week's journey away. She wouldn't have to invoke any magic to create what was already done.

Even in the sewers, the sounds of battle above filtered

down. The fighting seemed to be citywide. The explosions that morning, and the battle in the square, were just the beginning. When fleeing the mages in the square, they'd passed several businesses under attack, looters running out with goods, before they dropped down through an open grate to escape the chaos.

They'd encountered no rebels underground. They must be all above, fighting.

Portia's boots made solid slaps on the tunnel floor, while the sounds of Peter's footsteps were much softer. She wondered if his feet hurt from only having rags to protect them.

He didn't complain.

Peter cleared his throat. "I felt bad over what happened. It grew worse over time. Someone even worse than Deyelna tried to take over the gang. Did take over the gang. Nothing good came of it." He kicked at the water, then grabbed the wrap around his foot and tucked it in tighter.

"Came of what?" Portia asked, confused.

"Just going along with whoever was in charge. I promised myself in that stupid cage back there, if I ever got out, I'd live a better life," said Peter. "Today apparently was the day."

Portia laughed despite herself. "Lucky me to get to see it."

Peter laughed himself in a soft self-deprecating way. "I guess."

She knew she'd hate admitting it less than not thanking him. Barely less. "No, really, your magic helped a lot."

Her face flushed from the admission, a stark contrast to the chills she felt everywhere else from the cold breeze blowing through her sweat-soaked robes. Nothing felt comfortable.

"It's so hard to do magic here," Peter said.

"You mean you never tried before?" Portia asked, incredulous. "I'd think it'd be the first thing you'd do to escape."

"I tried. Once, and got beat soundly for it. And then a terrifying mage made it clear if I did it again I'd be burned alive, starting at my feet so my head could watch and feel," Peter said. He rubbed his shoulders and gave a shake, as if banishing the memory.

Portia stepped in front of Peter and stopped. "Wait, you understand their language?" Portia asked. He reluctantly stopped, looking back is if they would be immediately overtaken.

"They found a way to make me understand. Well enough." Peter rubbed his arm as if it hurt.

It was a story Portia didn't want to hear just then. She stepped out of his way. They continued walking on, not speaking, listening to the dim sounds of battle above.

Was she an idiot for continuing on here with Peter? Portia snuck a glance. He looked the same as he had back in the gang. Tall, thin, beautiful in a dangerous, aloof way. It had always seemed smarter to keep her distance, especially since he'd been such a favorite of Deyelna's. A voice in the back of her mind said run, leave him there to die.

Except he'd helped her.

Maybe Mark's help would have been enough to fight off the mages, but she'd never know because Peter shoved him through the portal.

This guy was making her more nervous than the Dragonoid fighters. At least she knew what they wanted, and whose side they were on. It took all her efforts to keep her hands from checking her weapons over and over again. He'd notice that.

"Now what?" Peter asked.

This was a question she was used to getting from Magisend. The thought of the tiny girl with the dark hair gave Portia's heart a start. Hopefully Magisend was all right.

Suddenly she really missed the school and all her friends there.

That seemed a lifetime ago. Would she ever get back?

The school. That was the last place she'd seen Peter.

"Wait, how did you get back to the gang in Valencia?" Portia asked, stepping in front of Peter yet again and forcing him to stop with a hand on his chest. She couldn't keep the accusation out of her voice and hated it. It sounded so weak. But the last time she'd seen Peter the school guards had him in custody for nearly killing her. Surely the queen wouldn't just let him go.

Peter smirked at her in the darkness. "Even for all my faults, I am still a *good* thief. Sometimes what you steal away is yourself."

IN A STROKE OF LUCK, or the effect of the rebellion, no guards stood at the gates to the city. One half of the wide iron-barred gate stood shut, and the other half only partially closed, as if the guards had tried to shut them before being drawn away.

No wagons or horses stood in the yellow stone courtyard just inside the gate, where normally the guards inspected every vehicle.

Portia's scalp tingled. This felt too easy, like a trap.

A scream came from behind them. High-pitched, nearly high enough to be human, but it curled up at the end in a tone no human could reach. A Dragonoid scream.

Looking back, Portia adjusted her robes. They covered her skin completely.

Peter had no such garment.

They stood hiding just behind a building close to the gate. Out of view of the guards, if there had been any.

"Wait here," Portia said to Peter, then walked off before he could object.

She ran to the guard house attached to the gate. Like the gate, the door stood half open. Listening at the door, she heard nothing. She peered inside. A pitcher and cups rested on a large table that took up most of the room. One of the cups laid on its side, its contents dripping onto the floor. No candles burned against the coming evening darkness.

Peter watched her disappear inside the structure, then appear a moment later with a large bundle.

She ran back to him.

"Here, put this on," she said. He stared at her, uncomprehending. Nerves shot from exhaustion, she didn't bother trying to explain, just grabbed a robe from the pile of goods at her feet and threw it over his head and belted it around his middle before he could get a protest out.

Enormous boots followed. She tied the tops of the boots tightly with strips of material torn from the bottom of the too big robe, making them look like enormous leather bags on his feet.

Ridiculous.

But effective.

Peter grunted as he looked down at himself.

"Don't thank me. I'm not going to get caught because of something so stupid as you not being dressed right," Portia said. "Now let's get out of here."

Peter followed her across the center of the courtyard and directly out of the city. The cool evening air washed over them both as the sun set into deep oranges and purples in the high mountain air.

———

THE DAY HAD COOLED PLEASANTLY AS the sun set over the little grove of tall yellow trees and thick gray-green bushes. Portia finished the remains of some berries and picked at the last of the cheese she'd stolen from the guardhouse. The soldiers had been well fed, apparently, at least compared to Portia.

A small fire now smoldered as mere coals in the center of the clearing. They'd risked a fire since they'd not seen anyone else for days. After the initial rush of fleeing vehicles, there had been no one sharing the road with them. Apparently few had walked out of the capital after the rebellion.

Once down the steep mountain the road passed through lands with sparse patches of trees and brush. Judging by the old charred smears on the ground in the tiny clearing, they had not been the first to take shelter there.

Peter waved away her offer of the dry white crumbly substance. "I hope to never eat that again. Ever."

"It's a few more days until the portal," Portia warned.

"We've done okay so far. This land isn't completely barren." Peter pulled the end of a small bone he'd been chewing out of his mouth and tossed it into the fire, meeting her eyes over the glowing remains. He stared.

"What?" Portia said, turning away from him.

"Nothing," Peter said, not looking away.

She threw a rock into the fire, sending the glowing embers scattering in Peter's direction. He calmly brushed off his robes. In the chill of the night, they were both tightly wrapped in their clothes. The heat of the day fled surprisingly fast once the sun went below the horizon.

"You're something special now, aren't you?" Peter said. It didn't sound like a question.

"What do you mean by that?" Portia shifted again on the ground, looking for something to lean against. All the trees were too far from the remaining heat of the fire.

"I mean, *the queen* cared about what happened to you," Peter said.

"Why didn't you?" Portia asked, blurting the question out

and immediately regretting it. It sounded pathetic to even care what Peter thought.

At least it got him to look away.

Portia's breath sounded loudly in her ears.

The embers in the fire pit glowed a deep red with a passing breeze, then cooled back down to near black.

"It's not that I didn't care," Peter said finally. He picked at something on the leg of his robe as he stretched out on his side. "I was just being practical. I figured you'd find a way to get along with her, eventually. I didn't think she'd really go that far."

"No?" Portia said. "Even after she had you hunt me down?" She threw another rock. This one bounced a coal out of the pit that flicked up and landed on Peter's arm.

He flicked it off quickly, shooting her a look.

"Oh dear, did that hit you. I'm sorry," Portia said. She tried to be sarcastic, but it just came out as angry. "I care too. About you getting hurt, I mean, but I'm just being practical."

"What's your problem?" Peter asked. His brows furrowed as he glared at her.

"What's my problem? *You* tried to kill me," Portia said. It took a lot of effort not to yell.

"Not recently. Besides, it wasn't really me, it was Deyelna. You've done so well, why do you care about me? Didn't my help mean anything at all?" Peter asked.

"No. Yes. I don't know," Portia answered, flustered, and even angrier that he got her flustered.

Not recently? Did it matter how long ago someone tried to kill you?

"You found a place now," Peter said. "I have nothing."

Portia's mouth fell open. "Am I supposed to feel bad for you?"

"No. Just appreciate what you have. Don't run away again."

Portia threw another rock, this time directly at Peter. It hit his chest, hard, drawing a grunt from him. Holding a hand to his heart, he looked down at his chest, then back up at her, hurt in his eyes. More hurt than that rock had earned.

She had to look away.

***

THEY CLIMBED the steep hill leading to the portal under a low crescent moon. The extra leather on Peter's loose shoes kept getting caught in the shallow roots clinging to the hillside, tripping him to his knees, sending loose dirt and rocks bounding down the slope behind him. Portia had learned to keep some distance behind him and to avert her eyes the moment he slipped to keep the rocks from hitting her face. It would've been better to be ahead, above the debris he sent down the hillside, but he had insisted on going first in case there was any danger.

Portia had been too annoyed to argue, merely snorted and let him go. She didn't remind him who was rescuing who from that world.

The floral fragrance Portia remembered from the last time on that hillside hung in the air. The thin yellow tree waved above at the crest of the hill.

The dwarves could take care of themselves, Portia firmly told herself as they climbed. The day had been a long agony of wondering if those back in her world needed them. If the Dragonoids had found the portal.

Wondering and dreading what they would find when they topped the hill.

She'd wanted to get to the portal earlier, but caution dictated they wait. They had even scouted the back side of the hill earlier that morning to see if another hidden route was possible and found the back of the hill impossibly steep for as far as they could see. Unclimbable for two humans.

No, the only approach was from the front, facing the city below. So they'd settled in to wait for half a long hot day in the scrub just within sight of the walled city. There was no sense going in daylight and helping their enemy to spot them climbing the steep hill if the Dragonoids had by chance found the magic hiding the portal, or the portal itself.

Finally, they reached the top. Peter stood at the edge, panting, until Portia caught up to him. She grabbed his ankle and tugged. He looked down. She motioned him down. Realization crossed his face, and he squatted quickly, no longer a silhouette against the night sky above.

Staying low to the ground, they ran away from the edge of the hill to where the trees thickened ahead. It was still insufficient cover, but better than the low scraggly growth behind them.

Portia ran ahead. When Peter started to object, she turned around with one finger to her lips, hushing him. Annoyance crossed his face, but he stopped talking.

The trees waved gently in the night breeze, the leaves high above creating moving shadows on the ground.

Squinting, Portia examined a line of trees until she found what she was looking for, a thin cut in the soft wood above her head. Checking the trees around, she found the second one. That was enough to know which direction to go.

They followed the line of cuts Portia had left when leaving the portal the first time.

The hillock, covered with the debris and low thorny bushes, looked just the same as when Portia had left it with Mark and Magisend.

There were no guards. Were there supposed to be guards? The dwarves had left some the first time they had gone exploring. She hissed in exasperation at herself, and at Kerat and Vermeil for not discussing this.

Creeping up to where the magical illusion began, Portia slowly leaned in, keeping her body low to the ground, and not at the height anyone would expect of someone walking into the magic. As she pressed forward, the illusion faded to nothing, leaving the shimmering portal ahead of her. It seemed to glow with its own light, competing with the moonlight above.

Breathing a sigh of relief, she leaned back out and motioned for Peter to join her. He too crouched and moved forward slowly, imitating Portia. Once inside, he saw the deserted portal. He exhaled and stood, straightening his clothes as if getting ready to enter a party, then stepped forward to enter the portal.

Hissing in fright, Portia tackled his legs, toppling the tall boy. They fell in a tumble of arms and legs just shy of the portal entrance. Portia tried to pull him back, yanking at his robe, but he was too heavy and all that happened was the robe started to slip over his head. He yanked it back.

"What are you doing?" he said, his voice a low hiss of frustration and confusion.

"You can't just enter," Portia said.

He looked at the portal, then back at Portia. The oval of swirling mists looked just like the portal she'd closed in the capital city.

He started to stand, but she grabbed the back of his robe and yanked sharply, pulling him off-balance to land on his rear next to her.

"Come over here, and watch," Portia said. She scooted off to one side of the portal. Annoyed, Peter joined her.

Portia grabbed a rock and threw it inside the oval of swirling mists.

A second later, a cloud of arrows poured out of the mists, spreading in a wide fan, the closest arrow landing at the dirt by Peter's foot. He danced back. "What the blasted thing is this?" he asked, his eyes wide. He moved behind Portia, putting her between him and the opening. "Have the Dragonoids invaded?"

Portia looked back at him, barely hiding her annoyance. "I don't know. But whoever is on the other side is a little anxious about someone coming through."

18

Portia quickly grabbed the nearest arrow, feeling the smooth wood under her fingers as she pulled it from the loose dirt. She sat back, away from the spray of arrows, trying to get behind the portal so no angle of attack could reach her.

The flint arrowhead was carved wide and notched wickedly on either edge. If it had struck either one of them, it would have lodged firmly within their flesh and been nearly impossible to remove without a great deal of cutting or tearing.

If the bolt hadn't gone through them entirely.

Portia shivered.

The fletch of the arrow shimmered in the moonlight. Dark feathers set deeply into notches in the wood. They looked like crow feathers. Did they have crows in the Dragonoid land? She thought of the strange looking horses they'd seen. Perhaps there were similarly distorted crows flying around.

But she'd seen none. Adrenaline made it difficult to think as she tried to remember if she'd seen any birds at all.

At least it wasn't a metal ball, or any of the black powder magic the Dragonoids possessed, so that at least was hopeful. If something like that had come shooting out of the portal, they'd known for sure the Dragonoids were within.

Portia sighed, exhausted. It'd be so much simpler if she could just poke her head inside and look around. They were so close to getting home.

There was to be some signal from the outside to alert the dwarves within but she couldn't remember hearing of the final decision. Mark would have known, but he was not there.

Looking down at her own garments, bag, and sword, she saw nothing she could bear to part with, nothing to send through as a signal to those waiting inside. If the Dragonoids had invaded, throwing in one of her precious knives and losing it to whomever was within would be stupidity itself.

She leaned forward, her head in her hands, her hair falling down to hide her face. She stared unseeing as she scrambled for an idea.

"Now what?" Peter asked.

Portia was beginning to hate that question.

"Go grab a thick stick," Portia said, waving to the direction behind the portal, safely out of the range of anything that might come flying out of it.

"A what?" Peter asked.

"A stick. A stick! Just go get a big stick and don't argue with me," Portia said.

Peter backed up, his hands held up. "Whoa. No problem."

He returned a moment later with a dried branch half the thickness of one of the tall yellow trees. Portia pulled her sword and with three cuts chopped off a section as long as her forearm and notched a shallow cut in the middle of it, identical to the markings she had left in the trees. Grabbing a length of her hair with her left hand, she used the tip of her sword to slice it off near the root. She tied the hair tightly to the stick, knotting it twice.

It was a strange bundle of wood and hair.

"What are you doing?" Peter asked, staring at Portia's creation.

"I don't know. Sending a calling card. Seeing who recognizes it, if anyone."

She scrambled to her feet, then edged forward to the face of the splinter, carefully keeping out of the angle the arrows had gone. Whipping the stick forward, she risked swinging her arm out and forward towards the portal, sending the stick catapulting end over end towards the swirling mists. It disappeared inside. She quickly backed away in case another volley of weapons came out at them.

But nothing did.

The moments ticked by. She sat, trying to be patient. The moonlight, the shifting shadows in the breeze, and Peter's labored breathing coming from behind her filled her senses as she waited for something, some signal, from those on the other side of the portal.

High-pitched chittering made Portia jump. It was so unexpected she didn't know what it was at first. Turning to the portal, she saw a tiny little furry face looking at her, and yelling in its chittering way.

Even Portia could understand it was saying hurry up and get inside, now.

The furry face disappeared back in the swirling mists.

Portia blinked and shook her head. Had she really seen that? Had it really happened? She looked back up at Peter, who was standing behind her. He was staring at the portal, his jaw hanging open.

If it was a vision, he'd seen it too.

The face reappeared at the portal, then the tiny creature ran out completely, bouncing over in a strange run to Portia's leg and then biting her soundly on the thigh.

"Ouch!" Portia said, getting to her feet and away from the feisty animal.

The tiny creature ran at Peter, who yelped, and ran away.

The creature wasn't having it. It ran faster than Peter, blocking his every escape, until finally it had corralled him to the portal, picking up Portia on the way.

Portia laughed. "I recognize this one. I think we're safe to go inside," she said.

"We're certainly not safe to stay," Peter said, aggrieved.

Portia nodded at that and then walked to the portal and stepped through. She thought to grab Peter on the way, but the last thing she heard was a high-pitched yelp from him as the creature must have nipped his ankle. He was a step behind her entering the portal.

An array of impressive weapons pointed directly at them, from massive arrow shooters, holding dozens of arrows at once, to catapults loaded with boulders, notched and ready to shoot. A line of sword-bearing dwarves stood at the front, their gleaming blades drawn and ready.

Portia had never seen such a beautiful sight in her life. They were back in Morgani.

———

PORTIA AND PETER sat at the table in the common room. Portia's eyelids kept drooping shut, the low candlelight and the warmth of the room nearly lulling her to sleep, especially after the hour-long hot bath the dwarves had kindly drawn for her.

The remains of several roasted birds, hearty brown bread, and roasted beets sat in the dishes on the table. The dwarves had brought enough to feed twenty people, or so it seemed. The maids had struggled under the huge wooden tray of dishes, laying everything out and covering most of the huge table with steaming piles of food, all while stealing covert glances at Peter and Portia before running off. Portia wondered at the riches spread out before them. There were even several bottles of wine. The dwarves they had seen in the cavern and in the caves looked as thin as ever. Peter did not hesitate. He grabbed a wing of one of the birds, tore it off and took a bite before he'd even sat down. Portia lost count of how many times he refilled his plate, eating just as fast as he could. At one point he stopped, looked white, and belched alarmingly.

"Might want to slow down. When was the last time you

had enough to eat?" Portia asked.

He glared at her, then stuffed a bird leg into his mouth, barely able to chew over the enormous bite. "Shut up. I've been dreaming about this for months." Another belch followed, then a hiccup. Portia stood, went behind Peter and thumped him soundly on the back. After a few choked noises, he breathed easier. Then took another bite. Portia sighed, sat back down.

Footsteps thumped down the hall, coming furiously.

Archmage Vermeil rounded the doorway, nearly colliding with the guard outside in his haste. "You closed the splinter," he said to Portia, his words an angry accusation. His hands clenched and unclenched.

Portia looked up, surprised. "Nice to see you again, too. I'm happy to be back safe."

Vermeil waved her greeting away. "The splinter. Why did you close it? We need that."

"Why?" Portia asked, staring at him calmly. She crossed her arms over her chest.

"Because... because... because..." he stammered.

"Would it be because you want to go and get the weapons your king and father tried to get?" Portia said, drawling out the words.

Archmage Vermeil's mouth opened and closed. He stammered, looked back as if for someone to give him a good reason to use as an argument, then, having found no one, back at Portia again. "Maybe," he finally said, crossing his own arms to glare at Portia.

"Yeah, I'm going to have to say no to that," Portia said.

Peter coughed, nearly spitting out his food. Portia turned slightly and thumped him on the back without breaking eye contact with Vermeil.

Vermeil turned an interesting shade of red, then almost purple, his eyes bulging. Portia had no idea dwarves could do that with their faces.

"How dare you? Who said you could do such a thing?" Vermeil asked, his voice rising to near hysteria.

"My abilities," said Portia. "Now, please calm down. You're upsetting the guard."

Vermeil looked at her, confused enough by her comment to stop talking.

Portia flicked her head back at the guard by the door. Vermeil looked in the direction of her motion. The guard stood in the doorway, his feet wide and sword ready, tense and glancing anxiously between Portia and Vermeil.

Who exactly would the guard strike if a fight broke out, Portia wondered. Probably her, unfortunately, even if she had brought back his king.

Portia patted the spot next to her on the bench, giving Vermeil her best effort at a warm smile.

He controlled himself with visible effort, his shoulders slowly dropping, and his hands opening. He breathed in deeply several times, then looked down and walked over to sit next to Portia. "You shouldn't have done that," he said, unable to let it go.

"I disagree," said Portia. "But it doesn't matter now, it's done. I'll not be opening another one unless..."

Vermeil looked at her hopefully. "Unless?"

Portia shook her head. "Not what you think. What were the words of your queen? We have some conditions. Well, I have some conditions, too. For my people. And your people. I've had a week to think about this."

Vermeil looked away, the tension returning to his shoulders.

"Easy," Portia said softly, reminding him of the guard still standing in the doorway, watching them intently. Vermeil nodded once without looking at her, his shoulders once again slowly lowering.

Turning to the table behind her, Portia pulled an empty glass towards herself and grabbed the bottle of wine. There was still enough for a mostly full cup. She poured it and gave it to Vermeil. He took it, meeting her gaze, then downed the wine in one gulp, putting the cup down behind him with a solid thump.

"How is your father?" Portia asked, keeping her tone light.

"He is well. Weak. But well," Vermeil said.

"And the king?" Portia asked.

"Better, as well. Have you not spoken to him yet?" Vermeil asked.

Portia shook her head. "We were told tomorrow, after we had rested and eaten. I think he had something to do with the amount of food we got."

Vermeil glanced at the table behind her, seeing the huge serving platters. A smile crossed his face, then quickly disappeared, as if he was remembering he was mad at Portia. "I'd say so."

Peter, his mouth full of food, and a wing held up, ready to

be consumed as soon as there was room in his mouth, stared at Vermeil. "Hey, wasn't your father the head magic guy? Does that mean now that he's back, you're demoted."

Vermeil stared at Peter with an expression of horror, and shock, and something else Portia couldn't name. She put a hand up to her mouth to hide the laughter that wanted to come out. She'd never seen the mage so flustered, even at his most irate at her.

"That's not how it works," Vermeil said, spluttering out the words.

Peter stared back at him, unperturbed, taking another enormous bite. "Then how does it work?" he asked, nearly unintelligible around the mouth full of food.

For the second time, Vermeil's mouth opened and then closed and opened and closed like a fish.

"Maybe we can talk about this tomorrow," Portia said, trying to smooth things over.

"Exactly," Vermeil said. "It's complicated. And you're tired. I'm sure you'd understand better in the morning."

Peter opened his mouth to argue again, disgustingly full of food, but Portia cut him off. "Tomorrow sounds good."

Peter shrugged his shoulders, pulled the plate of beets closer, stabbing a fork directly into the pile of thick red slices left on the serving platter, and shoved them into his mouth.

"Wake up, sleepyhead," said a voice drifting down into the dark warmth of Portia's dreams. Portia tried to ignore it, enjoying the dream of a feast in a brilliant sunny meadow. Snuggling deeper into the blankets, Portia smiled in her sleep.

Tiny hands shoved at her harshly, moving Portia's entire body, ruining the remnants of her dream the unpleasant intrusion of consciousness. Portia groaned as the dream of beautiful food, and even more beautiful people as company, slipped away.

Where were these interruptions when she was having nightmares?

Portia fended off the hands, opened her eyes, and blinked slowly, trying to figure out where she was. She'd sunk deeply into the rush pallet in a four-poster wooden bed, in the corner of a dim room. Heavy wool and linen blankets covered her, adding to the feeling of being in a deep nest. The only light came from the doorway which was currently mostly blocked by several people she could only see as shadowy outlines.

She focused on the face closest to her, partially covered by a swoop of dark straight hair.

Magisend.

"What?" Portia said, now grumpy at the unexpected company. She sat up.

"Aren't you happy to see me?" Magisend said, her voice sickly sweet. She placed her hands on her hips.

Portia rubbed her face. "Sure. Why not? Did you have to wake me for that?"

The laugh came from the back of the room. "Do you know how long you've been sleeping for?" Mark said. He came forward, pushing his way between people to stand next to Magisend and smirk down at Portia.

"Not long enough, apparently," Portia said, scowling at how closely Mark and Magisend stood.

"For near two days," Mark said. "We didn't know what we'd find when we finally got here, but sleeping beauty wasn't on the list."

Portia crossed her arms. She felt trapped in the bed. Being woken up was a poor experience on a good day. Being woken up by Magisend meant it wasn't a good day.

She focused on the other faces around her, and her irritation faded to amazement. Ella, Mia, Richard, and Liam were all there. Ella gave her a little wave, while Mia nodded. Richard and Liam were too busy examining the room to actually pay Portia much attention.

Was she still in Morgani, the Dwarven kingdom? Her heart started racing in a panic. Did something happen she couldn't remember?

Her alarm must have shown on her face, for Mark's expression changed. "Mayhaps we shouldn't have woken you," Mark said, his tone gentle this time. "You'll forgive us for being excited to see you, won't you?"

"Yes," Portia said tentatively. She looked around. "Are... we're in Morgani, right?"

Magisend laughed her pretty delicate laugh. "Yes, you underachiever, you're still here, while we have crossed the lands and back."

Confused, Portia stared at Magisend.

"Perhaps we could catch up over breakfast," Mark said.

MARK PULLED a sticky roll from a pan of now cold pastries, the sugary topping breaking and crumbling over his fingers. He made eye contact with Portia and gave her a wink.

They were in the common room given to them by the dwarves. Portia stared down at her clothing. Not only had it been washed, it had been pressed into sharp creases. It hadn't looked so good since the day long ago when she first got the outfit in Holne.

Richard and Liam sat next to each other, whispering furiously. Liam's hair was an unlikely shade of purple fading into white, flipped over to one side and hiding one eye rakishly. His outfit was different shades of purple to match. Richard, as ever, wore his hair dark and plain, though his face was clean shaved this time, exposing an impressively sharp jawline. He wore dark black leather, surprising Portia by looking almost regal. Both of them looked years older, something Portia could not understand. It had only been a month since she'd seen them last. Richard even looked ages older than Mark, who sat on the same bench as the twins, with Magisend on his other side.

Portia, Ella, and Mia sat across the table from them. Ella was also dressed in finery Portia had never seen before, diaphanous blue silks over fine cream linen. Looking down at the wondrous materials of Ella's outfit, Portia restrained herself from touching. Roommates or not, Ella might think that was too much. Even quiet Mia had an outfit in shades of fiery red that matched her hair, making her look like a living embodiment of a slender, and rather pretty, bonfire.

Unlike her normal sunny smiles, Ella had a strange sour

look on her face. She kept glancing at Magisend. Mia seemed oblivious to everything except for Portia's words. At least Portia could count on the tiny noble to pay attention.

Portia picked at the eggs on her plate, tiny little spotted shells cut in half after being soft-boiled, arrayed on a bed of fresh greens. The greens alone were a preciously rare commodity in this underground kingdom. The luxurious meals reassured Portia of the kingdom's continued support, despite not seeing either royal since their return. None of the visiting students had met with the royals either.

"I don't understand," Portia said. "How did you get everybody," she motioned to those at the table, "and get back here so quickly?"

"It wasn't all that quick," Magisend said. "You've just been lazy." Her soft tone belayed the taunting words. "Vermeil's father, King Morgani, and the rest had barely a word for us. Once through the portal, and assured of where they were, the dwarves took off near running for Morgani. Apparently they have far better sense of direction than us mere mortals. We wasted a bit of time getting our bearings." Magisend grimaced at the memory.

"Besides, we had to escort the captives back. Most were in pretty bad shape. Some of them might not have made it, or even figured out where they were," said Mark. He chewed on the roll while eyeing more leftovers further down the table. Everyone else had finished eating.

"There are lots of grateful people in the kingdom for your work," Mia said to Portia, giving rare praise. "I don't think I've ever seen anyone cry as much as Magisend's nurse's family when she was returned."

Magisend's what?

Portia turned to stare at Magisend, who was glaring at Mia. Mia jumped back, clutching at her knee under the table.

"You want to die?" Magisend said to Mia, her black eyes burning. From calm to angry in a breath.

"That woman was your nurse?" Portia said, stuck on Mia's word, incredulous. "The one you rescued. You mean she was a commoner? You went to a strange land and risked your life over a *lowly commoner?*"

Magisend slowly turned her gaze to Portia. If looks could kill, Portia would have been grilled alive over a bonfire.

Portia couldn't stop herself. "Commoner?" She drawled out slowly in an imitation of the way Magisend talked to her all those times.

Mark put a hand over his mouth, stifling a laugh.

"You're gonna die too," said Magisend. She rose, a butter knife in her hand, but Mark quickly put an arm around her and whispered in her ear, drawing her back down to the seat. Magisend pulled away from Mark's embrace and then glared at him, then back to Portia. "Maybe not right now, but you're going to die."

The rest watched the exchange with wide eyes. Portia didn't know why they were so surprised. Surely they'd all heard Magisend taunt her. Of course Portia wouldn't let this go, not when she had a chance to finally return the favor to the girl who'd made her so miserable for being a commoner.

Even though Portia wasn't actually a commoner.

Not that it should matter.

Magisend breathed heavily, looked around at all the staring faces. It looked like she would either start crying or yelling—her face twisted in an awkward expression Portia could not recall ever seeing before. Mark rubbed Magisend's back, his laughter gone, replaced by a look of concern for her.

Why did that make Portia feel jealous?

And Ella, too, apparently. Ella's mouth hung open as she stared at Mark and Magisend. Portia nudged Ella under the table with her foot. Ella looked at Portia, who motioned closing her own mouth. Ella shut her mouth, then looked away, annoyed.

A moment of awkward silence hung over the table. Portia felt uncomfortable, both with Mark's concern, and how much she had managed to upset Magisend. It had seemed like such fun to tease the girl, but now it left her stomach queasy. It was so much easier when Magisend was an imperturbable bastion of meanness.

It felt strange to actually worry about her feelings.

Portia rubbed her hands briskly, then clapped them, getting everyone's attention. "Okay, so that explains how the archmage and King Morgani got back here so quickly, but why did you bring everyone else—"

"Hey, what's this? You ate without me?" Peter said from the doorway, staring at Portia. Instead of the dirty rags she'd seen him in last, he was dressed in fine burgundy linens, custom-made for his tall, narrow body since none of the dwarves could wear anything close to that, except perhaps the unusually tall Archmage Vermeil. His hair, now clean and combed, shone in the candlelight, his face shaved and clean. He looked almost handsome. He *was* handsome. Portia was appalled at herself for even thinking it.

His gaze shifted to the rest of the people, stopping at Mark. Peter stood straighter, while Mark stiffened.

"Hello, Mark," said Peter. "Glad you made it okay."

"Made it okay?" Mark asked, momentarily confused. He looked Peter up and down, then nodded in recognition. "That was you. The ungrateful one that shoved me through the portal."

"I was just helping," said Peter. "Ask Portia."

Mark's eyes turned to Portia. She squirmed in her seat. "Yes, well, he did help, a lot. Actually."

This got everyone's attention.

"Seems there is a lot of catching up we need to do. I want to hear all about this," Liam said, a twinkle in his eye.

Even Mia and Richard, the quiet ones in the group, leaned in to hear more.

Portia groaned. She did not relish having all eyes on her, unlike Ella or Liam who loved all the social attention they could get.

"Besides, you could have still come back and fought with us," Peter said, entering the room and sitting down next to Portia. He grabbed the tray of rolls from in front of Mark and pulled it to himself, grabbing one of the soft rolls and shoving it in his mouth. He chewed while staring at Mark.

Red-faced, Mark glared back at Peter. "I was only there for a moment, waiting for her to run through so we could defend it from the far side, where our magic worked better. And then it suddenly closed. There was nothing I could do."

"I don't remember it being that quick while we were fighting for our lives," said Peter. He shoved another roll in his mouth.

"Then why did you push me through?" Mark asked, his voice rising. This time Magisend grabbed him and held him back.

Portia turned sideways to glare at Peter. Did he have a point?

No.

She'd made the decision to close the portal quickly. It felt like ages because of the fighting, and the rush of adrenaline, but really it had been right after they'd created all the duplicates. Just a few breaths after Peter shoved Mark.

Besides, it didn't matter now, anyway. They were all safe. That's all she cared about.

Peter leaned in to grab another serving tray of eggs, moving even closer to Portia, his warmth coming through the sleeve of her tunic. Mark watched closely, staring at Peter's arm as it brushed Portia's. She shifted uncomfortably, wishing both of them were a little further away.

There were too many people in the room. Most staring at her.

"Back to my question," Portia said, trying to change the subject. "Why are you all here?"

"Yes, well, there is a bit of a problem with the queen," Magisend said, while everyone else found something to look at besides Portia's questioning look.

That solved the staring problem, but it felt even worse. Portia waited for Magisend to continue. Magisend only gave her a small smirk.

Portia shifted awkwardly in her seat. She probably deserved that as payback for giving Magisend such a hard time. "Okay, what?" Portia demanded finally, unable to take it any longer.

"When the queen found out about the refugees returning, she was thrilled, until someone told her that one of the students opened a portal for them," Magisend said. "And we all know there is only one student who can do that."

Portia sucked in her breath.

"Yeah, they corralled all the teachers up at the palace. It's not good," Liam said from the end of the bench, his expression grim.

"But I wasn't there," Portia said, protesting. "She sent me away."

"Apparently she thinks you had collaborators," Mia said. She tilted her head sympathetically and reached over Ella and patted Portia's hand.

"Well, she did, didn't she?" a high-pitched voice said from the door. General Lyren stood in the entrance way, smiling broadly. The only smile in the room. Vermeil stood behind her in the hallway, still wearing the scowl from the other day. Apparently he had not yet forgiven Portia for closing the portal. "And you've all incriminated yourself by coming here, don't you think, young humans?" Lyren said.

Now everyone turned and scowled at General Lyren.

19

Portia paced the fortified room where the Dwarven portal had been. Mark, Vermeil, and Lyren watched bemused while sitting at the impressive machinery left behind by the dwarves after Portia had closed the access to the Dragonoid world. Mark played with a huge arrow, twirling the shaft in his fingers, poking at the dirt with the sharp arrowhead. Lyren had already inspected all the weaponry, complementing Vermeil on the fine Dwarven craftwork. The dwarf had been barely civil enough to grunt in return.

The rest of the students had taken advantage of a mushroom farm tour. It sounded dreadful to Portia, but she suspected it was merely an excuse to escape while she grappled with what she was going to do.

"I can't stay here forever," Portia said. She narrowed her eyes at Vermeil. "Can I?"

He laughed bitterly. "Even those not as angry at you as I

am would begrudge the food you take from their mouth. Even with the king's patronage.

"Why are you still so angry at me? Can you not understand? Those weapons are too dangerous for anyone in our lands to have," Portia said.

"Are you sure it's for *anyone* to have, or just not for the dwarves to have?" Vermeil said.

"How can you say such a thing? I risked my life for your people," Portia said.

Vermeil slammed a fist on the stone shelf he sat on. "For *your* people. Ours just happened to be there."

"They wouldn't have been there if they hadn't been greedy trying to get that black powder magic stuff," Portia said, waving off his words.

"Greedy? You try living your whole life underground because you've been chased out by some murderous invaders, not once, but twice." Vermeil stood, then strode to Portia to look down at her. "And now we're starving, because a third such invader has pushed humans onto our lands—what little we had left!"

Portia and Vermeil glared at each other, neither one budging.

"Come on, guys," Mark said. "This isn't helping."

Portia and Vermeil ignored him, still staring daggers at each other.

Lyren's musical laugh broke the mood. Both Portia and Vermeil turned to glare at the tiny elf, whose eyes twinkled in honest merriment.

"What is so funny?" Portia demanded.

"You two. Your impossible mission was a complete success. King Morgani is back. Your," Lyren pointed at Vermeil, "father is back. You don't have to carry the burden of being the archmage for the entire kingdom anymore, not without a lot of serious help. Humans and elves and dwarves have worked together for the first time in our history. And yet, you two fight like siblings battling it out over the last pie."

Mark let out a long low whistle.

Portia had never looked at it like that. Her face reddened at the silliness of their fighting after what they had accomplished.

"Are you calling the needs of my people *pie?*" Vermeil said, not at all appeased.

"I'm sure some of them would like *pie*," Lyren said, winking at Vermeil. At the archmage's stoic expression, Lyren relented and grew serious. "No, of course I'm not belittling the needs of your people. But in light of all that has been accomplished, don't you think we can find a way to work this out? If we've cooperated once, cannot it be done again?"

"Maybe if you turn me over to Queen Lorica and she burned me at the stake, that would satisfy all parties," Portia said, bitterness filling her stomach with once again being in the position of losing her home, or at least it looking like it.

"That we would not do, young human. We'll have to think of something better," Lyren said. The tiny elf gave her a warm smile.

Portia and Mark walked in the Dwarven hall of kings and queens. The soft golden light from the hanging moss reflected on their faces, making them look like angels walking between the two rows of busts of past Dwarven rulers, each statue carved out of red stone and placed high on its own pedestal. On the far side of each line of statues ran the twin channels of the sacred water of Morgani. More water ran down the walls to join the channels, making the walls shimmer in the dim light. The water rushed along its paths, mostly silent except for the occasional burble. It was a peaceful place.

Flat tribute squares, laden with gifts, lay next to the channels, set between the statues at regular intervals. This time, her second in the hall, Portia picked up one of the carvings to examine closer. The craftwork was so intricate on the Dwarven soldier she held that she could see laugh lines around its eyes, folds in the military cape it wore. Was it a real dwarf, or just a figure out of someone's imagination? She put the tribute back thoughtfully.

The statues and tribute squares went on for as far as the eye could see.

Morgani was an old kingdom.

Everyone else had gone to bed, but Portia had not been able to sleep. Mark caught her sneaking out and had joined her on her walk. Surprisingly, the guard had acquiesced to taking them here. So much had changed since they had gone back to the Dragonoid lands and retrieved their king. Now the soldiers were more of honor guards and less of prison wardens.

"Any ideas?" Mark asked.

"No, not yet," said Portia. She stared at her feet as they walked, lost in thought.

"I wonder what these rulers would have done?" Mark asked, staring at the nearest statue of an especially chubby faced dwarf with long hair so flowing that the artist had it coming down over the edge of the column holding it up. The statue was crafted perfectly to the size of its stand, an impressive feat of stonework.

"They are kings and queens. This would have been easy for them," Portia said, dismissively.

"Really?" Mark stopped, staring at Portia.

Reluctantly she stopped too, then faced him. "Of course, they must know what to do because they're... royal."

Mark crossed his arms and pursed his lips. "Really?"

Portia threw up her hands. "Of course."

"Come on. Don't you think they were just regular dwarves put on the spot and had to come up with something?" Mark said.

"No. There's a special line of dwarves that must be better at being rulers or something," Portia said. Why was Mark being so strange about this? It was not helping her at all. Next time she wanted to sneak out for a walk, she'd have to work on being quieter.

"I don't agree," Mark said. Portia gritted her teeth but didn't retort.

Mark smiled at her, his best attempt at charm, she knew. "I think they're just regular folk who have to make decisions and work things out," he said.

He started walking again, slowly, swinging each leg forward in an exaggerated fashion, making a show of it.

"What does that have to do with me?" Portia said, walking with him.

"Don't you have to make some decisions after being put in a difficult spot?"

"Yes. So?" She didn't need to be reminded. It was all she could think about.

Mark didn't answer for the longest time. They kept pace with each other, their footsteps an accompaniment to the sound of the streams running on either side of them.

Just when she thought he wasn't going to answer, Mark finally spoke. "And don't you have royal blood, anyhow? This should be easy for you."

Portia turned to Mark. "What?" Her hands fisted despite herself. What was he saying?

"Callac blood. The original rulers of Haulstatt. Of all the human kingdoms. If making choices was easy for these folk," he motioned to the statues in front of them, "that should be easy for you too. And even if it's not, if they could do it, so can you."

"That's different," Portia said, flustered.

"How?" Mark asked.

"It just is. Why are you being so impossible?" Portia asked, her voice rising. She looked back and forth down the hall, anywhere but at Mark.

"I'm not. I'm trying to help."

Exasperated, Portia walked off, not looking or caring if Mark followed. Her long strides burned off some of her anger and frustration. Surely none of these rulers felt so confused and unsure what to do. Kings and queens weren't supposed to be like that. How could you reassure your people if you were so scared?

"Portia, wait." Mark ran to catch up with her.

"Leave me alone, Mark. I need to figure this out."

"Just don't run away again. You can face this," Mark said, his voice getting breathy as he tried to keep up with Portia.

"And what if I can't?" Portia said.

"Last time you ran away from someone, you ended up killing her in the end." Mark said, stopping. "You have to deal with this head-on if you want to prevent bloodshed." His voice echoed after Portia as she walked down the long hall even faster, but not fast enough to escape his words.

Portia sat with her back to a pillar at the end the hall. It'd taken longer than she thought to walk to the end of the long cavern, but once she determined to go all the way, she wasn't going to quit early.

The statues had changed the further she went; from polished red stone carvings, to rougher ones, to finally a whiter stone set on rough stands. The opulence of the latter statues nowhere to be found.

The tributes too had changed. Some piles of dust on the tribute squares spoke of non-stone offerings that had long ago disintegrated. The kingdom looked like it had been much poorer when it started. Portia wondered that the statues had never been redone with finer materials, but the way it was now did speak of the history of the land.

She'd also checked the dates inscribed on the bases as she went. It wasn't clear at first if the time spanned was the age of the ruler, or just the length of their rule, but one such status had the period of only a year. Unless they let infants ascend the throne, it was the span of the rule.

One year. One short year to be queen.

Portia had stared at the statue. It was one of the rougher ones. A pretty female dwarf. Young, but smiling, unlike most of the other statues.

The tribute squares around it lay nearly empty except for the piles of dust. Even the golden light from the moss above seemed dimmer here. It was almost as if even the hall was sad about this period.

What could have happened to have a rule of only a year? Disease? War?

A chill ran down Portia's spine when the next thought came. Invasion. Was this ruler's death another price paid for the invasion of others through a splinter? Elves? Or humans?

If so, many more would have died than just the ruler.

The statue of the smiling queen stood closer to the end of the hall than the middle. If that represented the time the dwarves lived in this world, then the newcomers could have been the elves.

The dwarves hadn't lived underground when the elves came. Portia looked around at all the statues. It must have been created after these rulers had long since been dead. The dwarves must not want to forget their history. She wished the humans would be the same.

She herself was something someone wanted forgotten. If she'd not been a Jack of Magic, she'd have lived and died on the streets, known only as a thief and a lowlife, her own royal blood not known to anyone, not even herself. Her grave would have been lucky to have any marking at all, much less a statue to her existence.

How many others suffered and died in ignominy?

And yet, this ruler smiled. Portia stared at the statue. It seemed to look right at her, as if it were a live thing and knew she was there. A chill ran down her spine.

***

THE GUARD to the common room leaned on her short pike, nearly dozing. Portia nudged her gently, sharing a soft smile as the dwarf jerked and her eyes opened. The dwarf nodded her thanks and straightened, holding the pike at attention once again. Portia turned the corner into the common room.

Lyren and Vermeil sat in two chairs pulled from the corners of the room, the elf's delicate features and jewelry a strong contrast to the dwarf's near perpetual scowl. And yet, they looked like a pair. Mark and Magisend sat backwards at the bench by the table, their backs leaning against the table with their feet kicked out, another study in contrasts with his golden features and hers dark. The rest of the students sprawled on the floor, most changed into rougher wear, their finery of the day put away.

A more motley crew Portia could not have dreamed up.

They were all clearly waiting up for her.

All eyes turned to her as she entered. She stood straighter and smoothed down her tunic, and took in a deep breath. "I'm ready. I know what we need to do."

Magisend stood. "About time."

Vermeil and Lyren stood as the rest of the students roused themselves to all surround Portia as she started speaking.

Portia nudged her horse forward, through the thick crowd filling the streets of Holne. Strange accents filled the air, from the sharp clipped notes of the northern kingdom of Jukhnovo, to the rolling lazy tongue of Lusatiana, and even stranger ones from the west, from visitors rarely seen in these parts. The pedestrians crowding the street dressed in everything from rags, to the bright red shawls and dangling gold jewelry of travelers, to the soft velvets of nobles who pushed through the crowd in the wake their retainers made for them.

Keeping the large hood of her cloak down, Portia surreptitiously watched the crowd. Her horse raised his head and made a soft whinny at the strong, musky, sometimes floral, perfume smells of the humans around him, and the occasional unwanted touch. Portia patted his neck, reassuring him. She only had one task in town. It wouldn't take long.

Behind her, also cloaked, rode Magisend and Mark. The three had ventured from their camp hidden in the woods outside of the hamlet that morning. The rest stayed behind, awaiting the last of the newcomers.

Street vendors hawked their wares in the central square. The smell of fresh cooked food overwhelmed Portia, sending her stomach into spasms. Rock-hard chunks of stale bread soaked in water held nothing to the spits of fresh vegetables and chunks of meat sizzling over open flames that seemed to be everywhere she looked.

Soon. Soon, she could eat freely in a town.

Once in the square, Portia dismounted. Mark and Magisend paused by her for a moment, giving her a nod before riding on to the far side of the square, their saddlebags full. They would meet up again back in the camp.

They'd set their tents days before in the forest far outside town. It hung further back from the hamlet than planned, for when they reached the central location in the kingdom of Coverack, it had been completely transformed from the previous tent city around the sleepy hamlet. Where the refugee tents had stood was now completely filled with solid wood structures, and a new outer circle of tents and construction laid out around them, swallowing up even more of the farmland outside the hamlet. It must have taken a pretty coin to convince the farmers to let go of so much black dirt.

Portia tied up her horse to a small pole. Glancing around at the crowd of so many, she put a hand over the reins on the posts and laid out a quick spell in a magical node. If any thief made a try for the horse, they'd find a frozen hand the reward. Sparks were more entertaining for spectators, but Portia liked her horse far too much for that.

The clothing shop stood facing the busy square. It looked the same as always. The hamlet had grown around it, stores getting new paint jobs on the outside as their business grew, others changing from selling seeds and farmer's equipment to now selling fancy shawls and fans for the well-to-do ladies. The clothing shop's face never changed. The gray painted wood in plain planks, from the roof to ground, well-made, solid. The windows dark, but not unwelcoming, not to Portia anyhow. She felt a vibration in her bones when she saw it, the same as she did when her sword felt talkative, or even more often, bossy.

She pulled open the door, the inside cool and dim against the brilliant sunshine outside. The quiet enveloped Portia like a comforting blanket. The door shut with a whisper , and the last of the crowd's noise outside cut out into nothingness.

Portia exhaled, feeling her shoulders drop, not even aware until then how tense she'd been outside. She pulled back her hood.

"Hello, Portia," Alice said. She sat on a stool facing the door, looking ageless as always, her hair pulled back into a bun that was both blonde and gray at the same time. Portia blinked, nudging her eyes to focus in the dim light. Behind Alice, a worktable held sets of luxurious clothes of matching pinks, oranges, golds, reds and blues. In the center stood a stuffed dummy clothed in a dress of the deepest purple velvet, threaded through with gold embroidery in the shapes of stars, a moon, and wispy tendrils connecting all in an intricate scrolling pattern. The train flowed off the table and back to the room beyond it. On the bottom of the train, two moons embroidered nestled in a detailed constellation of stars.

It was the most magnificent dress Portia had ever seen.

"Hello, Alice," Portia said. No one else roamed the shop. Portia knew it would be so, and that it was no accident. "You knew I was coming."

Alice nodded. "I did. I am so glad you've changed your mind."

Portia hesitated for a minute, then stepped forward, her head held high.

Alice opened one arm to put around Portia's shoulders as she stepped to her future.

———

THE COOL MIST of the morning came into the tent, despite the brasiers set against the chill. The canvas walls of the enormous tent flapped in the early morning breeze that came just after the sun came over the horizon.

A huge mirror stood in one corner, while rugs piled deep on the ground. Portia had never been in such a luxurious room, never mind slept in one as part of a traveling camp. One tent in the midst of many more of the same scale, or even larger.

Royalty traveled in a different style than thieves and refugees.

The Dwarven maid motioned for Portia to bend forward, for the maid's arms were too short to place the intricate gold circle of twined leaves and flower buds on Portia's head, and

Portia dared not kneel and damage the thick silk chiffon underskirts that held up the velvet overdress.

The circlet placed, its weight unfamiliar to Portia, she stood. She held a hand up, afraid it would fall as she moved her head, but it did not budge at all. It fit perfectly.

She went to stand in front of the mirror, then sucked in her breath.

It was her. And not her. The slender girl in the mirror no longer had the soft cheeks of youth, but the strong lines of an adult. Her dark eyes stared back at her, a stranger.

The new her.

She looked like the most imposing court lady she had even seen.

Royal, even. She better look royal, Portia thought, then grimaced, the twist of her lips ruining the effect in the mirror. Portia laughed at that and felt the sick tension in her stomach relax. She might look different, but she was still herself.

Portia motioned to the sword and baldric. The maid gave her a questioning look. What lady wore a sword?

This one, thought Portia.

Alice had crafted a new baldric and scabbard for her blade. It had been waiting, along with the dress. Again, Portia was not surprised, only grateful when she saw the dark purple leather, almost a luminous black. It went with the dress, yet did not clash with the emeralds on the hilt of her copper sword.

The blade settled, Portia finally felt fully dressed.

Outside, Mark and Magisend bickered over the coffee by the fire. Ella's laugh rang out, distinct and heartwarming.

Other servants ran between the tents, their shadows passing by as they ran errands for their masters, the camp abuzz with preparations for the day. Portia's bathwater had come when it was still full dark out. She wondered if the servants had gotten any sleep at all.

The maid held the flap of the tent open. Portia exited.

Outside, the buzz of activity slowed as individuals caught sight of Portia. An ostler stopped mid-step, his bucket of dirty water sloshing its complaint. Mark paused in his drinking, his coffee cup held midway to his lips, the steam wrapping around eyes firmly fixed on Portia. Ella and Mia exited their tent at the strange silence, then stopped to stare, their mouths round with surprise.

Ella clapped her hands. "Oh, Portia, that is worth missing school for!" She gushed forward, breaking the spell of those around them. Ella walked around Portia, shamelessly eyeing her up and down, delight on her face.

"You look like a different person," Ella said, missing Portia's wince.

"I think she looks like the same person," Mark said gently, instantly understanding Portia's reaction. He set his coffee on the camp table and came to stand by Portia.

He, too, dressed quite fine. His chosen colors of red and orange suited his fair skin and golden hair. The only contrast the fine armband of purple velvet that perfectly matched Portia's dress.

"Well, well, well, the commoner cleans up well," Magisend said, an unfamiliar but much welcomed approval in her voice.

Portia raised her eyebrows.

Magisend cleared her throat. "Yes, well, I shall have to come up with a new pet name, I see, *My Lady*." The last words, though spoken sarcastically, came with a smile.

Portia smirked. "You could call me Jack."

"I could, though I highly doubt that I will," Magisend replied. She walked off in a fake huff, her own golden skirts flaring. A word to Magisend's house in Coverack had been enough for tents, trunks of outfits, and servants, all borne swiftly by carriage and horse, to meet them in Holne.

Mia had done nearly as well and had even thought to have items sent for Ella and Peter. The girl was a marvel with measurements, for the items that came back fit as if tailored directly on their bodies.

The whole camp looked splendid. And that was just the humans.

Lyren sauntered into the common area of the camp, her eyes glittering as she stared at Portia. Lyren had chosen to remain in her dress uniform, rather than a dress. The medals on her chest shone so brightly, they sent off daggers of light from the low morning sun. They would be absolutely blinding in the full day. No one could miss her rank, and import, to her Elven kingdom of Rocabarra. Even her earrings shone more brightly. With a soft gasp, Portia wondered if they were enchanted to be so brilliant. If so, what a clever tool indeed. Even Alice would be impressed with that.

"The young human cleans up well," Lyren said.

"Thank you, *elf*," Portia said saucily. "Tell me, how old would I have to be to lose that particular nickname of young?"

"Oh, about a hundred. At least," Lyren answered.

It sounded like a joke, but Portia had a feeling that was an honest answer. Did she even know how old Lyren was? She shook her head, forgetting about the circlet about her brow, only to reflexively reach up to catch it. A completely unnecessary action.

"That will not move until you want it off," Lyren assured her, eyeing the circlet.

Portia nodded her thanks.

"Our gift suits you," a deep voice said behind Portia. She turned, then curtsied quickly, along with all others present. King Magnus and Queen Ceola of the elves entered the common area between tents. Their servants and attendants tried to squeeze in too, but only a few of each of the queen's and the king's retainers found space in the now crowded clearing. The king waved the rest back. One of the tallest male attendants, dressed in a glaring brilliant orange, glared at the humans at being left out.

King Magnus and Queen Ceola wore matching cream coats of a fine feather material that moved around their bodies like a living creature. It looked warm. Fine blue taffeta poked up from beneath Queen Ceola's cloak. They, too, were ready for the journey.

Liam, Richard, and Peter bounded into the square like three peas in a pod, even dressed the same in the blue-greens of fine young succulents. Preoccupied with their own joking, they nearly tripped into the royalty. An elf attendant not so subtly pushed Liam back, but the ever-sunny boy, *man*, Portia corrected herself, only smiled warmly in returned. The trio of human males bowed together, further cementing the impression of a unit.

"Your Majesties," Liam said. He glanced at Portia, unsure how to address her.

"My Lady will work. Or My Jack," Portia said, helping him. One of the Elven attendants had the audacity to glare at her. Apparently, there were servants for those sorts of corrections. Portia looked down and cleared her throat to keep the laughter from burbling out.

"My Lady," Liam said, with a bold wink and another smile. "We've had much luck. People affiliated with all sorts of animals have come far and wide to our side."

Animals?

Peter put a hand to his mouth and turned, but not fast enough to hide his smile.

Ah, animals.

This was going to be a good day indeed.

"I think it is nearly time. Once everyone is here, we go," King Magnus said. Portia nodded.

The eyes of the others shifted. Portia turned to follow their gaze.

King and Queen Morgani stood behind them, also attended. The Dwarven king looked better than Portia had ever seen, the steady diet on their journey having done him well, his cheekbones no longer so sharp they looked like they could slice hide. A sparkle danced in his eyes. Both the queen and king of the dwarves wore finer outfits than anything she'd seen in their own lands, rich leathers and fine linen in matching deep burgundy. Alice, mysteriously, and as always, had just what was needed in a pinch. Even for a Dwarven king and his queen.

Behind and to the left stood Commander Kerat, who had insisted on coming, along with enough men to protect the ruler they'd just gotten back.

Finally, Vermeil shyly peered into the square over the heads of the Morganis' attendants. When not scowling at someone, he actually looked quite nice. Now he just looked uncomfortable. The tiny animal wrapped around his neck patted his cheek with one petite paw, like a tiny mother reassuring her enormous baby. The archmage leaned into the affection.

THEIR ENORMOUS CARAVAN set out on the road, Portia in the lead. The train of her dress, even tucked up and pinned, still hung along the sides of the rear legs of her enormous horse. The maids had clucked and fussed, making sure the fabric was nowhere near the hooves, or worse, the rear of the horse. The others followed, all mounted on their own horses. The coats of the horses shone in the sun, speaking to hours of currying and grooming by an army of ostlers. Fine braid cords and tassels hung from the reins, matching the outfits of the owners. Even the livery of the retainers matched the new outfits of their houses.

Behind, slowly moving wagons groaned, pulled to the road by sturdy pairs of work horses, their muscles rippling in the sun. The backs of the open wagons were loaded with fist sized linen-wrapped bundles. Servants not only drove the wagons, but several sat in the back beds of the wagons, within easy reach of the parcels.

More wagons behind those carried supplies in boxes and barrels, guarded by the soldiers of both Morgani and Rocabarra, as well as the house guards of Riddlepit, Magisend's house. She'd even promised more houses were on their way.

Mark nudged his horse up to pace Portia's. The hamlet of Holne spread out before them, just beyond the stretch of open road they rode upon. Beyond it, lay the road to the capital city of Coverack. "I'm rather amazed we've not been caught out," he said, glancing back at the huge procession behind them.

"I, too," Portia said. She shifted in her saddle, trying to find a more comfortable position. She'd never worn so many clothes while riding before. It felt like being smothered by silks.

"Stop squirming. It's not very ladylike," Mark said.

Portia huffed, turned to glare at Mark, only to find him smirking. She flipped her head, pretending to ignore him further.

"Honestly, I thought King Morgani was going to give us away," Mark said.

"He is a *king*," Portia said stiffly.

"And didn't Magisend just love telling him what to do to get past the border guards." His voice held admiration.

Portia was going to ignore that.

"Yes, well, some of us were busy doing the magic to make

him look..." What could she say that would not be disrespectful?

"Less king like? Less dwarf like?" Mark asked.

Portia knew he was fishing. She would never tell him what the Haulstatt guards saw when they looked at King and Queen Morgani. Regardless of how much she trusted Mark, some things you just didn't share about royalty. "Something like that," she admitted. That is all he would ever know.

He sighed, knowing that was a firm no to his curiosity.

They rode on, enjoying the morning birdsong as the sun drove the mists away. It was a fine morning.

A yell ahead told that they'd been spotted. By the ones and twos, curious people came to the edge of the road, whispering and muttering amongst themselves. They watched with rounded eyes as the procession went by. Happy cries greeted the gifts of the linen packages from the servants in the backs of the wagons. Small boys and girls unwrapped the bundles to find fruits and nuts, which were swiftly devoured.

A crier, brought by King Magnus, took his place riding ahead of the group, repeatedly calling out "The refugees are returned. All hail the new era!" in common, with only a hint of an elvish accent. He wore all the colors of the leaders behind him, in a rainbow of fabrics sewn together, a visual representation of the group, all on one body.

The crowd behind them grew as they traveled to the hamlet.

Some of the people tried to touch Portia, staring up at her with awe and admiration, as if she was a miracle. Or as if she had worked one, for she had—she'd brought back their loved ones. They stared at her face, to memorize its features for all time, as they crowded around her horse. The guards the kings and queens had set about her gently nudged the crowd back, but Portia reached out and let her fingers graze the fingertips of as many admirers as she could. Their happiness and gratitude fortified her.

Once in the hamlet, groups of young men and women, dressed as fancily as they could manage, waited in groups under homemade banners. The crudely stitched triangles of fabric depicted animals: black cats, brown hares, orange lynx, and others. Gangs. The gangs of Valencia, now scattered across the lands. A message from Mark weeks ago, and the promises of a bright future, had brought them here to pledge their allegiance and support. They'd brought other gangs with them, from other cities, their banners wholly unfamiliar to Portia.

She stared at the groups assembled in the central square and spilling off into the streets beyond. So many more than she ever imagined ever existed. And this was after the slaughter of war, and the scattering of the gang members to the winds. For too long, the young people of these lands had been left to their own devices for survival after wars, plagues, and blights had taken their parents. No more. She blinked rapidly, having to look away to control herself.

***

THEY LEFT the hamlet of Holne behind and made their way on the road to Coverack. The crowd behind them grew, many now with their own horses and supplies, not just those on foot. At their crawling pace, it would take two days to reach the capital city. They had one night of camping ahead. Portia was grateful their own camp would be ready and waiting for them, a group of servants having been sent ahead, along with the supplies and guards. Riding for two full days with such a caravan of chaos around her wore on her nerves, but she smiled for all.

But also waiting for them at the second day camp were tents from the houses of Ladock, Kelynack, and Hayle—all the great houses of Coverack. Other camps, from other cities and houses outside the capital, dotted the huge field obtained from a farmer, his herd elsewhere for the day in exchange for a goodly sum of silver.

That night passed a blur of greeting travelers from far away, nobles and commoner alike.

THE NEXT MORNING, Portia rose early, unable to sleep. She took her sword out into the predawn dimness and found an empty spot to practice, walking through the still sleeping camp to a grassy spot near the edge of the field of tents, dark trees marking the edge of the property. Only a few servants walked carefully in the darkness in the sprawling moving city, their morning chores already underway.

When the sweat ran down her back and soaked her rough practice linens, and her breath pulled raggedly from her lungs, she found herself finally calm enough to stand and enjoy the beginnings of the sun coming over the horizon.

"The sword of the kings," a voice said behind Portia, startling her.

Magnus stood, holding a steaming cup, even now trailed by several sleepy servants.

"What?" Portia asked. "Your Majesty," she added, remembering herself.

"That sword is ancient. We did not forge it, but rather took it from the first landers of the humans."

Portia's eyes widened.

"It was said to be magicked so that only the human rulers could wield it. I figured that was mere myth when you chose it, since you'd already told us of your simple background."

Portia didn't know what to say to that, opening her mouth to speak and then shutting it again.

"Then again, why tell someone they like a sword stolen from their own people when you're trying to get them to save your world for you?" He winked at Portia, then turned and disappeared into the maze of tents behind him, his servants stumbling after him.

She looked down at the copper blade in her hands. It vibrated as if in confirmation.

THE SMELL of the salt water met them long before they could see the city, the tang in the air piercing through the smells of horses, humans, dwarves, and elves sweating under the hot midday sun.

The crowds with them, no longer boisterous, walked more subdued towards the capital, as even the common folk knew a confrontation was coming. Acid bit the inside of Portia's stomach. She tried to not see their anxious glances.

Coming back here to face the queen. This was not her style at all.

Wasn't. Hadn't been.

That was the old Portia. Now, she had to be something new.

She thought back to the smiling Dwarven queen, who had ruled for only one short year, yet still wore the happiness of being alive, the love of her people with their tribute. If she could do it, so could Portia.

Her horse snuffed, raising its head, as if it could sense Portia straightening in the saddle, the arch of its neck beautiful to see. It knew it was a beauty and was not shy about showing off. Portia patted its neck with admiration.

The procession mounted the base of the long hill that crested further ahead into the first view of the city. Scouts had reported back earlier that morning that lookouts had been spotted at the top of the hill, not careful enough to hide themselves completely. Not careful enough, or else simply confident they could deal with anything that came. Stealth was only needed if you took your enemy seriously.

Not that they were enemies.

Not exactly.

Portia kept her eyes straight ahead, forcing herself not to

search the skyline for faces peering down at them. Her hands tightened on the reins.

The horses huffed with the effort it took to climb the slope. At the rear of the procession, the workhorses had an easier time, their loads of gifts mostly gone, now the wagons only giving the occasional tired child a ride. Tears of exhaustion dried quickly while watching the fascinating entertainment of strange elves and dwarves playing puppet games for their amusement. Grateful mothers and fathers walked next to the wagons.

Those wagons were far from the dangerous lead position. The position Portia held.

"Halt," a voice cried from ahead. The plume of a soldier's helmet crested the hill. He rode down, followed by an arrowhead formation of mounted soldiers, riding the road and spreading to the fields on either side. They were taking no chances with any of Portia's group getting around them.

Portia pulled back the reins of her horse. It stopped, impatient at the delay and the sight of those blocking his path.

She felt rather than saw Queen Morgani and King Morgani come up on her left side, and Queen Ceola and King Ceola come up on her right. The five of them waited in a line for the soldiers from Coverack to approach.

His gallop slowed to a trot, then halted. Underneath his helmet his eyes shifted from the dwarves to the elves to Portia's eyes, his surprise unhidden on his wide, strong face. They had been successful in keeping the presence of the royalty hidden long enough to catch the city unawares, for there was no mistake who was queen and king, nor the soldier's surprise at it. The elves' and dwarves' crowns shone brightly under the sun. Portia's circlet, not exactly a crown, and not exactly *not* a crown, also shone. The soldier looked nonplussed and irritated, not expecting what stood in front of him.

"Halt in the name of Queen Lorica," the soldier repeated inanely, for everyone already stood still.

"We have done so," King Magnus said. His voice light, but also the edge of authority there. He sounded like a king.

The soldier swallowed and glanced back the way he had come. More soldiers stood at the crest of the hill, their pikes and banners silhouetted against the clear blue sky. Reassured, he turned back.

"The queen has forbidden you to come further," said the soldier.

"We are here to speak to the queen," said Portia, speaking softly.

Surprised, the soldier pulled his eyes from King Magnus and looked at Portia. His eyes flicked up and down. His eyebrows rose.

Was he one of the soldiers that had rebuffed her from the palace gates all that time ago? Portia wondered, amused. Amazing how things can change.

"Perhaps," King Magnus said, his low voice commanding attention, "the queen will favor us with a meeting out here. We have journeyed a long way to meet with her."

The soldier stared at the Dwarven king, taking in the king's unusually wide features—the broad cheekbones, the width of shoulders and body appropriate for a man twice his height—for the king's small stature was clear, even mounted high upon a horse. The soldier's horse danced back and forth, betraying the agitation his rider felt and was so desperately trying to hide.

Portia breathed a sigh of relief as she entered the large tent, escaping the heat of the sun. It was not nearly so bakingly hot as the Dragonoid world, especially with the cool breeze of the ocean cresting the hill from the capital and washing inland, but it was still a lot to bear wearing so many clothes. She had a newfound respect for court ladies who had to wear these outfits day in and day out, with no respite, ever. Only the metal-plated knights were worse off for garment comfort.

A large circular table dominated the tent, chairs spread around it, leaving no obvious power position. More chairs filled the tent right up to the edges. This table, cut into sections, and loaded in a wagon, had been brought especially for this purpose. Portia nodded at Archmage Vermeil and Peter, who sat in chairs in the back of the tent. Peter smiled, an unfamiliar expression on his face.

Portia puzzled it until she recognized what that lopsided grin was—pride. Peter and his obsession with history had insisted this table be brought, if any table at all. He'd spoken at length of some famous old table and king he'd read about in his history books. Vermeil, of all allies, had backed him, and Morgani had the table made. Now she could feel even more than see the wisdom of it. There was no prized seat to be fought over, save perhaps the ones that faced the doorway. It was large enough that the seats with their backs to the door could be left empty and there was still enough room for those that needed to be there.

Lyren was already there too. She sat in the first row of chairs behind the table, with other senior advisors. She winked at Portia and motioned to the table.

Self-conscious, Portia took a seat at the round table. She was the first there. It felt audacious to sit at its polished planks, in a seat of leadership, even if she knew it was the plan. Her guts had not yet adjusted to the new reality.

The tent filled. The students, all dressed in their house colors, took seats behind the table. If Portia had not known them, she would have thought them all much older, not mere teens.

All stood as the queens and kings entered, then took their seats at the table. They had decided to wait in the cool shade while Queen Lorica and King Consort Aldis traveled from the city. Around them, the camp scrambled to be ready to receive them.

Finally, after a thick silence, broken only by the insects calling in the dry grass outside, trumpets announced the arrival of the queen. Portia's heart pounded. She glanced around at all the friendly faces, but still felt alone. This was all her doing, for good or for ill.

What if it was all for ill?

Portia forced herself to smile. Perhaps if she wore it on her face, the feeling would find its way into her heart.

The tent flaps opened, pulled back by two servants. All rose within the tent, pushing heavy chairs back on the thick carpet as Queen Lorica's figure silhouetted against the bright light, the queen's curls piled even higher, her crown taller. If clothing could be a weapon, Lorica had brought out her best equipment.

The queen's lips twitched up in the smallest of smiles as she nodded to greet the other rulers. The smile slipped for a second when her eyes came to Portia and took in her elaborate dress and circlet of gold. Only the tiniest of tension around Lorica's eyes gave away her reaction, which Portia imagined to be rage. The messenger to the castle had no doubt told Queen Lorica about the kings and queens present. What had he said about Portia? When he'd asked, they had only told him to let the queen know that her Jack of Magic was returned.

King Consort Aldis followed his queen into the tent, his face more easily creased into a smile that somehow felt thin. His eyes raced around the room, taking in all who were present.

Their attendants and advisors followed, including General Bancrot, who boldly gave Portia a wink. Or at least Portia thought she had. Portia glanced at the kings and queens standing around her, but their faces remained unreadable. Once all inside, the tent flaps dropped, taking away the golden sunshine and leaving the tent to the dim light provided by the candles.

Queen Lorica slowly sat in the chair held out for her at the table. All the other rulers, and Portia, sat with her.

They watched each other. No one was in a hurry to speak.

Portia held her hands tight under the table, forcing herself to not talk first, to not burst out in explanation, or worse, to beg forgiveness.

Those choices were long past.

A servant circled the table, pouring watered wine into hammered gold goblets. When he finished, Lorica reached out and took hers. She held it, gazing into the dark liquid.

King Morgani reached out and took his own. Giving Lorica a meaningful look, he held up the goblet. "To a new future," he said in a voice so deep it was almost a growl. He swallowed the wine in one gulp, put the vessel down with a thump.

Lorica nodded, satisfied the wine was not poisoned. She sipped from her own cup, then leisurely placed it back on the table.

"You have brought armies into my lands without warning, or permission," Lorica said, her voice steady and low. A shiver ran down Portia's spine. It couldn't have been more terrifying if the queen had shouted.

"Just a few fellows to help carry our pillows," King Magnus said, taking on an appeasing, if not joking tone. "We mean no harm by it. Surely you can understand a person's need for comfort?"

Lorica continued as if the Elven monarch had not spoken. "Any reasonable ruler would accept that as a declaration of war."

Next to Lorica, Aldis shifted uncomfortably in his seat, stopping the second Lorica's eyes flicked in his direction.

No one spoke.

Queen Ceola, sitting next to Portia, reached out under the table and gently squeezed Portia's hand, much more softly than Portia was squeezing her own. Portia gasped, then briefly shut her eyes with a small nod.

"Your Majesty," Portia said.

Queen Lorica's eyes slid to Portia.

"Your Majesty, this is no offer of war." Portia willed her voice to not quaver or crack. "We have proposals of a lands-wide alliance, of all the kingdoms."

Queen Lorica tilted her head, giving Portia permission to continue. "We only survived this war through the unity of our magic, and through a cooperative effort. If we had but two of the three magics, we would not be safe, and our people returned. We survive as a unit..." Portia's words stumbled to a halt under the unwavering gaze of her queen. She swallowed, her throat unbearably dry.

Having lost all joking, King Magnus spoke. "We believe we can only thrive as a whole. Dwarves," he nodded to King and Queen Morgani, "humans," he gestured to Queen Lorica, "and elves," he motioned to himself. "This union is for magic, for learning, for lands."

"Lands?" Queen Lorica repeated, her voice sharp. "So you do mean to invade."

"No," Queen Ceola said. "We mean to work together. Our brothers in this world, the dwarves, must survive by living underground. What justice is there in that, when we are all saved by their magic? If it was not for them, we'd be lucky to be alive at all."

"What happened to the dwarves happened long ago," Queen Lorica said, waving off Ceola's speech.

"When were your people taken, and then saved? Was that long ago too? Even if it was, can you honestly say there is a time limit to justice?" King Magnus asked, his voice steel. He'd taken his wife's hand. "We have only recently allowed your own people refuge, after millennia of running from them. Of constructing the biggest structures in the land to protect ourselves from them. From humans. From brutal, grisly deaths at their hands."

Portia sucked in her breath. The tension crackled in the air.

Queen Lorica leaned back.

Unable to bear the silence any longer, Portia cleared her throat. "Your Majesty, we propose a system of magic academies. Human, dwarf and elf. Those capable will learn all that they can. Those capable have a duty to all." Portia forced herself to speak loudly enough that those behind her could hear as well. Some few representatives from the gangs had been allowed to join the negotiating tent. She wanted them to know the promises made to them were real.

"Academies. We cannot spare so many students," Queen Lorica began.

"Not true." Portia recoiled at the look Lorica gave her, tried again. "Your Majesty, there are many talented young people wasted on the streets. Enough to send to school here, and to do learning tours in the other kingdoms and lands. The young folk from other kingdoms will come here to learn as well, and to work the farms, and in the cities. Each going to other lands for service. If we are not shut off from each other by gates and by weapons, we will understand each other much better."

Lorica stared at Portia until she was sure she was done, then her eyes met all the others at the table. She thrummed the arm of her chair. "I am not sure how I have become the enemy here."

"I assure you, Queen Lorica, no such thought has crossed our minds," Magnus said. "We simply saw an opportunity and are bringing it to you. We are *all* bringing it to you as a show of respect."

Lorica nodded at that, pleased with the flattery. "That is a gratifying way to put it."

"We brought gifts," King Morgani spoke gruffy, startling everyone. Someone in the back chuckled.

Lorica was not so easily won over. She turned back to Portia. "First, I will take my Jack back. We have much to discuss."

"No," Portia said. A small nugget of anger filled her stomach, giving her courage, even though her hands shook.

Lorica looked at Portia, incredulous. "You speak to your queen this way?"

"You are not my queen, any more than Queen Ceola, or Queen Morgani is my queen and my ruler. I recognize you as the Queen of Haulstatt, yes. This is your kingdom. But I am of House Callac, the original house over all human lands. All the kingdoms. Srubna, Jukhnovo, Lusatiana... and Haulstatt." Portia's heart beat so fast it felt as if it vibrated in her chest. She made herself breathe in deeply, when her instinct was to hold her breath. She forced herself on. "I belong to all the lands beyond that too, to Morgani, and to Rocabarra. My responsibility is to the safety of all. I cannot, I will not, answer only to you."

Queen Lorica's black eyes blazed at Portia. For a brief second Portia saw Deyelna's eyes overlaid on the queen's, and felt the same fear of dying, of exile. She made herself concentrate on the air flowing in and out of her lungs.

Deyelna was dead.

Portia now older and stronger. And wiser.

She just wished her terrified heart would listen to her brain when it said these things.

"You are the Jack of *Haulstatt*. You will do as I say. I am your ruler. You are my subject." The queen's voice was thick with barely repressed anger.

Magisend stood at the back of the tent, her chair clattering against others tightly packed around it. "The Houses of Coverack support Portia of House Callac."

Queen Lorica looked to Magisend, then scoffed. "You are a child, what do you speak of the houses of Coverack?"

"She speaks by my authority." A short dark man stood—an older male version of Magisend. Her father.

He stood unwavering under the queen's regard.

"And mine." Another nobleman stood, joining the head of the house of Riddlepit.

"And mine." An older woman in dowager robes stood.

"And mine." Yet another noblewoman.

Several more chimed in, more than Portia thought existed in Coverack, until she heard a voice like Mia's. These were not just the houses of Coverack, the capital. They were houses from other cities in Haulstatt.

Portia nudged her eyes with the back of her knuckles, then shook her head. The shaking in her hands lessened just enough for her to smooth her dress as she sat straighter.

"The Hares of Valencia support Portia of Callac", a young man chimed in, his voice breaking halfway through his speech.

Another young woman's voice called out, announcing the support of another gang.

The chorus continued.

Queen Lorica turned to Portia, her eyes narrowed.

Portia met her gaze. She did not look away.

The sun rose through the tiny window in Portia and Ella's dorm room. Portia patted the bed she sat on, amused at how tiny it looked now. The spot where her trunk used to stand now only held her small overnight bag, tiny in the unfaded spot on the wooden floor. Ella's trunk, painted with stick figures and other childish items as a gift from her brothers, still sat on its spot on the floor next to her desk. Ella's side of the room was a maze of tossed clothes, school books, and more items than Portia could count. Portia's heart felt warm just looking at it.

Ella came in from the bathroom, holding a towel high by the corners in front of her, obscuring her head and upper body. "Portia."

Portia stared at her roommate, or at least at the towel hiding most of her, only showing a beautiful shimmering blue-green dress below. A new one. Ella, like Portia, had not come from a noble house or royalty when she arrived at the school. New dresses were hard to come by.

But today was a special day.

"Yes, Ella, dear. I don't know if you've realized it, but there is a towel in front of your face," Portia said, bemused.

"Oh, hush, girl. I wanted to get your attention," said Ella.

"And?" Portia prompted, because she knew that was what Ella wanted.

Ella dropped the towel.

Her hair shimmered, a brilliant blue at the top and fading down to shades of lighter and darker green. With her dress, she looked like some exotic sea creature.

"Ella!"

Ella smirked. "I know. Isn't it great?"

"You didn't?" Portia asked, shock and delight in her voice.

"I did. That terrible, horrible, wonderful, handsome boy gave me his secret."

Portia leapt up from the bed, rushing in to give Ella a hug. Ella accepted it for a brief moment, then pushed Portia back.

"Stop now, you'll ruin the look and we aren't even at the party yet!" Ella protested, smoothing her dressing, then stepping to the mirror to check her hair.

Portia stood next to Ella to see them side by side in the reflection of the mirror, Portia's purple velvet dress and golden circlet a good complement to the greens of Ella. They looked like two sophisticated women, and not the young girls who had started at the Academy all that time ago.

New buildings lined the harbor of Coverack, painted in brilliant reds, greens, blues and every other shade anyone had ever thought of, all competing to stand out. Thin woven banners ran from building to building. Wrought iron and wooden posts lined the edge of the walkway bordering the harbor, set with candles and lanterns, ready to light the party long after the sun went down.

People crowded the streets, all dressed in their finest. Common folk in their best linen pushed up against nobles. Servants, released from duty for the day, looked uncomfortable in their civilian clothes, but loosened up the moment a glass of ale was pressed into their hands and they bade to drink.

Ships moored within the harbor themselves stood decorated for celebration, from the lacquered and decorated queen's ship, to the merchant cutters, to the smallest of fishing vessels. Tiny triangle flags, strung on ropes ran from mast to stern and prow, made even the most fearsome warship look like a fancy decorative item belonging on some lady's table. The celebration from the streets poured even into the decks of the ships themselves, with smaller rowboats ferrying the celebrants back and forth from the shore.

The entire city of Coverack celebrated, as did the entirety of the kingdom of Haulstatt, and all the other kingdoms. Today celebrated one full season of the unity of the world and its citizens, the work for their new order well underway.

The worst of the crisis was over: food had reached all, new trade structures were working themselves well into form, and even the cult members had been brought back into society, most grateful for the chance to earn an honest living and have enough for them and their families.

For that reason, all the kings and queens of the unified kingdoms had declared a full day of celebration to happen this day, and on every year forward. To mark what they had done so far, and what was to come.

"I can't believe they let you stay at the house," Ella whispered to Portia. They walked arm in arm, fighting their way through the crowds.

"It was just for one night," Portia said while looking at all the fancy people around them, and at the new construction on the harbor. "Besides, I'm in charge." She squeezed Ella's arm.

"Must be nice," Ella said.

"Not as nice as you might think."

They walked through the crowd. Handsome young men stopped and stared at Ella, along with a few scandalized young women. The women touched their own hair as they stared at Ella's unnatural and luminous locks.

"So tell me again, how did Grania not catch you all and throw you in the dungeon?" Ella asked.

Portia laughed. No matter how many times she'd told Ella, Ella always wanted to hear again how the Dwarven General Seren and human General Bancrot had led the spymaster all over the kingdom for two days before the now famous meeting on the hill, leaving her queen without critical information. "Are you ever going to tell me why you dislike our beloved spymaster so?" Portia asked.

Ella stopped in her tracks, dropping Portia's arm and staring at her. "Beloved? I don't care what house you come from, I will wash your mouth out with lye if you say that again." Ella's sunny smile gone, Portia wondered just how serious Ella was.

She was not going to find out.

"Apologies, my friend. I was only teasing," Portia said, giving Ella a small bow of respect.

Ella looked Portia up and down. "Hrmp." Ella flounced off, but not so fast that Portia could not catch up with two quick steps. A moment later, Ella glanced sideways at Portia and gave her a quick smile, all forgiven.

Ahead, a cluster of students stood out in the moving crowd, like a boulder in the middle of a stream. Portia waved high overhead to get their attention.

A thin voice piped up over the crowd. "Look, that *lady* comes."

Portia looked down and laughed. Somehow Magisend's new insult just didn't have the same ring as her old one of 'commoner.'

Magisend, Mark, Liam, Ella, Richard, and Peter stood in a circle, talking and sipping from the large tankards they held. Most people in the crowd had their own mugs, the ladies having strung theirs from their wrists with fine lengths of lace. Some of the sloppier men had theirs attached to their wrists with leather thongs, most likely from their irate wives not wanting to lose another precious cup in the chaos of the wonderful night.

Mark's fingers laced with Magisend's. Portia glanced at their hands, then away. She wasn't sure she'd ever get used to that, but she'd not begrudge either one their happiness.

Today, Liam's wild hair was shades of blue and green. The exact same shades as Ella. Ella looked at him shyly. He had no such restraint as he broke away from the other students to come and kiss Ella's hand. Portia walked on to the rest of the students to give them a moment of privacy.

"It's so good to see you again, Portia," Mia said, a true smile on her face. Mia's flame-red hair flowed around her, down the beautiful orange dress she wore. A new look for Mia, but it suited.

"It's good to be back, even for a short time," said Portia, accepting the offering of mead from a passing vendor. Today, the queen paid for all food and drinks. The people celebrated for free, with the vendors eager to give more to all, for they were paid by what was consumed.

"How goes the school in Rocabarra?" Peter asked. "When can we send some Cats up there?" He meant some of their old thieving gang. The gang had chosen that kingdom for their work, one that surprised Portia. She liked to think it was because it was the first kingdom she'd visited outside of Haulstatt.

"It coming. We've a new headmaster, and he's quite picky about things. But soon you and the others will have the fun of trying to ride a Sika deer without losing your head to a branch." Portia meant it as a joke, but had enough close calls on her own to have the occasional pang of worry for the new students.

No matter. They all had to go through the process.

Peter raised his glass to Portia's words.

"Young humans!" a high-pitched voice called out. Portia whirled, searching for the source.

Lyren wore an outfit of brilliant yellow, leaving her uniform far behind. Even her earrings were gold and yellow lacquered metal, wrapping in bands around her pointed ears. She leaned heavily on a tall dwarf with a tiny white animal on his neck. Vermeil, the dwarf in question, tried to keep a serious face but ended up only looking silly with a half smile, half scowl for an expression. Portia's heart leapt.

"Lyren, Vermeil, Chit!" Portia called. She tried to hug them all at once, nearly falling over when Lyren staggered into her. Chit put her little paws on Portia's face, wiggling her nose and whiskers right up against Portia's nose, making Portia sneeze. Portia wanted to grab the adorable little thing and squeeze, but knew that was bad form.

Portia backed up, letting Lyren stumble forward, then recover.

"Lyren, I've never seen you like this," Portia said, laughing a little.

"And you'll never again," Lyren said, sloshing around the last of the drink in her cup and swallowing it down. "Ok, a break for a while. Us professors need to think about our dignity."

Professors, Portia mouthed.

Professor Hilda and Professor Aelric came up the street, having been walking behind Vermeil and Lyren. Hilda curtsied, while Aelric bowed at Portia. She waved them to stop. It felt weird to have her old teachers treat her in this new way. But they insisted, a proud glint in their eyes.

"Yes, professors," Aelric said, gesturing to Vermeil and Lyren. "They've agreed to come teach for at least a year here in Coverack. In exchange, we'll go to their kingdoms, something I'm very much looking forward to." He looked much more enthusiastic about the adventure than Hilda.

Portia laughed. "Are you going to raid their libraries?"

"No! Never, how could you say such a thing?" Aelric asked, putting a hand over his heart in consternation. He looked around to see if anyone was paying attention, then leaned into Portia to fake whisper in her ear. "I'm going to need some maps before you leave again."

Portia laughed again, her stomach muscles pulling delightfully against the stays in her dress. It was so good to see everyone again.

Aelric went off to talk to the other students, while Hilda sidled next to Portia. "Has your mother written you lately?" she asked.

Portia shook her head. Was there a problem?

Hilda quickly rushed on, seeing the look on Portia's face. "Oh, nothing bad, my dear, nothing bad. Henry took one of the tests from the traveling groups and he's to be trained in swordsmanship. All courtesy of the kingdom."

Henry? Her seven-year-old half brother. Portia clapped her hand over her mouth, delighted. Those traveling tests were to find the most talented of the talented, no matter what part of the country they were in. Cecelia and William must be thunderstruck. The problem with Portia traveling so much was that sometimes the correspondence could not keep up.

She needed to go back and visit her mother more often. "He passed in swordmanship? Really?"

Hilda nodded. "They say it's a real talent for him. Cecelia's words nearly leapt off the page. She's also pushing to get Isolde in the academy and off the farm. Apparently farm life is not for her," Hilda said.

Portia nodded, looking at Mark and Magisend while Hilda spoke. It was probably not the only reason Isolde wanted to come to Coverack. No matter, there were many other young men at the academy. Somehow Portia had no doubt her step-sister would land on her feet just fine. Now, like for all the young people of the lands, new and amazing opportunities awaited her.

"Hey. Hey!" a tiny voice called. Someone tugged at the sleeve of Portia's arm. She looked down to see a darling little girl, her face shiny and scrubbed clean. The little girl's other hand was lost in a large hand. Portia followed the hand and arm up to see a huge man, his smile a larger version of the girl's. He pulled a small cart full of skewers of roast meat and vegetables, kept warm over a tiny stove of candles.

"This is my Pa," the girl said to Portia, both earnestly and beaming with pride. "I told you that was his shop." The little girl pointed to a new building, painted a deep rich red, proclaiming food and ale for all.

Portia knelt down so as to be face level with the girl. "And so you were right." She glanced up at the man who beamed down at his girl. "Aren't you glad we all worked to clean it up, so it'd be ready for him when he came back?"

The girl nodded seriously. Portia grabbed her and gave

her a huge bear hug, feeling the warmth and love from the girl, while the sounds of Portia's friends talking and laughing filled her ears. Portia felt so happy she thought if one more speck of joy came into her life, she'd burst into a million pieces.